Edward Gilpin Johnson, Charles Lamb

The Best Letters of Charles Lamb

Edward Gilpin Johnson, Charles Lamb

The Best Letters of Charles Lamb

ISBN/EAN: 9783337017149

Printed in Europe, USA, Canada, Australia, Japan

Cover: Foto ©Andreas Hilbeck / pixelio.de

More available books at **www.hansebooks.com**

OF

HARLES LAMB

Edited with an Introduction

By EDWARD GILPIN JOHNSON

CHICAGO
A. C. McCLURG AND COMPANY
1892

CONTENTS.

CONTENTS.

CONTENTS.

INTRODUCTION.

— ◆ —

No writer, perhaps, since the days of Dr. Johnson has been oftener brought before us in biographies, essays, letters, etc., than Charles Lamb. His stammering speech, his gaiter-clad legs, — " almost immaterial legs," Hood called them, — his frail wisp of a body, topped by a head " worthy of Aristotle," his love of punning, of the Indian weed, and, alas! of the kindly production of the juniper-berry (he was not, he owned, " constellated under Aquarius "), his antiquarianism of taste, and relish of the crotchets and whimsies of authorship, are as familiar to us almost as they were to the group he gathered round him Wednesdays at No. 4, Inner Temple Lane, where " a clear fire, a clean hearth, and the rigor of the game " awaited them. Talfourd has unctuously celebrated Lamb's " Wednesday Nights." He has kindly left ajar a door through which posterity peeps in upon the company, — Hazlitt, Leigh Hunt, " Barry Cornwall," Godwin, Martin Burney, Crabb Robinson (a ubiquitous shade, dimly suggestive of that figment, " Mrs. Harris "), Charles Kemble, Fanny Kelly (" Barbara S."), on red-letter occasions Coleridge and Wordsworth, — and sees them discharging the severer offices of the whist-table (" cards were cards " then), and, later, unbending their minds over poetry, criticism, and metaphysics. Elia was no Barmecide host, and the serjeant dwells not without regret upon the solider business of the evening, — " the cold roast lamb or boiled beef, the heaps of smoking roasted potatoes, and the

vast jug of porter, often replenished from the foaming
pots which the best tap of Fleet Street supplied," hos-
pitably presided over by "the most quiet, sensible, and
kind of women," Mary Lamb.

The *literati* of Talfourd's day were clearly hardier
of digestion than their descendants are. Roast lamb,
boiled beef, "heaps of smoking roasted potatoes," pots
of porter, — a noontide meal for a hodman, — and the
hour midnight! One is reminded, *à propos* of Miss
Lamb's robust viands, that Elia somewhere confesses
to "an occasional nightmare;" "but I do not," he
adds, "keep a whole stud of them." To go deeper into
this matter, to speculate upon the possible germs, the
first vague intimations to the mind of Coleridge of the
weird spectra of "The Ancient Mariner," the phantas-
magoria of "Kubla Khan," would be, perhaps, over-
refining. "Barry Cornwall," too, Lamb tells us, "had
his tritons and his nereids gambolling before him in
nocturnal visions." No wonder!

It is not intended here to re-thresh the straw left by
Talfourd, Fitzgerald, Canon Ainger, and others, in the
hope of discovering something new about Charles Lamb.
In this quarter, at least, the wind shall be tempered to
the reader, — shorn as he is by these pages of a charm
ing letter or two. So far as fresh facts are concerned,
the theme may fairly be considered exhausted. Num-
berless writers, too, have rung the changes upon "poor
Charles Lamb," "dear Charles Lamb," "gentle Charles
Lamb," and the rest, — the final epithet, by the way,
being one that Elia, living, specially resented:

"For God's sake," he wrote to Coleridge, "don't make me
ridiculous any more by terming me gentle-hearted in print,
or do it in better verses. It did well enough five years ago,
when I came to see you, and was moral coxcomb enough at
the time you wrote the lines to feed upon such epithets; but
besides that the meaning of 'gentle' is equivocal at best, and
almost always means poor-spirited, the very quality of gen-

tleness is abhorrent to such vile trumpetings. My sentiment is long since vanished. I hope my *virtues* have done *sucking.* I can scarce think but you meant it in joke. I hope you did, for I should be ashamed to believe that you could think to gratify me by such praise, fit only to be a cordial to some green-sick sonneteer."

The indulgent pity conventionally bestowed upon Charles Lamb — one of the most manly, self-reliant of characters, to say nothing of his genius — is absurdly misplaced.

Still farther be it from us to blunt the edge of appetite by sapiently essaying to " analyze " and account for Lamb's special zest and flavor, as though his writings, or any others worth the reading, were put together upon principles of clockwork. We are perhaps over-fond of these arid pastimes nowadays. It is not the " sweet musk-roses," the " apricocks and dewberries " of literature that please us best: like Bottom the Weaver, we prefer the " bottle of hay." What a mockery of right enjoyment our endless prying and sifting, our hunting of riddles in metaphors, innuendoes in tropes, ciphers in Shakspeare! Literature exhausted, we may turn to art, and resolve, say, the Sistine Madonna (I deprecate the Manes of the " Divine Painter ") into some ingenious and recondite rebus. For such critical chopped-hay — sweeter to the modern taste than honey of Hybla — Charles Lamb had little relish. " I am, sir," he once boasted to an analytical, unimaginative proser who had insisted upon *explaining* some quaint passage in Marvell or Wither, " I am, sir, a matter-of-lie man." It was his best warrant to sit at the Muses' banquet. Charles Lamb was blessed with an intellectual palate as fine as Keats's, and could enjoy the savor of a book (or of that dainty, " in the whole *mundus edibilis* the most delicate," Roast Pig, for that matter) without pragmatically asking, as the king did of the apple in the dumpling, " how the devil it got there." His value as a critic is grounded in this capacity of *naive* enjoyment (not of pig, but of literature), of discerning beauty and making *us* discern it, — thus adding to the known treasures and pleasures of mankind.

Suggestions not unprofitable for these later days lurk in these traits of Elia the student and critic. How worthy the imitation, for instance, of those disciples who band together to treat a fine poem (of Browning, say, or Shelley) as they might a chapter in the Revelation, — speculating sagely upon the import of the seven seals and the horns of the great beast, instead of enjoying the obvious beauties of their author. To the school-master — whose motto would seem too often to be the counsel of the irate old lady in Dickens, " Give him a meal of chaff ! " — Charles Lamb's critical methods are rich in suggestion. How many ingenuous boys, lads in the very flush and hey-day of appreciativeness of the epic virtues, have been parsed, declined, and conjugated into an utter detestation of the melodious names of Homer and Virgil ! Better far for such victims had they, instead of aspiring to the vanities of a " classical educa-tion," sat, like Keats, unlearnedly at the feet of quaint Chapman, or Dryden, or even of Mr. Pope.

Perhaps, by way of preparative to the reading of Charles Lamb's letters, it will be well to run over once more the leading facts of his life. First let us glance at his outward appearance. Fortunately there are a number of capital pieces of verbal portraiture of Elia. Referring to the year 1817, " Barry Cornwall " wrote:

" Persons who had been in the habit of traversing Covent Garden at that time of night, by extending their walk a few yards into Russell Street have noticed a small, spare man clothed in black, who went out every morning, and returned every afternoon as the hands of the clock moved toward certain hours. You could not mistake him. He was some-what stiff in his manner, and almost clerical in dress, which indicated much wear. He had a long, melancholy face, with

keen, penetrating eyes; and he walked with a short, resolute
step citywards. He looked no one in the face for more than
a moment, yet contrived to see everything as he went on.
No one who ever studied the human features could pass him
by without recollecting his countenance; it was full of sensibility, and it came upon you like new thought, which you
could not help dwelling upon afterwards: it gave rise to
meditation, and did you good. This small, half-clerical man
was — Charles Lamb."

His countenance is thus described by Thomas Hood:

" His was no common face, none of those willow-pattern
ones which Nature turns out by thousands at her potteries,
but more like a chance specimen of the Chinese ware, — one
to the set ; unique, antique, quaint, you might have sworn to
it piecemeal, — a separate affidavit to each feature."

Mrs. Charles Mathews, wife of the comedian, who
met Lamb at a dinner, gives an amusing account of
him : —

" Mr. Lamb's first appearance was not prepossessing. His
figure was small and mean, and no man was certainly ever
less beholden to his tailor. His 'bran' new suit of black
cloth (in which he affected several times during the day to
take great pride, and to cherish as a novelty that he had
looked for and wanted) was drolly contrasted with his very
rusty silk stockings, shown from his knees, and his much too
large, thick shoes, without polish. His shirt rejoiced in a wide,
ill-plaited frill, and his very small, tight, white neckcloth was
hemmed to a fine point at the ends that formed part of a little bow. His hair was black and sleek, but not formal, and
his face the gravest I ever saw, but indicating great intellect,
and resembling very much the portraits of Charles I."

From this sprightly and not too flattering sketch we
may turn to Serjeant Talfourd's tender and charming
portrait, — slightly idealized, no doubt; for the man of
the coif held a brief for his friend, and was a poet
besides : —

" Methinks I see him before me now as he appeared then,
and as he continued without any perceptible alteration to me,

during the twenty years of intimacy which followed, and were closed by his death. A light frame, so fragile that it seemed as if a breath would overthrow it, clad in clerk-like black, was surmounted by a head of form and expression the most noble and sweet. His black hair curled crisply about an expanded forehead; his eyes, softly brown, twinkled with varying expression, though the prevalent expression was sad; and the nose, slightly curved, and delicately carved at the nostril, with the lower outline of the face delicately oval, completed a head which was finely placed upon the shoulders, and gave importance and even dignity to a diminutive and shadowy stem. Who shall describe his countenance, catch its quivering sweetness, and fix it forever in words? There are none, alas! to answer the vain desire of friendship. Deep thought, striving with humor; the lines of suffering wreathed into cordial mirth, and a smile of painful sweetness, present an image to the mind it can as little describe as lose. His personal appearance and manner are not unjustly characterized by what he himself says in one of his letters to Manning,[1] 'a compound of the Jew, the gentleman, and the angel.'"

The writings of Charles Lamb abound in passages of autobiography. "I was born," he tells us in that delightful sketch, "The Old Benchers of the Inner Temple," "and passed the first seven years of my life in the Temple. Its church, its halls, its gardens, its fountain, its river, I had almost said, — for in those young years what was this king of rivers to me but a stream that watered our pleasant places? — these are of my oldest recollections." His father, John Lamb, the "Lovel" of the essay cited, had come up a little boy from Lincolnshire to enter the service of Samuel Salt, — one of those "Old Benchers" upon whom the pen of Elia has shed immortality, a stanch friend and patron to the Lambs, the kind proprietor of that "spacious closet of good old English reading" upon whose "fair and wholesome pasturage" Charles and his sister, as children, "browsed at will."

[1] Letter L..

John Lamb had married Elizabeth Field, whose mother was for fifty years housekeeper at the country-seat of the Plumers. Blakesware. in Hertfordshire, the "Blakesmoor" of the Essays. frequent scene of Lamb's childish holiday sports. — a spacious mansion, with its park and terraces and "firry wilderness. the haunt of the squirrel and day-long murmuring wood-pigeon;" an Eden it must have seemed to the London-bred child, in whose fancy the dusty trees and sparrows and smoke-grimed fountain of Temple Court had been a pastoral. Within the cincture of its excluding garden-walls, wrote Elia in later years, " I could have exclaimed with that garden-loving poet,[1] —

> "' Bind me, ye woodbines, in your twines ;
> Curl me about, ye gadding vines;
> And oh, so close your circles lace
> That I may never leave this place :
> But lest your fetters prove too weak,
> Ere I your silken bondage break,
> Do you, O brambles, chain me too,
> And, courteous briers, nail me through.' "

At Blakesware. too, was the room whence the spirit of Sarah Battle — that " gentlewoman born " — winged its flight to a region where revokes and "luke-warm gamesters " are unknown.

To John and Elizabeth Lamb were born seven children, only three of whom. John, Mary, and Charles, survived their infancy. Of the survivors, Charles was the youngest, John being twelve and Mary ten years his senior, — a fact to be weighed in estimating the heroism of Lamb's later life. At the age of seven, Charles Lamb, "son of John Lamb, scrivener, and Elizabeth, his wife," was entered at the school of Christ's Hospital, — " the antique foundation of that godly and royal child King Edward VI." Of his life

[1] Cowley.

at this institution he has left us abundant and charming
memorials in the Essays, " Recollections of Christ's
Hospital," and " Christ's Hospital Five-and-thirty Years
Ago," — the latter sketch corrective of the rather op-
timistic impressions of the former.

With his schoolfellows Charles seems to have been,
despite his timid and retiring disposition (he said of
himself, " while the others were all fire and play, he
stole along with all the self-concentration of a young
monk "), a decided favorite. " Lamb," wrote C. V. Le
Grice, a schoolmate often mentioned in essay and
letter, " was an amiable, gentle boy, very sensible and
keenly observing, indulged by his schoolfellows and
by his master on account of his infirmity of speech.
. . . I never heard his name mentioned without the
addition of Charles, although, as there was no other
boy of the name of Lamb, the addition was unneces-
sary ; but there was an implied kindness in it, and it
was a proof that his gentle manners excited that
kindness."

For us the most important fact of the Christ's Hospital school-days is the commencement of Lamb's life-long
friendship with Samuel Taylor Coleridge, two years his
senior, and the object of his fervent hero-worship.
Most of us, perhaps, can find the true source of whatever of notable good or evil we have effected in life in
the moulding influence of one of these early friendships
or admirations. It is the boy's hero, the one he loves
and reverences among his schoolfellows, — not his taskmaster, — that is his true teacher, the setter of the
broader standards by which he is to abide through life.
Happy the man the feet of whose early idols have not
been of clay.

It was under the quickening influence of the eloquent,
precocious genius of the " inspired charity boy " that
Charles Lamb's ideals and ambitions shaped themselves
out of the haze of a child's conceptions. Coleridge at

sixteen was already a poet, his ear attuned to the subtlest melody of verse, and his hand rivalling, in preluding fragments. the efforts of his maturer years; he was already a philosopher, rapt in Utopian schemes and mantling hopes as enchanting — and as chimerical — as the pleasure-domes and caves of ice decreed by Kubla Khan; and the younger lad became his ardent disciple.

Lamb quitted Christ's Hospital, prematurely, in November. 1787, and the companionship of the two friends was for a time interrupted. To part with Coleridge, to exchange the ease and congenial scholastic atmosphere of the Hospital for the *res angusta domi*, for the intellectual starvation of a life of counting-house drudgery, must have been a bitter trial for him. But the shadow of poverty was upon the little household in the Temple; on the horizon of the future the blackening clouds of anxieties still graver were gathering; and the youngest child was called home to share the common burden.

Charles Lamb was first employed in the South Sea House, where his brother John[1] — a cheerful optimist, a *dilettante* in art. genial, prosperous. thoroughly selfish, in so far as the family fortunes were concerned an outsider — already held a lucrative post. It was not long before Charles obtained promotion in the form of a clerkship with the East India Company, — one of the last kind services of Samuel Salt, who died in the same year, 1792, — and with the East India Company he remained for the rest of his working life.

Upon the death of their generous patron the Lambs removed from the Temple and took lodgings in Little Queen Street, Holborn; and for Charles the battle of life may be said to have fairly begun. His work as a junior clerk absorbed, of course, the greater part of his day and of his year. Yet there were breathing-spaces: there were the long evenings with the poets; with Mar-

---

[1] The James Elia of the essay " My Relations."

2

lowe, Drayton, Drummond of Hawthornden, and Cowley, — "the sweetest names, which carry a perfume in the mention;" there were the visits to the play, the yearly vacation jaunts to sunny Hertfordshire. The intercourse with Coleridge, too, was now occasionally renewed. The latter had gone up to Cambridge early in 1791, there to remain — except the period of his six months' dragooning — for the next four years. During his visits to London it was the habit of the two schoolfellows to meet at a tavern near Smithfield, the "Salutation and Cat," to discuss the topics dear to both ; and it was about this time that Lamb's sonnet to Mrs Siddons, his first appearance in print, was published in the "Morning Chronicle."

The year 1796 was a terribly eventful one for the Lambs. There was a taint of insanity in the family on the father's side, and on May 27, 1796, we find Charles writing to Coleridge these sad words, — doubly sad for the ring of mockery in them :—

"My life has been somewhat diversified of late. The six weeks that finished last year and began this, your very humble servant spent very agreeably in a madhouse at Hoxton. I am got somewhat rational now, and don't bite any one. But mad I was !" [1]

Charles, thanks to the resolution with which he combated the tendency, and to the steadying influence of his work at the desk, — despite his occasional murmurs, his best friend and sheet-anchor in life, — never again succumbed to the family malady ; but from that moment, over his small household, Madness — like Death in Milton's vision — continually "shook its dart," and at best only "delayed to strike." [2]

It was in the September of 1796 that the calamity befell which has tinged the story of Charles and Mary

1 Letter I.   2 Talfourd's Memoir.

Lamb with the sombrest hues of the Greek tragedy. The family were still in the Holborn lodgings, — the mother an invalid, the father sinking into a second childhood. Mary, in addition to the burden of ministering to her parents, was working for their support with her needle.

At this point it will be well to insert a prefatory word or two as to the character of Mary Lamb; and here the witnesses are in accord. There is no jarring of opinion, as in her brother's case; for Charles Lamb has been sorely misjudged, — often, it must be admitted, with ground of reason; sometimes by persons who might and should have looked deeper. In a notable instance, the heroism of his life has been meanly overlooked by one who preached to mankind with the eloquence of the Prophets the prime need and virtue of recognizing the hero. If self-abnegation lies at the root of true heroism, Charles Lamb — that "sorry phenomenon" with an "insuperable proclivity to gin"[1] — was a greater hero than was covered by the shield of Achilles. The character of Mary Lamb is quickly summed up. She was one of the most womanly of women. "In all its essential sweetness," says Talfourd, "her character was like her brother's; while, by a temper more placid, a spirit of enjoyment more serene, she was enabled to guide, to counsel, to cheer him, and to protect him on the verge of the mysterious calamity, from the depths of which she rose so often unruffled to his side. To a friend in any difficulty she was the most comfortable of advisers, the wisest of consolers." Hazlitt said that "he never met with a woman who could reason, and had met with only one thoroughly reasonable, — Mary Lamb." The writings of Elia are strewn, as we know, with the tenderest tributes to her worth. "I wish," he says, "that I could throw into a heap the

---

[1] Carlyle.

remainder of our joint existences, that we might share
them in equal division."

The psychology of madness is a most subtle inquiry.
How slight the mysterious touch that throws the
smooth-running human mechanism into a chaos of
jarring elements, that transforms, in the turn of an
eyelash, the mild humanity of the gentlest of beings
into the unreasoning ferocity of the tiger.

The London "Times" of September 26, 1796, contained the following paragraph : —

"On Friday afternoon the coroner and a jury sat on the
body of a lady in the neighborhood of Holborn, who died in
consequence of a wound from her daughter the preceding day.
It appeared by the evidence adduced that while the family
were preparing for dinner, the young lady seized a case-knife
lying on the table, and in a menacing manner pursued a little
girl, her apprentice, round the room. On the calls of her
infirm mother to forbear, she renounced her first object, and
with loud shrieks approached her parent. The child, by her
cries, quickly brought up the landlord of the house, but too
late.[1] The dreadful scene presented him the mother lifeless,
pierced to the heart, on a chair, her daughter yet wildly standing over her with the fatal knife, and the old man, her father,
weeping by her side, himself bleeding at the forehead from
the effects of a severe blow he received from one of the forks
she had been madly hurling about the room.

"For a few days prior to this, the family had observed
some symptoms of insanity in her, which had so much increased on the Wednesday evening that her brother, early
the next morning, went to Dr. Pitcairn ; but that gentleman
was not at home.

"The jury of course brought in their verdict, — *Lunacy.*"

I need not supply the omitted names of the actors in
this harrowing scene. Mary Lamb was at once placed

---

[1] It would seem from Lamb's lettter to Coleridge (Letter IV.) that
it was *he*, not the landlord, who appeared thus too late, and who
snatched the knife from the unconscious hand.

in the Asylum at Hoxton, and the victim of her frenzy was laid to rest in the churchyard of St. Andrew's, Holborn. It became necessary for Charles and his father to make an immediate change of residence, and they took lodgings at Pentonville. There is a pregnant sentence in one of Lamb's letters that flashes with the vividness of lightning into the darkest recesses of those early troubles and embarrassments. "We are," he wrote to Coleridge, "*in a manner marked.*"

Charles Lamb after some weeks obtained the release of his sister from the Hoxton Asylum by formally undertaking her future guardianship,— a charge which was borne, until Death released the compact, with a steadfastness, a cheerful renunciation of what men regard as the crowning blessings of manhood,[1] that has shed a halo more radiant even than that of his genius about the figure — it was "small and mean," said sprightly Mrs. Mathews — of the India House clerk.

As already stated, the mania that had once attacked Charles never returned; but from the side of Mary Lamb this grimmest of spectres never departed. "Mary is again *from home;*" " Mary is *fallen ill* again : " how often do such tear-fraught phrases — tenderly veiled, lest some chance might bring them to the eye of the blameless sufferer — recur in the Letters ! Brother and sister were ever on the watch for the symptoms premonitory of the return of this " their sorrow's crown of sorrows." Upon their little holiday excursions, says Talfourd, a strait-waistcoat, carefully packed by Miss Lamb herself, was their constant companion. Charles Lloyd relates that he once met them slowly pacing together a little footpath in Hoxton fields, both weeping bitterly, and found on joining them that they were taking their solemn way to the old asylum. Thus, upon this guiltless pair were visited the sins of their fathers.

[1] The reader is referred to Lamb's beautiful essay, " Dream Children."

With the tragical events just narrated, the storm of calamity seemed to have spent its force, and there were thenceforth plenty of days of calm and of sunshine for Charles Lamb. The stress of poverty was lightened and finally removed by successive increases of salary at the India House; the introductions of Coleridge and his own growing repute in the world of letters gathered about him a circle of friends — Southey, Wordsworth, Hazlitt, Manning, Barton, and the rest — more congenial, and certainly more profitable, than the vagrant *intimados*, " to the world's eye a ragged regiment," who had wasted his substance and his leisure in the early Temple days.

Lamb's earliest avowed appearance as an author was in Coleridge's first volume of poems, published by Cottle, of Bristol, in 1796. " The effusions signed C. L.," says Coleridge in the preface, " were written by Mr. Charles Lamb, of the India House. Independently of the signature, their superior merit would have sufficiently distinguished them." The " effusions " were ,four sonnets, two of them — the most noteworthy — touching upon the one love-romance of Lamb's life,[1] — his early attachment to the " fair-haired " Hertfordshire girl, the " Anna " of the Sonnets, the " Alice W——n " of the Essays. We remember that Elia in describing the gallery of old family portraits, in the essay, " Blakesmoor in H —— shire," dwells upon " that beauty with the cool, blue, pastoral drapery, and a lamb, that hung next the great bay window, with the bright yellow Hertfordshire hair, *so like my Alice.*"

In 1797 Cottle issued a second edition of Coleridge's poems, this time with eleven additional pieces by Lamb, — making fifteen of his in all, — and containing verses by their friend Charles Lloyd. " It is unlikely," observes

---

[1] If we except his passing tenderness for the young Quakeress, Hester Savory. Lamb admitted that he had never spoken to the lady in his life.

Canon Ainger, "that this little venture brought any profit to its authors, or that a subsequent volume of blank verse by Lamb and Lloyd in the following year proved more remunerative." In 1798 Lamb, anxious for his sister's sake to add to his slender income, composed his "miniature romance," as Talfourd calls it, "Rosamund Gray;" and this little volume, which has not yet lost its charm, proved a moderate success. Shelley, writing from Italy to Leigh Hunt in 1819, said of it: "What a lovely thing is his 'Rosamund Gray'! How much knowledge of the sweetest and deepest part of our nature in it! When I think of such a mind as Lamb's, when I see how unnoticed remain things of such exquisite and complete perfection, what should I hope for myself if I had not higher objects in view than fame?"

It is rather unpleasant, in view of this generous — if overstrained — tribute, to find the object of it referring later to the works of his encomiast as "thin sown with profit or delight."[1]

In 1802 Lamb published in a small duodecimo his blank-verse tragedy, "John Woodvil," — it had previously been declined by John Kemble as unsuited to the stage, — and in 1806 was produced at the Drury Lane Theatre his farce "Mr. H.," the summary failure of which is chronicled with much humor in the Letters.[2]

The "Tales from Shakspeare," by Charles and Mary Lamb, were published by Godwin in 1807, and a second edition was called for in the following year. Lamb was now getting on surer — and more remunerative — ground; and in 1808 he prepared for the firm of Longmans his masterly "Specimens of the English Dramatic Poets contemporary with Shakspeare." Concerning this work he wrote to Manning : —

"Specimens are becoming fashionable. We have Specimens of Ancient English Poets, Specimens of Modern Eng-

---

[1] Letter LXXXIII   [2] Letters LXVII., LXVIII., LXIX.

lish Poets, Specimens of Ancient English Prose Writers, without end. They used to be called 'Beauties.' You have seen Beauties of Shakspeare? so have many people that never saw any beauties *in* Shakspeare."

From Charles Lamb's "Specimens" dates, as we know, the revival of the study of the old English dramatists other than Shakespeare. He was the first to call attention to the neglected beauties of those great Elizabethans, Webster, Marlowe, Ford, Dekker, Massinger, — no longer accounted mere "mushrooms that sprang up in a ring under the great oak of Arden."[1] The opportunity that was to call forth Lamb's special faculty in authorship came late in life. In January, 1820, Baldwin, Cradock, and Joy, the publishers, brought out the first number of a new monthly journal under the name of an earlier and extinct periodical, the "London Magazine," and in the August number appeared an article, "Recollections of the South Sea House," over the signature *Elia.*[2] With this delightful sketch the essayist Elia may be said to have been born. In none of Lamb's previous writings had there been more than a hint of that unique vein, — wise, playful, tender, fantastic, "everything by starts, and nothing long," exhibited with a felicity of phrase certainly unexcelled in English prose literature, — that we associate with his name. The careful reader of the Letters cannot fail to note that it is *there* that Lamb's peculiar quality in authorship is first manifest. There is a letter to Southey, written as early as 1798, that has the true Elia ring.[3] With the "London Magazine," which was discontinued in 1826,

---

[1] W. S. Landor.

[2] In assuming this pseudonym Lamb borrowed the name of a fellow-clerk who had served with him thirty years before in the South Sea House, — an Italian named Elia. The name has probably never been pronounced as Lamb intended "*Call him Ellia,*" he said in a letter to J. Taylor, concerning this old acquaintance.

[3] Letter XVII.

Elia was born, and with it he may be said to have died, — although some of his later contributions to the " New Monthly "[1] and to the " Englishman's Magazine " were included in the " Last Essays of Elia," collected and published in 1833. The first series of Lamb's essays under the title of Elia had been published in a single volume by Taylor and Hessey, of the " London Magazine," in 1823.

The story of Lamb's working life — latterly an uneventful one, broken chiefly by changes of abode and by the yearly holiday jaunts, "migrations from the blue bed to the brown" — from 1796, when the correspondence with Coleridge begins, is told in the letters. For thirty-three years he served the East India Company, and he served it faithfully and steadily. There is, indeed, a tradition that having been reproved on one occasion for coming to the office late in the morning, he pleaded that he always left it " so very early in the evening." Poets, we know, often "heard the chimes at midnight " in Elia's day, and the plea has certainly a most Lamb-like ring. That the Company's directors, however, were more than content with the service of their literate clerk, the sequel shows.

It is manifest in certain letters, written toward the close of 1824 and in the beginning of 1825, that Lamb's confinement was at last telling upon him, and that he was thinking of a release from his bondage to the " desk's dead wood." In February, 1825, he wrote to Barton, —

" Your gentleman brother sets my mouth watering after liberty. Oh that I were kicked out of Leadenhall with every mark of indignity, and a competence in my fob! The birds of the air would not be so free as I should. How I would prance and curvet it, and pick up cowslips, and ramble about purposeless as an idiot!"

[1] The rather unimportant series, " Popular Fallacies," appeared in the " New Monthly."

Later in March we learn that he had signified to the directors his willingness to resign.

" I am sick of hope deferred. The grand wheel is in agitation that is to turn up my fortune ; but round it rolls, and will turn up nothing. I have a glimpse of freedom, of becoming a gentleman at large, but I am put off from day to day. I have offered my resignation, and it is neither accepted nor rejected. Eight weeks am I kept in this fearful suspense. Guess what an absorbing state I feel it. I am not conscious of the existence of friends, present or absent. The East India directors alone can be that thing to me. I have just learned that nothing will be decided this week. Why the next ? Why any week ? "

But the " grand wheel " was really turning to some purpose, and a few days later, April 6, 1825, he joyfully wrote to Barton, —

" My spirits are so tumultuary with the novelty of my recent emancipation that I have scarce steadiness of hand, much more mind, to compose a letter. 1 am free, B. B., — free as air !

> " ' The little bird that wings the sky
> Knows no such liberty.'

I was set free on Tuesday in last week at four o'clock. I came home forever ! "

The quality of the generosity of the East India directors was not strained in Lamb's case. It should be recorded as an agreeable commercial phenomenon that these officials, men of business acting in " a business matter," — words too often held to exclude all such Quixotic matters as sentiment, gratitude, and Christian equity between man and man, — were not only just, but munificent.[1] From the path of Charles and Mary Lamb — already beset with anxieties grave enough —

[1] In the essay " The Superannuated Man " Lamb describes, with certain changes and modifications, his retirement from the India House.

they removed forever the shadow of want. Lamb's
salary at the time of his retirement was nearly seven
hundred pounds a year, and the offer made to him was
a pension of four hundred and fifty, with a deduction
of nine pounds a year for his sister, should she survive
him. '

Lamb lived to enjoy his freedom and the Company's
bounty nearly nine years. Soon after his retirement he
settled with his sister at Enfield, within easy reach of
his loved London, removing thence to the neighboring
parish of Edmonton, — his last change of residence.
Coleridge's death, in July, 1834, was a heavy blow to
him. "When I heard of the death of Coleridge," he
wrote, " it was without grief. It seemed to me that he
had long been on the confines of the next world, that
he had a hunger for eternity. I grieved then that I could
not grieve ; but since, I feel how great a part he was of
me. His great and dear spirit haunts me. I cannot
think a thought, I cannot make a criticism on men or
books, without an ineffectual turning and reference to
him. He was the proof and touchstone of all my cogi-
tations." Lamb did not long outlive his old schoolfellow.
Walking in the middle of December along the London
road, he stumbled and fell, inflicting a slight wound upon
his face. The injury at first seemed trivial ; but soon
after, erysipelas appearing, it became evident that his
general health was too feeble to resist. On the 27th of
December, 1834, he passed quietly away, whispering in
his last moments the names of his dearest friends.

Mary Lamb survived her brother nearly thirteen years,
dying, at the advanced age of eighty-two, on May 20,
1847. With increasing years her attacks had become
more frequent and of longer duration, till her mind became permanently weakened. After leaving Edmonton, she lived chiefly in a pleasant house in St. John's
Wood, surrounded by old books and prints, under the
care of a nurse. Her pension, together with the income

from her brother's savings, was amply sufficient for her support.

Talfourd, who was present at the burial of Mary Lamb, has eloquently described the earthly reunion of the brother and sister : —

" A few survivors of the old circle, then sadly thinned, attended her remains to the spot in Edmonton churchyard where they were laid, above those of her brother. In accordance with Lamb's own feeling, so far as it could be gathered from his expressions on a subject to which he did not often or willingly refer, he had been interred in a deep grave, simply dug and wattled round, but without any affectation of stone or brickwork to keep the human dust from its kindred earth. So dry, however, is the soil of the quiet churchyard that the excavated earth left perfect walls of stiff clay, and permitted us just to catch a glimpse of the still untarnished edges of the coffin, in which all the mortal part of one of the most delightful persons who ever lived was contained, and on which the remains of her he had loved with love ' passing the love of woman ' were henceforth to rest, — the last glances we shall ever have even of that covering, — concealed from us as we parted by the coffin of the sister. We felt, I believe, after a moment's strange shuddering, that the reunion was well accomplished ; although the true-hearted son of Admiral Burney, who had known and loved the pair we quitted from a child, and who had been among the dearest objects of existence to him, refused to be comforted."

There are certain handy phrases, the legal-tender of conversation, that people generally use without troubling themselves to look into their title to currency. It is often said, for instance, with an air of deploring a phase of general mental degeneracy, that " letter-writing is a lost art." And so it is, — not because men nowadays, if they were put to it, could not, on the average, write as good letters as ever (the average, although we certainly have no Lambs, and perhaps no Walpoles or Southeys to raise it, would probably be higher), but because the conditions that call for and develop the epistolary art have largely passed away. With our modern facility of communication, the letter has lost the pristine dignity of its function. The earth has dwindled strangely since the advent of steam and electricity, and in a generation used to Mr. Edison's devices, Puck's girdle presents no difficulties to the imagination. In Charles Lamb's time the expression "from Land's End to John O'Groat's" meant something: to-day it means a few comfortable hours by rail, a few minutes by telegraph. Wordsworth in the North of England was to Lamb, so far as the chance of personal contact was concerned, nearly as remote as Manning in China. Under such conditions a letter was of course a weighty matter; it was a thoughtful summary of opinion, a rarely re- curring budget of general intelligence, expensive to send, and paid for by the recipient ; and men put their minds and energies into composing it. " One wrote at that time," says W. C. Hazlitt, " a letter to an acquaint- ance in one of the home counties which one would only write nowadays to a settler in the Colonies or a relative in India."

But to whatever conditions or circumstances we may owe the existence of Charles Lamb's letters, their qual- ity is of course the fruit of the genius and temperament of the writer. Unpremeditated as the strain of the sky- lark, they have almost to excess (were that possible) the prime epistolary merit of spontaneity. From the brain of the writer to the sheet before him flows an unbroken Pactolian stream. Lamb, at his best, ranges with Shakspearian facility the gamut of human emotion, exclaiming, as it were at one moment, with Jaques, " Motley's the only wear ! " — in the next probing the source of tears. He is as ejaculatory with his pen as other men are with their tongues. Puns, quotations, con- ceits, critical estimates of the rarest insight and sug- gestiveness, chase each other over his pages like clouds over a summer sky; and the whole is leavened with the sterling ethical and æsthetic good sense that renders Charles Lamb one of the wholesomest of writers.

As to the plan on which the selections for this volume have been made, it needs only to be said that, in general, the editor has aimed to include those letters which exhibit most fully the writer's distinctive charm and quality. This plan leaves, of course, a residue of considerable biographical and critical value; but it is believed that to all who really love and appreciate him, Charles Lamb's "Best Letters" are those which are most uniquely and unmistakably Charles Lamb's.

E. G. J.

September, 1891.

THE BEST LETTERS

OF

CHARLES LAMB.

———•———

I.

TO SAMUEL TAYLOR COLERIDGE.

May 27, 1796.

DEAR COLERIDGE, — Make yourself perfectly easy
about May. I paid his bill when I sent your
clothes. I was flush of money, and am so still to
all the purposes of a single life; so give yourself
no further concern about it. The money would
be superfluous to me if I had it.

When Southey becomes as modest as his prede-
cessor, Milton, and publishes his Epics in duodecimo, I will read 'em; a guinea a book is somewhat
exorbitant, nor have I the opportunity of borrowing
the work. The extracts from it in the " Monthly
Review," and the short passages in your " Watchman," seem to me much superior to anything in his
partnership account with Lovell.[1] Your poems I
shall procure forthwith. There were noble lines in

---

[1] Southey had just published his " Joan of Arc," in quarto.
He and Lovell had published jointly, two years before,
" Poems by Bion and Moschus."

what you inserted in one of your numbers from "Religious Musings," but I thought them elaborate. I am somewhat glad you have given up that paper; it must have been dry, unprofitable, and of dissonant mood to your disposition. I wish you success in all your undertakings, and am glad to hear you are employed about the "Evidences of Religion." There is need of multiplying such books a hundred-fold in this philosophical age, to *prevent* converts to atheism, for they seem too tough disputants to meddle with afterwards. . . .

Coleridge, I know not what suffering scenes you have gone through at Bristol. My life has been somewhat diversified of late. The six weeks that finished last year and began this, your very humble servant spent very agreeably in a madhouse at Hoxton. I am got somewhat rational now, and don't bite any one. But mad I was! and many a vagary my imagination played with me, — enough to make a volume, if all were told. My sonnets I have extended to the number of nine since I saw you, and will some day communicate to you. I am beginning a poem in blank verse, which, if I finish, I publish. White[1] is on the eve of publishing (he took the hint from Vortigern) "Original Letters of Falstaff, Shallow," etc.; a copy you shall have when it comes out. They are without exception the best imitations I ever saw. Coleridge, it may convince you of my regards for you when I tell you my head ran on you in my madness as much almost

[1] A Christ's Hospital schoolfellow, the "Jem" White of the Elia essay, "The Praise of Chimney-Sweepers."

as on another person, who I am inclined to think was the more immediate cause of my temporary frenzy.

The sonnet I send you has small merit as poetry; but you will be curious to read it when I tell you it was written in my prison-house in one of my lucid intervals.

TO MY SISTER.

If from my lips some angry accents fell,
　Peevish complaint, or harsh reproof unkind,
　'T was but the error of a sickly mind
And troubled thoughts, clouding the purer well
　And waters clear of Reason; and for me
　Let this my verse the poor atonement be,—
　My verse, which thou to praise wert e'er inclined
Too highly, and with partial eye to see
No blemish. Thou to me didst ever show
　Kindest affection; and wouldst oft-times lend
　An ear to the desponding love-sick lay,
　Weeping my sorrows with me, who repay
But ill the mighty debt of love I owe,
　Mary, to thee, my sister and my friend.

With these lines, and with that sister's kindest remembrances to Cottle, I conclude.

　　　　　　Yours sincerely,

　　　　　　　　　　LAMB

II.

TO COLERIDGE.

(*No month*) 1796.

Tuesday night. — Of your " Watchman," the review of Burke was the best prose. I augured great things from the first number. There is some

3

exquisite poetry interspersed. I have re-read the extract from the " Religious Musings," and retract whatever invidious there was in my censure of it as elaborate. There are times when one is not in a disposition thoroughly to relish good writing. I have re-read it in a more favorable moment, and hesitate not to pronounce it sublime. If there be anything in it approaching to tumidity (which I meant not to infer ; by " elaborate " I meant simply " labored "), it is the gigantic hyperbole by which you describe the evils of existing society : " snakes, lions, hyenas, and behemoths," is carrying your resentment beyond bounds. The pictures of " The Simoom," of " Frenzy and Ruin," of " The Whore of Babylon," and " The Cry of Foul Spirits disinherited of Earth," and " The Strange Beatitude " which the good man shall recognize in heaven, as well as the particularizing of the children of wretchedness (I have unconsciously included every part of it), form a variety of uniform excellence. I hunger and thirst to read the poem complete. That is a capital line in your sixth number, —

" This dark, frieze-coated, hoarse, teeth-chattering month."

They are exactly such epithets as Burns would have stumbled on, whose poem on the ploughed-up daisy you seem to have had in mind. Your complaint that of your readers some thought there was too much, some too little, original matter in your numbers, reminds me of poor dead Parsons in the " Critic." " Too little incident ! Give me leave to tell you, sir, there is too much incident." I had

like to have forgot thanking you for that exquisite
little morsel, the first Sclavonian Song. The expression in the second, " more happy to be unhappy in hell," is it not very quaint? Accept my
thanks, in common with those of all who love good
poetry, for "The Braes of Yarrow." I congratulate
you on the enemies you must have made by your
splendid invective against the barterers in human
flesh and sinews. Coleridge, you will rejoice to
hear that Cowper is recovered from his lunacy, and
is employed on his translation of the Italian, etc.,
poems of Milton for an edition where Fuseli pre-
sides as designer. Coleridge, to an idler like
myself, to write and receive letters are both very
pleasant; but I wish not to break in upon your
valuable time by expecting to hear very frequently
from you. Reserve that obligation for your moments of lassitude, when you have nothing else to
do; for your loco-restive and all your idle propen-
sities, of course, have given way to the duties of
providing for a family. The mail is come in, but
no parcel; yet this is Tuesday. Farewell, then,
till to-morrow; for a niche and a nook I must leave
for criticisms. By the way, I hope you do not send
your own only copy of " Joan of Arc;" I will in
that case return it immediately.

Your parcel *is* come; you have been *lavish* of
your presents.

Wordsworth's poem I have hurried through, not
without delight. Poor Lovell! my heart almost
accuses me for the light manner I lately spoke of
him, not dreaming of his death. My heart bleeds

for your accumulated troubles; God send you
through 'em with patience. I conjure you dream
not that I will ever think of being repaid; the very
word is galling to the ears. I have read all your
"Religious Musings" with uninterrupted feelings
of profound admiration. You may safely rest your
fame on it. The best remaining things are what I
have before read, and they lose nothing by my
recollection of your manner of reciting 'em, for I
too bear in mind "the voice, the look," of absent
friends, and can occasionally mimic their manner
for the amusement of those who have seen 'em.
Your impassioned manner of recitation I can recall
at any time to mine own heart and to the ears
of the bystanders. I rather wish you had left the
monody on Chatterton concluding, as it did, ab-
ruptly. It had more of unity. The conclusion
of your "Religious Musings," I fear, will entitle you
to the reproof of your beloved woman, who wisely
will not suffer your fancy to run riot, but bids you
walk humbly with your God. The very last words, "I
exercise my young novitiate thought in ministeries
of heart-stirring song," though not now new to me,
cannot be enough admired. To speak politely, they
are a well-turned compliment to poetry. I hasten
to read "Joan of Arc," etc. I have read your lines
at the beginning of second book; [1] they are worthy
of Milton, but in my mind yield to your "Religious
Musings." I shall read the whole carefully, and
in some future letter take the liberty to particularize

---

[1] Coleridge contributed some four hundred lines to the
second book of Southey's epic.

my opinions of it. Of what is new to me among
your poems next to the "Musings," that beginning
"My Pensive Sara" gave me most pleasure. The
lines in it I just alluded to are most exquisite ; they
made my sister and self smile, as conveying a
pleasing picture of Mrs. C. checking your wild
wanderings, which we were so fond of hearing you
indulge when among us. It has endeared us more
than anything to your good lady, and your own self-
reproof that follows delighted us. _'T is_ a charming
poem throughout (you have well remarked that
charming, admirable, exquisite are the words ex-
pressive of feelings more than conveying of ideas,
else I might plead very well want of room in my
paper as excuse for generalizing). I want room
to tell you how we are charmed with your verses in
the manner of Spenser, etc. I am glad you resume
the "Watchman." Change the name ; leave out
all articles of news, and whatever things are peculiar to newspapers, and confine yourself to ethics,
verse, criticism ; or, rather, do not confine yourself. Let your plan be as diffuse as the "Specta-
tor," and I 'll answer for it the work prospers. If
I am vain enough to think I can be a contributor,
rely on my inclinations. Coleridge, in reading
your "Religious Musings," I felt a transient supe-
riority over you. I _have_ seen Priestley. I love to
see his name repeated in your writings. I love
and honor him almost profanely. You would be
charmed with his _Sermons_, if you never read 'em.
You have doubtless read his books illustrative of the
doctrine of Necessity. Prefixed to a late work of

his in answer to Paine, there is a preface giving an account of the man and his services to men, written by Lindsey, his dearest friend, well worth your reading.

Tuesday Eve. — Forgive my prolixity, which is yet too brief for all I could wish to say. God give you comfort, and all that are of your household! Our loves and best good-wishes to Mrs. C.

C. LAMB.

III.

TO COLERIDGE.

June 10, 1796.

WITH "Joan of Arc" I have been delighted, amazed. I had not presumed to expect anything of such excellence from Southey. Why, the poem is alone sufficient to redeem the character of the age we live in from the imputation of degenerating in poetry, were there no such beings extant as Burns, and Bowles, Cowper, and ——, — fill up the blank how you please; I say nothing. The subject is well chosen; it opens well. To become more particular, I will notice in their order a few passages that chiefly struck me on perusal. Page 26 : " Fierce and terrible Benevolence ! " is a phrase full of grandeur and originality. The whole context made me feel *possessed*, even like Joan herself. Page 28 : " It is most horrible with the keen sword to gore the finely fibred human frame," and what follows, pleased me mightily. In the second book, the first forty lines in particular are majestic and high-sounding. Indeed, the whole vision of the Palace of Ambition and what follows are supremely excellent. Your simile of the Laplander, " By Niemi's lake, or Balda Zhiok, or the mossy stone of Solfar-Kapper,"[1] will bear comparison with any in Milton for fulness of circumstance and lofty-pacedness of versification. Southey's similes, though many of 'em are capital, are all inferior. In one of his books, the simile of the oak in the storm occurs, I think, four times. To return : the light in which you view the heathen deities is accurate and beautiful. Southey's personifications in this book are so many fine and faultless pictures. I was much pleased with your manner of accounting for the reason why monarchs take delight in war. At the 447th line you have placed Prophets and Enthusiasts cheek by jowl, on too intimate a footing for the dignity of the former. Necessarian-like-speaking, it is correct. Page 98 : " Dead is the Douglas ! cold thy warrior frame, illustrious Buchan," etc., are of kindred excellence with Gray's " Cold is Cadwallo's tongue," etc. How famously the Maid baffles the Doctors, Seraphic and Irrefragable, " with all their trumpery ! " Page 126 : the procession, the appearances of the Maid, of the Bastard Son of Orleans, and of Tremouille, are full of fire and fancy, and exquisite melody of versification. The personifications from line 303 to 309, in the heat of the battle, had better been omitted ; they are not very striking, and only encumber. The converse which Joan and Conrade hold on the banks

[1] Lapland mountains. From Coleridge's " Destiny of Nations."

of the Loire is altogether beautiful. Page 313 :
the conjecture that in dreams " all things are that
seem," is one of those conceits which the poet delights to admit into his creed, — a creed, by the way,
more marvellous and mystic than ever Athanasius
dreamed of.   Page 315 : I need only *mention* those
lines ending with " She saw a serpent gnawing at
her heart ! "   They are good imitative lines : " he
toiled and toiled, of toil to reap no end, but endless
toil and never-ending woe."   Page 347 : Cruelty is
such as Hogarth might have painted her.   Page
361 : all the passage about Love (where he seems to
confound conjugal love with creating and preserving
love) is very confused, and sickens me with a load
of useless personifications ; else that ninth book is
the finest in the volume, — an exquisite combination
of the ludicrous and the terrible.   I have never read
either, even in translation, but such I conceive to
be the manner of Dante or Ariosto.   The tenth
book is the most languid.

On the whole, considering the celerity wherewith
the poem was finished, I was astonished at the
unfrequency of weak lines.   I had expected to find
it verbose.   Joan, I think, does too little in battle.
Dunois perhaps the same ; Conrade too much.   The
anecdotes interspersed among the battles refresh the
mind very agreeably, and I am delighted with the
very many passages of simple pathos abounding
throughout the poem, — passages which the author of
" Crazy Kate " might have written.   Has not Master
Southey spoke very slightingly in his preface and
disparagingly of Cowper's Homer?   What makes

him reluctant to give Cowper his fame? And does not Southey use too often the expletives " did " and " does "? They have a good effect at times, but are too inconsiderable, or rather become blemishes when they mark a style. On the whole, I expect Southey one day to rival Milton; I already deem him equal to Cowper, and superior to all living poets besides. What says Coleridge? The " Monody on Henderson " is *immensely good;* the rest of that little volume is *readable and above mediocrity.*[1] I proceed to a more pleasant task, — pleasant because the poems are yours; pleasant because you impose the task on me; and pleasant, let me add, because it will confer a whimsical importance on me to sit in judgment upon your rhymes. First, though, let me thank you again and again, in my own and my sister's name, for your invitations. Nothing could give us more pleasure than to come; but (were there no other reasons) while my brother's leg is so bad, it is out of the question. Poor fellow! he is very feverish and light-headed; but Cruikshanks has pronounced the symptoms favourable, and gives us every hope that there will be no need of amputation. God send not! We are necessarily confined with him all the afternoon and evening till very late, so that I am stealing a few minutes to write to you.

Thank you for your frequent letters; you are the only correspondent and, I might add, the only friend I have in the world. I go nowhere, and

---

[1] The " Monody " referred to was by Cottle, and appeared in a volume of poems published by him at Bristol in 1795. Coleridge had forwarded the book to Lamb for his opinion.

have no acquaintance. Slow of speech and reserved of manners, no one seeks or cares for my society, and I am left alone. Austin calls only occasionally, as though it were a duty rather, and seldom stays ten minutes. Then judge how thankful I am for your letters! Do not, however, burden yourself with the correspondence. I trouble you again so soon only in obedience to your injunctions. Complaints apart, proceed we to our task. I am called away to tea, — thence must wait upon my brother; so must delay till to-morrow. Farewell! — *Wednesday.*

Thursday. — I will first notice what is new to me. Thirteenth page : "The thrilling tones that concentrate the soul" is a nervous line, and the six first lines of page 14 are very pretty, the twenty-first effusion a perfect thing. That in the manner of Spenser is very sweet, particularly at the close ; the thirty-fifth effusion is most exquisite, — that line in particular, "And, tranquil, muse upon tranquillity." It is the very reflex pleasure that distinguishes the tranquillity of a thinking being from that of a shepherd, — a modern one I would be understood to mean, — a Damœtas ; one that keeps other people's sheep. Certainly, Coleridge, your letter from Shurton Bars has less merit than most things in your volume ; personally it may chime in best with your own feelings, and therefore you love it best. It has, however, great merit. In your fourth epistle that is an exquisite paragraph, and fancy-full, of " A stream there is which rolls in lazy flow," etc. " Murmurs sweet undersong 'mid jasmin bowers " is a

sweet line, and so are the three next. The concluding simile is far-fetched ; " tempest-honored "
is a quaintish phrase.

Yours is a poetical family. I was much surprised
and pleased to see the signature of Sara to that
elegant composition, the fifth epistle. I dare not
criticise the " Religious Musings ; " I like not to
select any part, where all is excellent. I can only
admire, and thank you for it in the name of a Christian, as well as a lover of good poetry ; only let me
ask, is not that thought and those words in Young,
" stands in the sun," — or is it only such as Young,
in one of his *better moments*, might have writ ?

> " Believe thou, O my soul,
> Life is a vision shadowy of Truth ;
> And vice, and anguish, and the wormy grave,
> Shapes of a dream ! "

I thank you for these lines in the name of a necessarian, and for what follows in next paragraph, in
the name of a child of fancy. After all, you cannot
nor ever will write anything with which I shall be so
delighted as what I have heard yourself repeat. You
came to town, and I saw you at a time when your
heart was yet bleeding with recent wounds. Like
yourself, I was sore galled with disappointed hope ;
you had

> " Many an holy lay
> That, mourning, soothed the mourner on his way."

I had ears of sympathy to drink them in, and they
yet vibrate pleasant on the sense. When I read in
your little volume your nineteenth effusion, or the
twenty-eighth or twenty-ninth, or what you call the

"Sigh," I think I hear *you* again. I image to my-self the little smoky room at the "Salutation and Cat," where we have sat together through the winter nights, beguiling the cares of life with poesy. When you left London, I felt a dismal void in my heart. I found myself cut off, at one and the same time, from two most dear to me. "How blest with ye the path could I have trod of quiet life!" In your conversation you had blended so many pleasant fan-cies that they cheated me of my grief; but in your absence the tide of melancholy rushed in again, and did its worst mischief by overwhelming my reason. I have recovered, but feel a stupor that makes me indifferent to the hopes and fears of this life. I sometimes wish to introduce a religious turn of mind; but habits are strong things, and my religious fervours are confined, alas! to some fleeting mo-ments of occasional solitary devotion.

A correspondence, opening with you, has roused me a little from my lethargy and made me conscious of existence. Indulge me in it; I will not be very troublesome! At some future time I will amuse you with an account, as full as my memory will per-mit, of the strange turn my frenzy took. I look back upon it at times with a gloomy kind of envy; for while it lasted, I had many, many hours of pure happiness. Dream not, Coleridge, of having tasted all the grandeur and wildness of fancy till you have gone mad! All now seems to me vapid, — compar-atively so. Excuse this selfish digression. Your "Monody"[1] is so superlatively excellent that I can

---

[1] The Monody on Chatterton.

only wish it perfect, which I can't help feeling it is not quite. Indulge me in a few conjectures; what I am going to propose would make it more compressed and, I think, more energetic, though, I am sensible, at the expense of many beautiful lines. Let it begin, " Is this the land of song-ennobled line ? " and proceed to " Otway's famished form ; " then, " Thee, Chatterton," to " blaze of Seraphim ; " then, " clad in Nature's rich array," to " orient day ; " then, " but soon the scathing lightning," to " blighted land ; " then, " sublime of thought," to " his bosom glows ; " then

> " But soon upon his poor unsheltered head
> Did Penury her sickly mildew shed ;
> Ah ! where are fled the charms of vernal grace,
> And joy's wild gleams that lightened o'er his face."

Then " youth of tumultuous soul " to " sigh," as before. The rest may all stand down to " gaze upon the waves below." What follows now may come next as detached verses, suggested by the " Monody," rather than a part of it. They are, indeed, in themselves, very sweet ;

> " And we, at sober eve, would round thee throng,
> Hanging enraptured on thy stately song ! "

in particular, perhaps. If I am obscure, you may understand me by counting lines. I have proposed omitting twenty-four lines ; I feel that thus compressed it would gain energy, but think it most likely you will not agree with me ; for who shall go about to bring opinions to the bed of Procrustes, and introduce among the sons of men a monotony

of identical feelings?   I only propose with diffidence.
Reject you, if you please, with as little remorse as
you would the color of a coat or the pattern of a
buckle, where our fancies differed.

The "Pixies" is a perfect thing, and so are the
"Lines on the Spring," page 28.   The "Epitaph
on an Infant," like a Jack-o'-lantern, has danced
about (or like Dr. Forster's[1] scholars) out of the
"Morning Chronicle" into the "Watchman," and
thence back into your collection.   It is very pretty,
and you seem to think so, but, may be, o'erlooked
its chief merit, that of filling up a whole page.   I
had once deemed sonnets of unrivalled use that way,
but your Epitaphs, I find, are the more diffuse.
"Edmund" still holds its place among your best
verses.   "Ah! fair delights" to "roses round," in
your poem called "Absence," recall (none more
forcibly) to my mind the tones in which *you recited
it*.   I will not notice, in this tedious (to you) manner, verses which have been so long delightful to me,
and which you already know my opinion of.   Of
this kind are Bowles, Priestley, and that most exquisite and most Bowles-like of all, the nineteenth effusion.   It would have better ended with "agony of
care;" the last two lines are obvious and unneces-
sary; and you need not now make fourteen lines of
it, now it is rechristened from a Sonnet to an
Effusion.

Schiller might have written the twentieth effusion; 't is worthy of him in any sense.   I was glad
to meet with those lines you sent me when my

---

[1] Dr. Faustus's.

sister was so ill; I had lost the copy, and I felt
not a little proud at seeing my name in your verse.
The "Complaint of Ninathoma" (first stanza in particular) is the best, or only good, imitation of
Ossian I ever saw, your "Restless Gale" excepted.
"To an Infant" is most sweet; is not "foodful,"
though, very harsh? Would not "dulcet" fruit
be less harsh, or some other friendly bi-syllable?
In "Edmund," "Frenzy! fierce-eyed child" is not
so well as "frantic," though that is an epithet adding nothing to the meaning. Slander *couching* was
better than "squatting." In the "Man of Ross"
it *was* a better line thus, —

"If 'neath this roof thy wine-cheered moments pass,"

than as it stands now. Time nor nothing can
reconcile me to the concluding five lines of "Kos-
ciusko;" call it anything you will but sublime.
In my twelfth effusion I had rather have seen what
I wrote myself, though they bear no comparison
with your exquisite lines, —

"On rose-leaf'd beds amid your faery bowers," etc.

I love my sonnets because they are the reflected
images of my own feelings at different times. To
instance, in the thirteenth, —

"How reason reeled," etc.,

are good lines, but must spoil the whole with me,
who know it is only a fiction of yours, and that the
"rude dashings" did in fact not "rock me to
repose." I grant the same objection applies not
to the former sonnet; but still I love my own feelings, — they are dear to memory, though they now

and then wake a sigh or a tear. "Thinking on
divers things fordone," I charge you, Coleridge,
spare my ewe-lambs; and though a gentleman may
borrow six lines in an epic poem (I should have
no objection to borrow five hundred, and without
acknowledging), still, in a sonnet, a personal poem,
I do not "ask my friend the aiding verse;" I
would not wrong your feelings by proposing any
improvements (did I think myself capable of sug-
gesting 'em) in such personal poems as "Thou
bleedest, my poor heart," — 'od so, — I am caught,
— I have already done it; but that simile I propose
abridging would not change the feeling or introduce
any alien ones. Do you understand me? In the
twenty-eighth, however, and in the "Sigh," and
that composed at Clevedon, things that come from
the heart direct, not by the medium of the fancy,
I would not suggest an alteration.

When my blank verse is finished, or any long
fancy poem, "propino tibi alterandum, cut-up-
andum, abridgeandum," just what you will with it;
but spare my ewe-lambs! That to "Mrs. Siddons,"
now, you were welcome to improve, if it had been
worth it; but I say unto you again, Coleridge, spare
my ewe-lambs! I must confess, were they mine,
I should omit, *in editione secunda*, effusions two and
three, because satiric and below the dignity of the
poet of "Religious Musings," fifth, seventh, half
of the eighth, that "Written in early youth," as far
as "thousand eyes," — though I part not unreluc-
tantly with that lively line, —

"Chaste joyance dancing in her bright blue eyes,"

and one or two just thereabouts. But I would substitute for it that sweet poem called " Recollection,"
in the fifth number of the " Watchman," better,
I think, than the remainder of this poem, though
not differing materially ; as the poem now stands,
it looks altogether confused. And do not omit those
lines upon the " Early Blossom " in your sixth number of the " Watchman ; " and I would omit the
tenth effusion, or what would do better, alter and
improve the last four lines. In fact, I suppose,
if they were mine, I should *not* omit 'em ; but your
verse is, for the most part, so exquisite that I
like not to see aught of meaner matter mixed with
it. Forgive my petulance and often, I fear, ill-
founded criticisms, and forgive me that I have,
by this time, made your eyes and head ache with
my long letter; but I cannot forego hastily the
pleasure and pride of thus conversing with you.
You did not tell me whether I was to include the
" Conciones ad Populum " in my remarks on your
poems. They are not unfrequently sublime, and
I think you could not do better than to turn 'em
into verse, — if you have nothing else to do. Austin, I am sorry to say, is a *confirmed* atheist. Stoddart, a cold-hearted, well-bred, conceited disciple of
Godwin, does him no good. His wife has several
daughters (one of 'em as old as himself). Surely
there is something unnatural in such a marriage.

How I sympathize with you on the dull duty of
a reviewer, and heartily damn with you Ned Evans
and the Prosodist ! I shall, however, wait impa-
tiently for the articles in the " Critical Review "

4

next month, because they are *yours.* Young Evans
(W. Evans, a branch of a family you were once
so intimate with) is come into our office, and sends
his love to you. Coleridge, I devoutly wish that
Fortune, who has made sport with you so long, may
play one freak more, throw you into London or
some spot near it, and there snug-ify you for life.
'T is a selfish but natural wish for me, cast as I am
" on life's wide plain, friendless." Are you acquainted with Bowles? I see by his last Elegy (written at Bath) you are near neighbors. — *Thursday.*

"And I can think I can see the groves again;"
"Was it the voice of thee;" "Turns not the voice
of thee, my buried friend;" "Who dries with her
dark locks the tender tear," — are touches as true
to Nature as any in his other Elegy, written at the
Hot Wells, about poor Kassell, etc. You are doubtless acquainted with it.

I do not know that I entirely agree with you in
your stricture upon my sonnet "To Innocence."
To men whose hearts are not quite deadened by
their commerce with the world, innocence (no
longer familiar) becomes an awful idea. So I felt
when I wrote it. Your other censures (qualified
and sweetened, though, with praises somewhat ex-
travagant) I perfectly coincide with; yet I choose
to retain the word "lunar," — indulge a "lunatic"
in his loyalty to his mistress the moon! I have just
been reading a most pathetic copy of verses on
Sophia Pringle, who was hanged and burned for coin-
ing. One of the strokes of pathos (which are very
many, all somewhat obscure) is, "She lifted up her

guilty forger to heaven." A note explains, by " forger," her right hand, with which she forged or coined the base metal. For " pathos " read " bathos." You have put me out of conceit with my blank verse by your " Religious Musings." I think it will come to nothing. I do not like 'em enough to send 'em. I have just been reading a book, which I may be too partial to, as it was the delight of my childhood ; but I will recommend it to you, — it is Izaak Walton's " Complete Angler." All the scientific part you may omit in reading. The dialogue is very simple, full of pastoral beauties, and will charm you. Many pretty old verses are interspersed. This letter, which would be a week's work reading only, I do not wish you to answer in less than a month. I shall be richly content with a letter from you some day early in July ; though, if you get anyhow *settled* before then, pray let me know it immediately ; 't would give me much satisfaction. Concerning the Unitarian chapel, the salary is the only scruple that the most rigid moralist would admit as valid. Concerning the tutorage, is not the salary low, and absence from your family unavoidable? London is the only fostering soil for genius. Nothing more occurs just now ; so I will leave you, in mercy, one small white spot empty below, to repose your eyes upon, fatigued as they must be with the wilderness of words they have by this time painfully travelled through. God love you, Coleridge, and prosper you through life ! though mine will be loss if your lot is to be cast at Bristol, or at Nottingham, or anywhere but London. Our loves to Mrs. C———. C. L.

IV.

TO COLERIDGE.

June 14, 1796.

I am not quite satisfied now with the Chatterton,[1] and with your leave will try my hand at it again.   A master-joiner, you know, may leave a cabinet to be finished, when his own hands are full.   To your list of illustrative personifications, into which a fine imagination enters, I will take leave to add the following from Beaumont and Fletcher's " Wife for a Month ; " 't is the conclusion of a description of a sea-fight : " The game of *death* was never played so nobly ; the meagre thief grew wanton in his mischiefs, and his shrunk, hollow eyes smiled on his ruins."   There is fancy in these of a lower order from " Bonduca " : " Then did I see these valiant men of Britain, like boding owls creep into tods of ivy, and hoot their fears to one another nightly."   Not that it is a personification, only it just caught my eye in a little extract-book I keep, which is full of quotations from B. and F. in particular, in which authors I can't help thinking there is a greater richness of poetical fancy than in any one, Shakspeare excepted.   Are you acquainted with Massinger?   At a hazard I will trouble you with a passage from a play of his called " A Very Woman."   The lines are spoken by a lover (disguised) to his faithless mistress.   You will remark the fine effect of the double endings.   You

---

[1] Coleridge's " Monody " on Chatterton.

will by your ear distinguish the lines, for I write 'em
as prose. "Not far from where my father lives, *a
lady*, a neighbor by, blest with as great a *beauty* as
Nature durst bestow without *undoing*, dwelt, and
most happily, as I thought then, and blest the
house a thousand times she *dwelt* in. This beauty,
in the blossom of my youth, when my first fire knew
no adulterate *incense*, nor I no way to flatter but my
fondness; in all the bravery my friends could *show
me*, in all the faith my innocence could *give me*, in
the best language my true tongue could *tell me*, and
all the broken sighs my sick heart *lend me*, I sued
and served ; long did I serve this *lady*, long was my
travail, long my trade to *win her ;* with all the duty
of my soul I SERVED HER." "Then she must love."
"She did, but never me : she could not *love me ;*
she would not love, she hated, — more, she *scorn'd
me ;* and in so a poor and base a way *abused me* for
all my services, for all my *bounties*, so bold neglects
flung on me." "What out of love, and worthy love,
I *gave her* (shame to her most unworthy mind !),
to fools, to girls, to fiddlers and her boys she flung,
all in disdain of me." One more passage strikes
my eye from B. and F.'s "Palamon and Arcite."
One of 'em complains in prison : "This is all our
world ; we shall know nothing here but one another,
hear nothing but the clock that tells us our woes ;
the vine shall grow, but we shall never see it," etc.
Is not the last circumstance exquisite? I mean not
to lay myself open by saying they exceed Milton,
and perhaps Collins in sublimity. But don't you
conceive all poets after Shakspeare yield to 'em in

variety of genius? Massinger treads close on their heels; but you are most probably as well acquainted with his writings as your humble servant. My quotations, in that case, will only serve to expose my barrenness of matter. Southey in simplicity and tenderness is excelled decidedly only, I think, by Beaumont and F. in his "Maid's Tragedy," and some parts of "Philaster" in particular, and elsewhere occasionally; and perhaps by Cowper in his "Crazy Kate," and in parts of his translation, such as the speeches of Hecuba and Andromache. I long to know your opinion of that translation. The Odyssey especially is surely very Homeric. What nobler than the appearance of Phœbus at the beginning of the Iliad, — the lines ending with "Dread sounding, bounding on the silver bow!"

I beg you will give me your opinion of the translation; it afforded me high pleasure. As curious a specimen of translation as ever fell into my hands, is a young man's in our office, of a French novel. What in the original was literally "amiable delusions of the fancy," he proposed to render "the fair frauds of the imagination." I had much trouble in licking the book into any meaning at all. Yet did the knave clear fifty or sixty pounds by subscription and selling the copyright. The book itself not a week's work! To-day's portion of my journalizing epistle has been very dull and poverty-stricken. I will here end.

Tuesday night.

I have been drinking egg-hot and smoking Oronooko (associated circumstances, which ever forci-

bly recall to my mind our evenings and nights at
the "Salutation"). My eyes and brain are heavy
and asleep, but my heart is awake; and if words
came as ready as ideas, and ideas as feelings, I
could say ten hundred kind things. Coleridge, you
know not my supreme happiness at having one
on earth (though counties separate us) whom I can
call a friend. Remember you those tender lines
of Logan? —

> " Our broken friendships we deplore,
>   And loves of youth that are no more ;
>   No after friendships e'er can raise
>   Th' endearments of our early days,
>   And ne'er the heart such fondness prove,
>   As when we first began to love."

I am writing at random, and half-tipsy, what you
may not *equally* understand, as you will be sober
when you read it ; but *my* sober and *my* half-tipsy
hours you are alike a sharer in.   Good night.

> " Then up rose our bard, like a prophet in drink,
>   Craigdoroch, thou 'lt soar when creation shall sink."
>   BURNS.

V.

TO COLERIDGE.

September 27, 1796.

MY DEAREST FRIEND, — White, or some of my
friends, or the public papers, by this time may have
informed you of the terrible calamities that have
fallen on our family.   I will only give you the out-
lines : My poor dear, dearest sister, in a fit of

insanity, has been the death of her own mother.
I was at hand only time enough to snatch the knife
out of her grasp. She is at present in a madhouse,
from whence I fear she must be moved to an hospital. God has preserved to me my senses, — I eat.
and drink, and sleep, and have my judgment, I
believe, very sound. My poor father was slightly
wounded, and I am left to take care of him and my
aunt. Mr. Norris, of the Blue-coat School, has been
very kind to us, and we have no other friend ; but,
thank God, I am very calm and composed, and able
to do the best that remains to do. Write as religious a letter as possible, but no mention of what is
gone and done with. With me " the former things
are passed away," and I have something more to do
than to feel.

God Almighty have us all in his keeping !

C. Lamb.

Mention nothing of poetry. I have destroyed
every vestige of past vanities of that kind. Do as
you please, but if you publish, publish mine (I give
free leave) without name or initial, and never send
me a book, I charge you.

Your own judgment will convince you not to take
any notice of this yet to your dear wife. You look
after your family ; I have my reason and strength
left to take care of mine. I charge you, don't think
of coming to see me. Write. I will not see you, if
you come. God Almighty love you and all of us !

C. Lamb.

VI.

October 3, 1796.

MY DEAREST FRIEND, — Your letter was an inestimable treasure to me. It will be a comfort to you,
I know, to know that our prospects are somewhat
brighter. My poor dear, dearest sister, the unhappy
and unconscious instrument of the Almighty's judgments on our house, is restored to her senses, to a
dreadful sense and recollection of what has past,
awful to her mind and impressive (as it must be to
the end of life), but tempered with religious resignation and the reasonings of a sound judgment, which
in this early stage knows how to distinguish between
a deed committed in a transient fit of frenzy, and
the terrible guilt of a mother's murder. I have seen
her. I found her, this morning, calm and serene ;
far, very, very far, from an indecent, forgetful serenity.
She has a most affectionate and tender concern for
what has happened. Indeed, from the beginning,
frightful and hopeless as her disorder seemed, I had
confidence enough in her strength of mind and religious principle to look forward to a time when *even
she* might recover tranquillity. God be praised,
Coleridge, wonderful as it is to tell, I have never
once been otherwise than collected and calm ; even
on the dreadful day and in the midst of the terrible
scene, I preserved a tranquillity which bystanders
may have construed into indifference,— a tranquil-

lity not of despair. Is it folly or sin in me to say that it was a religious principle that *most* supported me? I allow much to other favorable circumstances. I felt that I had something else to do than to regret. On that first evening my aunt was lying insensible, to all appearance like one dying; my father with his poor forehead plastered over, from a wound he had received from a daughter dearly loved by him, and who loved him no less dearly; my mother a dead and murdered corpse in the next room, — yet was I wonderfully supported. I closed not my eyes in sleep that night, but lay without terrors and without despair. I have lost no sleep since. I had been long used not to rest in things of sense, — had endeavored after a comprehension of mind unsatisfied with the " ignorant present time ; " and *this* kept me up. I had the whole weight of the family thrown on me; for my brother,[1] little disposed (I speak not without tenderness for him) at any time to take care of old age and infirmities, had now, with his bad leg, an exemption from such duties; and I was now left alone.

One little incident may serve to make you understand my way of managing my mind. Within a day or two after the fatal one, we dressed for dinner a tongue which we had had salted for some weeks in the house. As I sat down, a feeling like remorse struck me : this tongue poor Mary got for me, and can I partake of it now, when she is far away? A thought occurred and relieved me : if I give in

[1] John Lamb, the " James Elia " of the essay " My Relations."

to this way of feeling, there is not a chair, a room,
an object in our rooms, that will not awaken the
keenest griefs; I must rise above such weaknesses.
I hope this was not want of true feeling. I did not
let this carry me, though, too far. On the very
second day (I date from the day of horrors), as is
usual in such cases, there were a matter of twenty
people, I do think, supping in our room; they pre-
vailed on me to eat *with them* (for to eat I never
refused). They were all making merry in the room !
Some had come from friendship, some from busy
curiosity, and some from interest. I was going to
partake with them, when my recollection came that
my poor dead mother was lying in the next room, —
the very next room; a mother who through life
wished nothing but her children's welfare. Indignation, the rage of grief, something like remorse, rushed
upon my mind. In an agony of emotion I found my
way mechanically to the adjoining room, and fell on
my knees by the side of her coffin, asking forgive-
ness of Heaven, and sometimes of her, for forgetting
her so soon. Tranquillity returned, and it was the
only violent emotion that mastered me ; and I think
it did me good.

I mention these things because I hate conceal-
ment, and love to give a faithful journal of what
passes within me. Our friends have been very
good. Sam Le Grice,[1] who was then in town, was
with me the three or four first days, and was as
a brother to me, gave up every hour of his time,
to the very hurting of his health and spirits, in

---

[1] A Christ's Hospital schoolfellow.

constant attendance and humoring my poor father;
talked with him, read to him, played at cribbage
with him (for so short is the old man's recollection
that he was playing at cards, as though nothing had
happened, while the coroner's inquest was sitting
over the way!). Samuel wept tenderly when he
went away, for his mother wrote him a very severe
letter on his loitering so long in town, and he was
forced to go. Mr. Norris, of Christ's Hospital, has
been as a father to me, Mrs. Norris as a mother,
though we had few claims on them. A gentleman,
brother to my god-mother, from whom we never
had right or reason to expect any such assistance,
sent my father twenty pounds; and to crown all
these God's blessings to our family at such a time,
an old lady, a cousin of my father and aunt's, a
gentlewoman of fortune, is to take my aunt and
make her comfortable for the short remainder of
her days. My aunt is recovered, and as well as
ever, and highly pleased at thoughts of going, and
has generously given up the interest of her little
money (which was formerly paid my father for her
board) wholely and solely to my sister's use.
Reckoning this, we have, Daddy and I, for our
two selves and an old maid-servant to look after
him when I am out, which will be necessary, £170,
or £180 rather, a year, out of which we can spare
£50 or £60 at least for Mary while she stays at
Islington, where she must and shall stay during her
father's life, for his and her comfort. I know John
will make speeches about it, but she shall not go
into an hospital. The good lady of the madhouse

and her daughter, an elegant, sweet-behaved young
lady, love her, and are taken with her amazingly;
and I know from her own mouth she loves them,
and longs to be with them as much. Poor thing,
they say she was but the other morning saying she
knew she must go to Bethlem for life ; that one
of her brothers would have it so, but the other
would wish it not, but be obliged to go with the
stream ; that she had often, as she passed Bethlem,
thought it likely, " here it may be my fate to end
my days," conscious of a certain flightiness in her
poor head oftentimes, and mindful of more than
one severe illness of that nature before. A legacy
of £100 which my father will have at Christmas,
and this £20 I mentioned before, with what is in
the house, will much more than set us clear. If
my father, an old servant-maid, and I can't live, and
live comfortably, on £130 or £120 a year, we
ought to burn by slow fires ; and I almost would,
that Mary might not go into an hospital.

Let me not leave one unfavorable impression on
your mind respecting my brother. Since this has
happened, he has been very kind and brotherly;
but I fear for his mind. He has taken his ease
in the world, and is not fit himself to struggle with
difficulties, nor has much accustomed himself to
throw himself into their way ; and I know his language is already, " Charles, you must take care of
yourself, you must not abridge yourself of a single
pleasure you have been used to," etc., and in
that style of talking. But you, a necessarian, can
respect a difference of mind, and love what *is ami-*

able in a character not perfect.   He has been very
good, but I fear for his mind.   Thank God, I
can unconnect myself with him, and shall manage
all my father's moneys in future myself, if I take
charge of Daddy, which poor John has not even
hinted a wish, at any future time even, to share
with me.   The lady at this madhouse assures me
that I may dismiss immediately both doctor and
apothecary, retaining occasionally a composing
draught or so for a while ; and there is a less expensive establishment in her house, where she will
only not have a room and nurse to herself, for £50
or guineas a year, — the outside would be £60.
You know, by economy, how much more even I
shall be able to spare for her comforts.   She will, I
fancy, if she stays, make one of the family rather
than of the patients ; and the old and young ladies I
like exceedingly, and she loves dearly ; and they,
as the saying is, take to her very extraordinarily,
if it is extraordinary that people who see my sister
should love her.

Of all the people I ever saw in the world, my
poor sister was most and thoroughly devoid of the
least tincture of selfishness.   I will enlarge upon her
qualities, poor dear, dearest soul, in a future letter, for my own comfort, for I understand her
thoroughly ; and if I mistake not, in the most trying situation that a human being can be found in,
she will be found (I speak not with sufficient humility, I fear, but humanly and foolishly speaking), —
she will be found, I trust, uniformly great and amiable.   God keep her in her present mind, to whom

be thanks and praise for all His dispensations to mankind !

C. Lamb.

These mentioned good fortunes and change of prospects had almost brought my mind over to the extreme the very opposite to despair. I was in danger of making myself too happy. Your letter brought me back to a view of things which I had entertained from the beginning. I hope (for Mary I can answer) — but I hope that *I* shall through life never have less recollection, nor a fainter impression, of what has happened than I have now. 'T is not a light thing, nor meant by the Almighty to be received lightly. I must be serious, circumspect, and deeply religious through life ; and by such means may *both* of us escape madness in future, if it so please the Almighty !

Send me word how it fares with Sara. I repeat it, your letter was, and will be, an inestimable treasure to me. You have a view of what my situation demands of me, like my own view, and I trust a just one.

Coleridge, continue to write, but do not forever offend me by talking of sending me cash. Sincerely and on my soul, we do not want it. God love you both !

I will write again very soon. Do you write directly.

VII.

TO COLERIDGE.

October 17, 1796.

MY DEAREST FRIEND, — I grieve from my very soul
to observe you in your plans of life veering about
from this hope to the other, and settling nowhere.
Is it an untoward fatality (speaking humanly) that
does this for you, — a stubborn, irresistible concur-
rence of events, — or lies the fault, as I fear it does,
in your own mind? You seem to be taking up
splendid schemes of fortune only to lay them down
again ; and your fortunes are an *ignis fatuus* that has
been conducting you in thought from Lancaster
Court, Strand, to somewhere near Matlock ; then
jumping across to Dr. Somebody's, whose son's tutor
you were likely to be ; and would to God the dancing demon *may* conduct you at last in peace and
comfort to the "life and labours of a cottager" !
You see from the above awkward playfulness of
fancy that my spirits are not quite depressed. I
should ill deserve God's blessings, which, since the
late terrible event, have come down in mercy upon
us, if I indulge in regret or querulousness. Mary
continues serene and cheerful. I have not by me a
little letter she wrote to me ; for though I see her
almost every day, yet we delight to write to one another, for we can scarce see each other but in company with some of the people of the house. I have
not the letter by me, but will quote from memory
what she wrote in it : "I have no bad, terrifying

dreams. At midnight, when I happen to awake, the nurse sleeping by the side of me, with the noise of the poor mad people around me, I have no fear. The spirit of my mother seems to descend and smile upon me, and bid me live to enjoy the life and reason which the Almighty has given me. I shall see her again in heaven; she will then understand me better. My grandmother, too, will understand me better, and will then say no more, as she used to do, ' Polly, what are those poor crazy, moythered brains of yours thinking of always?'" Poor Mary! my mother indeed *never understood* her right. She loved her, as she loved us all, with a mother's love; but in opinion, in feeling and sentiment and disposition, bore so distant a resemblance to her daughter that she never understood her right, — never could believe how much *she* loved her, but met her caresses, her protestations of filial affection, too frequently with coldness and repulse. Still, she was a good mother. God forbid I should think of her but *most* respectfully, *most* affectionately. Yet she would always love my brother above Mary, who was not worthy of one tenth of that affection which Mary had a right to claim. But it is my sister's gratifying recollection that every act of duty and of love she could pay, every kindness (and I speak true, when I say to the hurting of her health, and most probably in great part to the derangement of her senses) through a long course of infirmities and sickness she could show her, she ever did. I will some day, as I promised, enlarge to you upon my sister's excellences; 't will seem like exaggeration, but I will do it. At present,

short letters suit my state of mind best. So take my
kindest wishes for your comfort and establishment
in life, and for Sara's welfare and comforts with you.
God love you ; God love us all !

C. LAMB.

VIII.

TO COLERIDGE.

November 14, 1796.

COLERIDGE, I love you for dedicating your poetry
to Bowles.[1] Genius of the sacred fountain of tears,
it was he who led you gently by the hand through
all this valley of weeping, showed you the dark green
yew-trees and the willow shades where, by the fall of
waters, you might indulge in uncomplaining melancholy, a delicious regret for the past, or weave fine
visions of that awful future, —

> " When all the vanities of life's brief day
> Oblivion's hurrying hand hath swept away,
> And all its sorrows, at the awful blast
> Of the archangel's trump, are but as shadows past."

I have another sort of dedication in my head for
my few things, which I want to know if you approve
of and can insert.[2] I mean to inscribe them to my
sister. It will be unexpected, and it will give her
pleasure ; or do you think it will look whimsical

---

[1] The earliest sonnets of William Lisle Bowles were published in 1789, the year of Lamb's removal from Christ's
Hospital.

[2] Alluding to the prospective joint volume of poems (by
Coleridge, Lamb, and Charles Lloyd) to be published by Cottle
in 1797. This was Lamb's second serious literary venture, he
and Coleridge having issued a joint volume in 1796.

at all? As I have not spoke to her about it, I can easily reject the idea. But there is a monotony in the affections which people living together, or as we do now, very frequently seeing each other, are apt to give in to, — a sort of indifference in the expression of kindness for each other, which demands that we should sometimes call to our aid the trickery of surprise. Do you publish with Lloyd, or without him? In either case my little portion may come last, and after the fashion of orders to a country correspondent, I will give directions how I should like to have 'em done. The title-page to stand thus : —

POEMS
BY
CHARLES LAMB, OF THE INDIA HOUSE.

Under this title the following motto, which, for want of room, I put over-leaf, and desire you to insert whether you like it or no. May not a gentleman choose what arms, mottoes, or armorial bearings the herald will give him leave, without consulting his republican friend, who might advise none? May not a publican put up the sign of the Saracen's Head, even though his undiscerning neighbor should prefer, as more genteel, the Cat and Gridiron?

[MOTTO.]

" This beauty, in the blossom of my youth,
When my first fire knew no adulterate incense,
Nor I no way to flatter but my fondness,
In the best language my true tongue could tell me,
And all the broken sighs my sick heart lend me,
I sued and served. Long did I love this lady."[1]

MASSINGER.

[1] From "A Very Woman."

THE DEDICATION.

THE FEW FOLLOWING POEMS,
CREATURES OF THE FANCY AND THE FEELING
IN LIFE'S MORE VACANT HOURS,
PRODUCED, FOR THE MOST PART, BY
LOVE IN IDLENESS,
ARE,
WITH ALL A BROTHER'S FONDNESS,
INSCRIBED TO

MARY ANN LAMB,

THE AUTHOR'S BEST FRIEND AND SISTER.

This is the pomp and paraphernalia of parting, with which I take my leave of a passion which has reigned so royally (so long) within me ; thus, with its trappings of laureateship, I fling it off, pleased and satisfied with myself that the weakness troubles me no longer. I am wedded, Coleridge, to the fortunes of my sister and my poor old father. Oh, my friend, I think sometimes, could I recall the days that are past, which among them should I choose? Not those " merrier days," not the " plea-sant days of hope," not "those wanderings with a fair-hair'd maid,"[1] which I have so often and so feelingly regretted, but the days, Coleridge, of a *mother's* fondness for her *schoolboy*. What would I give to call her back to earth for *one* day, on my knees to ask her pardon for all those little asperities of temper which from time to time have

---

[1] An allusion to Lamb's first love, — the " Anna " of his sonnets, and the original, probably, of " Rosamund Gray " and of " Alice W——n " in the beautiful essay " Dream Children."

given her gentle spirit pain. And the day, my friend, I trust will come; there will be "time enough" for kind offices of love, if "Heaven's eternal year" be ours. Hereafter, her meek spirit shall not reproach me. Oh, my friend, cultivate the filial feelings, and let no man think himself released from the kind "charities" of relationship. These shall give him peace at the last; these are the best foundation for every species of benevolence. I rejoice to hear, by certain channels, that you, my friend, are reconciled with all your relations. 'T is the most kindly and natural species of love, and we have all the associated train of early feelings to secure its strength and perpetuity. Send me an account of your health; *indeed* I am solicitous about you. God love you and yours!

C. LAMB.

IX.

TO COLERIDGE.

[Fragment.]

Dec. 5, 1796.

AT length I have done with verse-making, — not that I relish other people's poetry less : theirs comes from 'em without effort ; mine is the difficult operation of a brain scanty of ideas, made more difficult by disuse. I have been reading "The Task" with fresh delight. I am glad you love Cowper. I could forgive a man for not enjoying Milton ; but I would not call that man my friend who should be offended with the "divine chit-chat of Cowper." Write to me. God love you and yours!

C. L.

X.

TO COLERIDGE.

Dec. 10, 1796.

I HAD put my letter into the post rather hastily, not expecting to have to acknowledge another from you so soon. This morning's present has made me alive again. My last night's epistle was childishly querulous; but you have put a little life into me, and I will thank you for your remembrance of me, while my sense of it is yet warm; for if I linger a day or two, I may use the same phrase of acknowledgment, or similar, but the feeling that dictates it now will be gone; I shall send you a *caput mortuum*, not a *cor vivens*. Thy "Watchman's," thy bellman's verses, I do retort upon thee, thou libellous varlet, — why, you cried the hours yourself, and who made you so proud? But I submit, to show my humility, most implicitly to your dogmas. I reject entirely the copy of verses you reject. With regard to my leaving off versifying,[1] you have said so many pretty things, so many fine compliments, ingeniously decked out in the garb of sincerity, and undoubtedly springing from a present feeling somewhat like sincerity, that you might melt the most un-muse-ical soul, did you not (now for a Rowland compliment for your profusion of Olivers), — did you not in your very epistle, by the many pretty fancies and profusion of heart displayed in

---

[1] See preceding letter.

it, dissuade and discourage me from attempting anything after you. At present I have not leisure to make verses, nor anything approaching to a fondness for the exercise. In the ignorant present time, who can answer for the future man? "At lovers' perjuries Jove laughs," — and poets have sometimes a disingenuous way of forswearing their occupation. This, though, is not my case. The tender cast of soul, sombred with melancholy and subsiding recollections, is favorable to the Sonnet or the Elegy; but from —

> "The sainted growing woof
> The teasing troubles keep aloof."

The music of poesy may charm for a while the importunate, teasing cares of life; but the teased and troubled man is not in a disposition to make that music.

You sent me some very sweet lines relative to Burns; but it was at a time when, in my highly agitated and perhaps distorted state of mind, I thought it a duty to read 'em hastily and burn 'em. I burned all my own verses, all my book of extracts from Beaumont and Fletcher and a thousand sources; I burned a little journal of my foolish passion which I had a long time kept, —

> "Noting, ere they past away,
> The little lines of yesterday."

I almost burned all your letters; I did as bad, — I lent 'em to a friend to keep out of my brother's sight, should he come and make inquisition into our papers; for much as he dwelt upon your conversation while you were among us, and delighted to be with you, it has been his fashion ever since to depreciate and cry you down, — you were the cause of my madness, you and your damned foolish sensibility and melancholy; and he lamented with a true brotherly feeling that we ever met,— even as the sober citizen, when his son went astray upon the mountains of Parnassus, is said to have cursed wit, and poetry, and Pope.[1] I quote wrong, but no matter. These letters I lent to a friend to be out of the way for a season; but I have claimed them in vain, and shall not cease to regret their loss. Your packets posterior to the date of my misfortunes, commencing with that valuable consolatory epistle, are every day accumulating, — they are sacred things with me.

Publish your *Burns* [2] when and how you like; it will be new to me, — my memory of it is very confused, and tainted with unpleasant associations. Burns was the god of my idolatry, as Bowles of yours. I am jealous of your fraternizing with Bowles, when I think you relish him more than Burns or my old favorite, Cowper. But you conciliate matters when you talk of the "divine chit-chat" of the latter; by the expression I see you thoroughly relish him. I love Mrs. Coleridge for her excuses an hundred-fold more dearly than if she heaped "line upon line," out-Hannah-ing Hannah More, and had

---

[1] Epistle to Arbuthnot : —

> "Poor Cornus sees his frantic wife elope,
>   And curses wit, and poetry, and Pope."

[2] The lines on him which Coleridge had sent to Lamb, and which the latter had burned.

rather hear you sing " Did a very little baby " by
your family fireside, than listen to you when you
were repeating one of Bowles's sweetest sonnets in
your sweet manner, while we two were indulging
sympathy, a solitary luxury, by the fireside at the
" Salutation." Yet have I no higher ideas of heaven.
Your company was one " cordial in this melancholy
vale,"--- the remembrance of it is a blessing partly,
and partly a curse. When I can abstract myself
from things present, I can enjoy it with a freshness of relish ; but it more constantly operates to
an unfavorable comparison with the uninterest-
ing converse I always and *only* can partake in. Not
a soul loves Bowles here ; scarce one has heard of
Burns ; few but laugh at me for reading my Testa-
ment, — they talk a language I understand not ; I
conceal sentiments that would be a puzzle to them.
I can only converse with you by letter, and with the
dead in their books. My sister, indeed, is all I can
wish in a companion ; but our spirits are alike
poorly, our reading and knowledge from the self-
same sources, our communication with the scenes of
the world alike narrow. Never having kept separate
company, or any " company " *together;* never having read separate books, and few books *together,* —
what knowledge have we to convey to each other?
In our little range of duties and connections, how few
sentiments can take place without friends, with few
books, with a taste for religion rather than a strong
religious habit ! We need some support, some
leading-strings to cheer and direct us. You talk
very wisely ; and be not sparing of *your advice.*

Continue to remember us, and to show us you do
remember us; we will take as lively an interest in
what concerns you and yours. All I can add to
your happiness will be sympathy. You can add to
mine *more:* you can teach me wisdom. I am indeed an unreasonable correspondent; but I was
unwilling to let my last night's letter go off without
this qualifier: you will perceive by this my mind is
easier, and you will rejoice. I do not expect or
wish you to write till you are moved; and of course
shall not, till you announce to me that event, think
of writing myself. Love to Mrs. Coleridge and
David Hartley, and my kind remembrance to
Lloyd, if he is with you.

C. LAMB.

XI.

TO COLERIDGE.

January 5, 1797.

Sunday Morning.— You cannot surely mean to
degrade the Joan of Arc into a pot-girl.[1] You are
not going, I hope, to annex to that most splendid
ornament of Southey's poem all this cock-and-a-bull

---

[1] Coleridge, in later years, indorsed Lamb's opinion of this
portion of his contribution to " Joan of Arc." " I was really
astonished," he said, " (1) at the schoolboy, wretched, alle-
goric machinery; (2) at the transmogrification of the fanatic
virago into a modern novel-pawing proselyte of the " Age of
Reason,"— a Tom Paine in petticoats; (3) at the utter want
of all rhythm in the verse, the monotony and dead plumb-down
of the pauses, and the absence of all bone, muscle, and sinew
in the single lines."

story of Joan, the publican's daughter of Neufchâtel,
with the lamentable episode of a wagoner, his wife,
and six children. The texture will be most lamenta-
bly disproportionate. The first forty or fifty lines of
these addenda are no doubt in their way admirable
too ; but many would prefer the Joan of Southey.

> " On mightiest deeds to brood
> Of shadowy vastness, such as made my heart
> Throb fast ; anon I paused, and in a state
> Of half expectance listened to the wind."

> " They wondered at me, who had known me once
> A cheerful, careless damsel."
> "The eye,
> That of the circling throng and of the visible world,
> Unseeing, saw the shapes of holy phantasy."

I see nothing in your description of the Maid equal
to these. There is a fine originality certainly in those
lines, —

> " For she had lived in this bad world
> As in a place of tombs,
> And touched not the pollutions of the dead ; "

but your "fierce vivacity" is a faint copy of the
"fierce and terrible benevolence" of Southey;
added to this, that it will look like rivalship in you,
and extort a comparison with Southey, — I think
to your disadvantage. And the lines, considered in
themselves as an addition to what you had before
written (strains of a far higher mood), are but such
as Madame Fancy loves in some of her more familiar moods, — at such times as she has met Noll
Goldsmith, and walked and talked with him, calling
him " old acquaintance." Southey certainly has no

pretensions to vie with you in the sublime of poetry ; but he tells a plain tale better than you. I will enumerate some woful blemishes, some of 'em sad deviations from that simplicity which was your aim. "Hailed who might be near" (the "canvas-coverture moving," by the by, is laughable) ; "a woman and six children" (by the way, why not nine children? It would have been just half as pathetic again) ; "statues of sleep they seemed ; " "frost-mangled wretch ; " "green putridity ; " "hailed him immortal" (rather ludicrous again) ; "voiced a sad and simple tale" (abominable !) ; "unprovendered ; " "such his tale ; " "Ah, suffering to the height of what was sufffered" (a most *insufferable line*) ; "amazements of affright ; " "The hot, sore brain attributes its own hues of ghastliness and torture" (what shocking confusion of ideas !).

In these delineations of common and natural feelings, in the familiar walks of poetry, you seem to resemble Montauban dancing with Roubigné's tenants,[1] "*much of his native loftiness remained in the execution.*"

I was reading your "Religious Musings" the other day, and sincerely I think it the noblest poem in the language next after the "Paradise Lost ; " and even that was not made the vehicle of such grand truths. "There is one mind," etc., down to "Almighty's throne," are without a rival in the whole compass of my poetical reading.

> "Stands in the sun, and with no partial gaze
> Views all creation."

[1] In Mackenzie's tale, "Julia de Roubigné."

I wish I could have written those lines. I rejoice that I am able to relish them. The loftier walks of Pindus are your proper region. There you have no compeer in modern times. Leave the lowlands, unenvied, in possession of such men as Cowper and Southey. Thus am I pouring balsam into the wounds I may have been inflicting on my poor friend's vanity.

In your notice of Southey's new volume you omit to mention the most pleasing of all, the " Miniature."

> " There were
> Who formed high hopes and flattering ones of thee,
> Young Robert ! "

> " Spirit of Spenser ! was the wanderer wrong ? "

Fairfax I have been in quest of a long time. Johnson, in his " Life of Waller," gives a most delicious specimen of him, and adds, in the true manner of that delicate critic, as well as amiable man, " It may be presumed that this old version will not be much read after the elegant translation of my friend Mr. Hoole." I endeavored — I wished to gain some idea of Tasso from this Mr. Hoole, the great boast and ornament of the India House, but soon desisted. I found him more vapid than smallest small beer " sun-vinegared." Your " Dream," down to that exquisite line, —

> " I can't tell half his adventures,"

is a most happy resemblance of Chaucer. The remainder is so-so. The best line, I think, is, " He belong'd, I believe, to the witch Melancholy." By

the way, when will our volume come out ? Don't
delay it till you have written a new "Joan of Arc."
Send what letters you please by me, and in any way
you choose, single or double. The India Company
is better adapted to answer the cost than the gener-
ality of my friend's correspondents, — such poor and
honest dogs as John Thelwall particularly. I cannot say I know Coulson, — at least intimately ; I once
supped with him and Austin ; I think his manners
very pleasing. I will not tell you what I think of
Lloyd, for he may by chance come to see this letter ;
and that thought puts a restraint on me. I cannot
think what subject would suit your epic genius, —
some philosophical subject, I conjecture, in which
shall be blended the sublime of poetry and of
science. Your proposed " Hymns " will be a fit
preparatory study wherewith " to discipline your
young novitiate soul." I grow dull ; I 'll go walk
myself out of my dulness.

Sunday Night. — You and Sara are very good
to think so kindly and so favorably of poor Mary ;
I would to God all did so too. But I very much
fear she must not think of coming home in my
father's lifetime. It is very hard upon her, but
our circumstances are peculiar, and we must submit
to them. God be praised she is so well as she is.
She bears her situation as one who has no right to
complain. My poor old aunt, whom you have seen,
the kindest, goodest creature to me when I was at
school ; who used to toddle there to bring me good
things, when I, schoolboy-like, only despised her for
it, and used to be ashamed to see her come and sit

herself down on the old coal-hole steps as you went into the old grammar-school. and open her apron, and bring out her basin, with some nice thing she had caused to be saved for me, [1] — the good old creature is now lying on her death-bed. I cannot bear to think on her deplorable state. To the shock she received on that our evil day, from which she never completely recovered, I impute her illness. She says, poor thing, she is glad she is come home to die with me. I was always her favourite ;

> " No after friendship e'er can raise
> The endearments of our early days ;
> Nor e'er the heart such fondness prove,
> As when it first began to love."

.   .   .   .   .

XII.

TO COLERIDGE.

January 10, 1797.

I NEED not repeat my wishes to have my little sonnets printed *verbatim* my last way. In particular, I fear lest you should prefer printing my first sonnet, as you have done more than once, " did the wand of Merlin wave," it looks so like Mr. Merlin,[2] the ingenious successor of the immortal Merlin, now living in good health and spirits, and flourishing in magical reputation, in Oxford Street ; and, on my life, one half who read it would understand it so.

---

[1] See the essay, " Christ's Hospital Five-and-Thirty Years Ago."

[2] A well-known conjuror of the time.

Do put 'em forth finally, as I have, in various letters,
settled it; for first a man's self is to be pleased, and
then his friends, — and of course the greater number of his friends, if they differ *inter se.* Thus taste
may safely be put to the vote. I do long to see
our names together, — not for vanity's sake, and
naughty pride of heart altogether; for not a living
soul I know, or am intimate with, will scarce read
the book, — so I shall gain nothing, *quoad famam;*
and yet there is a little vanity mixes in it, I cannot
help denying. — I am aware of the unpoetical cast
of the last six lines of my last sonnet, and think myself unwarranted in smuggling so tame a thing into
the book; only the sentiments of those six lines are
thoroughly congenial to me in my state of mind,
and I wish to accumulate perpetuating tokens of my
affection to poor Mary. That it has no originality
in its cast, nor anything in the feelings but what
is common and natural to thousands, nor ought
properly to be called poetry, I see ; still, it will tend
to keep present to my mind a view of things which
I ought to indulge. These six lines, too, have not,
to a reader, a connectedness with the foregoing.
Omit it if you like. — What a treasure it is to my
poor, indolent, and unemployed mind thus to lay
hold on a subject to talk about, though 't is but
a sonnet, and that of the lowest order! How
mournfully inactive I am! — 'T is night; good
night.

My sister, I thank God, is nigh recovered; she
was seriously ill. Do, in your next letter, and that
right soon, give me some satisfaction respecting

your present situation at Stowey. Is it a farm that you have got? and what does your worship know about farming?

Coleridge, I want you to write an epic poem. Nothing short of it can satisfy the vast capacity of true poetic genius. Having one great end to direct all your poetical faculties to, and on which to lay out your hopes, your ambition will show you to what you are equal. By the sacred energies of Milton! by the dainty, sweet, and soothing phantasies of honey-tongued Spenser! I adjure you to attempt the epic, or do something more ample than the writing an occasional brief ode or sonnet; something "to make yourself forever known, — to make the age to come your own." But I prate; doubtless you meditate something. When you are exalted among the lords of epic fame, I shall recall with pleasure and exultingly the days of your humility, when you disdained not to put forth, in the same volume with mine, your "Religious Musings" and that other poem from the "Joan of Arc," those promising first-fruits of high renown to come. You have learning, you have fancy, you have enthusiasm, you have strength and amplitude of wing enow for flights like those I recommend. In the vast and unexplored regions of fairy-land there is ground enough unfound and uncultivated: search there, and realize your favorite Susquehanna scheme. In all our comparisons of taste, I do not know whether I have ever heard your opinion of a poet very dear to me, — the now-out-of-fashion Cowley. Favor me with your judgment of him, and tell me if his prose essays, in particular, as well as no inconsiderable part of his verse, be not delicious. I prefer the graceful rambling of his essays even to the courtly elegance and ease of Addison, abstracting from this the latter's exquisite humor.

When the little volume is printed, send me three or four, at all events not more than six, copies, and tell me if I put you to any additional expense by printing with you. I have no thought of the kind, and in that case must reimburse you.

Priestley, whom I sin in almost adoring, speaks of " such a choice of company as tends to keep up that right bent and firmness of mind which a necessary intercourse with the world would otherwise warp and relax. . . . Such fellowship is the true balsam of life ; its cement is infinitely more durable than that of the friendships of the world, and it looks for its proper fruit and complete gratification to the life beyond the grave." Is there a possible chance for such an one as I to realize in this world such friendships? Where am I to look for 'em? What testimonials shall I bring of my being worthy of such friendship? Alas ! the great and good go together in separate herds, and leave such as I to lag far, far behind in all intellectual and, far more grievous to say, in all moral accomplishments. Coleridge, I have not one truly elevated character among my acquaintance, — not one Christian ; not one but undervalues Christianity. Singly what am I to do? Wesley (have you read his life?), was *he* not an elevated character? Wesley has said, " Religion is not a solitary thing." Alas ! it necessarily

is so with me, or next to solitary. 'T is true you
write to me. But correspondence by letter and
personal intimacy are very widely different. Do,
do write to me, and do some good to my mind, already how much " warped and relaxed " by the
world ! 'T is the conclusion of another evening.
Good night ; God have us all in His keeping !

If you are sufficiently at leisure, oblige me with
an account of your plan of life at Stowey ; your
literary occupations and prospects, — in short, make
me acquainted with every circumstance which, as
relating to you, can be interesting to me. Are you
yet a Berkleyan? Make me one. I rejoice in
being, speculatively, a necessarian. Would to God
I were habitually a practical one ! Confirm me in
the faith of that great and glorious doctrine, and
keep me steady in the contemplation of it. You
some time since expressed an intention you had of
finishing some extensive work on the Evidences of
Natural and Revealed Religion. Have you let that
intention go? Or are you doing anything towards
it? Make to yourself other ten talents. My letter
is full of nothingness. I talk of nothing. But I
must talk. I love to write to you. I take a pride
in it. It makes me think less meanly of myself. It
makes me think myself not totally disconnected
from the better part of mankind. I know I am too
dissatisfied with the beings around me ; but I cannot help occasionally exclaiming, " Woe is me, that
I am constrained to dwell with Meshech, and to
have my habitation among the tents of Kedar." I
know I am noways better in practice than my neigh-

bors, but I have a taste for religion, an occasional earnest aspiration after perfection, which they have not. I gain nothing by being with such as myself, — we encourage one another in mediocrity. I am always longing to be with men more excellent than myself. All this must sound odd to you; but these are my predominant feelings when I sit down to write to you, and I should put force upon my mind, were I to reject them. Yet I rejoice, and feel my privilege with gratitude, when I have been reading some wise book, such as I have just been reading, — Priestley on Philosophical Necessity, — in the thought that I enjoy a kind of communion, a kind of friendship even, with the great and good. Books are to me instead of friends. I wish they did not resemble the latter in their scarceness.

And how does little David Hartley? " Ecquid in antiquam virtutem?" Does his mighty name work wonders yet upon his little frame and opening mind? I did not distinctly understand you, — you don't mean to make an actual ploughman of him? Is Lloyd with you yet? Are you intimate with Southey? What poems is he about to publish? He hath a most prolific brain, and is indeed a most sweet poet. But how can you answer all the various mass of interrogation I have put to you in the course of the sheet? Write back just what you like, only write something, however brief. I have now nigh finished my page, and got to the end of another evening (Monday evening), and my eyes are heavy and sleepy, and my brain unsuggestive. I have just heart enough awake to say good night once

more, and God love you, my dear friend ; God love
us all !   Mary bears an affectionate remembrance of
you.

CHARLES LAMB.

XIII.

TO COLERIDGE.

February 13, 1797.

YOUR poem is altogether admirable — parts of it
are even exquisite ; in particular your personal account of the Maid far surpasses anything of the
sort in Southey.[1]   I perceived all its excellences,
on a first reading, as readily as now you have been
removing a supposed film from my eyes.   I was
only struck with a certain faulty disproportion in
the matter and the *style*, which I still think I perceive, between these lines and the former ones.   I
had an end in view, — I wished to make you reject
the poem, only as being discordant with the other ;
and, in subservience to that end, it was politically
done in me to over-pass, and make no mention of,
merit which, could you think me capable of *over-
looking*, might reasonably damn forever in your
judgment all pretensions in me to be critical.   There,
I will be judged by Lloyd whether I have not made
a very handsome recantation.   I was in the case of
a man whose friend has asked him his opinion of a
certain young lady ; the deluded wight gives judgment against her *in toto*, — don't like her face, her

---

[1] See Letter VIII.

walk, her manners; finds fault with her eyebrows;
can see no wit in her.   His friend looks blank;
he begins to smell a rat; wind veers about; he acknowledges her good sense, her judgment in dress,
a certain simplicity of manners and honesty of heart,
something too in her manners which gains upon you
after a short acquaintance, — and then her accurate
pronunciation of the French language, and a pretty,
uncultivated taste in drawing.   The reconciled gentleman smiles applause, squeezes him by the hand,
and hopes he will do him the honor of taking a bit
of dinner with Mrs. —— and him — a plain family
dinner — some day next week; " for, I suppose,
you never heard we were married.   I 'm glad to
see you like my wife, however; you 'll come and
see her, ha?"   Now am I too proud to retract entirely?   Yet I do perceive I am in some sort strait-
ened ; you are manifestly wedded to this poem, and
what fancy has joined, let no man separate.   I turn
me to the " Joan of Arc," second book.

The solemn openings of it are with sounds which,
Lloyd would say, " are silence to the mind."   The
deep preluding strains are fitted to initiate the mind,
with a pleasing awe, into the sublimest mysteries of
theory concerning man's nature and his noblest
destination, — the philosophy of a first cause; of
subordinate agents in creation superior to man;
the subserviency of pagan worship and pagan faith
to the introduction of a purer and more perfect religion, which you so elegantly describe as winning,
with gradual steps, her difficult way northward from
Bethabara.   After all this cometh Joan, a *publican's*

daughter, sitting on an ale-house *bench*, and marking
the *swingings* of the *signboard*, finding a poor man,
his wife and six children, starved to death with cold,
and thence roused into a state of mind proper to
receive visions emblematical of equality, — which,
what the devil Joan had to do with, I don't know,
or indeed with the French and American revolu-
tions; though that needs no pardon, it is executed
so nobly. After all, if you perceive no disproportion, all argument is vain; I do not so much object
to parts. Again, when you talk of building your
fame on these lines in preference to the " Religious
Musings," I cannot help conceiving of you and of
the author of that as two different persons, and I
think you a very vain man.

I have been re-reading your letter. Much of it I
could dispute; but with the latter part of it, in which
you compare the two Joans with respect to their
predispositions for fanaticism, I *toto corde* coincide;
only I think that Southey's strength rather lies in
the description of the emotions of the Maid under
the weight of inspiration. These (I see no mighty
difference between *her* describing them or *you* describing them),— these if you only equal, the previous admirers of his poem, as is natural, will prefer
his; if you surpass, prejudice will scarcely allow it,
and I scarce think you will surpass, though your
specimen at the conclusion (I am in earnest) I think
very nigh equals them. And in an account of a
fanatic or of a prophet the description of her *emotions* is expected to be most highly finished. By
the way, I spoke far too disparagingly of your lines,

and, I am ashamed to say, purposely. I should like
you to specify or particularize ; the story of the
" Tottering Eld," of " his eventful years all come
and gone," is too general ; why not make him a
soldier, or some character, however, in which he
has been witness to frequency of " cruel wrong and
strange distress " ?   I think I should.   When I
laughed at the " miserable man crawling from
beneath the coverture," I wonder I did not perceive
it was a laugh of horror,— such as I have laughed
at Dante's picture of the famished Ugolino.   Without falsehood, I perceive an hundred beauties in
your narrative.   Yet I wonder you do not perceive
something out-of-the-way, something unsimple and
artificial, in the expression, " voiced a sad tale."   I
hate made-dishes at the muses' banquet.   I believe I was wrong in most of my other objections.
But surely " hailed him immortal " adds nothing to
the terror of the man's death, which it was your
business to heighten, not diminish by a phrase
which takes away all terror from it.   I like that line,
" They closed their eyes in sleep, nor knew 't was
death."   Indeed, there is scarce a line I do not like.
" *Turbid* ecstasy " is surely not so good as what
you *had* written, — " troublous."   " Turbid " rather
suits the muddy kind of inspiration which London
porter confers.   The versification is throughout, to
my ears, unexceptionable, with no disparagement to
the measure of the " Religious Musings," which is
exactly fitted to the thoughts.

    You were building your house on a rock when
you rested your fame on that poem.   I can scarce

bring myself to believe that I am admitted to a familiar correspondence, and all the license of friendship, with a man who writes blank verse like Milton. Now, this is delicate flattery, *indirect* flattery. Go on with your " Maid of Orleans," and be content to be second to yourself. I shall become a convert to it, when 't is finished.

This afternoon I attend the funeral of my poor old aunt, who died on Thursday. I own I am thankful that the good creature has ended all her days of suffering and infirmity. She was to me the " cherisher of infancy ; " and one must fall on these occasions into reflections, which it would be commonplace to enumerate, concerning death, " of chance and change, and fate in human life." Good God, who could have foreseen all this but four months back ! I had reckoned, in particular, on my aunt's living many years ; she was a very hearty old woman. But she was a mere skeleton before she died ; looked more like a corpse that had lain weeks in the grave, than one fresh dead. " Truly the light is sweet, and a pleasant thing it is for the eyes to behold the sun : but let a man live many days, and rejoice in them all ; yet let him remember the days of darkness, for they shall be many." Coleridge, why are we to live on after all the strength and beauty of existence are gone, when all the life of life is fled, as poor Burns expresses it? Tell Lloyd I have had thoughts of turning Quaker, and have been reading, or am rather just beginning to read, a most capital book, good thoughts in good language, William Penn's " No Cross, no Crown ; " I like it immensely. Unluckily

I went to one of his meetings, tell him, in St. John Street, yesterday, and saw a man under all the agitations and workings of a fanatic, who believed himself under the influence of some "inevitable presence." This cured me of Quakerism; I love it in the books of Penn and Woolman, but I detest the vanity of a man thinking he speaks by the Spirit, when what he says an ordinary man might say without all that quaking and trembling. In the midst of his inspiration,—and the effects of it were most noisy,—was handed into the midst of the meeting a most terrible blackguard Wapping sailor; the poor man, I believe, had rather have been in the hottest part of an engagement, for the congregation of broad-brims, together with the ravings of the prophet, were too much for his gravity, though I saw even he had delicacy enough not to laugh out. And the inspired gentleman, though his manner was so supernatural, yet neither talked nor professed to talk anything more than good sober sense, common morality, with now and then a declaration of not speaking from himself. Among other things, looking back to this childhood and early youth, he told the meeting what a graceless young dog he had been, that in his youth he had a good share of wit. Reader, if thou hadst seen the gentleman, thou wouldst have sworn that it must indeed have been many years ago, for his rueful physiognomy would have scared away the playful goddess from the meeting, where he presided, forever. A wit! a wit! what could he mean? Lloyd, it minded me of Falkland in the "Rivals," "Am I full of wit and humor? No, indeed, you are not. Am I the life and soul of every company I come into? No, it cannot be said you are." That hard-faced gentleman a wit! Why, Nature wrote on his fanatic forehead fifty years ago, " Wit never comes, that comes to all." I should be as scandalized at a *bon-mot* issuing from his oracle-looking mouth as to see Cato go down a country-dance. God love you all! You are very good to submit to be pleased with reading my nothings. 'T is the privilege of friendship to talk nonsense and to have her nonsense respected. Yours ever,

C. LAMB.

XIV.

TO COLERIDGE.

January 28, 1798.

You have writ me many kind letters, and I have answered none of them. I don't deserve your attentions. An unnatural indifference has been creeping on me since my last misfortunes, or I should have seized the first opening of a correspondence with *you*. To you I owe much under God. In my brief acquaintance with you in London, your conversations won me to the better cause, and rescued me from the polluting spirit of the world. I might have been a worthless character without you; as it is, I do possess a certain improvable portion of devotional feelings, though when I view myself in the light of divine truth, and not according to the common measures of human judgment, I am altogether corrupt and sinful. This is no cant. I am very sincere.

These last afflictions,[1] Coleridge, have failed to soften and bend my will. They found me unprepared. My former calamities produced in me a spirit of humility and a spirit of prayer. I thought they had sufficiently disciplined me; but the event ought to humble me. If God's judgments now fail to take away from me the heart of stone, what more grievous trials ought I not to expect? I have been very querulous, impatient under the rod, full of little jealousies and heartburnings. I had wellnigh quarrelled with Charles Lloyd, and for no other reason, I believe, than that the good creature did all he could to make me happy. The truth is, I thought he tried to force my mind from its natural and proper bent: he continually wished me to be from home; he was drawing me *from* the consideration of my poor dear Mary's situation, rather than assisting me to gain a proper view of it with religious consolations. I wanted to be left to the tendency of my own mind in a solitary state which, in times past, I knew had led to quietness and a patient bearing of the yoke. He was hurt that I was not more constantly with him; but he was living with White, — a man to whom I had never been accustomed to impart my *dearest feelings*, though from long habits of friendliness, and many a social and good quality, I loved him very much. I met company there sometimes, — indiscriminate company. Any society almost, when I am in afflic-

[1] Mary Lamb had fallen ill again.

tion, is sorely painful to me. I seem to breathe more freely, to think more collectedly, to feel more properly and calmly, when alone. All these things the good creature did with the kindest intentions in the world, but they produced in me nothing but soreness and discontent. I became, as he complained, " jaundiced " towards him. . . . But he has forgiven me ; and his smile, I hope, will draw all such humors from me. I am recovering, God be praised for it, a healthiness of mind, something like calmness ; but I want more religion, I am jealous of human helps and leaning-places. I rejoice in your good fortunes. May God at the last settle you ! You have had many and painful trials ; humanly speaking, they are going to end ; but we should rather pray that discipline may attend us through the whole of our lives. . . . A careless and a dissolute spirit has advanced upon *me* with large strides. Pray God that my present afflictions may be sanctified to me ! Mary is recovering ; but I see no opening yet of a situation for her. Your invitation went to my very heart ; but you have a power of exciting interest, of leading all hearts captive, too forcible to admit of Mary's being with you. I consider her as perpetually on the brink of madness. I think you would almost make her dance within an inch of the precipice ; she must be with duller fancies and cooler intellects. I know a young man of this description who has suited her these twenty years, and may live to do so still, if we are one day restored to each other. In answer to your suggestions of occupation for me, I must say that I do

not think my capacity altogether suited for disquisitions of that kind. . . . I have read little; I
have a very weak memory, and retain little of what
I read; am unused to composition in which any
methodizing is required. But I thank you sincerely
for the hint, and shall receive it as far as I am able,
— that is, endeavor to engage my mind in some constant and innocent pursuit. I know my capacities
better than you do.

Accept my kindest love, and believe me yours,
as ever.

C. L.

XV.

TO ROBERT SOUTHEY

(No month, 1798.)

DEAR SOUTHEY, — I thank you heartily for the
eclogue;[1] it pleases me mightily, being so full
of picture-work and circumstances. I find no fault
in it, unless perhaps that Joanna's ruin is a catastrophe too trite; and this is not the first or second
time you have clothed your indignation, in verse, in
a tale of ruined innocence. The old lady, spinning
in the sun, I hope would not disdain to claim some
kindred with old Margaret. I could almost wish
you to vary some circumstances in the conclusion.
A gentleman seducer has so often been described
in prose and verse: what if you had accomplished
Joanna's ruin by the clumsy arts and rustic gifts
of some country fellow? I am thinking, I believe,
of the song, —

---

[1] The eclogue was entitled " The Ruined Cottage."

> " An old woman clothed in gray,
>   Whose daughter was charming and young,
>   And she was deluded away
>   By Roger's false, flattering tongue."

A Roger-Lothario would be a novel character; I think you might paint him very well. You may think this a very silly suggestion, and so indeed it is; but, in good truth, nothing else but the first words of that foolish ballad put me upon scribbling my "Rosamund." [1] But I thank you heartily for the poem. Not having anything of my own to send you in return, — though, to tell truth, I am at work upon something which, if I were to cut away and garble, perhaps I might send you an extract or two that might not displease you; but I will not do that; and whether it will come to anything, I know not, for I am as slow as a Fleming painter when I compose anything. I will crave leave to put down a few lines of old Christopher Marlowe's; I take them from his tragedy, " The Jew of Malta." The Jew is a famous character, quite out of nature; but when we consider the terrible idea our simple ancestors had of a Jew, not more to be discommended for a certain discoloring (I think Addison calls it) than the witches and fairies of Marlowe's mighty successor. The scene is betwixt Barabas, the Jew, and Ithamore, a Turkish captive exposed to sale for a slave.

BARABAS.

(*A precious rascal.*)

" As for myself, I walk abroad o' nights,
  And kill sick people groaning under walls;

---

[1] His romance, " Rosamund Gray."

Sometimes I go about and poison wells;
And now and then, to cherish Christian thieves,
I am content to lose some of my crowns,
That I may, walking in my gallery,
See 'm go pinioned along by my door.
Being young, I studied physic, and began
To practise first upon the Italian ;
There I enriched the priests with burials,
And always kept the sexton's arms in ure[1]
With digging graves and ringing dead men's knells.
And after that, was I an engineer,
And in the wars 'twixt France and Germany,
Under pretence of serving Charles the Fifth,
Slew friend and enemy with my stratagems.
Then after that was I an usurer,
And with extorting, cozening, forfeiting,
And tricks belonging unto brokery,
I fill'd the jails with bankrupts in a year,
And with young orphans planted hospitals,
And every moon made some or other mad;
And now and then one hang'd himself for grief,
Pinning upon his breast a long great scroll,
How I with interest tormented him."

Now hear Ithamore, the other gentle nature, explain how he has spent his time : —

ITHAMORE.

(*A Comical Dog.*)

" Faith, master, in setting Christian villages on fire,
Chaining of eunuchs, binding galley-slaves.
One time I was an hostler in an inn,
And in the night-time secret would I steal
To travellers' chambers, and there cut their throats.
Once at Jerusalem, where the pilgrims kneel'd,
I strewèd powder on the marble stones,
And therewithal their knees would rankle so,

---

[1] Use.

That I have laugh'd a-good to see the cripples
Go limping home to Christendom on stilts."

BARABAS.

" Why, this is something."

There is a mixture of the ludicrous and the terrible in these lines, brimful of genius and antique invention, that at first reminded me of your old description of cruelty in hell, which was in the true Hogarthian style. I need not tell *you* that Marlowe was author of that pretty madrigal, " Come live with me, and be my Love," and of the tragedy of " Edward II.," in which are certain *lines* unequalled in our English tongue. Honest Walton mentions the said madrigal under the denomination of " certain smooth verses made long since by Kit Marlowe."

I am glad you have put me on the scent after old Quarles. If I do not put up those eclogues, and that shortly, say I am no true-nosed hound. I have had a letter from Lloyd; the young metaphysician of Caius is well, and is busy recanting the new heresy, metaphysics, for the old dogma Greek. My sister, I thank you, is quite well. She had a slight attack the other day, which frightened me a good deal; but it went off unaccountably. Love and respects to Edith.

Yours sincerely,

C. LAMB.

XVI.

TO SOUTHEY.

November 8, 1798.

I PERFECTLY accord with your opinion of old Wither. Quarles is a wittier writer, but Wither lays more hold of the heart. Quarles thinks of his audience when he lectures; Wither soliloquizes in company with a full heart. What wretched stuff are the "Divine Fancies" of Quarles! Religion appears to him no longer valuable than it furnishes matter for quibbles and riddles; he turns God's grace into wantonness. Wither is like an old friend, whose warm-heartedness and estimable qualities make us wish he possessed more genius, but at the same time make us willing to dispense with that want. I always love W., and sometimes admire Q. Still, that portrait is a fine one; and the extract from "The Shepherds' Hunting" places him in a starry height far above Quarles. If you wrote that review in "Crit. Rev.," I am sorry you are so sparing of praise to the "Ancient Marinere;"[1] so far from calling it, as you do, with some wit but more severity, "A Dutch Attempt," etc., I call it a right English attempt, and a successful one, to dethrone German sublimity. You have selected a passage fertile in unmeaning miracles, but have passed by fifty passages as miraculous as the

---

[1] The "Lyrical Ballads" of Wordsworth and Coleridge had just appeared. The volume contained four pieces, including the "Ancient Mariner," by Coleridge.

miracles they celebrate. I never so deeply felt the pathetic as in that part, —

> " A spring of love gush'd from my heart,
>   And I bless'd them unaware."

It stung me into high pleasure through sufferings. Lloyd does not like it ; his head is too metaphysical, and your taste too correct, — at least I must allege something against you both, to excuse my own dotage, —

> " So lonely 't was, that God himself
>   Scarce seemèd there to be ! " etc.

But you allow some elaborate beauties ; you should have extracted 'em. " The Ancient Marinere " plays more tricks with the mind than that last poem, which is yet one of the finest written. But I am getting too dogmatical ; and before I degenerate into abuse, I will conclude with assuring you that I am,   Sincerely yours,

C. LAMB.

XVII.

TO SOUTHEY.

November 28, 1798.

.   .   .   .

I SHOWED my " Witch " and " Dying Lover " to Dyer [1] last night ; but George could not compre-

---

[1] This quaint scholar, a marvel of simplicity and universal optimism, is a constantly recurring and delightfully humorous character in the Letters. Lamb and Dyer had been school-fellows at Christ's Hospital.

hend how that could be poetry which did not go
upon ten feet, as George and his predecessors had
taught it to do; so George read me some lectures
on the distinguishing qualities of the Ode, the Epi-
gram, and the Epic, and went home to illustrate his
doctrine by correcting a proof-sheet of his own
Lyrics.   George writes odes where the rhymes, like
fashionable man and wife, keep a comfortable distance of six or eight lines apart, and calls that "observing the laws of verse."   George tells you, before
he recites, that you must listen with great attention,
or you'll miss the rhymes.   I did so, and found
them pretty exact.   George, speaking of the dead
Ossian, exclaimeth, "Dark are the poet's eyes."   I
humbly represented to him that his own eyes were
dark, and many a living bard's besides, and recommended "Clos'd are the poet's eyes."   But that
would not do.   I found there was an antithesis between the darkness of his eyes and the splendor of
his genius, and I acquiesced.

Your recipe for a Turk's poison is invaluable
and truly Marlowish. . . . Lloyd objects to "shutting up the womb of his purse" in my Curse (which
for a Christian witch in a Christian country is not
too mild, I hope): do you object?   I think there
is a strangeness in the idea, as well as "shaking the
poor like snakes from his door," which suits the
speaker.   Witches illustrate, as fine ladies do, from
their own familiar objects, and snakes and shutting
up of wombs are in their way.   I don't know that
this last charge has been before brought against 'em,
nor either the sour milk or the mandrake babe; but

I affirm these be things a witch would do if she could.

My tragedy[1] will be a medley (as I intend it to be a medley) of laughter and tears, prose and verse, and in some places rhyme, songs, wit, pathos, humor, and if possible, sublimity. — at least, it is not a fault in my intention if it does not comprehend most of these discordant colors. Heaven send they dance not the "Dance of Death!" I hear that the Two Noble Englishmen[2] have parted no sooner than they set foot on German earth; but I have not heard the reason, — possibly to give novelists a handle to exclaim, "Ah me, what things are perfect!" I think I shall adopt your emendation in the "Dying Lover," though I do not myself feel the objection against "Silent Prayer."

My tailor has brought me home a new coat lapelled, with a velvet collar. He assures me everybody wears velvet collars now. Some are born fashionable, some achieve fashion, and others, like your humble servant, have fashion thrust upon them. The rogue has been making inroads hitherto by modest degrees, foisting upon me an additional button, recommending gaiters; but to come upon me thus in a full tide of luxury, neither becomes him as a tailor or the ninth of a man. | My meek gentleman was robbed the other day, coming with his wife and family in a one-horse shay from Hampstead; the villains rifled him of four guineas, some shillings and half-

---

[1] John Woodvil.

[2] Coleridge and Wordsworth, who started for Germany together.

pence, and a bundle of customers' measures, which they swore were bank-notes. They did not shoot him, and when they rode off he addressed them with profound gratitude, making a congee : " Gentlemen, I wish you good-night ; and we are very much obliged to you that you have not used us ill ! " And this is the cuckoo that has the audacity to foist upon me ten buttons on a side and a black velvet collar, — a cursed ninth of a scoundrel !

When you write to Lloyd, he wishes his Jacobin correspondents to address him as *Mr.* C. L. Love and respects to Edith. I hope she is well.

Yours sincerely,

C. Lamb.

XVIII.

TO SOUTHEY.

March 20, 1799.

I am hugely pleased with your " Spider," " your old freemason," as you call him. The three first stanzas are delicious ; they seem to me a compound of Burns and Old Quarles, those kind of home-strokes, where more is felt than strikes the ear, — a terseness, a jocular pathos which makes one feel in laughter. The measure, too, is novel and pleasing. I could almost wonder Rob Burns in his lifetime never stumbled upon it. The fourth stanza is less striking, as being less original. The fifth falls off. It has no felicity of phrase, no old-fashioned phrase or feeling.

" Young hopes, and love's delightful dreams,"

savor neither of Burns nor Quarles; they seem more like shreds of many a modern sentimental sonnet. The last stanza hath nothing striking in it, if I except the two concluding lines, which are Burns all over. I wish, if you concur with me, these things could be looked to. I am sure this is a kind of writing which comes tenfold better recommended to the heart, comes there more like a neighbor or familiar, than thousands of Hamnels and Zillahs and Madelons. I beg you will send me the "Holly-tree," if it at all resemble this, for it must please me. I have never seen it. I love this sort of poems, that open a new intercourse with the most despised of the animal and insect race. I think this vein may be further opened; Peter Pindar hath very prettily apostrophized a fly; Burns hath his mouse and his louse; Coleridge, less successfully, hath made overtures of intimacy to a jackass, — therein only following at unresembling distance Sterne and greater Cervantes. Besides these, I know of no other examples of breaking down the partition between us and our "poor earth-born companions." It is sometimes revolting to be put in a track of feeling by other people, not one's own immediate thoughts, else I would persuade you, if I could (I am in earnest), to commence a series of these animal poems, which might have a tendency to rescue some poor creatures from the antipathy of mankind. Some thoughts come across me : for instance, to a rat, to a toad, to a cockchafer, to a mole, — people bake moles alive by a slow oven-fire to cure consumption. Rats are, indeed,

the most despised and contemptible parts of God's
earth.   I killed a rat the other day by punching
him to pieces, and feel a weight of blood upon me
to this hour.   Toads, you know, are made to fly,
and tumble down and crush all to pieces.   Cock-
chafers are old sport;   then again to a worm, with
an apostrophe to anglers, — those patient tyrants,
meek inflictors of pangs intolerable, cool devils;[1] to
an owl; to all snakes, with an apology for their
poison; to a cat in boots or bladders.   Your own
fancy, if it takes a fancy to these hints, will suggest
many more.   A series of such poems, suppose them
accompanied with plates descriptive of animal tor-
ments,— cooks roasting lobsters, fishmongers crimp-
ing skates, etc., — would take excessively.   I will
willingly enter into a partnership in the plan with
you; I think my heart and soul would go with it
too, — at least, give it a thought.   My plan is but
this minute come into my head; but it strikes me
instantaneously as something new, good, and useful,
full of pleasure and full of moral.   If old Quarles
and Wither could live again, we would invite them
into our firm.   Burns hath done his part.

Poor Sam Le Grice!   I am afraid the world

---

[1] Leigh Hunt says : "Walton says that an angler does no
hurt but to fish; and this he counts as nothing. . . . Now,
fancy a Genius fishing for us.   Fancy him baiting a great
hook with pickled salmon, and twitching up old Izaac Walton
from the banks of the River Lee, with the hook through his
ear.   How he would go up, roaring and screaming, and
thinking the devil had got him!

> " ' Other joys
>   Are but toys.'

> WALTON."

and the camp and the university have spoiled him among them. 'T is certain he had at one time a strong capacity of turning out something better. I knew him, and that not long since, when he had a most warm heart. I am ashamed of the indifference I have sometimes felt towards him. I think the devil is in one's heart. I am under obligations to that man for the warmest friendship and heartiest sympathy,[1] even for an agony of sympathy expressed both by word and deed, and tears for me when I was in my greatest distress. But I have forgot that, — as, I fear, he has nigh forgot the awful scenes which were before his eyes when he served the office of a comforter to me. No service was too mean or troublesome for him to perform. I can't think what but the devil, "that old spider," could have suck'd my heart so dry of its sense of all gratitude. If he does come in your way, Southey, fail not to tell him that I retain a most affectionate remembrance of his old friendliness, and an earnest wish to resume our intercourse. In this I am serious. I cannot recommend him to your society, because I am afraid whether he be quite worthy of it. But I have no right to dismiss him from *my* regard. He was at one time, and in the worst of times, my own familiar friend, and great comfort to me then. I have known him to play at cards with my father, meal-times excepted, literally all day long, in long days too, to save me from being teased by the old man when I was not able to bear it.

God bless him for it, and God bless you, Southey !

C. L.

[1] See Letter VI.

XIX.

TO THOMAS MANNING.[1]

March 1, 1800.

I HOPE by this time you are prepared to say the "Falstaff's Letters" are a bundle of the sharpest, queerest, profoundest humors of any these juice-drained latter times have spawned. I should have advertised you that the meaning is frequently hard to be got at, — and so are the future guineas that now lie ripening and aurifying in the womb of some undiscovered Potosi; but dig, dig, dig, dig, Manning! I set to with an unconquerable propulsion to write, with a lamentable want of what to write. My private goings on are orderly as the movements of the spheres, and stale as their music to angels' ears. Public affairs, except as they touch upon me, and so turn into private, I cannot whip up my mind to feel any interest in. I grieve, indeed, that War and Nature and Mr. Pitt, that hangs up in Lloyd's best parlour, should have conspired to call up three

[1] To this remarkable person we are largely indebted for some of the best of Lamb's letters. He was mathematical tutor at Caius College, Cambridge, and in later years became somewhat famous as an explorer of the remoter parts of China and Thibet. Lamb had been introduced to him, during a Cambridge visit, by Charles Lloyd, and afterwards told Crabb Robinson that he was the most "wonderful man" he ever met. An account of Manning will be found in the memoir prefixed to his "Journey to Lhasa," in 1811–12. (George Bogle and Thomas Manning's Journey to Thibet and Lhasa, by C. R. Markham, 1876.)

necessaries, simple commoners as our fathers knew them, into the upper house of luxuries, — bread and beer and coals, Manning. But as to France and Frenchmen, and the Abbé Siéyès and his constitutions, I cannot make these present times present to me. I read histories of the past, and I live in them; although, to abstract senses, they are far less momentous than the noises which keep Europe awake. I am reading Burnet's "Own Times." Did you ever read that garrulous, pleasant history? He tells his story like an old man, past political service, bragging to his sons on winter evenings of the part he took in public transactions when "his old cap was new." Full of scandal, which all true history is. No palliatives; but all the stark wickedness that actually gives the *momentum* to national actors. Quite the prattle of age and outlived importance. Truth and sincerity staring out upon you perpetually in *alto relievo*. Himself a party man, he makes you a party man. None of the cursed philosophical Humeian indifference, so cold and unnatural and inhuman! None of the cursed Gibbonian fine writing, so fine and composite. None of Dr. Robertson's periods with three members. None of Mr. Roscoe's sage remarks, all so apposite, and coming in so clever, lest the reader should have had the trouble of drawing an inference. Burnet's good old prattle I can bring present to my mind; I can make the Revolution present to me: the French Revolution, by a converse perversity in my nature, I fling as far *from* me. To quit this tiresome subject, and to relieve you from two or three dismal yawns, which I hear in spirit, I here conclude my more than commonly obtuse letter, — dull up to the dulness of a Dutch commentator on Shakspeare.

My love to Lloyd and Sophia.

C. L.

XX.

TO COLERIDGE.

May 12, 1800.

MY DEAR COLERIDGE, — I don't know why I write, except from the propensity misery has to tell her griefs. Hetty[1] died on Friday night, about eleven o'clock, after eight days' illness; Mary, in consequence of fatigue and anxiety, is fallen ill again, and I was obliged to remove her yesterday. I am left alone in a house with nothing but Hetty's dead body to keep me company. To-morrow I bury her, and then I shall be quite alone, with nothing but a cat to remind me that the house has been full of living beings like myself. My heart is quite sunk, and I don't know where to look for relief. Mary will get better again ; but her constantly being liable to such relapses is dreadful; nor is it the least of our evils that her case and all our story is so well known around us. We are in a manner *marked.* Excuse my troubling you ; but I have nobody by me to speak to me. I slept out last night, not being able to endure the change and the stillness. But I did not sleep well, and I must come back to my own bed. I am going to try and get a friend to

[1] The Lambs' old servant.

come and be with me to-morrow. I am completely shipwrecked. My head is quite bad. I almost wish that Mary were dead. God bless you. Love to Sara and Hartley.

C. LAMB.

XXI.

TO MANNING.

Before June, 1800.

DEAR MANNING, — I feel myself unable to thank you sufficiently for your kind letter. It was doubly acceptable to me, both for the choice poetry and the kind, honest prose which it contained. It was just such a letter as I should have expected from Manning.

I am in much better spirits than when I wrote last. I have had a very eligible offer to lodge with a friend in town. He will have rooms to let at midsummer, by which time I hope my sister will be well enough to join me. It is a great object to me to live in town, where we shall be much more *private*, and to quit a house and neighborhood where poor Mary's disorder, so frequently recurring, has made us a sort of marked people. We can be nowhere private except in the midst of London. We shall be in a family where we visit very frequently; only my landlord and I have not yet come to a conclusion. He has a partner to consult. I am still on the tremble, for I do not know where we could go into lodgings that would not be, in many respects, highly exceptionable. Only God send Mary

well again, and I hope all will be well ! The prospect, such as it is, has made me quite happy. I
have just time to tell you of it, as I know it will give
you pleasure. Farewell.

C. LAMB.

XXII.

TO COLERIDGE.

August, 6, 1800.

DEAR COLERIDGE, — I have taken to-day and
delivered to Longman and Co., *Imprimis* : your
books, viz., three ponderous German dictiona-
ries, one volume (I can find no more) of German
and French ditto, sundry other German books un-
bound, as you left them, Percy's Ancient Poetry,
and one volume of Anderson's Poets. I specify
them, that you may not lose any. *Secundo :* a
dressing-gown (value, fivepence), in which you used
to sit and look like a conjuror when you were
translating " Wallenstein." A case of two razors
and a shaving-box and strap. This it has cost me a
severe struggle to part with. They are in a brown-
paper parcel, which also contains sundry papers
and poems, sermons, *some few Epic* poems, — one
about Cain and Abel, which came from Poole,
etc., and also your tragedy ; with one or two small
German books, and that drama in which Got-fader
performs. *Tertio :* a small oblong box containing
all your letters, collected from all your waste papers,
and which fill the said little box. All other waste

papers, which I judged worth sending, are in the
paper parcel aforesaid. But you will find *all* your
letters in the box by themselves. Thus have I discharged my conscience and my lumber-room of all
your property, save and except a folio entitled
Tyrrell's " Bibliotheca Politica," which you used to
learn your politics out of when you wrote for the Post,
— *mutatis mutandis, i. e.*, applying past inferences
to modern *data*. I retain that, because I am sensible I am very deficient in the politics myself; and I
have torn up — don't be angry; waste paper has
risen forty per cent, and I can't afford to buy it —
all Bonaparte's Letters, Arthur Young's Treatise
on Corn, and one or two more light-armed infantry,
which I thought better suited the flippancy of London discussion than the dignity of Keswick thinking.
Mary says you will be in a passion about them when
you come to miss them ; but you must study philosophy. Read Albertus Magnus de Chartis Amissis
five times over after phlebotomizing, — 't is Burton's
recipe, — and then be angry with an absent friend if
you can. Sara is obscure. Am I to understand by
her letter that she sends a *kiss* to Eliza Bucking-
ham? Pray tell your wife that a note of interrogation on the superscription of a letter is highly
ungrammatical ! She proposes writing my name
Lambe? *Lamb* is quite enough. I have had the
Anthology, and like only one thing in it, — *Lewti ;* but
of that the last stanza is detestable, the rest most
exquisite ! The epithet *enviable* would dash the
finest poem. For God's sake (I never was more
serious), don't make me ridiculous any more by

terming me gentle-hearted in print, or do it in
better verses.[1] It did well enough five years ago,
when I came to see you, and was moral coxcomb
enough at the time you wrote the lines, to feed upon
such epithets ; but, besides that, the meaning of
" gentle " is equivocal at best, and almost always
means " poor-spirited ; " the very quality of gentle-
ness is abhorrent to such vile trumpetings. My
sentiment is long since vanished. I hope my *virtues*
have done *sucking*. I can scarce think but you
meant it in joke. I hope you did, for I should
be ashamed to think you could think to gratify me
by such praise, fit only to be a cordial to some green-
sick sonneteer.

.   .   .   .

XXIII.

TO MANNING.

August, 1800.

DEAR MANNING, —I am going to ask a favor of
you, and am at a loss how to do it in the most delicate manner. For this purpose I have been looking
into Pliny's Letters, who is noted to have had the
best grace in begging of all the ancients (I read
him in the elegant translation of Mr. Melmoth) ; but
not finding any case there exactly similar with mine,
I am constrained to beg in my own barbarian way.
To come to the point, then, and hasten into the

---

[1] An allusion to Coleridge's lines, " This Lime-Tree Bower
my Prison," wherein he styles Lamb " my gentle-hearted
Charles."

middle of things, have you a copy of your Algebra[1] to give away? I do not ask it for myself; I have too much reverence for the Black Arts ever to approach thy circle, illustrious Trismegist! But that worthy man and excellent poet, George Dyer, made me a visit yesternight on purpose to borrow one, supposing, rationally enough, I must say, that you had made me a present of one before this; the omission of which I take to have proceeded only from negligence: but it is a fault. I could lend him no assistance. You must know he is just now diverted from the pursuit of BELL LETTERS by a paradox, which he has heard his friend Frend[2] (that learned mathematician) maintain, that the negative quantities of mathematicians were *meræ nugæ*,— things scarcely *in rerum naturâ*, and smacking too much of mystery for gentlemen of Mr. Frend's clear Unitarian capacity. However, the dispute, once set a-going, has seized violently on George's pericranick; and it is necessary for his health that he should speedily come to a resolution of his doubts. He goes about teasing his friends with his new mathematics: he even frantically talks of purchasing Manning's Algebra, which shows him far gone, for, to my knowledge, he has not been master of seven shillings a good time. George's pockets and ——'s brains are two things in nature which do not abhor a vacuum. . . . Now, if you could step in, in this

[1] Manning, while at Cambridge, published a work on Algebra.

[2] The Rev. William Frend, who was expelled from Cambridge for Unitarianism.

trembling suspense of his reason, and he should find
on Saturday morning, lying for him at the Porter's
Lodge, Clifford's Inn, — his safest address, — Manning's Algebra, with a neat manuscriptum in the
blank leaf, running thus, " FROM THE AUTHOR ! " it
might save his wits and restore the unhappy author
to those studies of poetry and criticism which are
at present suspended, to the infinite regret of the
whole literary world.   N. B. — Dirty books, smeared
leaves, and dogs' ears will be rather a recommendation than otherwise.   N. B. — He must have the
book as soon as possible, or nothing can withhold
him from madly purchasing the book on tick. . . .
Then shall we see him sweetly restored to the chair
of Longinus, — to dictate in smooth and modest
phrase the laws of verse; to prove that Theocritus
first introduced the Pastoral, and Virgil and Pope
brought it to its perfection ; that Gray and Mason
(who always hunt in couples in George's brain) have
shown a great deal of poetical fire in their lyric poetry ;
that Aristotle's rules are not to be servilely followed,
which George has shown to have imposed great
shackles upon modern genius.   His poems, I find,
are to consist of two vols., reasonable octavo ; and
a third book will exclusively contain criticisms, in
which he asserts he has gone *pretty deeply* into the
laws of blank verse and rhyme, epic poetry, dramatic and pastoral ditto, — all which is to come out
before Christmas.   But above all he has *touched*
most *deeply* upon the Drama, comparing the English
with the modern German stage, their merits and
defects.   Apprehending that his *studies* (not to

mention his *turn*, which I take to be chiefly towards the lyrical poetry) hardly qualified him for these disquisitions, I modestly inquired what plays he had read. I found by George's reply that he *had* read Shakspeare, but that was a good while since : he calls him a great but irregular genius, which I think to be an original and just remark. (Beaumont and Fletcher, Massinger, Ben Jonson, Shirley, Marlowe, Ford, and the worthies of Dodsley's Collection, — he confessed he had read none of them, but professed his *intention* of looking through them all, so as to be able to *touch* upon them in his book.) So Shakspeare, Otway, and I believe Rowe, to whom he was naturally directed by Johnson's Lives, and these not read lately, are to stand him in stead of a general knowledge of the subject. God bless his dear absurd head !

By the by, did I not write you a letter with something about an invitation in it? — but let that pass ; I suppose it is not agreeable.

N. B. It would not be amiss if you were to accompany your *present* with a dissertation on negative quantities.

C. L.

XXIV.

TO MANNING.

1800.

GEORGE DYER is an Archimedes and an Archimagus and a Tycho Brahé and a Copernicus ; and thou art the darling of the Nine, and midwife to their wandering babe also ! We take tea with that learned poet and critic on Tuesday night, at half-past five, in his neat library ; the repast will be light and Attic, with criticism. If thou couldst contrive to wheel up thy dear carcase on the Monday, and after dining with us on tripe, calves' kidneys, or whatever else the Cornucopia of St. Clare may be willing to pour out on the occasion, might we not adjourn together to the Heathen's, thou with thy Black Backs, and I with some innocent volume of the Bell Letters, — Shenstone, or the like ; it would make him wash his old flannel gown (that has not been washed, to my knowledge, since it has been *his*, — Oh, the long time !) with tears of joy. Thou shouldst settle his scruples, and unravel his cobwebs, and sponge off the sad stuff that weighs upon his dear wounded pia mater ; thou shouldst restore light to his eyes, and him to his friends and the public ; Parnassus should shower her civic crowns upon thee for saving the wits of a citizen ! I thought I saw a lucid interval in George the other night : he broke in upon my studies just at tea-time, and brought with him Dr. Anderson, an old gentleman who ties his breeches' knees with packthread, and boasts that he has been disappointed by ministers. The Doctor wanted to see *me ;* for, I being a poet, he thought I might furnish him with a copy of verses to suit his " Agricultural Magazine." The Doctor, in the course of the conversation, mentioned a poem, called the " Epigoniad," by one Wilkie, an epic poem, in which there is not one tolerable good line all through, but every incident and speech borrowed from Homer.

George had been sitting inattentive seemingly to what was going on, — hatching of negative quantities, — when, suddenly, the name of his old friend Homer stung his pericranicks, and, jumping up, he begged to know where he could meet with Wilkie's work. " It was a curious fact that there should be such an epic poem and he not know of it ; and he *must* get a copy of it, as he was going to touch pretty deeply upon the subject of the epic, — and he was sure there must be some things good in a poem of eight thousand lines! " I was pleased with this transient return of his reason and recurrence to his old ways of thinking ; it gave me great hopes of a recovery, which nothing but your book can completely insure. Pray come on Monday if you *can*, and stay your own time. I have a good large room, with two beds in it, in the handsomest of which thou shalt repose a-nights, and dream of spheroides. I hope you will understand by the nonsense of this letter that I am *not* melancholy at the thoughts of thy coming ; I thought it necessary to add this, because you love *precision*. Take notice that our stay at Dyer's will not exceed eight o'clock, after which our pursuits will be our own. But indeed I think a little recreation among the Bell Letters and poetry will do you some service in the interval of severer studies. I hope we shall fully discuss with George Dyer what I have never yet heard done to my satisfaction, — the reason of Dr. Johnson's malevolent strictures on the higher species of the Ode.

C. LAMB.

XXV.

TO COLERIDGE.

August 14, 1800.

My head is playing all the tunes in the world, ringing such peals! It has just finished the "Merry Christ Church Bells," and absolutely is beginning "Turn again, Whittington." Buz, buz, buz; bum, bum, bum; wheeze, wheeze, wheeze; fen, fen, fen; tinky, tinky, tinky; *cr'annch*. I shall certainly come to be condemned at last. I have been drinking too much for two days running. I find my moral sense in the last stage of a consumption, and my religion getting faint. This is disheartening, but I trust the devil will not overpower me. In the midst of this infernal torture Conscience is barking and yelping as loud as any of them. I have sat down to read over again, and I think I do begin to spy out something with beauty and design in it. I perfectly accede to all your alterations, and only desire that you had cut deeper, when your hand was in.

. . . . .

Now I am on the subject of poetry, I must announce to you, who, doubtless, in your remote part of the island, have not heard tidings of so great a blessing, that George Dyer hath prepared two ponderous volumes full of poetry and criticism. They impend over the town, and are threatened to fall in the winter. The first volume contains every sort of poetry except personal satire, which George, in his

truly original prospectus, renounceth forever, whim-
sically foisting the intention in between the price
of his book and the proposed number of subscribers.
(If I can, I will get you a copy of his *handbill.*) He
has tried his *vein* in every species besides, — the
Spenserian, Thomsonian, Masonic, and Akensidish
more especially. The second volume is all criticism ; wherein he demonstrates to the entire satisfaction of the literary world, in a way that must
silence all reply forever, that the pastoral was introduced by Theocritus and polished by Virgil and
Pope ; that Gray and Mason (who always hunt in
couples in George's brain) have a good deal of poetical fire and true lyric genius; that Cowley was
ruined by excess of wit (a warning to all moderns) ;
that Charles Lloyd, Charles Lamb, and William
Wordsworth, in later days, have struck the true
chords of poesy. Oh, George, George, with a head
uniformly wrong and a heart uniformly right, that I
had power and might equal to my wishes ; then
would I call the gentry of thy native island, and
they should come in troops, flocking at the sound
of thy prospectus-trumpet, and crowding who shall
be first to stand in thy list of subscribers ! I can
only put twelve shillings into thy pocket (which, I
will answer for them, will not stick there long) out
of a pocket almost as bare as thine. Is it not a pity
so much fine writing should be erased? But, to tell
the truth, I began to scent that I was getting into
that sort of style which Longinus and Dionysius
Halicarnassus fitly call "the affected."

C. L.

XXVI

August 22, 1800.

DEAR MANNING, — You need not imagine any apology necessary. Your fine hare and fine birds (which just now are dangling by our kitchen blaze) discourse most eloquent music in your justification. You just nicked my palate ; for, with all due decorum and leave may it be spoken, my worship hath taken physic to-day, and being low and puling, requireth to be pampered. Foh ! how beautiful and strong those buttered onions come to my nose ! For you must know we extract a divine spirit of gravy from those materials which, duly compounded with a consistence of bread and cream (yclept bread-sauce), each to each giving double grace, do mutually illustrate and set off (as skilful gold-foils to rare jewels) your partridge, pheasant, woodcock, snipe, teal, widgeon, and the other lesser daughters of the ark. My friendship, struggling with my carnal and fleshly prudence (which suggests that a bird a man is the proper allotment in such cases), yearneth sometimes to have thee here to pick a wing or so. I question if your Norfolk sauces match our London culinaric.

George Dyer has introduced me to the table of an agreeable old gentleman, Dr. Anderson, who gives hot legs of mutton and grape pies at his sylvan lodge at Isleworth, where, in the middle of a street,

he has shot up a wall most preposterously before his
small dwelling, which, with the circumstance of his
taking several panes of glass out of bedroom windows (for air), causeth his neighbors to speculate
strangely on the state of the good man's pericranicks. Plainly, he lives under the reputation of
being deranged. George does not mind this circumstance ; he rather likes him the better for it.
The Doctor, in his pursuits, joins agricultural to poetical science, and has set George's brains mad about
the old Scotch writers, Barbour, Douglas's Æneid,
Blind Harry, etc. We returned home in a return
postchaise (having dined with the Doctor) ; and
George kept wondering and wondering, for eight or
nine turnpike miles, what was the name, and striving
to recollect the name, of a poet anterior to Barbour.
I begged to know what was remaining of his works.
"There is nothing *extant* of his works, sir ; but by
all accounts he seems to have been a fine genius ! "
This fine genius, without anything to show for it or
any title beyond George's courtesy, without even a
name, and Barbour and Douglas and Blind Harry
now are the predominant sounds in George's pia
mater, and their buzzings exclude politics, criticism,
and algebra,— the late lords of that illustrious lumber-room. Mark, he has never read any of these
bucks, but is impatient till he reads them *all*, at the
Doctor's suggestion. Poor Dyer ! his friends should
be careful what sparks they let fall into such inflam-
mable matter.

Could I have my will of the heathen, I would
lock him up from all access of new ideas ; I would

exclude all critics that would not swear me first
(upon their Virgil) that they would feed him with
nothing but the old, safe, familiar notions and sounds
(the rightful aborigines of his brain),— Gray, Aken-
side, and Mason. In these sounds, reiterated as
often as possible, there could be nothing painful,
nothing distracting.

God bless me, here are the birds, smoking hot !

All that is gross and unspiritual in me rises at the
sight !

Avaunt friendship and all memory of absent
friends !

C. LAMB.

XXVII.

TO COLERIDGE.

August 26, 1800.

.   .   .   .

GEORGE DYER is the only literary character I am
happily acquainted with. The oftener I see him,
the more deeply I admire him. He is goodness
itself. If I could but calculate the precise date of
his death, I would write a novel on purpose to make
George the hero. I could hit him off to a hair.

George brought a Dr. Anderson [1] to see me. The
Doctor is a very pleasant old man, a great genius
for agriculture, one that ties his breeches-knees with
packthread, and boasts of having had disappoint-
ments from ministers. The Doctor happened to
mention an epic poem by one Wilkie, called the

---

[1] See preceding Letter.

" Epigoniad." in which he assured us there is not one tolerable line from beginning to end, but all the characters, incidents, etc., verbally copied from *Homer*. George, who had been sitting quite inattentive to the Doctor's criticism, no sooner heard the sound of *Homer* strike his pericraniks, than up he gets, and declares he must see that poem immediately : where was it to be had ? An epic poem of eight thousand lines, and *he* not hear of it ! There must be some things good in it, and it was necessary he should see it, for he had touched pretty deeply upon that subject in his criticisms on the Epic. George had touched pretty deeply upon the Lyric, I find ; he has also prepared a dissertation on the Drama, and the comparison of the English and German theatres. As I rather doubted his competency to do the latter, knowing that his peculiar *turn* lies in the lyric species of composition, I questioned George what English plays he had read. I found that he *had* read Shakspeare (whom he calls an original, but irregular, genius), but it was a good while ago ; and he has dipped into Rowe and Otway, I suppose having found their names in Johnson's Lives at full length ; and upon this slender ground he has undertaken the task. He never seemed even to have heard of Fletcher, Ford, Marlowe, Massinger, and the worthies of Dodsley's Collection ; but he is to read all these, to prepare him for bringing out his " Parallel " in the winter. I find he is also determined to vindicate poetry from the shackles which Aristotle and some others have imposed upon it, — which is very good-natured of

him, and very necessary just now!   Now I am
touching so *deeply* upon poetry, can I forget that
I have just received from Cottle a magnificent copy
of his Guinea Epic.[1]   Four-and-twenty books to
read in the dog days!   I got as far as the Mad
Monk the first day, and fainted.   Mr. Cottle's
genius strongly points him to the *Pastoral*, but his
inclinations divert him perpetually from his calling.
He imitates Southey, as Rowe did Shakspeare, with
his " Good morrow to ye, good master Lieutenant."
Instead of *a* man, *a* woman, *a* daughter, he constantly writes "one a man," "one a woman," "one
his daughter."   Instead of *the* king, *the* hero, he
constantly writes, " he the king," "he the hero," —
two flowers of rhetoric palpably from the "Joan."
But Mr. Cottle soars a higher pitch; and when he
is original, it is in a most original way indeed.
His terrific scenes are indefatigable.   Serpents, asps,
spiders, ghosts, dead bodies, staircases made of nothing, with adders' tongues for bannisters, — Good
Heaven, what a brain he must have!   He puts as
many plums in his pudding as my grandmother
used to do; and then his emerging from Hell's
horrors into light, and treading on pure flats of this
earth — for twenty-three books together!

C. L.

---

[1] Alfred.

XXVIII.

TO COLERIDGE.

October 9, 1800.

I SUPPOSE you have heard of the death of Amos Cottle. I paid a solemn visit of condolence to his brother, accompanied by George Dyer, of burlesque memory. I went, trembling, to see poor Cottle so immediately upon the event. He was in black, and his younger brother was also in black. Everything wore an aspect suitable to the respect due to the freshly dead. For some time after our entrance, nobody spake, till George modestly put in a question, whether "Alfred" was likely to sell. This was Lethe to Cottle, and his poor face wet with tears, and his kind eye brightened up in a moment. Now I felt it was my cue to speak. I had to thank him for a present of a magnificent copy, and had promised to send him my remarks, — the least thing I could do; so I ventured to suggest that I perceived a considerable improvement he had made in his first book since the state in which he first read it to me. Joseph, who till now had sat with his knees cowering in by the fireplace, wheeled about, and with great difficulty of body shifted the same round to the corner of a table where I was sitting, and first stationing one thigh over the other, which is his sedentary mood, and placidly fixing his benevolent face right against mine, waited my observations. At that moment it came strongly into my mind that

I had got Uncle Toby before me, he looked so kind and so good. I could not say an unkind thing of " Alfred." So I set my memory to work to recollect what was the name of Alfred's queen, and with some adroitness recalled the well-known sound to Cottle's ears of Alswitha. At that moment I could perceive that Cottle had forgot his brother was so lately become a blessed spirit. In the language of mathematicians, the author was as 9, the brother as 1. I felt my cue, and strong pity working at the root, I went to work and beslabber'd " Alfred " with most unqualified praise, or only qualifying my praise by the occasional polite interposition of an exception taken against trivial faults, slips, and human imperfections, which, by removing the appearance of insincerity, did but in truth heighten the relish. Perhaps I might have spared that refinement, for Joseph was in a humor to hope and believe *all things.* What I said was beautifully supported, corroborated, and confirmed by the stupidity of his brother on my left hand, and by George on my right, who has an utter incapacity of comprehending that there can be anything bad in poetry. All poems are *good* poems to George; all men are *fine geniuses.* So what with my actual memory, of which I made the most, and Cottle's own helping me out, for I *really* had forgotten a good deal of " Alfred," I made shift to discuss the most essential parts entirely to the satisfaction of its author, who repeatedly declared that he loved nothing better than *candid* criticism. Was I a candid greyhound now for all this? or did I do right? I believe I did. The effect was luscious to my conscience. For all the rest of the evening Amos was no more heard of, till George revived the subject by inquiring whether some account should not be drawn up by the friends of the deceased to be inserted in " Phillips's Monthly Obituary ; " adding, that Amos was estimable both for his head and heart, and would have made a fine poet if he had lived. To the expediency of this measure Cottle fully assented, but could not help adding that he always thought that the qualities of his brother's heart exceeded those of his head. I believe his brother, when living, had formed precisely the same idea of him ; and I apprehend the world will assent to both judgments. I rather guess that the brothers were poetical rivals. I judged so when I saw them together. Poor Cottle, I must leave him, after his short dream, to muse again upon his poor brother, for whom I am sure in secret he will yet shed many a tear. Now send me in return some Greta news.

C. L.

XXIX.

TO MANNING.

October 16, 1800.

DEAR MANNING, — Had you written one week before you did, I certainly should have obeyed your injunction ; you should have seen me before my letter. I will explain to you my situation. There are six of us in one department. Two of us (within these four days) are confined with severe fevers; and two more, who belong to the Tower Militia, expect to have marching orders on Friday. Now, six are absolutely necessary. I have already asked and obtained two young hands to supply the loss of the *feverites;* and with the other prospect before me, you may believe I cannot decently ask leave of absence for myself. All I can promise (and I do promise with the sincerity of Saint Peter, and the contrition of sinner Peter if I fail) [is] that I will come *the very first spare week,* and go nowhere till I have been at Cambridge. No matter if you are in a state of pupilage when I come; for I can employ myself in Cambridge very pleasantly in the mornings. Are there not libraries, halls, colleges, books, pictures, statues? I wish you had made London in your way. There is an exhibition quite uncommon in Europe, which could not have escaped *your genius,* — a live rattlesnake, ten feet in length, and the thickness of a big leg. I went to see it last night by candlelight. We were ushered into a room very little bigger than ours at Pentonville. A man and woman and four boys live in this room, joint tenants with nine snakes, most of them such as no remedy has been discovered for their bite. We walked into the middle, which is formed by a half-moon of wired boxes, all mansions of *snakes,* — whip-snakes, thunder-snakes, pig-nose-snakes, American vipers, and *this monster.* He lies curled up in folds; and immediately a stranger enters (for he is used to the family, and sees them play at cards) he set up a rattle like a watchman's in London, or near as loud, and reared up a head, from the midst of these folds, like a toad, and shook his head, and showed every sign a snake can show of irritation. I had the foolish curiosity to strike the wires with my finger, and the devil flew at me with his toad-mouth wide open : the inside of his mouth is quite white. I had got my finger away, nor could he well have bit me with his big mouth, which would have been certain death in five minutes. But it frightened me so much that I did not recover my voice for a minute's space. I forgot, in my fear, that he was secured. You would have forgot too, for 't is incredible how such a monster can be confined in small gauzy-looking wires. I dreamed of snakes in the night. I wish to Heaven you could see it. He absolutely swelled with passion to the bigness of a large thigh. I could not retreat without infringing on another box, and just behind, a little devil, not an inch from my back, had got his nose out, with some difficulty and pain, quite through the bars! He was soon taught better manners. All the snakes were curious, and objects of terror; but this monster, like Aaron's serpent, swallowed up the impression of the rest. He opened his cursed mouth, when he made at me, as wide as his head was broad. I hallooed out quite loud, and felt pains all over my body with the fright.

I have had the felicity of hearing George Dyer read out one book of "The Farmer's Boy." I thought it rather childish. No doubt, there is originality in it (which, in your self-taught geniuses, is a most rare quality, they generally getting hold of

some bad models in a scarcity of books, and form-
ing their taste on them), but no *selection*. *All* is
described.

Mind, I have only heard read one book.

Yours sincerely,
Philo-Snake,
C. L.

XXX.

TO MANNING.

November 3, 1800.

Ecquid meditatur Archimedes ? What is Euclid
doing? What has happened to learned Trismegist?
Doth he take it in ill part that his humble friend
did not comply with his courteous invitation? Let
it suffice, I could not come. Are impossibilities
nothing? — be they abstractions of the intellects,
or not (rather) most sharp and mortifying realities?
nuts in the Will's mouth too hard for her to crack?
brick and stone walls in her way, which she can by
no means eat through? sore lets, *impedimenta via-
rum*, no thoroughfares? *racemi nimium alte pen-
dentes ?* Is the phrase classic? I allude to the
grapes in Æsop, which cost the fox a strain, and
gained the world an aphorism. Observe the superscription of this letter. In adapting the size of the
letters which constitute *your* name and Mr. *Crisp's*
name respectively, I had an eye to your different
stations in life. 'T is really curious, and must be
soothing to an *aristocrat*. I wonder it has never
been hit on before my time. I have made an ac-

quisition latterly of a *pleasant hand*, one Rickman,[1]
to whom I was introduced by George Dyer, — not
the most flattering auspices under which one man
can be introduced to another. George brings all
sorts of people together, setting up a sort of agra-
rian law, or common property, in matter of society; but for once he has done me a great pleasure,
while he was only pursuing a principle, as *ignes
fatui may* light you home. This Rickman lives in
our Buildings, immediately opposite our house; the
finest fellow to drop in a' nights, about nine or ten
o'clock, — cold bread-and-cheese time, — just in
the *wishing* time of the night, when you *wish* for
somebody to come in, without a distinct idea of a
probable anybody. Just in the nick, neither too
early to be tedious, nor too late to sit a reasonable
time. He is a most pleasant hand, — a fine, rat-
tling fellow, has gone through life laughing at solemn apes; himself hugely literate, oppressively full
of information in all stuff of conversation, from matter of fact to Xenophon and Plato; can talk Greek
with Porson, politics with Thelwall, conjecture with
George Dyer, nonsense with me, and anything with
anybody; a great farmer, somewhat concerned in
an agricultural magazine; reads no poetry but
Shakspeare, very intimate with Southey, but never
reads his poetry; relishes George Dyer, thoroughly
penetrates into the ridiculous wherever found, un-
derstands the *first time* (a great desideratum in

---

[1] John Rickman, clerk-assistant at the table of the House
of Commons, an eminent statistician, and the intimate friend
of Lamb, Southey, and others of their set

common minds), — you need never twice speak
to him; does not want explanations, translations,
limitations, as Professor Godwin does when you
make an assertion; *up* to anything, *down* to everything, — whatever *sapit hominem.* A perfect *man.*
All this farrago, which must perplex you to read,
and has put me to a little trouble to *select*, only
proves how impossible it is to describe a *pleasant
hand.* You must see Rickman to know him, for he
is a species in one, — a new class; an exotic, any
slip of which I am proud to put in my garden-pot.
The clearest-headed fellow; fullest of matter, with
least verbosity. If there be any alloy in my fortune
to have met with such a man, it is that he commonly divides his time between town and country,
having some foolish family ties at Christchurch, by
which means he can only gladden our London
hemisphere with returns of light. He is now going
for six weeks.

.   .   .   .

XXXI.

TO MANNING.

November 28, 1800

DEAR MANNING, — I have received a very kind
invitation from Lloyd and Sophia to go and spend
a month with them at the Lakes. Now, it fortunately happens (which is so seldom the case) that
I have spare cash by me enough to answer the
expenses of so long a journey; and I am determined to get away from the office by some means.

The purpose of this letter is to request of you (my dear friend) that you will not take it unkind if I decline my proposed visit to Cambridge *for the present.* Perhaps I shall be able to take Cambridge *in my way*, going or coming. (I need not describe to you the expectations which such an one as myself, pent up all my life in a dirty city, have formed of a tour to the Lakes. Consider Grasmere ! Ambleside ! Wordsworth ! Coleridge ! Hills, woods, lakes, and mountains, to the devil ! I will eat snipes with thee, Thomas Manning. Only confess, confess, a *bite.*) . . .

P. S. — I think you named the 16th ; but was it not modest of Lloyd to send such an invitation ! It shows his knowledge of *money* and *time.* I would be loth to think he meant

> " Ironic satire sidelong sklented
> On my poor pursie."[1]

For my part, with reference to my friends northward, I must confess that I am not romance-bit about *Nature.* The earth and sea and sky (when all is said) is but as a house to dwell in. · · If the inmates be courteous, and good liquors flow like the conduits at an old coronation, if they can talk sensibly and feel properly, I have no need to stand staring upon the gilded looking-glass (that strained my friend's purse-strings in the purchase), nor his five-shilling print over the mantelpiece of old Nabbs the carrier (which only betrays his false taste). · · Just as important to me (in a sense) is all the furniture of my world, — eye-pampering, but satisfies

---

[1] Burns.

no heart. Streets, streets, streets, markets, theatres, churches, Covent Gardens, shops sparkling
with pretty faces of industrious milliners, neat semp-
stresses, ladies cheapening, gentlemen behind coun-
ters lying, authors in the street with spectacles,
George Dyers (you may know them by their gait),
lamps lit at night, pastry-cooks' and silversmiths'
shops, beautiful Quakers of Pentonville, noise of
coaches, drowsy cry of mechanic watchman at night,
with bucks reeling home drunk; if you happen to
wake at midnight, cries of " Fire ! " and " Stop
thief ! " inns of court, with their learned air, and
halls, and butteries, just like Cambridge colleges;
old book-stalls, Jeremy Taylors, Burtons on Melancholy, and Religio Medicis on every stall. These
are thy pleasures, O London with-the-many-sins !
O City abounding in ——, for these may Keswick
and her giant brood go hang !

C. L.

XXXII.

TO MANNING.

December 27, 1800.

At length George Dyer's phrenitis has come to
a crisis; he is raging and furiously mad. I waited
upon the Heathen, Thursday was a se'nnight; the
first symptom which struck my eye and gave me in-
controvertible proof of the fatal truth was a pair of
nankeen pantaloons four times too big for him,
which the said Heathen did pertinaciously affirm to
be new.

They were absolutely ingrained with the accumulated dirt of ages; but he affirmed them to be clean. He was going to visit a lady that was nice about those things, and that's the reason he wore nankeen that day. And then he danced, and capered, and fidgeted, and pulled up his pantaloons, and hugged his intolerable flannel vestment closer about his poetic loins; anon he gave it loose to the zephyrs which plentifully insinuate their tiny bodies through every crevice, door, window, or wainscot, expressly formed for the exclusion of such impertinents. Then he caught at a proof-sheet, and catched up a laundress's bill instead; made a dart at Bloomfield's Poems, and threw them in agony aside. I could not bring him to one direct reply; he could not maintain his jumping mind in a right line for the tithe of a moment by Clifford's Inn clock. He must go to the printer's immediately,—the most unlucky accident; he had struck off five hundred impressions of his Poems, which were ready for delivery to subscribers, and the Preface must all be expunged. There were eighty pages of Preface, and not till that morning had he discovered that in the very first page of said Preface he had set out with a principle of criticism fundamentally wrong, which vitiated all his following reasoning. The Preface must be expunged, although it cost him £30, —the lowest calculation, taking in paper and printing! In vain have his real friends remonstrated against this Midsummer madness; George is as obstinate as a Primitive Christian, and wards and parries off all our thrusts with one unanswerable fence, — "Sir, it's of great consequence that the *world* is not *misled!*"

.   .   .   .

Man of many snipes, I will sup with thee, *Deo volente et diabolo nolente*, on Monday night the 5th of January, in the new year, and crush a cup to the infant century.

A word or two of my progress. Embark at six o'clock in the morning, with a fresh gale, on a Cambridge one-decker; very cold till eight at night; land at St. Mary's lighthouse, muffins and coffee upon table (or any other curious production of Turkey or both Indies), snipes exactly at nine, punch to commence at ten, with *argument;* difference of opinion is expected to take place about eleven; perfect unanimity, with some haziness and dimness, before twelve. N. B. — My single affection is not so singly wedded to snipes; but the curious and epicurean eye would also take a pleasure in beholding a delicate and well-chosen assortment of teals, ortolans, the unctuous and palate-soothing flesh of geese wild and tame, nightingales' brains, the sensorium of a young sucking-pig, or any other Christmas dish, which I leave to the judgment of you and the cook of Gonville.

C. LAMB.

XXXIII.

TO COLERIDGE.

(End of 1800)

I SEND you, in this parcel, my play, which I beg you to present in my name, with my respect and love, to Wordsworth and his sister. You blame us for giving your direction to Miss Wesley; the woman has been ten times after us about it, and we gave it her at last, under the idea that no further harm would ensue, but she would *once* write to you, and you would bite your lips and forget to answer it, and so it would end. You read us a dismal homily upon "Realities." We know quite as well as you do what are shadows and what are realities. You, for instance, when you are over your fourth or fifth jorum, chirping about old school occurrences, are the best of realities. Shadows are cold, thin things, that have no warmth or grasp in them. Miss Wesley and her friend, and a tribe of author-esses, that come after you here daily, and, in defect of you, hive and cluster upon us, are the shadows. You encouraged that mopsey, Miss Wesley, to dance after you, in the hope of having her nonsense put into a nonsensical Anthology. We have pretty well shaken her off, by that simple expedient of referring her to you; but there are more burrs in the wind. I came home t'other day from business, hungry as a hunter, to dinner, with nothing, I am sure, of *the author but hunger* about me, and whom found I closeted with Mary but a friend of this Miss Wesley, one Miss Benje, or Bengey,[1] — I don't know how she spells her name.   I just came in time enough, I believe, luckily, to prevent them from exchanging vows of eternal friendship.   It seems she is one of your authoresses, that you first foster, and then upbraid us with.   But I forgive you.   "The rogue has given me potions to make me love him."   Well ; go she would not, nor step a step over our threshold, till we had promised to come and drink tea with her next night.   I had never seen her before, and could not tell who the devil it was that was so familiar.   We went, however, not to be impolite.   Her lodgings are up two pairs of stairs in East Street.   Tea and coffee and macaroons — a kind of cake — I much love.   We sat down.   Presently Miss Benje broke the silence by declaring herself quite of a different opinion from D'Israeli, who supposes the differences of human intellect to be the mere effect of organization.   She begged to know my opinion.   I attempted to carry it off with a pun upon organ ; but that went off very flat.   She immediately conceived a very low opinion of my metaphysics ; and turning round to Mary, put some question to her in French, — possibly having heard that neither Mary nor I understood French.   The explanation that took place occasioned some embarrassment and much wondering.   She then fell into an insulting conversation about the comparative genius and merits of all modern languages, and concluded with asserting

[1] Miss Elizabeth Benger   See "Dictionary of National Biography," iv. 221.

that the Saxon was esteemed the purest dialect in Germany. From thence she passed into the subject of poetry, where I, who had hitherto sat mute and a hearer only, humbly hoped I might now put in a word to some advantage, seeing that it was my own trade in a manner. But I was stopped by a round assertion that no good poetry had appeared since Dr. Johnson's time. It seems the Doctor had suppressed many hopeful geniuses that way by the severity of his critical strictures in his "Lives of the Poets." I here ventured to question the fact, and was beginning to appeal to *names ;* but I was assured "it was certainly the case." Then we discussed Miss More's book on education, which I had never read. It seems Dr. Gregory, another of Miss Bengey's friends, has found fault with one of Miss More's metaphors. Miss More has been at some pains to vindicate herself, — in the opinion of Miss Bengey, not without success. It seems the Doctor is invariably against the use of broken or mixed metaphor, which he reprobates against the authority of Shakspeare himself. We next discussed the question whether Pope was a poet. I find Dr. Gregory is of opinion he was not, though Miss Seward does not at all concur with him in this. We then sat upon the comparative merits of the ten translations of " Pizarro," and Miss Bengey, or Benje, advised Mary to take two of them home ; she thought it might afford her some pleasure to compare them *verbatim ;* which we declined. It being now nine o'clock, wine and macaroons were again served round, and we parted, with a promise to go again next week, and meet the Miss Porters, who, it seems, have heard much of Mr. Coleridge, and wish to meet *us*, because we are *his* friends. I have been preparing for the occasion. I crowd cotton in my ears. I read all the reviews and magazines of the past month against the dreadful meeting, and I hope by these means to cut a tolerable second-rate figure.

Pray let us have no more complaints about shadows. We are in a fair way, *through you*, to surfeit sick upon them.

Our loves and respects to your host and hostess. Our dearest love to Coleridge.

Take no thought about your proof-sheets; they shall be done as if Woodfall himself did them. Pray send us word of Mrs. Coleridge and little David Hartley, your little reality.

Farewell, dear Substance. Take no umbrage at anything I have written.

C. LAMB, Umbra.

XXXIV.

TO WORDSWORTH.

January, 1801.

THANKS for your letter and present. I had already borrowed your second volume.[1] What pleases one most is "The Song of Lucy." *Simon's sickly*

---

[1] Of the "Lyrical Ballads," then just published. For certain results of Lamb's strictures in this letter, see Letter xxxvii.

Daughter, in "The Sexton," made me *cry.* Next
to these are the description of these continuous
echoes in the story of "Joanna's Laugh," where the
mountains and all the scenery absolutely seem alive ;
and that fine Shakspearian character of the "happy
man" in the "Brothers,"—

> "That creeps about the fields,
> Following his fancies by the hour, to bring
> Tears down his cheek, or solitary smiles
> Into his face, until the setting sun
> Write Fool upon his forehead!"

I will mention one more,—the delicate and curious feeling in the wish for the "Cumberland Beggar" that he may have about him the melody of
birds, although he hear them not. Here the mind
knowingly passes a fiction upon herself, first substi-
tuting her own feeling for the Beggar's, and in the
same breath detecting the fallacy, will not part with
the wish. The "Poet's Epitaph" is disfigured, to
my taste, by the common satire upon parsons and
lawyers in the beginning, and the coarse epithet of
"pin-point," in the sixth stanza. All the rest is
eminently good, and your own. I will just add that
it appears to me a fault in the "Beggar" that the
instructions conveyed in it are too direct, and like
a lecture : they don't slide into the mind of the
reader while he is imagining no such matter. An
intelligent reader finds a sort of insult in being told,
"I will teach you how to think upon this subject."
This fault, if I am right, is in a ten-thousandth worse
degree to be found in Sterne, and in many novelists
and modern poets, who continually put a sign-post

up to show where you are to feel. They set out
with assuming their readers to be stupid, — very different from "Robinson Crusoe," the "Vicar of
Wakefield," "Roderick Random," and other beautiful, bare narratives. There is implied an un-
written compact between author and reader: "I
will tell you a story, and I suppose you will understand it." Modern novels, "St. Leons" and the
like, are full of such flowers as these, — "Let not
my reader suppose;" "Imagine, if you can, modest," etc. I will here have done with praise and
blame. I have written so much only that you may
not think I have passed over your book without
observation. . . . I am sorry that Coleridge has
christened his "Ancient Marinere," a "Poet's Reve-
rie;" it is as bad as Bottom the Weaver's declaration that he is not a lion, but only the scenical
representation of a lion. What new idea is gained
by this title but one subversive of all credit — which
the tale should force upon us — of its truth !

For me, I was never so affected with any human
tale. After first reading it, I was totally possessed
with it for many days. I dislike all the miraculous
part of it; but the feelings of the man under the
operation of such scenery, dragged me along like
Tom Pipe's magic whistle. I totally differ from
your idea that the "Marinere" should have had a
character and a profession. This is a beauty in
"Gulliver's Travels," where the mind is kept in a
placid state of little wonderments; but the "Ancient Marinere" undergoes such trials as overwhelm
and bury all individuality or memory of what he

was,—like the state of a man in a bad dream, one terrible peculiarity of which is, that all consciousness of personality is gone. Your other observation is, I think as well, a little unfounded: the "Marinere," from being conversant in supernatural events, *has* acquired a supernatural and strange cast of *phrase*, eye, appearance, etc., which frighten the "wedding guest." You will excuse my remarks, because I am hurt and vexed that you should think it necessary, with a prose apology, to open the eyes of dead men that cannot see.

To sum up a general opinion of the second volume, I do not feel any one poem in it so forcibly as the "Ancient Marinere" and "The Mad Mother," and the "Lines at Tintern Abbey" in the first.

C. L.

XXXV.

TO WORDSWORTH.

January 30, 1801.

I OUGHT before this to have replied to your very kind invitation into Cumberland. With you and your sister I could gang anywhere; but I am afraid whether I shall ever be able to afford so desperate a journey. Separate from the pleasure of your company, I don't much care if I never see a mountain in my life. I have passed all my days in London, until I have formed as many and intense local attachments as any of you mountaineers can have done with dead nature. The lighted shops of the Strand and Fleet Street; the innumerable trades,

tradesmen, and customers; coaches, wagons, playhouses; all the bustle and wickedness round about
Covent Garden; the very women of the town; the
watchmen, drunken scenes, rattles; life awake, if
you awake, at all hours of the night; the impossibility of being dull in Fleet Street; the crowds, the
very dirt and mud, the sun shining upon houses and
pavements; the print-shops, the old-book stalls,
parsons cheapening books; coffee-houses, steams
of soups from kitchens; the pantomimes, London
itself a pantomime* and a masquerade, — all these
things work themselves into my mind, and feed me
without a power of satiating me. The wonder of
these sights impels me into night-walks about her
crowded streets, and I often shed tears in the motley Strand from fulness of joy at so much life. All
these emotions must be strange to you; so are
your rural emotions to me. But consider what must
I have been doing all my life, not to have lent great
portions of my heart with usury to such scenes?

My attachments are all local, purely local, — I
have no passion (or have had none since I was in
love, and then it was the spurious engendering of
poetry and books) to groves and valleys. The
rooms where I was born, the furniture which has
been before my eyes all my life, a bookcase which
has followed me about like a faithful dog (only
exceeding him in knowledge), wherever I have
moved; old chairs, old tables; streets, squares,
where I have sunned myself; my old school, —
these are my mistresses. Have I not enough without your mountains? I do not envy you. I should

pity you, did I not know that the mind will make friends with anything. Your sun and moon, and skies and hills and lakes, affect me no more or scarcely come to be in more venerable characters, than as a gilded room with tapestry and tapers, where I might live with handsome visible objects. I consider the clouds above me but as a roof beautifully painted, but unable to satisfy the mind, and at last, like the pictures of the apartment of a connoisseur, unable to afford him any longer a pleasure. So fading upon me, from disuse, have been the beauties of Nature, as they have been confidently called ; so ever fresh and green and warm are all the inventions of men and assemblies of men in this great city. I should certainly have laughed with dear Joanna.

Give my kindest love *and my sister's* to D. and yourself. And a kiss from me to little Barbara Lewthwaite.[1] Thank you for liking my play !

C. L.

XXXVI.

TO MANNING

February, 1801.

.   .   .   .

I AM going to change my lodgings, having received a hint that it would be agreeable, at our Lady's next feast. I have partly fixed upon most delectable rooms, which look out (when you stand a-tiptoe) over the Thames and Surrey Hills, at the

---

[1] The child in Wordsworth's " The Pet Lamb."

upper end of King's Bench Walks, in the Temple. There I shall have all the privacy of a house without the encumbrance, and shall be able to lock my friends out as often as I desire to hold free converse with my immortal mind; for my present lodgings resemble a minister's levee, I have so increased my acquaintance (as they call 'em), since I have resided in town. Like the country mouse, that had tasted a little of urban manners, I long to be nibbling my own cheese by my dear self without mousetraps and time-traps. By my new plan, I shall be as airy, up four pair of stairs, as in the country; and in a garden, in the midst of enchanting, more than Mahometan paradise, London, whose dirtiest drab-frequented alley, and her lowest-bowing tradesman, I would not exchange for Skiddaw, Helvellyn, James, Walter, and the parson into the bargain. Oh, her lamps of a night; her rich goldsmiths, print-shops, toy-shops, mercers, hardwaremen, pastry-cooks; St. Paul's Churchyard; the Strand; Exeter 'Change; Charing Cross, with a man *upon* a black horse! These are thy gods, O London! Ain't you mightily moped on the banks of the Cam? Had not you better come and set up here? You can't think what a difference. All the streets and pavements are pure gold, I warrant you, — at least, I know an alchemy that turns her mud into that metal: a mind that loves to be at home in crowds.

'Tis half-past twelve o'clock, and all sober people ought to be a-bed. Between you and me, the L. Ballads are but drowsy performances.

C. LAMB (as you may guess).

XXXVII.

February 15, 1801.

I HAD need be cautious henceforward what opinion I give of the "Lyrical Ballads." All the North of England are in a turmoil. Cumberland and Westmoreland have already declared a state of war. I lately received from Wordsworth a copy of the second volume, accompanied by an acknowledgment of having received from me many months since a copy of a certain tragedy, with excuses for not having made any acknowledgment sooner, it being owing to an "almost insurmountable aversion from letter-writing." This letter I answered in due form and time, and enumerated several of the passages which had most affected me, adding, unfortunately, that no single piece had moved me so forcibly as the "Ancient Mariner," "The Mad Mother," or the "Lines at Tintern Abbey." The Post did not sleep a moment. I received almost instantaneously a long letter of four sweating pages from my Reluctant Letter-Writer, the purport of which was that he was sorry his second volume had not given me more pleasure (Devil a hint did I give that it had *not pleased me*), and "was compelled to wish that my range of sensibility was more extended, being obliged to believe that I should receive large influxes of happiness and happy thoughts" (I suppose from the L. B.), — with a deal of stuff about a certain Union of Tenderness and Imagination, which, in the sense he used Imagination, was not the characteristic of Shakspeare, but which Milton possessed in a degree far exceeding other Poets; which union, as the highest species of poetry, and chiefly deserving that name, " he was most proud to aspire to ; " then illustrating the said union by two quotations from his own second volume (which I had been so unfortunate as to miss.) First specimen : A father addresses his son : —

> " When thou
> First camest into the World, as it befalls
> To new-born infants, thou didst sleep away
> Two days ; *and blessings from thy father's tongue*
> *Then fell upon thee.*"

The lines were thus undermarked, and then followed, " This passage, as combining in an extraordinary degree that union of tenderness and imagination which I am speaking of, I consider as one of the best I ever wrote."

Second specimen : A youth, after years of absence, revisits his native place, and thinks (as most people do) that there has been strange alteration in his absence, —

> " And that the rocks
> And everlasting hills themselves were changed."

You see both these are good poetry; but after one has been reading Shakspeare twenty of the best years of one's life, to have a fellow start up and prate about some unknown quality which Shakspeare possessed in a degree inferior to Milton and

somebody else! This was not to be *all* my castiga-
tion. Coleridge, who had not written to me for
some months before, starts up from his bed of sickness to reprove me for my tardy presumption; four
long pages, equally sweaty and more tedious, came
from him, assuring me that when the works of a
man of true genius, such as W. undoubtedly was,
do not please me at first sight, I should expect the
fault to lie "in me, and not in them," etc. What
am I to do with such people? I certainly shall
write them a very merry letter. Writing to *you*, I
may say that the second volume has no such pieces
as the three I enumerated. It is full of original
thinking and an observing mind; but it does not
often make you laugh or cry. It too artfully aims
at simplicity of expression. And you sometimes
doubt if simplicity be not a cover for poverty. The
best piece in it I will send you, being *short.* I
have grievously offended my friends in the North
by declaring my undue preference; but I need
not fear you.

> " She dwelt among the untrodden ways
>   Beside the Springs of Dove, —
>   A maid whom there were few (*sic*) to praise,
>   And very few to love.
>
> " A violet, by a mossy stone
>   Half hidden from the eye,
>   Fair as a star when only one
>   Is shining in the sky.
>
> " She lived unknown; and few could know
>   When Lucy ceased to be;
>   But she is in the grave, and oh,
>   The difference to me!"

This is choice and genuine, and so are many, many more. But one does not like to have 'em rammed down one's throat. " Pray take it, — it 's very good ; let me help you, — eat faster."

XXXVIII.

TO MANNING.

September 24, 1802

MY DEAR MANNING, — Since the date of my last letter, I have been a traveller. A strong desire seized me of visiting remote regions. My first impulse was to go and see Paris. It was a trivial objection to my aspiring mind that I did not understand a word of the language, since I certainly intend some time in my life to see Paris, and equally certainly never intend to learn the language ; therefore that could be no objection. However, I am very glad I did not go, because you had left Paris (I see) before I could have set out. I believe Stoddart promising to go with me another year prevented that plan. My next scheme (for to my restless, ambitious mind London was become a bed of thorns) was to visit the far famed peak in Derbyshire, where the Devil sits, they say, without breeches. *This* my purer mind rejected as indelicate. And my final resolve was a tour to the Lakes. I set out with Mary to Keswick, without giving Coleridge any notice ; for my time, being precious, did not admit of it. He received us with all the hospitality in the world, and gave up his time to show us all the wonders of the country. He dwells upon a small hill by the side of Keswick, in a comfortable house, quite enveloped on all sides by a net of mountains, — great floundering bears and monsters they seemed, all couchant and asleep. We got in in the evening, travelling in a post-chaise from Penrith, in the midst of a gorgeous sunshine, which transmuted all the mountains into colors, purple, etc. We thought we had got into fairy-land. But that went off (as it never came again ; while we stayed, we had no more fine sunsets) ; and we entered Coleridge's comfortable study just in the dusk, when the mountains were all dark, with clouds upon their heads. Such an impression I never received from objects of sight before, nor do I suppose that I can ever again. Glorious creatures, fine old fellows, Skiddaw, etc. I never shall forget ye, how ye lay about that night, like an intrenchment ; gone to bed, as it seemed for the night, but promising that ye were to be seen in the morning. Coleridge had got a blazing fire in his study, which is a large, antique, ill-shaped room, with an old-fashioned organ, never played upon, big enough for a church, shelves of scattered folios, an Æolian harp, and an old sofa, half-bed, etc. ; and all looking out upon the last fading view of Skiddaw and his broad-breasted brethren. What a night ! Here we stayed three full weeks, in which time I visited Wordsworth's cottage, where we stayed a day or two with the Clarksons (good people and most hospitable, at whose house we tarried one day and night), and saw Lloyd. The Wordsworths were gone to Calais. They have since been in London, and passed much time with us: he has now gone into Yorkshire to be married. So we have seen Keswick, Grasmere, Ambleside, Ulswater (where the Clarksons live), and a place at the other end of Ulswater, — I forget the name,[1] — to which we travelled on a very sultry day, over the middle of Helvellyn. We have clambered up to the top of Skiddaw, and I have waded up the bed of Lodore. In fine, I have satisfied myself that there is such a thing as that which tourists call *romantic*, which I very much suspected before; they make such a spluttering about it, and toss their splendid epithets around them, till they give as dim a light as at four o'clock next morning the lamps do after an illumination. Mary was excessively tired when she got about half way up Skiddaw; but we came to a cold rill (than which nothing can be imagined more cold, running over cold stones), and with the reinforcement of a draught of cold water she surmounted it most manfully. Oh, its fine black head, and the bleak air atop of it, with a prospect of mountains all about and about, making you giddy; and then Scotland afar off, and the border countries so famous in song and ballad! It was a day that will stand out like a mountain, I am sure, in my life. But I am returned (I have now been come home near three weeks; I was a month out), and you cannot conceive the degradation I felt at first, from being accustomed to wander free as air among mountains, and bathe in rivers without being controlled by any

[1] Patterdale.

one, to come home and *work*. I felt very *little*.
I had been dreaming I was a very great man. But
that is going off, and I find I shall conform in time
to that state of life to which it has pleased God to
call me. Besides, after all, Fleet Street and the
Strand are better places to live in for good and all
than amidst Skiddaw. Still, I turn back to those
great places where I wandered about, participating
in their greatness. After all, I could not *live* in
Skiddaw. I could spend a year, — two, three years
among them ; but I must have a prospect of seeing
Fleet Street at the end of that time, or I should
mope and pine away, I know. Still, Skiddaw is a
fine creature.

My habits are changing, I think, — *i. e.*, from
drunk to sober. Whether I shall be happier or
not, remains to be proved. I shall certainly be
more happy in a morning ; but whether I shall
not sacrifice the fat and the marrow and the kidneys, — *i. e.*, the night, — glorious, care-drowning
night, that heals all our wrongs, pours wine into our
mortifications, changes the scene from indifferent
and flat to bright and brilliant? O Manning, if I
should have formed a diabolical resolution, by the
time you come to England, of not admitting any
spirituous liquors into my house, will you be my guest
on such shameworthy terms? Is life, with such limitations, worth trying? The truth is, that my liquors
bring a nest of friendly harpies about my house, who
consume me. This is a pitiful tale to be read at St.
Gothard ; but it is just now nearest my heart.

XXXIX.

TO COLERIDGE.

October 23, 1802.

I READ daily your political essays. I was particularly pleased with " Once a Jacobin ; " though the argument is obvious enough, the style was less swelling than your things sometimes are, and it was plausible *ad populum.* A vessel has just arrived from Jamaica with the news of poor Sam Le Grice's death. He died at Jamaica of the yellow fever. His course was rapid, and he had been very foolish ; but I believe there was more of kindness and warmth in him than in almost any other of our schoolfellows. The annual meeting of the Blues is to-morrow, at the London Tavern, where poor Sammy dined with them two years ago, and attracted the notice of all by the singular foppishness of his dress. When men go off the stage so early, it scarce seems a noticeable thing in their epitaphs, whether they had been wise or silly in their lifetime.

I am glad the snuff and Pi-pos's books please. " Goody Two Shoes " is almost out of print. Mrs. Barbauld's stuff has banished all the old classics of the nursery ; and the shopman at Newberry's hardly deigned to reach them off an old exploded corner of a shelf, when Mary asked for them. Mrs. B.'s and Mrs. Trimmer's nonsense lay in piles about. Knowledge insignificant and vapid as Mrs. B.'s books convey, it seems, must come to the child in the *shape* of *knowledge*, and his empty noddle must be turned with conceit of his own powers when he has learned that a horse is an animal, and Billy is better than a horse, and such like ; instead of that beautiful interest in wild tales which made the child a man, while all the time he suspected himself to be no bigger than a child. Science has succeeded to poetry no less in the little walks of children than with men. Is there no possibility of averting this sore evil? Think what you would have been now, if instead of being fed with tales and old wives' fables in childhood, you had been crammed with geography and natural history !

Hang them ! — I mean the cursed Barbauld crew, those blights and blasts of all that is human in man and child.   .

As to the translations, let me do two or three hundred lines, and then do you try the nostrums upon Stuart in any way you please. If they go down, I will bray more. In fact, if I got or could but get £50 a year only, in addition to what I have, I should live in affluence.

Have you anticipated it, or could not you give a parallel of Bonaparte with Cromwell, particularly as to the contrast in their deeds affecting *foreign* States? Cromwell's interference for the Albigenses, B[onaparte]'s against the Swiss. Then religion would come in ; and Milton and you could rant about our countrymen of that period. This is a hasty suggestion, the more hasty because I want my supper. I have just finished Chapman's Homer. Did you ever read it?   It has most the continuous

power of interesting you all along, like a rapid
original, of any, and in the uncommon excellence of
the more finished parts goes beyond Fairfax or any
of 'em. The metre is fourteen syllables, and capable of all sweetness and grandeur. Cowper's
ponderous blank verse detains you every step with
some heavy Miltonism; Chapman gallops off with
you his own free pace. Take a simile, for example.
The council breaks up, —

> " Being abroad, the earth was overlaid
> With flockers to them, that came forth ; as when of frequent
>   bees
> Swarms rise out of a hollow rock, repairing the degrees
> *Of their egression endlessly, with ever rising new*
> From forth their sweet nest ; as their store, still as it faded,
>   grew,
> *And never would cease sending forth her clusters to the spring,*
> They still crowd out so : this flock here, that there, belaboring
> The loaded flowers. So," etc.

What *endless egression of phrases* the dog commands !

Take another, — Agamemnon, wounded, bearing
his wound heroically for the sake of the army (look
below) to a woman in labor : —

> "He with his lance, sword, mighty stones, poured his heroic
>   wreak
>   On other squadrons of the foe, whiles yet warm blood did
>   break
>   Thro' his cleft veins : but when the wound was quite ex-
>   haust and crude,
>   The eager anguish did approve his princely fortitude.
>   As when most sharp and bitter pangs distract a laboring
>   dame,
>   Which the divine Ilithiæ, that rule the painful frame

Of human childbirth, pour on her ; the Ilithiæ that are
The daughters of Saturnia ; with whose extreme repair
The woman in her travail strives to take the worst it gives ;
With thought, *it must be, 't is love's fruit, the end for which
   she lives ;*
The mean to make herself new born, what comforts will re-
   dound !
So," etc.

I will tell you more about Chapman and his pecu-
liarities in my next.   I am much interested in him.

Yours ever affectionately, and Pi-Pos's,

C. L.

XL.

TO MANNING.

November, 1802.

My dear Manning, — I must positively write, or
I shall miss you at Toulouse.   I sit here like a
decayed minute-hand (I lie ; *that* does not *sit*), and
being myself the exponent of no time, take no
heed how the clocks about me are going.   You
possibly by this time may have explored all Italy,
and toppled, unawares, into Etna, while you went
too near those rotten-jawed, gap-toothed, old worn-
out chaps of hell, — while I am meditating a quies-
cent letter to the honest postmaster at Toulouse.
But in case you should not have been *felo de se*, this
is to tell you that your letter was quite to my palate ;
in particular your just remarks upon Industry,
cursed Industry (though indeed you left me to
explore the reason), were highly relishing.

I 've often wished I lived in the Golden Age,

before doubt, and propositions, and corollaries, got into the world. *Now*, as Joseph Cottle, a Bard of Nature, sings, going up Malvern Hills,—

> " How steep, how painful the ascent !
> It needs the evidence of *close deduction*
> To know that ever I shall gain the top."

You must know that Joe is lame, so that he had some reason for so singing. These two lines, I assure you, are taken *totidem literis* from a very *popular* poem. Joe is also an epic poet as well as a descriptive, and has written a tragedy, though both his drama and epopoiea are strictly *descriptive*, and chiefly of the *beauties of nature*, for Joe thinks *man*, with all his passions and frailties, not a proper subject of the *drama*. Joe's tragedy hath the following surpassing speech in it. Some king is told that his enemy has engaged twelve archers to come over in a boat from an enemy's country and way-lay him ; he thereupon pathetically exclaims,—

> " *Twelve*, dost thou say ? Curse on those dozen villains ! "

Cottle read two or three acts out to us, very gravely on both sides, till he came to this heroic touch, — and then he asked what we laughed at ? I had no more muscles that day. A poet that chooses to read out his own verses has but a limited power over you. There is a bound where his authority ceases.

.   .   .   .

XLI

February 19, 1803.

MY DEAR MANNING, — The general scope of your letter afforded no indications of insanity, but some particular points raised a scruple. For God's sake, don't think any more of " Independent Tartary." [1] What are you to do among such Ethiopians? Is there no *lineal descendant* of Prester John? Is the chair empty? Is the sword unswayed? Depend upon it, they'll never make you their king as long as any branch of that great stock is remaining. I tremble for your Christianity. They will certainly circumcise you. Read Sir John Mandeville's travels to cure you, or come over to England. There is a Tartar man now exhibiting at Exeter 'Change. Come and talk with him, and hear what he says first. Indeed, he is no very favorable specimen of his countrymen ! But perhaps the best thing you can do is to *try* to get the idea out of your head. For this purpose repeat to yourself every night, after you have said your prayers, the words " Independent Tartary, Independent Tartary," two or three times, and associate with them the *idea* of *oblivion* ('t is Hartley's method with obstinate memories) ; or say " Independent, Independent, have I not already got an *independence ?* " That was

---

[1] Manning had evidently written to Lamb as to his cherished project of exploring remoter China and Thibet.

a clever way of the old Puritans, — pun-divinity.
My dear friend, think what a sad pity it would be
to bury such *parts* in heathen countries, among
nasty, unconversable, horse-belching, Tartar people!
Some say they are cannibals; and then conceive
a Tartar fellow *eating* my friend, and adding the
cool malignity of mustard and vinegar! I am
afraid 't is the reading of Chaucer has misled you;
his foolish stories about Cambuscan and the ring,
and the horse of brass. Believe me, there are no
such things, — 't is all the poet's *invention;* but if
there were such darling things as old Chaucer sings,
I would *up* behind you on the horse of brass, and
frisk off for Prester John's country. But these are
all tales; a horse of brass never flew, and a king's
daughter never talked with birds! The Tartars
really are a cold, insipid, smouchy set. You 'll be
sadly moped (if you are not eaten) among them.
Pray *try* and cure yourself. Take hellebore (the
counsel is Horace's; 't was none of my thought
originally). Shave yourself oftener. Eat no saf-
fron, for saffron-eaters contract a terrible Tartar-
like yellow. Pray to avoid the fiend. Eat nothing
that gives the heartburn. *Shave the upper lip.* Go
about like an European. Read no book of voyages
(they are nothing but lies); only now and then a
romance, to keep the fancy *under*. Above all,
don't go to any sights of *wild beasts*. *That has
been your ruin*. Accustom yourself to write familiar letters on common subjects to your friends in
England, such as, are of a moderate understanding.
And think about common things more. I supped

last night with Rickman, and met a merry *natural* captain, who pleases himself vastly with once having made a pun at Otaheite in the O. language. 'T is the same man who said Shakspeare he liked, because he was so *much of the gentleman.* Rickman is a man "absolute in all numbers." I think I may one day bring you acquainted, if you do not go to Tartary first; for you 'll never come back. Have a care, my dear friend, of Anthropophagi! their stomachs are always craving. 'T is terrible to be weighed out at fivepence a pound. To sit at table (the reverse of fishes in Holland), not as a guest, but as a meat!

God bless you! do come to England. Air and exercise may do great things. Talk with some minister. Why not your father?

God dispose all for the best! I have discharged my duty.

Your sincere friend,

C. LAMB.

XLII.

TO MANNING.

February, 1803.

NOT a sentence, not a syllable, of Trismegistus shall be lost through my neglect. I am his word-banker, his storekeeper of puns and syllogisms. You cannot conceive (and if Trismegistus cannot, no man can) the strange joy which I felt at the receipt of a letter from Paris. It seemed to give me a learned importance which placed me above

all who had not Parisian correspondents. Believe
that I shall carefully husband every scrap, which
will save you the trouble of memory when you
come back. You cannot write things so trifling,
let them only be about Paris, which I shall not
treasure.   In particular, I must have parallels of
actors and actresses.   I must be told if any building in Paris is at all comparable to St. Paul's, which,
contrary to the usual mode of that part of our
nature called admiration, I have looked up to with
unfading wonder every morning at ten o'clock, ever
since it has lain in my way to business. At noon
I casually glance upon it, being hungry; and hunger has not much taste for the fine arts.   Is any
night-walk comparable to a walk from St. Paul's
to Charing Cross, for lighting and paving, crowds
going and coming without respite, the rattle of
coaches, and the cheerfulness of shops?   Have you
seen a man guillotined yet? is it as good as hang-
ing?   Are the women *all* painted, and the men *all*
monkeys? or are there not a *few* that look like
rational of *both sexes?*   Are you and the First
Consul *thick?*   All this expense of ink I may fairly
put you to, as your letters will not be solely for my
proper pleasure, but are to serve as memoranda
and notices, helps for short memory, a kind of
Rumfordizing recollection, for yourself on your return. Your letter was just what a letter should
be, — crammed and very funny. Every part of it
pleased me, till you came to Paris, and your philosophical indolence or indifference stung me. You
cannot stir from your rooms till you know the

language! What the devil! are men nothing but word-trumpets? Are men all tongue and ear? Have these creatures, that you and I profess to know *something about,* no faces, gestures, gabble ; no folly, no absurdity, no induction of French education upon the abstract idea of men and women ; no similitude nor dissimilitude to English? Why, thou cursed Smellfungus! your account of your landing and reception, and Bullen (I forget how you spell it, — it was spelt my way in Harry the Eighth's time), was exactly in that minute style which strong impressions INSPIRE (writing to a Frenchman, I write as a Frenchman would). It appears to me as if I should die with joy at the first landing in a foreign country. It is the nearest pleasure which a grown man can substitute for that unknown one, which he can never know, — the pleasure of the first entrance into life from the womb. I daresay, in a short time, my habits would come back like a "stronger man" armed, and drive out that new pleasure ; and I should soon sicken for known objects. Nothing has transpired here that seems to me of sufficient importance to send dry-shod over the water ; but I suppose you will want to be told some news. The best and the worst to me is, that I have given up two guineas a week at the "Post," and regained my health and spirits, which were upon the wane. I grew sick, and Stuart unsatisfied. *Ludisti satis, tempus abire est;* I must cut closer, that's all. Mister Fell — or as you, with your usual facetiousness and drollery, call him, Mr. F + ll — has stopped short in the middle

of his play. Some *friend* has told him that it has
not the least merit in it. Oh that I had the recti-
fying of the Litany! I would put in a *Libera nos*
(*Scriptores videlicet*) *ab amicis!* That's all the
news. *A propos* (is it pedantry, writing to a
Frenchman, to express myself sometimes by a
French word, when an English one would not do
as well? Methinks my thoughts fall naturally into
it) —

In all this time I have done but one thing which I
reckon tolerable, and that I will transcribe, because
it may give you pleasure, being a picture of *my*
humors. You will find it in my last page. It
absurdly is a first number of a series, thus strangled
in its birth.

More news! The Professor's Rib[1] has come out
to be a disagreeable woman, so much so as to drive
me and some more old cronies from his house.
He must not wonder if people are shy of coming
to see him because of the *Snakes.*

C. L.

XLIII.

TO WILLIAM GODWIN.

November 10, 1803.

DEAR GODWIN, — You never made a more unlucky
and perverse mistake than to suppose that the reason of my not writing that cursed thing was to be
found in your book. I assure you most sincerely

---

[1] Mrs. Godwin.

that I have been greatly delighted with "Chaucer." [1]
I may be wrong, but I think there is one considerable error runs through it, which is a conjecturing
spirit, a fondness for filling out the picture by supposing what Chaucer did and how he felt, where the
materials are scanty. So far from meaning to withhold from you (out of mistaken tenderness) this
opinion of mine, I plainly told Mrs. Godwin that I
did find a *fault*, which I should reserve naming until
I should see you and talk it over. This she may
very well remember, and also that I declined naming this fault until she drew it from me by asking
me if there was not too much fancy in the work.
I then confessed generally what I felt, but refused to
go into particulars until I had seen you. I am never
very fond of saying things before third persons, because in the relation (such is human nature) something is sure to be dropped. If Mrs. Godwin has
been the cause of your misconstruction, I am very
angry, tell her; yet it is not an anger unto death. I
remember also telling Mrs. G. (which she may have
dropt) that I was by turns considerably more delighted than I expected. But I wished to reserve
all this until I saw you. I even had conceived an
expression to meet you with, which was thanking
you for some of the most exquisite pieces of criticism I had ever read in my life. In particular, I
should have brought forward that on "Troilus and
Cressida" and Shakspeare, which, it is little to say,

---

[1] Godwin's "Life of Chaucer," —a work, says Canon
Ainger, consisting of "four fifths ingenious guessing to one
fifth of material having any historic basis."

delighted me and instructed me (if not absolutely *in-structed* me, yet put into *full-grown sense* many conceptions which had arisen in me before in my most discriminating moods). All these things I was preparing to say, and bottling them up till I came, thinking to please my friend and host the author, when lo ! this deadly blight intervened.

I certainly ought to make great allowances for your misunderstanding me. You, by long habits of composition and a greater command gained over your own powers, cannot conceive of the desultory and uncertain way in which I (an author by fits) sometimes cannot put the thoughts of a common letter into sane prose. Any work which I take upon myself as an engagement will act upon me to torment ; *e.g.,* when I have undertaken, as three or four times I have, a school-boy copy of verses for Merchant Taylors' boys, at a guinea a copy, I have fretted over them in perfect inability to do them, and have made my sister wretched with my wretchedness for a week together. The same, till by habit I have acquired a mechanical command, I have felt in making paragraphs. As to reviewing, in particular, my head is so whimsical a head that I cannot, after reading another man's book, let it have been never so pleasing, give any account of it in any methodical way. I cannot follow his train. Something like this you must have perceived of me in conversation. Ten thousand times I have confessed to you, talking of my talents, my utter inability to remember in any comprehensive way what I read. I can vehemently applaud, or perversely stickle, at *parts ;* but I can-

not grasp at a whole. This infirmity (which is nothing to brag of) may be seen in my two little compositions, the tale and my play, in both which no reader,
however partial, can find any story. I wrote such
stuff about Chaucer, and got into such digressions,
quite irreducible into 1½ column of a paper, that I
was perfectly ashamed to show it you. However, it
is become a serious matter that I should convince
you I neither slunk from the task through a wilful
deserting neglect, or through any (most imaginary
on your part) distaste of " Chaucer ; " and I will try
my hand again,— I hope with better luck. My health
is bad, and my time taken up ; but all I can spare
between this and Sunday shall be employed for you,
since you desire it : and if I bring you a crude,
wretched paper on Sunday, you must burn it, and
forgive me ; if it proves anything better than I pre-
dict, may it be a peace-offering of sweet incense
between us !

C. LAMB.

XLIV.

TO MANNING.

February 24, 1805

DEAR MANNING, — I have been very unwell since
I saw you. A sad depression of spirits, a most un-
accountable nervousness ; from which I have been
partially relieved by an odd accident. You knew
Dick Hopkins, the swearing scullion of Caius?
This fellow, by industry and agility, has thrust himself into the important situations (no sinecures, be-

lieve me) of cook to Trinity Hall and Caius College ;
and the generous creature has contrived, with the
greatest delicacy imaginable, to send me a present
of Cambridge brawn. What makes it the more
extraordinary is, that the man never saw me in his
life that I know of. I suppose he has *heard* of me.
I did not immediately recognize the donor ; but one
of Richard's cards, which had accidentally fallen into
the straw, detected him in a moment. Dick, you
know, was always remarkable for flourishing. His
card imports that "orders [to wit, for brawn] from
any part of England, Scotland, or Ireland, will be
duly executed," etc. At first I thought of declin-
ing the present ; but Richard knew my blind side
when he pitched upon brawn. 'T is of all my hob-
bies the supreme in the eating way. He might have
sent sops from the pan, skimmings, crumpets, chips,
hog's lard, the tender brown judiciously scalped
from a fillet of veal (dexterously replaced by a
salamander), the tops of asparagus, fugitive livers,
runaway gizzards of fowls, the eyes of martyred pigs,
tender effusions of laxative woodcocks, the red
spawn of lobsters, leverets' ears, and such pretty
filchings common to cooks ; but these had been
ordinary presents, the everyday courtesies of dish-
washers to their sweethearts. Brawn was a noble
thought. It is not every common gullet-fancier that
can properly esteem it. It is like a picture of
one of the choice old Italian masters. Its gusto is
of that hidden sort. As Wordsworth sings of a
modest poet, "you must love him, ere to you he
will seem worthy of your love," so brawn, you must

taste it, ere to you it will seem to have any taste at all. But 'tis nuts to the adept, — those that will send out their tongues and feelers to find it out. It will be wooed, and not unsought be won. Now, ham-essence, lobsters, turtle, such popular minions, absolutely *court you*, lay themselves out to strike you at first smack, like one of David's pictures (they call him *Darveed*), compared with the plain russet-coated wealth of a Titian or a Correggio, as I illustrated above. Such are the obvious glaring heathen virtues of a corporation dinner, compared with the reserved collegiate worth of brawn. Do me the favour to leave off the business which you may be at present upon, and go immediately to the kitchens of Trinity and Caius, and make my most respectful compliments to Mr. Richard Hopkins, and assure him that his brawn is most excellent, and that I am moreover obliged to him for his innuendo about salt water and bran, which I shall not fail to improve. I leave it to you whether you shall choose to pay him the civility of asking him to dinner while you stay in Cambridge, or in whatever other way you may best like to show your gratitude to *my friend*. Richard Hopkins, considered in many points of view, is a very extraordinary character. Adieu. I hope to see you to supper in London soon, where we will taste Richard's brawn, and drink his health in a cheerful but moderate cup. We have not many such men in any rank of life as Mr. R. Hopkins. Crisp the barber, of St. Mary's, was just such another. I wonder *he* never sent me any little token, — some chestnuts, or a puff, or two pound of hair just to remember him by; gifts are like nails. *Præsens ut absens*, that is, your *present* makes amends for your absence.

Yours,

C. LAMB.

XLV.

June 14, 1805.

MY DEAR MISS WORDSWORTH, — I have every reason to suppose that this illness, like all Mary's former ones, will be but temporary. But I cannot always feel so. Meantime she is dead to me, and I miss a prop. All my strength is gone, and I am like a fool, bereft of her co-operation. I dare not think, lest I should think wrong; so used am I to look up to her in the least and the biggest perplexity. To say all that I know of her, would be more than I think anybody could believe or ever understand; and when I hope to have her well again with me, it would be sinning against her feelings to go about to praise her; for I can conceal nothing that I do from her. She is older and wiser and better than I, and all my wretched imperfections I cover to myself by resolutely thinking on her goodness. She would share life and death, heaven and hell, with me. She lives but for me; and I know I have been wasting and teasing her life for five years past incessantly with my cursed ways of going on. But even in this upbraiding of myself I am offending against her, for I know that she has cleaved to me for better, for worse; and if the balance has been

against her hitherto, it was a noble trade. I am
stupid, and lose myself in what I write. I write
rather what answers to my feelings (which are sometimes sharp enough) than express my present ones,
for I am only flat and stupid. I am sure you will
excuse my writing any more, I am so very poorly.

I cannot resist transcribing three or four lines
which poor Mary made upon a picture (a Holy
Family) which we saw at an auction only one week
before she left home. They are sweet lines, and
upon a sweet picture. But I send them only as the
last memorial of her.

VIRGIN AND CHILD, L. DA VINCI.

> " Maternal Lady, with thy virgin-grace,
>   Heaven-born thy Jesus seemeth, sure,
>   And thou a virgin pure.
>   Lady most perfect, when thy angel face
>   Men look upon, they wish to be
>   A Catholic, Madonna fair, to worship thee."

You had her lines about the "Lady Blanch."
You have not had some which she wrote upon a copy
of a girl from Titian, which I had hung up where that
print of Blanch and the Abbess (as she beautifully
interpreted two female figures from L. da Vinci)
had hung in our room. 'Tis light and pretty.

> " Who art thou, fair one, who usurp'st the place
>   Of Blanch, the lady of the matchless grace ?
>   Come, fair and pretty, tell to me
>   Who in thy lifetime thou mightst be ?
>   Thou pretty art and fair,
>   But with the Lady Blanch thou never must compare.
>   No need for Blanch her history to tell,
>   Whoever saw her face, they there did read it well ;

But when I look on thee, I only know
There lived a pretty maid some hundred years ago."

This is a little unfair, to tell so much about ourselves, and to advert so little to your letter, so full
of comfortable tidings of you all. But my own cares
press pretty close upon me, and you can make allow-
ance. That you may go on gathering strength and
peace is my next wish to Mary's recovery.

I had almost forgot your repeated invitation.
Supposing that Mary will be well and able, there is
another *ability* which you may guess at, which I
cannot promise myself. In prudence we ought not
to come. This illness will make it still more pru-
dential to wait. It is not a balance of this way of
spending our money against another way, but an
absolute question of whether we shall stop now, or
go on wasting away the little we have got before-
hand, which my evil conduct has already encroached
upon one-half. My best love, however, to you all,
and to that most friendly creature, Mrs. Clarkson,
and better health to her, when you see or write
to her.

CHARLES LAMB.

XLVI.[1]

TO MANNING.

May 10, 1806.

MY DEAR MANNING, — I did n't know what your
going was till I shook a last fist with you, and then

---

[1] Addressed: "Mr. Manning, Passenger on Board the
'Thames,' East Indiaman, Portsmouth." Manning had set
out for Canton.

't was just like having shaken hands with a wretch on the fatal scaffold, and when you are down the ladder, you can never stretch out to him again. Mary says you are dead, and there's nothing to do but to leave it to time to do for us in the end what it always does for those who mourn for people in such a case. But she'll see by your letter you are not quite dead. A little kicking and agony, and then — Martin Burney *took me out* a walking that evening, and we talked of Manning; and then I came home and smoked for you, and at twelve o'clock came home Mary and Monkey Louisa from the play, and there was more talk and more smoking, and they all seemed first-rate characters, because they knew a certain person. But what's the use of talking about 'em? By the time you'll have made your escape from the Kalmuks, you'll have stayed so long I shall never be able to bring to your mind who Mary was, who will have died about a year before, nor who the Holcrofts were! Me perhaps you will mistake for Phillips, or confound me with Mr. Dawe, because you saw us together. Mary (whom you seem to remember yet) is not quite easy that she had not a formal parting from you. I wish it had so happened. But you must bring her a token, a shawl or something, and remember a sprightly little mandarin for our mantelpiece, as a companion to the child I am going to purchase at the museum. She says you saw her writings about the other day, and she wishes you should know what they are. She is doing for Godwin's bookseller twenty of Shakspeare's plays, to be made into chil-

dren's tales. Six are already done by her; to wit:
"The Tempest," "Winter's Tale," "Midsummer
Night's Dream," "Much Ado," "Two Gentlemen
of Verona," and "Cymbeline;" and "The Merchant of Venice" is in forwardness. I have done
"Othello" and "Macbeth," and mean to do all
the tragedies. I think it will be popular among
the little people, besides money. It's to bring in
sixty guineas. Mary has done them capitally, I
think you'd think.[1] These are the humble amuse-
ments we propose, while you are gone to plant the
cross of Christ among barbarous pagan anthropophagi. *Quam homo homini præstat!* but then,
perhaps, you'll get murdered, and we shall die in
our beds, with a fair literary reputation. Be sure, if
you see any of those people whose heads do grow
beneath their shoulders, that you make a draught of
them. It will be very curious. Oh, Manning, I
am serious to sinking almost, when I think that all
those evenings, which you have made so pleasant,
are gone perhaps forever. Four years you talk of,
maybe ten; and you may come back and find such
alterations! Some circumstances may grow up to
you or to me that may be a bar to the return of any

---

[1] Miss Lamb has amusingly described the progress of
their labors on this volume: "You would like to see us, as
we often sit writing on one table (but not on one cushion
sitting), like Hermia and Helena, in the 'Midsummer
Night's Dream;' or rather like an old literary Darby and
Joan, I taking snuff, and he groaning all the while, and saying he can make nothing of it, which he always says till he
has finished, and then he finds out that he has made something of it."

such intimacy. I daresay all this is hum, and that
all will come back; but indeed we die many deaths
before we die, and I am almost sick when I think
that such a hold as I had of you is gone. I have
friends, but some of 'em are changed. Marriage,
or some circumstance, rises up to make them not
the same. But I felt sure of you. And that last
token you gave me of expressing a wish to have my
name joined with yours, you know not how it
affected me, — like a legacy.

God bless you in every way you can form a wish!
May He give you health, and safety, and the accom-
plishment of all your objects, and return you again to
us to gladden some fireside or other (I suppose we
shall be moved from the Temple). I will nurse the
remembrance of your steadiness and quiet, which
used to infuse something like itself into our nervous
minds. Mary called you our ventilator. Farewell!
and take her best wishes and mine.

Good by.

C. L.

XLVII.

TO WORDSWORTH.

June, 1806.

DEAR WORDSWORTH, — We are pleased, you may
be sure, with the good news of Mrs. Wordsworth.[1]
Hope all is well over by this time. "A fine boy!
Have you any more? — One more and a girl, —
poor copies of me!" *vide* "Mr. H.," a farce which

---

[1] Wordsworth's son Thomas was born June 16, 1806.

the proprietors have done me the honor — But I
set down Mr. Wroughton's own words. N. B.— The
ensuing letter was sent in answer to one which I
wrote, begging to know if my piece had any chance,
as I might make alterations, etc.   I writing on
Monday, there comes this letter on the Wednesday.
Attend !

[*Copy of a letter from Mr. R. Wroughton.*]

Sir, — Your piece of " Mr. H.," I am desired to say,
is accepted at Drury Lane Theatre by the proprietors,
and if agreeable to you, will be brought forwards when
the proper opportunity serves.   The piece shall be sent
to you for your alterations in the course of a few days,
as the same is not in my hands, but with the proprietors.

I am, sir, your obedient servant,

RICHARD WROUGHTON.

[Dated]
66, Gower Street,
Wednesday, June 11th, 1806.

On the following Sunday Mr. Tobin comes.   The
scent of a manager's letter brought him.   He would
have gone farther any day on such a business.   I
read the letter to him.   He deems it authentic and
peremptory.   Our conversation naturally fell upon
pieces, different sorts of pieces, — what is the best
way of offering a piece ; how far the caprice of
managers is an obstacle in the way of a piece ; how
to judge of the merits of a piece ; how long a piece
may remain in the hands of the managers before it
is acted ; and my piece, and your piece, and my
poor brother's piece,— my poor brother was all his
life endeavoring to get a piece accepted.

I wrote that in mere wantonness of triumph. Have nothing more to say about it. The managers, I thank my stars, have decided its merits forever. They are the best judges of pieces, and it would be insensible in me to affect a false modesty, after the very flattering letter which I have received.

> ADMIT
>
> TO
>
> BOXES.
>
> MR. II.
>
> *Ninth Night.*
>
> CHARLES LAMB.

I think this will be as good a pattern for orders as I can think on. A little thin flowery border, round, neat, not gaudy, and the Drury Lane Apollo, with the harp at the top. Or shall I have no Apollo, — simply nothing? Or perhaps the Comic Muse?

The same form, only I think without the Apollo, will serve for the pit and galleries. I think it will be best to write my name at full length; but then if I give away a great many, that will be tedious. Perhaps *Ch. Lamb* will do.

BOXES, now I think on it, I 'll have in capitals; the rest, in a neat Italian hand. Or better, perhaps, Boxes in Old English characters, like Madoc or Thalaba?

A propos of Spenser (you will find him mentioned a page or two before, near enough for an *à propos*), I was discoursing on poetry (as one 's apt to deceive one's self, and when a person is willing to *talk* of what one likes, to believe that he also likes the same, as lovers do) with a young gentleman of my office, who is deep read in Anacreon Moore, Lord Strangford, and the principal modern poets, and I happened to mention Epithalamiums, and that I could show him a very fine one of Spenser's. At the mention of this my gentleman, who is a very fine gentleman, pricked up his ears and expressed great pleasure, and begged that I would give him leave to copy it; he did not care how long it was (for I objected the length), he should be very happy to see *anything by him.* Then pausing, and looking sad, he ejaculated, " POOR SPENCER ! " I begged to know the reason of his ejaculation, thinking that time had by this time softened down any calamities which the bard might have endured. " Why, poor fellow," said he, " he has lost his wife ! " " Lost his wife ! " said I, " who are you talking of? " " Why, Spencer ! " said he ; " I've read the Monody he wrote on the occasion, and *a very pretty thing it is.*" This led to an explanation (it could be delayed no longer) that the sound *Spenser*, which, when poetry is talked of, generally excites an image of an old bard in a ruff, and sometimes with it dim notions of Sir P. Sidney and perhaps Lord Burleigh, had raised in my gentleman a quite contrary image of the Honorable William Spencer, who has translated some things from the German very prettily, which are published with Lady Di Beauclerk's designs. Nothing like defining of terms when we talk. What blunders might I have fallen into of quite inapplicable criticism, but for this timely explanation !

N.B.— At the beginning of *Edm*. Spenser (to prevent mistakes), I have copied from my own copy,
and primarily from a book of Chalmers's on Shakspeare, a sonnet of Spenser's never printed among
his poems. It is curious, as being manly, and rather
Miltonic, and as a sonnet of Spenser's with nothing
in it about love or knighthood. I have no room for
remembrances, but I hope our doing your commission will prove we do not quite forget you.

C. L.

XLVIII.

TO MANNING

December 5, 1806.

MANNING, your letter, dated Hottentots, August
the what-was-it? came to hand. I can scarce hope
that mine will have the same luck. China, Canton, — bless us, how it strains the imagination and
makes it ache ! I write under another uncertainty
whether it can go to-morrow by a ship which I have
just learned is going off direct to your part of the
world, or whether the despatches may not be sealed
up and this have to wait ; for if it is detained here,
it will grow staler in a fortnight than in a five
months' voyage coming to you. It will be a point
of conscience to send you none but bran-new news
(the latest edition), which will but grow the better,
like oranges, for a sea-voyage. Oh that you should
be so many hemispheres off ! — if I speak incorrectly,
you can correct me. Why, the simplest death or
marriage that takes place here must be important

to you as news in the old Bastile. There's your
friend Tuthill has got away from France — you remember France? and Tuthill ? — ten to one but
he writes by this post, if he don't get my note in
time, apprising him of the vessel sailing.   Know,
then, that he has found means to obtain leave from
Bonaparte, without making use of any *incredible romantic pretences*, as some have done, who never
meant to fulfil them, to come home ; and I have
seen him here and at Holcroft's.   An't you glad
about Tuthill?   Now then be sorry for Holcroft,
whose new play, called " The Vindictive Man,"
was damned about a fortnight since.   It died in
part of its own weakness, and in part for being
choked up with bad actors.   The two principal
parts were destined to Mrs. Jordan and Mr. Bannister ; but Mrs. J. has not come to terms with the
managers, — they have had some squabble, — and
Bannister shot some of his fingers off by the going
off of a gun.   So Miss Duncan had her part, and Mr.
De Camp took his.   His part, the principal comic
hope of the play, was most unluckily Goldfinch,
taken out of the " Road to Ruin," — not only the
same character, but the identical Goldfinch ; the
same as Falstaff is in two plays of Shakspeare.   As
the devil of ill-luck would have it, half the audience
did not know that H. had written it, but were dis-
pleased at his stealing from the " Road to Ruin ; "
and those who might have borne a gentlemanly
coxcomb with his " That 's your sort," " Go it," —
such as Lewis is, — did not relish the intolerable
vulgarity and inanity of the idea stripped of his

manner. De Camp was hooted, more than hissed, — hooted and bellowed off the stage before the second act was finished; so that the remainder of his part was forced to be, with some violence to the play, omitted. In addition to this, a strumpet was another principal character, — a most unfortunate choice in this moral day. The audience were as scandalized as if you were to introduce such a personage to their private tea-tables. Besides, her action in the play was gross, — wheedling an old man into marriage. But the mortal blunder of the play was that which, oddly enough, H. took pride in, and exultingly told me of the night before it came out, that there were no less than eleven principal characters in it, and I believe he meant of the men only, for the play-bill expressed as much, not reckoning one woman and one —— ; and true it was, for Mr. Powell, Mr. Raymond, Mr. Bartlett, Mr. H. Siddons, Mr. Barrymore, etc., to the number of eleven, had all parts equally prominent, and there was as much of them in quantity and rank as of the hero and heroine, and most of them gentlemen who seldom appear but as the hero's friend in a farce, — for a minute or two, — and here they all had their ten-minute speeches, and one of them gave the audience a serious account how he was now a lawyer, but had been a poet; and then a long enumeration of the inconveniences of authorship, rascally booksellers, reviewers, etc. ; which first set the audience a-gaping. But I have said enough; you will be so sorry that you will not think the best of me for my detail: but news is

news at Canton.   Poor H. I fear will feel the disappointment very seriously in a pecuniary light.
From what I can learn, he has saved nothing.   You
and I were hoping one day that he had ; but I fear
he has nothing but his pictures and books, and a
no very flourishing business, and to be obliged to
part with his long-necked Guido that hangs opposite as you enter, and the game-piece that hangs
in the back drawing-room, and all those Vandykes,
etc. ! God should temper the wind to the shorn
connoisseur.   I hope I need not say to you that I
feel for the weather-beaten author and for all his
household.   I assure you his fate has soured a good
deal the pleasure I should have otherwise taken in
my own little farce being accepted, and I hope
about to be acted, — it is in rehearsal actually, and
I expect it to come out next week.   It is kept a
sort of secret, and the rehearsals have gone on pri-
vately, lest by many folks knowing it, the story
should come out, which would infallibly damn it.
You remember I had sent it before you went.
Wroughton read it, and was much pleased with it.
I speedily got an answer.   I took it to make alterations, and lazily kept it some months, then took
courage and furbished it up in a day or two and
took it.   In less than a fortnight I heard the principal part was given to Elliston, who liked it, and
only wanted a prologue, which I have since done
and sent ; and I had a note the day before yesterday from the manager, Wroughton (bless his fat face,
he is not a bad actor in some things), to say
that I should be summoned to the rehearsal after

the next, which next was to be yesterday. I had
no idea it was so forward. I have had no trouble,
attended no reading or rehearsal, made no interest ;
what a contrast to the usual parade of authors !
But it is peculiar to modesty to do all things without noise or pomp ! I have some suspicion it will
appear in public on Wednesday next, for W. says
in his note, it is so forward that if wanted it may
come out next week, and a new melodrama is an-
nounced for every day till then ; and " a new farce
is in rehearsal," is put up in the bills. Now, you 'd
like to know the subject. The title is " Mr. H.,"
no more ; how simple, how taking ! A great H.
sprawling over the play-bill and attracting eyes at
every corner. The story is a coxcomb appearing at
Bath, vastly rich, all the ladies dying for him, all
bursting to know who he is ; but he goes by no
other name than Mr. H., — a curiosity like that of
the dames of Strasburg about the man with the great
nose. But I won't tell you any more about it. Yes,
I will, but I can't give you an idea how I have done
it. I 'll just tell you that after much vehement admiration, when his true name comes out, " Hogs-
flesh," all the women shun him, avoid him, and not
one can be found to change their name for him, —
that 's the idea, — how flat it is here ;[1] but how
whimsical in the farce ! And only think how hard
upon me it is that the ship is despatched to-morrow,
and my triumph cannot be ascertained till the Wednesday after ; but all China will ring of it by and

---

[1] It was precisely this flatness, this slightness of plot and
catastrophe, that doomed " Mr. H." to failure. See next
letter.

by. N. B. (But this is a secret.) The Professor [1] has got a tragedy coming out, with the young Roscius in it, in January next, as we say, — January last it will be with you; and though it is a profound secret now, as all his affairs are, it cannot be much of one by the time you read this. However, don't let it go any farther. I understand there are dramatic exhibitions in China. One would not like to be forestalled. Do you find in all this stuff I have written anything like those feelings which one should send my old adventuring friend, that is gone to wander among Tartars, and may never come again? I don't; but your going away, and all about you, is a threadbare topic. I have worn it out with thinking, it has come to me when I have been dull with anything, till my sadness has seemed more to have come from it than to have introduced it. I want you, you don't know how much; but if I had you here in my European garret, we should but talk over such stuff as I have written, so — Those "Tales from Shakspeare" are near coming out, and Mary has begun a new work. Mr. Dawe is turned author; he has been in such a way lately, — Dawe the painter, I mean, — he sits and stands about at Holcroft's and says nothing, then sighs, and leans his head on his hand. I took him to be in love, but it seems he was only meditating a work, — "The Life of Morland:" the young man is not used to composition. Rickman and Captain Burney are well; they assemble at my house pretty regularly of a Wednesday, —

---

[1] Godwin. His tragedy of "Faulkner" was published in 1808.

a new institution. Like other great men, I have a
public day, — cribbage and pipes, with Phillips and
noisy Martin Burney.

Good Heaven, what a bit only I 've got left !
How shall I squeeze all I know into this morsel !
Coleridge is come home, and is going to turn
lecturer on taste at the Royal Institution. I shall
get £200 from the theatre if " Mr. H." has a good
run, and I hope £100 for the copyright. Nothing
if it fails ; and there never was a more ticklish thing.
The whole depends on the manner in which the
name is brought out, which I value myself on, as a
chef d'œuvre. How the paper grows less and less !
In less than two minutes I shall cease to talk to
you, and you may rave to the Great Wall of China.
N. B. — Is there such a wall ? Is it as big as Old
London Wall by Bedlam ? Have you met with a
friend of mine named Ball at Canton ? If you 're
acquainted, remember me kindly to him. Maybe
you 'll think I have not said enough of Tuthill and
the Holcrofts. Tuthill is a noble fellow, as far as I
can judge. The Holcrofts bear their disappointment pretty well, but indeed they are sadly mortified. Mrs. H. is cast down. It was well, if it
were but on this account, that Tuthill is come home.
N. B. — If my little thing don't succeed, I shall easily
survive, having, as it were, compared to H.'s venture,
but a sixteenth in the lottery. Mary and I are to
sit next the orchestra in the pit, next the tweedle-
dees. She remembers you. You are more to us
than five hundred farces, clappings, etc.

Come back one day.   C. LAMB.

XLIX.

December, 11, 1806.

MARY'S love to all of you; I would n't let her write.

DEAR WORDSWORTH, — "Mr. H." came out last night, and failed. I had many fears; the subject was not substantial enough. John Bull must have solider fare than a *letter*. We are pretty stout about it; have had plenty of condoling friends; but, after all, we had rather it should have succeeded. You will see the prologue in most of the morning papers. It was received with such shouts as I never witnessed to a prologue. It was attempted to be encored. How hard! a thing I did merely as a task, because it was wanted, and set no great store by; and "Mr. H." ! The quantity of friends we had in the house — my brother and I being in public offices, etc. — was astonishing; but they yielded at last to a few hisses.

A hundred hisses (Damn the word, I write it like kisses, — how different!) — a hundred hisses outweigh a thousand claps.[1] The former come more directly from the heart. Well, 't is withdrawn, and there is an end.

Better luck to us,

C. LAMB.

[1] Lamb was himself in the audience, and is said to have taken a conspicuous share in the storm of hisses that followed the dropping of the curtain.

L.

DEAR MANNING, — When I last wrote to you, I
was in lodgings. I am now in chambers, No. 4,
Inner Temple Lane, where I should be happy to see
you any evening. Bring any of your friends the
Mandarins with you. I have two sitting-rooms. I
call them so *par excellence*, for you may stand, or
loll, or lean, or try any posture in them ; but they are
best for sitting, — not squatting down Japanese fashion, but in the more decorous way which European
usage has consecrated. I have two of these rooms
on the third floor, and five sleeping, cooking, etc.,
rooms, on the fourth floor. In my best room is a
choice collection of the works of Hogarth, an English painter of some humor. In my next best are
shelves containing a small, but well-chosen library.
My best room commands a court, in which there
are trees and a pump, the water of which is excellent,
— cold with brandy, and not very insipid without.
Here I hope to set up my rest, and not quit till Mr.
Powell, the undertaker, gives me notice that I may
have possession of my last lodging. He lets lodgings
for single gentlemen. I sent you a parcel of books
by my last, to give you some idea of the state of
European literature. There comes with this two
volumes, done up as letters, of minor poetry, a
sequel to " Mrs. Leicester ; " the best you may sup-

pose mine; the next best are my coadjutor's. You may amuse yourself in guessing them out; but I must tell you mine are but one third in quantity of the whole. So much for a very delicate subject. It is hard to speak of one's self, etc. Holcroft had finished his life when I wrote to you, and Hazlitt has since finished his life, — I do not mean his own life, but he has finished a life of Holcroft, which is going to press. Tuthill is Dr. Tuthill. I continue Mr. Lamb. I have published a little book for children on titles of honor; and to give them some idea of the difference of rank and gradual rising, I have made a little scale, supposing myself to receive the following various accessions of dignity from the king, who is the fountain of honor, — as at first, 1, Mr. C. Lamb; 2, C. Lamb, Esq.; 3, Sir C. Lamb, Bart.; 4, Baron Lamb, of Stamford; 5, Viscount Lamb; 6, Earl Lamb; 7, Marquis Lamb; 8, Duke Lamb. It would look like quibbling to carry it on farther, and especially as it is not necessary for children to go beyond the ordinary titles of sub-regal dignity in our own country, otherwise I have sometimes in my dreams imagined myself still advancing, as 9th, King Lamb; 10th, Emperor Lamb; 11th, Pope Innocent, — higher than which is nothing. Puns I have not made many (nor punch much) since the date of my last; one I cannot help relating. A constable in Salisbury Cathedral was telling me that eight people dined at the top of the spire of the cathedral; upon which I remarked that they must be very sharp-set. But in general I cultivate the reasoning part of my mind more than the imaginative. I

am stuffed out so with eating turkey for dinner,
and another turkey for supper yesterday (turkey in
Europe and turkey in Asia), that I can't jog on. It
is New Year here. That is, it was New Year half a
year back, when I was writing this. Nothing puzzles
me more than time and space, and yet nothing
puzzles me less, for I never think about them. The
Persian ambassador is the principal thing talked of
now. I sent some people to see him worship the
sun on Primrose Hill at half-past six in the morning,
28th November; but he did not come, — which
makes me think the old fire-worshippers are a sect
almost extinct in Persia. The Persian ambassador's
name is Shaw Ali Mirza. The common people call
him Shaw Nonsense. While I think of it, I have
put three letters besides my own three into the
India post for you, from your brother, sister, and
some gentleman whose name I forget. Will they,
have they, did they come safe? The distance you
are at, cuts up tenses by the root. I think you said
you did not know Kate ********. I express her
by nine stars, though she is but one. You must
have seen her at her father's. Try and remember
her. Coleridge is bringing out a paper in weekly
numbers, called the " Friend," which I would send,
if I could; but the difficulty I had in getting the
packets of books out to you before deters me; and
you 'll want something new to read when you come
home. Except Kate, I have had no vision of excellence this year, and she passed by like the queen
on her coronation day; you don't know whether
you saw her or not. Kate is fifteen; I go about

moping, and sing the old, pathetic ballad I used to like in my youth, —

> " She 's sweet fifteen,
> I 'm *one year more.*"

Mrs. Bland sang it in boy's clothes the first time I heard it. I sometimes think the lower notes in my voice are like Mrs. Bland's. That glorious singer, Braham, one of my lights, is fled. He was for a season. He was a rare composition of the Jew, the gentleman, and the angel, yet all these elements mixed up so kindly in him that you could not tell which predominated ; but he is gone, and one Phillips is engaged instead. Kate is vanished, but Miss Burrell is always to be met with !

> "Queens drop away, while blue-legged Maukin thrives,
>   And courtly Mildred dies, while country Madge survives."

That is not my poetry, but Quarles's ; but have n't you observed that the rarest things are the least obvious? Don't show anybody the names in this letter. I write confidentially, and wish this letter to be considered as *private.* Hazlitt has written a *grammar* for Godwin ; Godwin sells it bound up with a treatise of his own on language : but the *gray mare is the better horse.* I don't allude to Mrs. Godwin, but to the word *grammar*, which comes near to *gray mare*, if you observe, in sound. That figure is called paranomasia in Greek. I am sometimes happy in it. An old woman begged of me for charity. " Ah, sir," said she, " I have seen better days ! " " So have I, good woman," I replied ; but

I meant literally, days not so rainy and overcast as that on which begged, — she meant more prosperous days.

.   .   .   .

LI.

TO MISS WORDSWORTH.

August, 1810.

MARY has left a little space for me to fill up with nonsense, as the geographers used to cram monsters in the voids of the maps, and call it *Terra Incognita.* She has told you how she has taken to water like a hungry otter. I too limp after her in lame imitation,[1] but it goes against me a little at first. I have been acquaintance with it now for full four days, and it seems a moon. I am full of cramps and rheumatisms, and cold internally, so that fire won't warm me; yet I bear all for virtue's sake. Must I then leave you, gin, rum, brandy, *aqua-vitæ*, pleasant, jolly fellows? Damn temperance and he that first invented it! — some Anti-Noahite. Coleridge has powdered his head, and looks like Bacchus, — Bacchus ever sleek and young. He is going to turn sober, but his clock has not struck yet; meantime he pours down goblet after goblet, the second to see where the first is gone, the third to see no harm happens to the second, a fourth to say there is another coming, and a fifth to say he is not sure he is the last. C. L.

---

[1] An experiment in total abstinence; it did not last long.

LII

October 19, 1810.

DEAR W., — Mary has been very ill, which you have heard, I suppose, from the Montagues. She is very weak and low-spirited now. I was much pleased with your continuation of the " Essay on Epitaphs." [1] It is the only sensible thing which has been written on that subject, and it goes to the bottom. In particular I was pleased with your translation of that turgid epitaph into the plain feeling under it. It is perfectly a test. But what is the reason we have no good epitaphs after all?

A very striking instance of your position might be found in the churchyard of Ditton-upon-Thames, if you know such a place. Ditton-upon-Thames has been blessed by the residence of a poet who, for love or money, I do not well know which, has dignified every gravestone for the last few years with brannew verses, all different and all ingenious, with the author's name at the bottom of each. This sweet Swan of Thames has so artfully diversified his strains and his rhymes that the same thought never occurs twice, — more justly, perhaps, as no thought ever occurs at all, there was a physical impossibility that the same thought should recur. It is long since I saw and read these inscriptions ; but I remember the

---

[1] Published in Coleridge's " Friend," Feb. 22, 1810.

impression was of a smug usher at his desk in the
intervals of instruction, levelling his pen. Of death,
as it consists of dust and worms, and mourners and
uncertainty, he had never thought; but the word
"death" he had often seen separate and conjunct
with other words, till he had learned to speak of all
its attributes as glibly as Unitarian Belsham will discuss you the attributes of the word "God" in a
pulpit, and will talk of infinity with a tongue that
dangles from a skull that never reached in thought
and thorough imagination two inches, or farther than
from his hand to his mouth, or from the vestry to
the sounding-board of the pulpit.

But the epitaphs were trim and sprag, and patent,
and pleased the survivors of Thames Ditton above
the old mumpsimus of "Afflictions sore." . . . To
do justice, though, it must be owned that even the
excellent feeling which dictated this dirge when new,
must have suffered something in passing through so
many thousand applications, many of them no doubt
quite misplaced, as I have seen in Islington churchyard (I think) an Epitaph to an Infant who died
"*Ætatis* four months," with this seasonable inscription appended, "Honor thy father and thy mother,
that thy days may be long in the land," etc. Sincerely wishing your children long life to honor, etc.,

I remain,

C. LAMB.

LIII

August 14, 1814.

DEAR WORDSWORTH, — I cannot tell you how
pleased I was at the receipt of the great armful of
poetry which you have sent me; and to get it
before the rest of the world, too! I have gone
quite through with it, and was thinking to have accomplished that pleasure a second time before I
wrote to thank you; but Martin Burney came in the
night (while we were out) and made holy theft of it:
but we expect restitution in a day or two. It is the
noblest conversational poem [1] I ever read, — a day in
heaven. The part (or rather main body) which
has left the sweetest odor on my memory (a bad
term for the remains of an impression so recent) is
the "Tales of the Churchyard," — the only girl
among seven brethren, born out of due time, and
not duly taken away again; the deaf man and the
blind man; the Jacobite and the Hanoverian, whom
antipathies reconcile; the Scarron-entry of the
rusticating parson upon his solitude, — these were
all new to me too. My having known the story of
Margaret (at the beginning), a very old acquaintance, even as long back as when I saw you first at
Stowey, did not make her reappearance less fresh.
I don't know what to pick out of this best of books
upon the best subjects for partial naming. That

---

[1] The Excursion.

gorgeous sunset is famous; I think it must have
been the identical one we saw on Salisbury Plain
five years ago, that drew Phillips from the card-
table, where he had sat from rise of that luminary to
its unequalled setting. But neither he nor I had
gifted eyes to see those symbols of common things
glorified, such as the prophets saw them in that sunset, — the wheel, the potter's clay, the washpot, the
wine-press, the almond-tree rod, the baskets of figs,
the four-fold-visaged head, the throne, and Him
that sat thereon.

One feeling I was particularly struck with, as
what I recognized so very lately at Harrow Church
on entering in it after a hot and secular day's pleasure,
— the instantaneous coolness and calming, almost
transforming, properties of a country church just
entered; a certain fragrance which it has, either
from its holiness, or being kept shut all the week, or
the air that is let in being pure country, — exactly
what you have reduced into words; but I am feeling that which I cannot express. The reading
your lines about it fixed me for a time a monument
in Harrow Church, — do you know it? — with its fine
long spire, white as washed marble, to be seen, by
vantage of its high site, as far as Salisbury spire
itself almost.

I shall select a day or two very shortly, when I am
coolest in brain, to have a steady second reading,
which I feel will lead to many more; for it will be
a stock book with me while eyes or spectacles shall
be lent me. There is a great deal of noble matter
about mountain scenery, yet not so much as to over-

power and discountenance a poor Londoner, or
south-countryman entirely, — though Mary seems
to have felt it occasionally a little too powerfully; for
it was her remark, during reading it, that by your
system it was doubtful whether a liver in towns had
a soul to be saved. She almost trembled for that
invisible part of us in her.

Save for a late excursion to Harrow, and a day or
two on the banks of the Thames this summer, rural
images were fast fading from my mind, and by the
wise provision of the Regent all that was countri-
fied in the parks is all but obliterated. The very
colour of green is vanished; the whole surface of
Hyde Park is dry, crumbling sand (*Arabia Are-
nosa*), not a vestige or hint of grass ever having
grown there; booths and drinking-places go all
round it, for a mile and a half, I am confident, —
I might say two miles in circuit; the stench of
liquors, *bad* tobacco, dirty people and provisions,
conquers the air, and we are all stifled and suffo-
cated in Hyde Park.[1]   Order after order has been
issued by Lord Sidmouth in the name of the Regent
(acting in behalf of his royal father) for the dis-
persion of the varlets; but in vain. The *vis unita*
of all the publicans in London, Westminster, Mary-
lebone, and miles round, is too powerful a force
to put down. The Regent has raised a phantom
which he cannot lay. There they'll stay probably

---

[1] Early in 1814 the London parks were thrown open to the
public, with fireworks, booths, illuminations, etc., in celebra-
tion of the peace between France and England.   It was two
or three years before they recovered their usual verdure.

forever. The whole beauty of the place is gone, —
that lake-look of the Serpentine (it has got foolish
ships upon it) ; but something whispers to have
confidence in Nature and its revival, —

> " At the coming of the *milder day*,
> These monuments shall all be overgrown:"

Meantime I confess to have smoked one delicious
pipe in one of the cleanliest and goodliest of the
booths, — a tent rather, —

> " Oh, call it not a booth ! "

erected by the public spirit of Watson, who keeps
the "Adam and Eve" at Pancras (the ale-houses
have all emigrated, with their train of bottles, mugs,
cork-screws, waiters, into Hyde Park, — whole ale-
houses, with all their ale !) in company with some of
the Guards that had been in France, and a fine
French girl, habited like a princess of banditti,
which one of the dogs had transported from the
Garonne to the Serpentine. The unusual scene in
Hyde Park, by candle-light, in open air, — good
tobacco, bottled stout, — made it look like an interval in a campaign, a repose after battle. I almost
fancied scars smarting, and was ready to club a story
with my comrades of some of my lying deeds.
After all, the fireworks were splendid ; the rockets
in clusters, in trees, and all shapes, spreading about
like young stars in the making, floundering about in
space (like unbroke horses), till some of Newton's
calculations should fix them ; but then they went
out. Any one who could see 'em, and the still finer

showers of gloomy rain-fire that fell sulkily and angrily from 'em, and could go to bed without dreaming of the last day, must be as hardened an atheist as —.

The conclusion of this epistle getting gloomy, I have chosen this part to desire *our* kindest loves to Mrs. Wordsworth and to Dorothea. Will none of you ever be in London again?

Again let me thank you for your present, and assure you that fireworks and triumphs have not distracted me from receiving a calm and noble enjoyment from it (which I trust I shall often), and I sincerely congratulate you on its appearance.

With kindest remembrances to you and household, we remain, yours sincerely,

C. LAMB and Sister.

LIV.

TO WORDSWORTH.

(1815.)

DEAR WORDSWORTH, — You have made me very proud with your successive book presents.[1] I have

[1] In 1815 Wordsworth published a new edition of his poems, with the following title : " Poems by William Wordsworth; including Lyrical Ballads, and the Miscellaneous Pieces of the Author. With Additional Poems, a new Preface, and a Supplementary Essay. In two Volumes." The new poems were " Yarrow Visited," " The Force of Prayer," " The Farmer of Tilsbury Vale," " Laodamia," " Yew-Trees," " A Night Piece," etc., and it was chiefly on these that Lamb made his comments.

been carefully through the two volumes to see that
nothing was omitted which used to be there. . I think
I miss nothing but a character in the antithetic manner, which I do not know why you left out, — the
moral to the boys building the giant, the omission
whereof leaves it, in my mind, less complete, — and
one admirable line gone (or something come instead
of it), "the stone-chat, and the glancing sand-
piper," which was a line quite alive. I demand
these at your hand. I am glad that you have not
sacrificed a verse to those scoundrels. I would not
have had you offer up the poorest rag that lingered
upon the stripped shoulders of little Alice Fell, to
have atoned all their malice; I would not have
given 'em a red cloak to save their souls. I am
afraid lest that substitution of a shell (a flat falsifi-
cation of the history) for the household implement,
as it stood at first, was a kind of tub thrown out
to the beast, or rather thrown out for him. The
tub was a good honest tub in its place, and nothing
could fairly be said against it. You say you made
the alteration for the "friendly reader;" but the
"malicious" will take it to himself. Damn 'em !
if you give 'em an inch, etc. The Preface is noble,
and such as you should write. I wish I could set
my name to it, *Imprimatur;* but you have set it
there yourself, and I thank you. I had rather be
a doorkeeper in your margin than have their proud-
est text swelling with my eulogies. The poems in
the volumes which are new to me are so much in
the old tone that I hardly received them as novelties. Of those of which I had no previous knowl-

edge, the " Four Yew-Trees " and the mysterious
company which you have assembled there most
struck me, — " Death the Skeleton, and Time the
Shadow." It is a sight not for every youthful poet
to dream of; it is one of the last results he must
have gone thinking on for years for. " Laodamia "
is a very original poem, — I mean original with
reference to your own manner. You have nothing like it. I should have seen it in a strange
place, and greatly admired it, but not suspected its
derivation.

Let me in this place, for I have writ you several
letters naming it, mention that my brother, who is
a picture-collector, has picked up an undoubtable
picture of Milton.[1] He gave a few shillings for it,
and could get no history with it, but that some old
lady had had it for a great many years. Its age is
ascertainable from the state of the canvas, and you
need only see it to be sure that it is the original
of the heads in the Tonson editions, with which we
are all so well familiar. Since I saw you, I have
had a treat in the reading way which comes not
every day, — the Latin poems of V. Bourne, which
were quite new to me. What a heart that man
had, all laid out upon town scenes ! — a proper
counterpoise to *some people's* rural extravaganzas.
Why I mention him is, that your " Power of Music "
reminded me of his poem of " The Ballad-singer
in the Seven Dials." Do you remember his epi-

---

[1] John Lamb afterwards gave the picture to Charles, who
made it a wedding present to Mrs. Moxon (Emma Isola).
It is now in the National Portrait Gallery.

gram on the old woman who taught Newton the
A B C, which, after all, he says, he hesitates not to
call Newton's "Principia"? I was lately fatiguing
myself with going through a volume of fine words
by Lord Thurlow, — excellent words; and if the
heart could live by words alone, it could desire no
better regales. But what an aching vacuum of matter! I don't stick at the madness of it, for that is
only a consequence of shutting his eyes and thinking he is in the age of the old Elizabeth poets.
From thence I turned to Bourne. What a sweet,
unpretending, pretty-mannered, *matterful* creature,
sucking from every flower, making a flower of everything, his diction all Latin, and his thoughts all
English! Bless him! Latin was n't good enough
for him. Why was n't he content with the language which Gay and Prior wrote in?

I am almost sorry that you printed extracts from
those first poems, or that you did not print them
at length. They do not read to me as they do
altogether. Besides, they have diminished the
value of the original (which I possess) as a curiosity. I have hitherto kept them distinct in my
mind, as referring to a particular period of your life.
All the rest of your poems are so much of a piece
they might have been written in the same week;
these decidedly speak of an earlier period. They
tell more of what you had been reading. We were
glad to see the poems "by a female friend."[1] The
one on the Wind is masterly, but not new to us.
Being only three, perhaps you might have clapped

---

[1] Dorothy Wordsworth.

a D. at the corner, and let it have past as a printer's mark to the uninitiated, as a delightful hint to the better instructed. As it is, expect a formal criticism on the poems of your female friend, and she must expect it. I should have written before; but I am cruelly engaged, and like to be. On Friday I was at office from ten in the morning (two hours dinner excepted) to eleven at night, last night till nine; my business and office business in general have increased so; I don't mean I am there every night, but I must expect a great deal of it. I never leave till four, and do not keep a holiday now once in ten times, where I used to keep all red-letter days, and some few days besides, which I used to dub Nature's holidays. I have had my day. I had formerly little to do. So of the little that is left of life I may reckon two thirds as dead, for time that a man may call his own is his life; and hard work and thinking about it taint even the leisure hours, — stain Sunday with work-day contemplations. This is Sunday; and the headache I have is part late hours at work the two preceding nights, and part later hours over a consoling pipe afterwards. But I find stupid acquiescence coming over me. I bend to the yoke, and it is almost with me and my household as with the man and his consort, —

> "To them each evening had its glittering star,
>   And every sabbath-day its golden sun!" [1]

to such straits am I driven for the life of life, Time! Oh that from that superfluity of holiday-leisure my

[1] Excursion, book v.

youth wasted, "Age might but take some hours youth wanted not " ! N. B. — I have left off spirituous liquors for four or more months, with a moral certainty of its lasting. Farewell, dear Wordsworth !

O happy Paris, seat of idleness and pleasure ! From some returned English I hear that not such a thing as a counting-house is to be seen in her streets, — scarce a desk. Earthquakes swallow up this mercantile city and its " gripple merchants," as Drayton hath it, " born to be the curse of this brave isle " ! I invoke this, not on account of any parsimonious habits the mercantile interest may have, but, to confess truth, because I am not fit for an office.

Farewell, in haste, from a head that is too ill to methodize, a stomach to digest, and all out of tune. Better harmonies await you !

C. LAMB.

LV.

TO WORDSWORTH.

EXCUSE this maddish letter ; I am too tired to write *in formâ*.

1815.

DEAR WORDSWORTH, — The more I read of your two last volumes, the more I feel it necessary to make my acknowledgments for them in more than one short letter. The " Night Piece," to which you refer me, I meant fully to have noticed ; but the fact is, I come so fluttering and languid from business, tired with thoughts of it, frightened with fears of it, that when I get a few minutes to sit down and scribble (an action of the hand now seldom natural to me, — I mean voluntary pen-work), I lose all presential memory of what I had intended to say, and say what I can, talk about Vincent Bourne or any casual image, instead of that which I had meditated (by the way, I must look out V. B. for you). So I had meant to have mentioned " Yarrow Visited," with that stanza, " But thou that didst appear so fair ; "[1] than which I think no lovelier stanza can be found in the wide world of poetry. Yet the poem, on the whole, seems condemned to leave behind it a melancholy of imperfect satisfaction, as if you had wronged the feeling with which, in what preceded it, you had resolved never to visit it, and as if the Muse had determined, in the most delicate manner, to make you, and *scarce make you*, feel it.   Else, it is far superior to the other, which has but one exquisite verse in it, — the last but one, or the last two : this is all fine, except, perhaps, that *that* of " studious ease and generous cares " has a little tinge of the *less romantic* about it.   " The Farmer of Tilsbury Vale " is a charming counterpart to " Poor Susan," with the addition of that delicacy towards aberrations from the strict path which is so fine in the " Old Thief and the Boy by his side," which always brings water into my eyes.   Perhaps it

[1] " But thou, that didst appear so fair
To fond imagination,
Dost rival in the light of day
Her delicate creation."

is the worse for being a repetition; "Susan" stood
for the representative of poor *Rus in Urbe*.   There
was quite enough to stamp the moral of the thing
never to be forgotten,— " bright volumes of vapor,"
etc.   The last verse of Susan was to be got rid of, at
all events.   It threw a kind of dubiety upon Susan's
moral conduct.   Susan is a servant-maid.   I see her
trundling her mop, and contemplating the whirling
phenomenon through blurred optics ; but to term
her " a poor outcast " seems as much as to say that
poor Susan was no better than she should be, — which
I trust was not what you meant to express.   Robin
Goodfellow supports himself without that *stick* of a
moral which you have thrown away ; but how I can
be brought in *felo de omittendo* for that ending to
the Boy-builders [1] is a mystery.   I can't say positively now, I only know that no line oftener or
readier occurs than that " Light-hearted boys, I will
build up a Giant with you."   It comes naturally
with a warm holiday and the freshness of the blood.
It is a perfect summer amulet, that I tie round my
legs to quicken their motion when I go out a-maying.   (N. B.) I don't often go out a-maying ;
must is the tense with me now.   Do you take the
pun?   *Young Romilly* is divine, the reasons of his
mother's grief being remediless, — I never saw
parental love carried up so high, towering above the
other loves, — Shakspeare had done something for
the filial in Cordelia, and, by implication, for the
fatherly too in Lear's resentment ; he left it for you
to explore the depths of the maternal heart.   I get

---

[1] Better known as " Rural Architecture."

stupid and flat, and flattering; what's the use of telling you what good things you have written, or — I hope I may add — that I know them to be good? *A propos,* when I first opened upon the just-mentioned poem, in a careless tone I said to Mary, as if putting a riddle, "What is good for a bootless bene?"[1] To which, with infinite presence of mind (as the jest-book has it) she answered, "A shoeless pea." It was the first joke she ever made. Joke the second I make. You distinguish well, in your old preface, between the verses of Dr. Johnson, of the "Man in the Strand," and that from "The Babes in the Wood." I was thinking whether, taking your own glorious lines, —

> "And from the love which was in her soul
> For her youthful Romilly,"

which, by the love I bear my own soul, I think have no parallel in any of the best old ballads, and just altering it to, —

> "And from the great respect she felt
> For Sir Samuel Romilly,"

would not have explained the boundaries of prose expression and poetic feeling nearly as well. Excuse my levity on such an occasion. I never felt deeply in my life if that poem did not make me, both lately and when I read it in MS. No alderman

---

[1] The first line of the poem on Bolton Abbey : —

> "'What is good for a bootless bene?'
> With these dark words begins my tale;
> And their meaning is, whence can comfort spring
> When Prayer is of no avail?"

ever longed after a haunch of buck venison more
than I for a spiritual taste of that " White Doe " you
promise.   I am sure it is superlative, or will be when
dressed, i. e., printed.   All things read raw to me in
MS. ; to compare *magna parvis,* I cannot endure my
own writings in that state.   The only one which I
think would not very much win upon me in print is
" Peter Bell ; " but I am not certain.   You ask me
about your preface.   I like both that and the
supplement, without an exception.   The account of
what you mean by imagination is very valuable to
me.   It will help me to like some things in poetry
better, which is a little humiliating in me to confess.
I thought I could not be instructed in that science
(I mean the critical), as I once heard old ob-
scene, beastly Peter Pindar, in a dispute on Milton,
say he thought that if he had reason to value himself upon one thing more than another, it was in
knowing what good verse was.   Who looked over
your proof-sheets and left *ordebo* in that line of
Virgil ?

My brother's picture of Milton is very finely
painted, — that is, it might have been done by a hand
next to Vandyke's.   It is the genuine Milton, and
an object of quiet gaze for the half-hour at a time.
Yet though I am confident there is no better one of
him, the face does not quite answer to Milton.
There is a tinge of *petit* (or *petite,* how do you spell
it ?) querulousness about it ; yet, hang it ! now I remember better, there is not, — it is calm, melancholy,
and poetical.   *One* of the copies of the poems you
sent has precisely the same pleasant blending of a

sheet of second volume with a sheet of first. I think it was page 245 ; but I sent it and had it rectified. It gave me, in the first impetus of cutting the leaves, just such a cold squelch as going down a plausible turning and suddenly reading " No thoroughfare." Robinson's is entire ; I wish you would write more criticism about Spencer, etc. I think I could say something about him myself; but, Lord bless me ! these " merchants and their spicy drugs," which are so harmonious to sing of, they lime-twig up my poor soul and body till I shall forget I ever thought myself a bit of a genius ! I can't even put a few thoughts on paper for a newspaper. I engross when I should pen a paragraph. Confusion blast all mercantile transactions, all traffic, exchange of commodities, intercourse between nations, all the consequent civilization, and wealth, and amity, and link of society, and getting rid of prejudices, and knowledge of the face of the globe; and rot the very firs of the forest that look so romantic alive, and die into desks ! *Vale.*

Yours, dear W., and all yours,

C. LAMB.

LVI.

TO SOUTHEY.

May 6, 1815

DEAR SOUTHEY, — I have received from Longman a copy of " Roderick," with the author's compliments, for which I much thank you. I don't know where I shall put all the noble presents I have lately received in that way ; the " Excursion," Wordsworth's

two last volumes, and now " Roderick," have come
pouring in upon me like some irruption from Heli-
con. The story of the brave Maccabee was already,
you may be sure, familiar to me in all its parts. I
have, since the receipt of your present, read it quite
through again, and with no diminished pleasure. I
don't know whether I ought to say that it has given
me more pleasure than any of your long poems.
" Kehama " is doubtless more powerful, but I don't
feel that firm footing in it that I do in " Roderick ; "
my imagination goes sinking and floundering in the
vast spaces of unopened-before systems and faiths ;
I am put out of the pale of my old sympathies ; my
moral sense is almost outraged ; I can't believe, or
with horror am made to believe, such desperate
chances against omnipotences, such disturbances of
faith to the centre. The more potent, the more
painful the spell. Jove and his brotherhood of
gods, tottering with the giant assailings, I can bear,
for the soul's hopes are not struck at in such con-
tests ; but your Oriental almighties are too much
types of the intangible prototype to be meddled with
without shuddering. One never connects what are
called the " attributes " with Jupiter. I mention only
what diminishes my delight at the wonder-workings
of " Kehama," not what impeaches its power, which
I confess with trembling.

But " Roderick " is a comfortable poem. It reminds me of the delight I took in the first reading
of the " Joan of Arc." It is maturer and better
than *that*, though not better to me now than that
was then. It suits me better than " Madoc." I am

14

at home in Spain and Christendom. I have a timid imagination, I am afraid; I do not willingly admit of strange beliefs or out-of-the-way creeds or places. I never read books of travel, at least not farther than Paris or Rome. I can just endure Moors, because of their connection as foes with Christians; but Abyssinians, Ethiops, Esquimaux, Dervises, and all that tribe, I hate; I believe I fear them in some manner. A Mahometan turban on the stage, though enveloping some well-known face (Mr. Cook or Mr. Maddox, whom I see another day good Christian and English waiters, innkeepers, etc.), does not give me pleasure unalloyed. I am a Christian, Englishman, Londoner, *Templar*. God help me when I come to put off these snug relations, and to get abroad into the world to come! I shall be like *the crow on the sand*, as Wordsworth has it; but I won't think on it, — no need, I hope, yet.

The parts I have been most pleased with, both on first and second readings, perhaps, are Florinda's palliation of Roderick's crime, confessed to him in his disguise; the retreat of Pelayo's family first discovered; his being made king, — " For acclamation one form must serve, *more solemn for* the *breach* of *old observances*." Roderick's vow is extremely fine, and his blessing on the vow of Alphonso, —

> " Towards the troop he spread his arms,
> As if the expanded soul diffused itself,
> And carried to all spirits, *with the act*,
> Its affluent inspiration."

It struck me forcibly that the feeling of these last lines might have been suggested to you by the Car-

toon of Paul at Athens. Certain it is that a better
motto or guide to that famous attitude can nowhere
be found. I shall adopt it as explanatory of that
violent but dignified motion.

I must read again Landor's " Julian ; " I have
not read it some time. I think he must have failed
in Roderick, for I remember nothing of him, nor of
any distinct character as a character, — only fine-
sounding passages. I remember thinking also he
had chosen a point of time after the event, as it
were, for Roderick survives to no use ; but my
memory is weak, and I will not wrong a fine poem
by trusting to it.

The notes to your poem I have not read again ;
but it will be a take-downable book on my shelf, and
they will serve sometimes at breakfast, or times too
light for the text to be duly appreciated, — though
some of 'em, one of the serpent Penance, is serious
enough, now I think on 't.

Of Coleridge I hear nothing, nor of the Morgans.
I hope to have him like a reappearing star, stand-
ing up before me some time when least expected in
London, as has been the case whilere.

I am *doing* nothing (as the phrase is) but reading
presents, and walk away what of the day-hours I can
get from hard occupation. Pray accept once more
my hearty thanks and expression of pleasure for
your remembrance of me. My sister desires her
kind respects to Mrs. S. and to all at Keswick.

Yours truly,

C. LAMB.

LVII.

October 19, 1815.

DEAR MISS H., — I am forced to be the replier to your letter, for Mary has been ill, and gone from home these five weeks yesterday. She has left me very lonely and very miserable. I stroll about, but there is no rest but at one's own fireside ; and there is no rest for me there now. I look forward to the worse half being past, and keep up as well as I can. She has begun to show some favorable symptoms. The return of her disorder has been frightfully soon this time, with scarce a six-months' interval. I am almost afraid my worry of spirits about the E. I. House was partly the cause of her illness ; but one always imputes it to the cause next at hand, — more probably it comes from some cause we have no control over or conjecture of. It cuts sad great slices out of the time, the little time, we shall have to live together. I don't know but the recurrence of these illnesses might help me to sustain her death better than if we had had no partial separations. But I won't talk of death. I will imagine us immortal, or forget that we are otherwise. By God's blessing, in a few weeks we may be making our meal together, or sitting in the front row of the pit at Drury Lane, or taking our evening walk past the theatres, to look at the outside of them, at least, if not to be tempted

[1] Mrs. Wordsworth's sister. ·

in. Then we forget we are assailable ; we are strong for the time as rocks, — "the wind is tempered to the shorn Lambs." Poor C. Lloyd and poor Priscilla ! I feel I hardly feel enough for him ; my own calamities press about me, and involve me in a thick integument not to be reached at by other folks' misfortunes. But I feel all I can, all the kindness I can, towards you all. God bless you ! I hear nothing from Coleridge.

Yours truly,

C. LAMB.

LVIII.

TO MANNING.

December 25, 1815.

DEAR OLD FRIEND AND ABSENTEE, — This is Christmas Day, 1815, with us ; what it may be with you I don't know, — the 12th of June next year, perhaps ; and if it should be the consecrated season with you, I don't see how you can keep it. You have no turkeys ; you would not desecrate the festival by offering up a withered Chinese bantam, instead of the savoury grand Norfolcian holocaust, that smokes all around my nostrils at this moment from a thousand firesides. Then what puddings have you? Where will you get holly to stick in your churches, or churches to stick your dried tea-leaves (that must be the substitute) in? What memorials you can have of the holy time, I see not. A chopped missionary or two may keep up the thin idea of Lent and the wilderness ; but what standing evi-

dence have you of the Nativity? 'T is our rosy-
cheeked, homestalled divines, whose faces shine to
the tune of *unto us a child was born*, — faces fragrant
with the mince-pies of half a century, that alone can
authenticate the cheerful mystery. I feel, I feel my
bowels refreshed with the holy tide; my zeal is
great against the unedified heathen. Down with the
Pagodas; down with the idols, — Ching-chong-fo
and his foolish priesthood! Come out of Babylon,
oh my friend, for her time is come, and the child
that is native, and the Proselyte of her gates, shall
kindle and smoke together! And in sober sense
what makes you so long from among us, Manning?
You must not expect to see the same England again
which you left.

Empires have been overturned, crowns trodden
into dust, the face of the Western world quite
changed; your friends have all got old, those you
left blooming, myself (who am one of the few that
remember you) — those golden hairs which you recollect my taking a pride in, turned to silvery and
gray. Mary has been dead and buried many years;
she desired to be buried in the silk gown you
sent her. Rickman, that you remember active and
strong, now walks out supported by a servant-maid
and a stick. Martin Burney is a very old man.
The other day an aged woman knocked at my door
and pretended to my acquaintance. It was long before I had the most distant cognition of her; but at
last together we made her out to be Louisa, the
daughter of Mrs. Topham, formerly Mrs. Morton,
who had been Mrs. Reynolds, formerly Mrs. Kenney,

whose first husband was Holcroft, the dramatic
writer of the last century. St. Paul's church is a
heap of ruins; the Monument is n't half so high as
you knew it, divers parts being successively taken
down which the ravages of time had rendered dan-
gerous; the horse at Charing Cross is gone, no one
knows whither, — and all this has taken place while
you have been settling whether Ho-hing-tong should
be spelled with a —— or a ——. For aught I see,
you had almost as well remain where you are, and
not come, like a Struldbrug, into a world where few
were born when you went away. Scarce here and
there one will be able to make out your face; all
your opinions will be out of date, your jokes obsolete, your puns rejected with fastidiousness as wit of
the last age. Your way of mathematics has already
given way to a new method which, after all, is, I believe, the old doctrine of Maclaurin new-vamped up
with what he borrowed of the negative quantity of
fluxions from Euler.

Poor Godwin! I was passing his tomb the other
day in Cripplegate churchyard. There are some
verses upon it, written by Miss ——, which if I
thought good enough I would send you. He was
one of those who would have hailed your return, not
with boisterous shouts and clamors, but with the
complacent gratulations of a philosopher anxious to
promote knowledge, as leading to happiness; but
his systems and his theories are ten feet deep in
Cripplegate mould. Coleridge is just dead, having
lived just long enough to close the eyes of Wordsworth, who paid the debt to nature but a week or

two before. Poor Col., but two days before he
died he wrote to a bookseller proposing an epic
poem on the "Wandering of Cain," in twenty-four
books. It is said he has left behind him more than
forty thousand treatises in criticism, metaphysics,
and divinity; but few of them in a state of comple-
tion. They are now destined, perhaps, to wrap up
spices. You see what mutation the busy hand of
Time has produced, while you have consumed in
foolish, voluntary exile that time which might have
gladdened your friends, benefited your country —
But reproaches are useless. Gather up the wretched
relics, my friend, as fast as you can, and come to
your old home. I will rub my eyes and try to
recognize you. We will shake withered hands together, and talk of old things, — of St. Mary's church
and the barber's opposite, where the young students
in mathematics used to assemble. Poor Crisp, that
kept it afterwards, set up a fruiterer's shop in
Trumpington Street, and for aught I know resides
there still; for I saw the name up in the last journey
I took there with my sister just before she died. I
suppose you heard that I had left the India House
and gone into the Fishmongers' Almshouses over the
bridge. I have a little cabin there, small and
homely; but you shall be welcome to it. You like
oysters, and to open them yourself; I'll get you
some if you come in oyster time. Marshall, Godwin's old friend, is still alive, and talks of the faces
you used to make.[1]

Come as soon as you can.   C. LAMB.

[1] The reversal of this serio-humorous mingling of fiction
and forecast will be found in the next letter.

LIX.

December 26, 1815.

DEAR MANNING, — Following your brother's example, I have just ventured one letter to Canton, and am now hazarding another (not exactly a duplicate) to St. Helena. The first was full of unprobable romantic fictions, fitting the remoteness of the mission it goes upon ; in the present I mean to confine myself nearer to truth as you come nearer home. A correspondence with the uttermost parts of the earth necessarily involves in it some heat of fancy ; it sets the brain agoing ; but I can think on the half-way house tranquilly. Your friends, then, are not all dead or grown forgetful of you through old age, — as that lying letter asserted, anticipating rather what must happen if you keep tarrying on forever on the skirts of creation, as there seemed a danger of your doing, — but they are all tolerably well, and in full and perfect comprehension of what is meant by Manning's coming home again. Mrs. Kenney never let her tongue run riot more than in remembrances of you. Fanny expends herself in phrases that can only be justified by her romantic nature. Mary reserves a portion of your silk, not to be buried in (as the false nuncio asserts), but to make up spick and span into a bran-new gown to wear when you come. I am the same as when you knew me, almost to a surfeiting identity. This very night I am going to

leave off tobacco! Surely there must be some other
world in which this unconquerable purpose shall be
realized. The soul hath not her generous aspirings
implanted in her in vain. One that you knew, and
I think the only one of those friends we knew much
of in common, has died in earnest. Poor Priscilla!
Her brother Robert is also dead, and several of the
grown-up brothers and sisters, in the compass of a
very few years. Death has not otherwise meddled
much in families that I know. Not but he has
his horrid eye upon us, and is whetting his infernal
feathered dart every instant, as you see him truly
pictured in that impressive moral picture, "The
good man at the hour of death." I have in trust
to put in the post four letters from Diss, and one
from Lynn, to St. Helena, which I hope will accompany this safe, and one from Lynn, and the one before spoken of from me, to Canton. But we all hope
that these letters may be waste paper. I don't know
why I have foreborne writing so long; but it is such
a forlorn hope to send a scrap of paper straggling
over wide oceans. And yet I know when you come
home, I shall have you sitting before me at our fireside just as if you had never been away. In such an
instant does the return of a person dissipate all the
weight of imaginary perplexity from distance of time
and space! I'll promise you good oysters. Cory
is dead, that kept the shop opposite St. Dunstan's,
but the tougher materials of the shop survive the
perishing frame of its keeper. Oysters continue to
flourish there under as good auspices. Poor Cory!
But if you will absent yourself twenty years together,

you must not expect numerically the same population to congratulate your return which wetted the sea-beach with their tears when you went away. Have you recovered the breathless stone-staring astonishment into which you must have been thrown upon learning at landing that an Emperor of France was living at St. Helena? What an event in the solitude of the seas, — like finding a fish's bone at the top of Plinlimmon; but these things are nothing in our Western world. Novelties cease to affect. Come and try what your presence can.

God bless you! Your old friend,

C. LAMB.

LX.

TO WORDSWORTH

April 9, 1816.

DEAR WORDSWORTH, — Thanks for the books you have given me, and for all the books you mean to give me. I will bind up the "Political Sonnets" and "Ode" according to your suggestion. I have not bound the poems yet; I wait till people have done borrowing them. I think I shall get a chain and chain them to my shelves, *more Bodleiano*, and people may come and read them at chain's length. For of those who borrow, some read slow; some mean to read but don't read; and some neither read nor meant to read, but borrow to leave you an opinion of their sagacity. I must do my money-borrowing friends the justice to say that there is nothing of this caprice or wantonness of alienation in

them ; when they borrow my money they never fail
to make use of it.   Coleridge has been here about a
fortnight.   His health is tolerable at present, though
beset with temptations.   In the first place, the Covent Garden Manager has declined accepting his
Tragedy,[1] though (having read it) I see no reason
upon earth why it might not have run a very fair
chance, though it certainly wants a prominent part
for a Miss O'Neil or a Mr. Kean.   However, he is
going to write to-day to Lord Byron to get it to
Drury.   Should you see Mrs. C., who has just written to C. a letter, which I have given him, it will be
as well to say nothing about its fate till some answer
is shaped from Drury.   He has two volumes printing
together at Bristol, both finished as far as the composition goes ; the latter containing his fugitive
poems, the former his Literary Life.   Nature, who
conducts every creature by instinct to its best end,
has skilfully directed C. to take up his abode at a
Chemist's Laboratory in Norfolk Street.   She might
as well have sent a *Helluo Librorum* for cure to the
Vatican.   God keep him inviolate among the traps
and pitfalls !   He has done pretty well as yet.[2]

Tell Miss Hutchinson my sister is every day wishing to be quietly sitting down to answer her very kind
letter ; but while C. stays she can hardly find a quiet
time.   God bless him !

Tell Mrs. Wordsworth her postscripts are always
agreeable.   They are legible too.   Your manual-
graphy is terrible, — dark as Lycophron.   " Likeli-

---

[1] Zapolya.

[2] Lamb alludes, of course, to Coleridge's opium habit.

hood," for instance, is thus typified. . . . I should not wonder if the constant making out of such paragraphs is the cause of that weakness in Mrs. W.'s eyes, as she is tenderly pleased to express it. Dorothy, I hear, has mounted spectacles; so you have deoculated two of your dearest relations in life. Well, God bless you, and continue to give you power to write with a finger of power upon our hearts what you fail to impress, in corresponding lucidness, upon our outward eyesight!

Mary's love to all; she is quite well.

I am called off to do the deposits on Cotton Wool. But why do I relate this to you, who want faculties to comprehend the great mystery of deposits, of interest, of warehouse rent, and contingent fund? Adieu!

C. LAMB.

LXI.

TO WORDSWORTH.

April 26, 1816.

DEAR W.,— I have just finished the pleasing task of correcting the revise of the poems and letter.[1] I hope they will come out faultless. One blunder I saw and shuddered at. The hallucinating rascal had

---

[1] Wordsworth's " Letter to a Friend of Burns " (London, 1816).

" Wordsworth had been consulted by a friend of Burns as to the best mode of vindicating the reputation of the poet, which, it was alleged, had been much injured by the publication of Dr. Currie's ' Life and Correspondence of Burns.' " — AINGER.

printed *battered* for *battened*, this last not conveying
any distinct sense to his gaping soul. The Reader
(as they call 'em) had discovered it, and given it the
marginal brand ; but the ‸ubstitutory *n* had not yet
appeared. I accompanied his notice with a most
pathetic address to the printer not to neglect the
correction. I know how such a blunder would
" batter at your peace." With regard to the works,
the Letter I read with unabated satisfaction. Such
a thing was wanted, called for. The parallel of
Cotton with Burns I heartily approve. Iz. Walton
hallows any page in which his reverend name appears. " Duty archly bending to purposes of general
benevolence " is exquisite. The poems I endeavored not to understand, but to read them with my
eye alone ; and I think I succeeded. (Some people
will do that when they come out, you 'll say.) As if I
were to luxuriate to-morrow at some picture-gallery
I was never at before, and, going by to-day by
chance, found the door open, and having but five
minutes to look about me, peeped in, — just such a
chastised peep I took with my mind at the lines my
luxuriating eye was coursing over unrestrained, not
to anticipate another day's fuller satisfaction. Coleridge is printing " Christabel," by Lord Byron's
recommendation to Murray, with what he calls a
vision, " Kubla Khan," which said vision he repeats
so enchantingly that it irradiates and brings heaven
and elysian bowers into my parlor while he sings or
says it ; but there is an observation, " Never tell thy
dreams," and I am almost afraid that " Kubla
Khan " is an owl that won't bear daylight. I fear

lest it should be discovered, by the lantern of typography and clear reducting to letters, no better than nonsense or no sense. When I was young, I used to chant with ecstasy " MILD ARCADIANS EVER BLOOM-ING," till somebody told me it was meant to be nonsense. Even yet I have a lingering attachment to it, and I think it better than "Windsor Forest," " Dying Christian's Address," etc. Coleridge has sent his tragedy to D. L. T.; it cannot be acted this season, and by their manner of receiving I hope he will be able to alter it to make them accept it for next. He is at present under the medical care of a Mr. Gilman (Killman?) at Highgate, where he plays at leaving off laud—m. I think his essentials not touched; he is very bad, but then he wonderfully picks up another day, and his face, when he repeats his verses, hath its ancient glory, — an archangel a little damaged. Will Miss H. pardon our not replying at length to her kind letter? We are not quiet enough; Morgan is with us every day, going betwixt Highgate and the Temple. Coleridge is absent but four miles; and the neighborhood of such a man is as exciting as the presence of fifty ordinary persons. 'T is enough to be within the whiff and wind of his genius for us not to possess our souls in quiet. If I lived with him or the *Author of the " Excursion,"* I should, in a very little time, lose my own identity, and be dragged along in the current of other people's thoughts, hampered in a net. How cool I sit in this office, with no possible interruption further than what I may term *material!* There is not as much metaphysics in thirty-six of

the people here as there is in the first page of
Locke's "Treatise on the Human Understanding," or
as much poetry as in any ten lines of the " Pleasures
of Hope," or more natural " Beggar's Petition."   I
never entangle myself in any of their speculations.
Interruptions, if I try to write a letter even, I have
dreadful.   Just now, within four lines, I was called
off for ten minutes to consult dusty old books for the
settlement of obsolete errors.   I hold you a guinea
you don't find the chasm where I left off, so excel-
lently the wounded sense closed again and was
healed.

N. B. — Nothing said above to the contrary, but
that I hold the personal presence of the two mentioned potent spirits at a rate as high as any ; but I
pay dearer : what amuses others robs me of myself ;
my mind is positively discharged into their greater
currents, but flows with a willing violence.   As to
your question about work, it is far less oppressive to
me than it was, from circumstances ; it takes all the
golden part of the day away, a solid lump, from ten
to four : but it does not kill my peace, as before.
Some day or other I shall be in a taking again.   My
head aches, and you have had enough.   God bless
you !

C. Lamb.

LXII.

July, 1816.

My dear Fellow, — I have been in a lethargy this long while, and forgotten London, Westminster, Marybone, Paddington, — they all went clean out of my head, till happening to go to a neighbor's in this good borough of Calne, for want of whist-players we fell upon *Commerce :* the word awoke me to a remembrance of my professional avocations and the long-continued strife which I have been these twenty-four years endeavoring to compose between those grand Irreconcilables, Cash and Commerce ; I instantly called for an almanac, which with some difficulty was procured at a fortune-teller's in the vicinity (for happy holiday people here, having nothing to do, keep no account of time), and found that by dint of duty I must attend in Leadenhall on Wednesy. morning next ; and shall attend accordingly. Does Master Hannah give maccaroons still, and does he fetch the Cobbetts from my attic? Perhaps it would n't be too much trouble for him to drop the enclosed up at my aforesaid chamber, and any letters, etc., with it ; but the enclosed should go without delay. N. B. — He is n't to fetch Monday's Cobbett, but it is to wait my reading when I come

---

[1] A fellow-clerk in the India House. This charming letter, written evidently during a vacation trip, was first published entire in Canon Ainger's edition (1887) of Lamb's Letters.

back.   Heigh-ho!   Lord have mercy upon me,
how many does two and two make?   I am afraid I
shall make a poor clerk in future, I am spoiled with
rambling among haycocks and cows and pigs.   Bless
me !   I had like to have forgot (the air is so temperate and oblivious here) to say I have seen your
brother, and hope he is doing well in the finest spot
of the world.   More of these things when I return.
Remember me to the gentlemen, — I forget names.
Shall I find all my letters at my rooms on Tuesday?
If you forget to send 'em never mind, for I don't
much care for reading and writing now; I shall
come back again by degrees, I suppose, into my
former habits.   How is Bruce de Ponthieu, and
Porcher and Co.? — the tears come into my eyes
when I think how long I have neglected —.

Adieu ! ye fields, ye shepherds and — herdesses,
and dairies and cream-pots, and fairies and dances
upon the green.

I come, I come.   Don't drag me so hard by the
hair of my head, Genius of British India !   I know
my hour is come, Faustus must give up his soul, O
Lucifer, O Mephistopheles !   Can you make out
what all this letter is about?   I am afraid to look
it over.

Ch. Lamb.

LXIII.

TO MRS. WORDSWORTH.

February 18, 1818.

My dear Mrs. Wordsworth, — I have repeatedly taken pen in hand to answer your kind

letter. My sister should more properly have done it ; but she having failed, I consider myself answerable for her debts. I am now trying to do it in the midst of commercial noises, and with a quill which seems more ready to glide into arithmetical figures and names of gourds, cassia, cardamoms, aloes, ginger, or tea, than into kindly responses and friendly recollections. The reason why I cannot write letters at home is that I am never alone. Plato's — (I write to W. W. now) — Plato's double-animal parted never longed more to be reciprocally re-united in the system of its first creation than I sometimes do to be but for a moment single and separate. Except my morning's walk to the office, which is like treading on sands of gold for that reason, I am never so. I cannot walk home from office, but some officious friend offers his unwelcome courtesies to accompany me. All the morning I am pestered. I could sit and gravely cast up sums in great books, or compare sum with sum, and write "paid" against this, and "unpaid" against t'other, and yet reserve in some corner of my mind "some darling thoughts all my own," — faint memory of some passage in a book, or the tone of an absent friend's voice, — a snatch of Miss Burrell's singing, or a gleam of Fanny Kelly's divine plain face. The two operations might be going on at the same time without thwarting, as the sun's two motions (earth's I mean) ; or as I sometimes turn round till I am giddy, in my back parlor, while my sister is walking longitudinally in the front ; or as the shoulder of veal twists round with the spit, while the smoke wreathes up the chimney. But

there are a set of amateurs of the Belles Lettres, —
the gay science, — who come to me as a sort of
rendezvous, putting questions of criticism, of British
Institutions, Lalla Rookhs, etc., — what Coleridge
said at the lecture last night, — who have the form
of reading men, but, for any possible use reading
can be to them but to talk of, might as well have
been Ante-Cadmeans born, or have lain, sucking out
the sense of an Egyptian hieroglyph as long as the
pyramids will last, before they should find it. These
pests worrit me at business and in all its intervals,
perplexing my accounts, poisoning my little salutary
warming-time at the fire, puzzling my paragraphs if
I take a newspaper, cramming in between my own
free thoughts and a column of figures, which had
come to an amicable compromise but for them.
Their noise ended, one of them, as I said, accom-
panies me home, lest I should be solitary for a
moment. He at length takes his welcome leave at
the door; up I go, mutton on table, hungry as hunter, hope to forget my cares and bury them in the
agreeable abstraction of mastication; knock at the
door! In comes Mr. Hazlitt, or Martin Burney, or
Morgan Demi-gorgon,[1] or my brother, or somebody,
to prevent my eating alone, — a process absolutely
necessary to my poor wretched digestion. Oh, the
pleasure of eating alone! Eating my dinner alone,
— let me think of it! But in they come, and make
it absolutely necessary that I should open a bottle
of orange; for my meat turns into stone when any
one dines with me, if I have not wine. Wine can

---

[1] John Morgan.

mollify stones; then *that* wine turns into acidity, acerbity, misanthropy, a hatred of my interrupters (God bless 'em! I love some of 'em dearly) ; and with the hatred, a still greater aversion to their going away. Bad is the dead sea they bring upon me, choking and deadening; but worse is the deader dry sand they leave me on, if they go before bed-time. Come never, I would say to these spoilers of my dinner; but if you come, never go! The fact is, this interruption does not happen very often; but every time it comes by surprise, that present bane of my life, orange wine, with all its dreary stifling consequences, follows. Evening company I should always like, had I any mornings; but I am saturated with human faces (*divine* forsooth!) and voices all the golden morning; and five evenings in a week would be as much as I should covet to be in company; but I assure you that is a wonderful week in which I can get two, or one, to myself. I am never C. L., but always C. L. & Co. He who thought it not good for man to be alone, preserve me from the more prodigious monstrosity of being never by myself! I forget bed-time; but even there these sociable frogs clamber up to annoy me. Once a week, generally some singular evening that, being alone, I go to bed at the hour I ought always to be a-bed, just close to my bed-room window is the club-room of a public-house, where a set of singers — I take them to be chorus-singers of the two theatres (it must be *both of them*) — begin their orgies. They are a set of fellows (as I conceive) who, being limited by their talents to the burden

of the song at the playhouses, in revenge have got
the common popular airs by Bishop or some cheap
composer, arranged for choruses, that is, to be sung
all in chorus,— at least, I never can catch any of the
text of the plain song, nothing but the Babylonish
choral howl at the tail on 't. " That fury being
quenched," — the howl I mean, — a burden suc-
ceeds of shouts and clapping and knocking of the
table.   At length over-tasked nature drops under it,
and escapes for a few hours into the society of the
sweet silent creatures of dreams, which go away with
mocks and mows at cockcrow.   And then I think
of the words Christabel's father used (bless me ! I
have dipt in the wrong ink) to say every morning
by way of variety when he awoke, —

> " Every knell, the Baron saith,
>   Wakes us up to a world of death," —

or something like it.   All I mean by this senseless
interrupted tale is, that by my central situation I am
a little over-companied.   Not that I have any ani-
mosity against the good creatures that are so anxious
to drive away the harpy Solitude from me.   I like 'em,
and cards, and a cheerful glass ; but I mean merely
to give you an idea, between office confinement and
after-office society, how little time I can call my own.
I mean only to draw a picture, not to make an inference.   I would not, that I know of, have it otherwise.   I only wish sometimes I could exchange some
of my faces and voices for the faces and voices
which a late visitation brought most welcome, and carried away, leaving regret, but more pleasure,— even

a kind of gratitude,— at being so often favored with that kind northern visitation. My London faces and noises don't hear me,— I mean no disrespect, or I should explain myself, that instead of their return 220 times a year, and the return of W. W., etc., seven times in 104 weeks, some more equal distribution might be found. I have scarce room to put in Mary's kind love and my poor name.

C. LAMB.

W. H[azlitt]. goes on lecturing against W. W., and making copious use of quotations from said W. W. to give a zest to said lectures. S. T. C. is lecturing with success. I have not heard either him or H.; but I dined with S. T. C. at Gilman's a Sunday or two since; and he was well and in good spirits. I mean to hear some of the course; but lectures are not much to my taste, whatever the lecturer may be. If *read*, they are dismal flat, and you can't think why you are brought together to hear a man read his works, which you could read so much better at leisure yourself; if delivered extempore, I am always in pain lest the gift of utterance should suddenly fail the orator in the middle, as it did me at the dinner given in honor of me at the London Tavern. "Gentlemen," said I, and there I stopped; the rest my feelings were under the necessity of supplying. Mrs. Wordsworth *will* go on, kindly haunting us with visions of seeing the lakes once more, which never can be realized. Between us there is a great gulf, not of inexplicable moral antipathies and distances, I hope, as there seemed to be between me and that gentleman concerned in the stamp-office that I so strangely recoiled from at Haydon's. I think I had an instinct that he was the head of an office. I hate all such people, — accountants'· deputy accountants. The mere abstract notion of the East India Company, as long as she is unseen, is pretty, rather poetical; but as she makes herself manifest by the persons of such beasts, I loathe and detest her as the scarlet what-do-you-call-her of Babylon. I thought, after abridging us of all our red-letter days, they had done their worst; but I was deceived in the length to which heads of offices, those true liberty-haters, can go, — they are the tyrants, not Ferdinand, nor Nero. By a decree passed this week, they have abridged us of the immemorially observed custom of going at one o'clock of a Saturday, — the little shadow of a holiday left us. Dear W. W., be thankful for liberty.

LXIV.

TO WORDSWORTH.

May, 1819.

DEAR WORDSWORTH,— I received a copy of " Peter Bell "[1] a week ago, and I hope the author will not

---

[1] Lamb alludes to a parody, ridiculing Wordsworth, by J. Hamilton Reynolds. The verses were entitled " Peter Bell: A Lyrical Ballad ; " and their drift and spirit may be inferred from the following lines from the preface : " It is now a period of one-and-twenty years since I first wrote some of the most perfect compositions (except certain pieces I have written in my later days) that ever dropped from

be offended if I say I do not much relish it. The
humor, if it is meant for humor, is forced ; and then
the price, — sixpence would have been dear for it.
Mind, I do not mean *your* " Peter Bell," but *a* " Peter
Bell," which preceded it about a week, and is in
every bookseller's shop-window in London, the type
and paper nothing differing from the true one, the
preface signed W. W., and the supplementary preface quoting as the author's words an extract from
the supplementary preface to the " Lyrical Ballads."
Is there no law against these rascals?   I would have
this Lambert Simnel whipped at the cart's tail. Who
started the spurious " P. B." I have not heard.   I
should guess, one of the sneering brothers, the vile
Smiths ; but I have heard no name mentioned.
" Peter Bell " (not the mock one) is excellent, —
for its matter, I mean.   I cannot say the style of it
quite satisfies me.   It is too lyrical.   The auditors,
to whom it is feigned to be told, do not *arride me*.
I had rather it had been told me, the reader, at once.
" Hart-leap Well " is the tale for me ; in matter as
good as this, in manner infinitely before it, in my
poor judgment. Why did you not add " The Wagoner "?   Have I thanked you, though, yet for
" Peter Bell "?   I would not *not have it* for a good
deal of money. Coleridge is very foolish to scribble
about books. Neither his tongue nor fingers are very

poetical pen. My heart hath been right and powerful all
its years. I never thought an evil or a weak thought in my
life. It has been my aim and my achievement to deduce
moral thunder from buttercups, daisies, celandines, and (as a
poet scarcely inferior to myself hath it) ' such small deer,' "
etc.

retentive. But I shall not say anything to him about
it. He would only begin a very long story with a
very long face, and I see him far too seldom to tease
him with affairs of business or conscience when I do
see him. He never comes near our house, and when
we go to see him he is generally writing or thinking ;
he is writing in his study till the dinner comes, and
that is scarce over before the stage summons us
away. The mock " P. B." had only this effect on
me, that after twice reading it over in hopes to find
something diverting in it, I reached your two books
off the shelf, and set into a steady reading of them,
till I had nearly finished both before I went to bed, —
the two of your last edition, of course, I mean.
And in the morning I awoke determined to take
down the " Excursion." I wish the scoundrel imi-
tator could know this. But why waste a wish on
him ? I do not believe that paddling about with a
stick in a pond, and fishing up a dead author, whom
his intolerable wrongs had driven to that deed of
desperation, would turn the heart of one of these
obtuse literary BELLS. There is no Cock for such
Peters, damn 'em ! I am glad this aspiration came
upon the red-ink line.[1] It is more of a bloody
curse. I have delivered over your other presents
to Alsager and G. Dyer. A., I am sure, will value
it, and be proud of the hand from which it came.
To G. D. a poem is a poem, — his own as good as
anybody's, and, God bless him ! anybody's as good
as his own ; for I do not think he has the most dis-

---

[1] The original letter is actually written in two inks,—
alternate black and red.

tant guess of the possibility of one poem being better than another. The gods, by denying him the very faculty itself of discrimination, have effectually cut off every seed of envy in his bosom. But with envy they excited curiosity also ; and if you wish the copy again, which you destined for him, I think I shall be able to find it again for you on his third shelf, where he stuffs his presentation copies, uncut, in shape and matter resembling a lump of dry dust ; but on carefully removing that stratum, a thing like a pamphlet will emerge. I have tried this with fifty different poetical works that have been given G. D. in return for as many of his own performances ; and I confess I never had any scruple in taking *my own* again, wherever I found it, shaking the adherences off; and by this means one copy of ' my works ' served for G. D., — and, with a little dusting, was made over to my good friend Dr. Geddes, who little thought whose leavings he was taking when he made me that graceful bow. By the way, the Doctor is the only one of my acquaintance who bows gracefully, — my town acquaintance, I mean. How do you like my way of writing with two inks? I think it is pretty and motley. Suppose Mrs. W. adopts it, the next time she holds the pen for you. My dinner waits. I have no time to indulge any longer in these laborious curiosities. God bless you, and cause to thrive and burgeon whatsoever you write, and fear no inks of miserable poetasters.

Yours truly,
CHARLES LAMB.

Mary's love.

LXV

TO MANNING.

May 28, 1819.

MY DEAR M., — I want to know how your brother is, if you have heard lately. I want to know about you. I wish you were nearer. How are my cousins, the Gladmans of Wheathampstead, and Farmer Bruton? Mrs. Bruton is a glorious woman.

"Hail, Mackery End!"[1]

This is a fragment of a blank-verse poem which I once meditated, but got no farther. The E. I. H. has been thrown into a quandary by the strange phenomenon of poor Tommy Bye, whom I have known, man and madman, twenty-seven years, he being elder here than myself by nine years and more. He was always a pleasant, gossiping, half-headed, muzzy, dozing, dreaming, walk-about, inoffensive chap, a little too fond of the creature, — who isn't at times? But Tommy had not brains to work off an overnight's surfeit by ten o'clock next morning, and unfortunately, in he wandered the other morning drunk with last night and with a superfœtation of drink taken in since he set out from bed. He came staggering under his double burden, like trees in Java, bearing at once blossom, fruit, and falling fruit, as I have heard you or some other traveller tell, with his face literally as blue as the bluest firmament. Some wretched calico that he

---

[1] See the Elia essay, " Mackery End, in H—shire."

had mopped his poor oozy front with, had rendered up its native dye, and the devil a bit would he consent to wash it, but swore it was characteristic, for he was going to the sale of indigo ; and set up a laugh which I did not think the lungs of mortal man were competent to. It was like a thousand people laughing, or the Goblin Page. He imagined afterwards that the whole office had been laughing at him, so strange did his own sounds strike upon his *non*sensorium. But Tommy has laughed his last laugh, and awoke the next day to find himself reduced from an abused income of £600 per annum to one sixth of the sum, after thirty-six years' tolerably good service. The quality of mercy was not strained in his behalf; the gentle dews dropped not on him from heaven. It just came across me that I was writing to Canton. Will you drop in to-morrow night? Fanny Kelly is coming, if she does not cheat us. Mrs. *Gold* is well, but proves " uncoined," as the lovers about Wheathampstead would say.

I have not had such a quiet half hour to sit down to a quiet letter for many years. I have not been interrupted above four times. I wrote a letter the other day in alternate lines, black ink and red, and you cannot think how it chilled the flow of ideas. Next Monday is Whit-Monday. What a reflection ! Twelve years ago, and I should have kept that and the following holiday in the fields a-maying. All of those pretty pastoral delights are over. This dead, everlasting dead desk, — how it weighs the spirit of a gentleman down ! This dead wood of the desk in-

stead of your living trees !   But then, again, I hate the
Joskins, *a name for Hertfordshire bumpkins.*   Each
state of life has its inconvenience ; but then, again,
mine has more than one.   Not that I repine, or
grudge, or murmur at my destiny.   I have meat and
drink, and decent apparel, — I shall, at least, when I
get a new hat.

A red-haired man just interrupted me.   He has
broke the current of my thoughts.   I have n't a
word to add.   I don't know why I send this letter,
but I have had a hankering to hear about you some
days.   Perhaps it will go off before your reply
comes.   If it don't, I assure you no letter was ever
welcomer from you, from Paris or Macao.

C. LAMB.

LXVI.

TO MISS WORDSWORTH.

November 25, 1819.

DEAR MISS WORDSWORTH, — You will think me
negligent, but I wanted to see more of Willy[1] before I ventured to express a prediction.   Till yesterday I had barely seen him, — *Virgilium tantum
vidi ;* but yesterday he gave us his small company to
a bullock's heart, and I can pronounce him a lad of
promise.   He is no pedant nor bookworm ; so far
I can answer.   Perhaps he has hitherto paid too
little attention to other men's inventions, preferring,

---

[1] Wordsworth's third son.   He was at the Charter-house
School in London, and the Lambs had invited him to spend
a half holiday with them.

like Lord Foppington, the " natural sprouts of his
own." But he has observation, and seems thoroughly
awake. I am ill at remembering other people's *bon
mots*, but the following are a few. Being taken over
Waterloo Bridge, he remarked that if we had no
mountains, we had a fine river, at least, — which was
a touch of the comparative ; but then he added in
a strain which augured less for his future abilities as
a political economist, that he supposed they must
take at least a pound a week toll. Like a curious
naturalist, he inquired if the tide did not come up
a little salty. This being satisfactorily answered,
he put another question, as to the flux and reflux ;
which being rather cunningly evaded than artfully
solved by that she-Aristotle Mary, who muttered
something about its getting up an hour sooner and
sooner every day, he sagely replied, " Then it must
come to the same thing at last," — which was a
speech worthy of an infant Halley ! The lion in the
'Change by no means came up to his ideal standard,
— so impossible is it for Nature, in any of her works,
to come up to the standard of a child's imagination !
The whelps (lionets) he was sorry to find were
dead ; and on particular inquiry, his old friend the
orang-outang had gone the way of all flesh also.
The grand tiger was also sick, and expected in no
short time to exchange this transitory world for another or none. But, again, there was a golden eagle
(I do not mean that of Charing) which did much
arride and console him. William's genius, I take
it, leans a little to the figurative ; for being at play
at tricktrack (a kind of minor billiard-table which

we keep for smaller wights, and sometimes refresh our own mature fatigues with taking a hand at), not being able to hit a ball he had iterate aimed at, he cried out, "I cannot hit that beast." Now, the balls are usually called men, but he felicitously hit upon a middle term, — a term of approximation and imaginative reconciliation; a something where the two ends of the brute matter (ivory) and their human and rather violent personification into men might meet, as I take it, — illustrative of that excellent remark in a certain preface about imagination, explaining "Like a sea-beast that had crawled forth to sun himself!" Not that I accuse William Minor of hereditary plagiary, or conceive the image to have come *ex traduce*. Rather he seemeth to keep aloof from any source of imitation, and purposely to remain ignorant of what mighty poets have done in this kind before him; for being asked if his father had ever been on Westminster Bridge,[1] he answered that he did not know!

It is hard to discern the oak in the acorn, or a temple like St. Paul's in the first stone which is laid; nor can I quite prefigure what destination the genius of William Minor hath to take. Some few hints I have set down, to guide my future observations. He hath the power of calculation in no ordinary degree for a chit. He combineth figures, after the first boggle, rapidly; as in the tricktrack board, where the hits are figured, at first he did not perceive that 15 and 7 made 22; but by

---

[1] "William Minor" was evidently forgetful of the exquisite sonnet, "Composed Upon Westminster Bridge."

a little use he could combine 8 with 25, and 33 again with 16, — which approacheth something in kind (far let me be from flattering him by saying in degree) to that of the famous American boy. I am sometimes inclined to think I perceive the future satirist in him, for he hath a sub-sardonic smile which bursteth out upon occasion, — as when he was asked if London were as big as Ambleside ; and indeed no other answer was given, or proper to be given, to so ensnaring and provoking a question. In the contour of skull certainly I discern something paternal ; but whether in all respects the future man shall transcend his father's fame, Time, the trier of Geniuses, must decide. Be it pronounced peremptorily at present that Willy is a well-mannered child, and though no great student, hath yet a lively eye for things that lie before him.

Given in haste from my desk at Leadenhall.

Yours, and yours most sincerely,

C. LAMB.

LXVII.

TO COLERIDGE.

March 9, 1822.

DEAR C., — It gives me great satisfaction to hear that the pig turned out so well,[1] — they are interesting creatures at a certain age ; what a pity such buds should blow out into the maturity of rank

---

[1] Some one had sent Coleridge a pig, and the gift was erroneously credited to Lamb.

bacon! You had all some of the crackling — and
brain sauce; did you remember to rub it with
butter, and gently dredge it a little, just before
the crisis? Did the eyes come away kindly, with
no Œdipean avulsion? Was the crackling the
color of the ripe pomegranate? Had you no
cursed complement of boiled neck of mutton before it, to blunt the edge of delicate desire? Did
you flesh maiden teeth in it? Not that I sent the
pig, or can form the remotest guess what part Owen
could play in the business. I never knew him give
anything away in my life. He would not begin
with strangers. I suspect the pig, after all, was
meant for me; but at the unlucky juncture of time
being absent, the present somehow went round to
Highgate. To confess an honest truth, a pig is one
of those things I could never think of sending away.
Teals, widgeons, snipes, barn-door fowl, ducks,
geese, — your tame villatic things, — Welsh mutton,
collars of brawn, sturgeon, fresh or pickled, your
potted char, Swiss cheeses, French pies, early
grapes, muscadines, I impart as freely unto my
friends as to myself. They are but self-extended;
but pardon me if I stop somewhere. Where the
fine feeling of benevolence giveth a higher smack
than the sensual rarity, there my friends (or any
good man) may command me; but pigs are pigs,
and I myself therein am nearest to myself. Nay,
I should think it an affront, an undervaluing done
to Nature, who bestowed such a boon upon me, if
in a churlish mood I parted with the precious gift.
One of the bitterest pangs I ever felt of remorse

was when a child. My kind old aunt [1] had strained her pocket-strings to bestow a sixpenny whole plum-cake upon me. In my way home through the Borough, I met a venerable old man, not a mendicant, but thereabouts, — a look-beggar, not a verbal petitionist ; and in the coxcombry of taught-charity, I gave away the cake to him. I walked on a little in all the pride of an Evangelical peacock, when of a sudden my old aunt's kindness crossed me, — the sum it was to her ; the pleasure she had a right to expect that I — not the old impostor — should take in eating her cake ; the cursed ingratitude by which, under the color of a Christian virtue, I had frustrated her cherished purpose. I sobbed, wept, and took it to heart so grievously that I think I never suffered the like ; and I was right. It was a piece of unfeeling hypocrisy, and proved a lesson to me ever after. The cake has long been masticated, consigned to dunghill with the ashes of that unseasonable pauper.

But when Providence, who is better to us all than our aunts, gives me a pig, remembering my temptation and my fall, I shall endeavor to act towards it more in the spirit of the donor's purpose.

Yours (short of pig) to command in everything,

C. L.

---

[1] Elia : "Christ's Hospital Five-and-Thirty Years Ago."

LXVIII.

March 20, 1822.

MY DEAR WORDSWORTH, — A letter from you is very grateful; I have not seen a Kendal postmark so long. We are pretty well, save colds and rheumatics, and a certain deadness to everything, which I think I may date from poor John's loss, and another accident or two at the same time, that has made me almost bury myself at Dalston, where yet I see more faces than I could wish. Deaths overset one and put one out long after the recent grief. Two or three have died within this last two twelve-months, and so many parts of me have been numbed. One sees a picture, reads an anecdote, starts a casual fancy, and thinks to tell of it to this person in preference to every other: the person is gone whom it would have peculiarly suited. It won't do for another. Every departure destroys a class of sympathies. There's Captain Burney gone! What fun has whist now? What matters it what you lead, if you can no longer fancy him looking over you?[1] One never hears anything, but the image of the particular person occurs with whom alone almost you would care to share the intelligence, — thus one distributes oneself about; and now for so many parts of me I have lost the market. Common natures do not

---

[1] Martin Burney was the grimy-fisted whist-player to whom Lamb once observed, "Martin, if dirt was trumps, what hands you would hold!"

suffice me. Good people, as they are called, won't
serve ; I want individuals. I am made up of queer
points, and I want so many answering needles.
The going-away of friends does not make the remainder more precious. It takes so much from
them, as there was a common link. A, B, and C
make a party. A dies. B not only loses A, but
all A's part in C. C loses A's part in B, and so
the alphabet sickens by subtraction of interchange-
ables. I express myself muddily, *capite dolente*. I
have a dulling cold. My theory is to enjoy life ;
but my practice is against it. I grow ominously
tired of official confinement. Thirty years have I
served the Philistines, and my neck is not subdued
to the yoke. You don't know how wearisome it is
to breathe the air of four pent walls without relief,
day after day, all the golden hours of the day between ten and four, without ease or interposition.
Tædet me harum quotidianarum formarum, these
pestilential clerk-faces always in one's dish. Oh for
a few years between the grave and the desk ! they
are the same, save that at the latter you are the
outside machine. The foul enchanter [Nick ?],
" letters four do form his name," — Busirane [1] is his
name in hell, — that has curtailed you of some domestic comforts, hath laid a heavier hand on me,
not in present infliction, but in the taking away the
hope of enfranchisement. I dare not whisper to
myself a pension on this side of absolute incapacita-
tion and infirmity, till years have sucked me dry, —
Otium cum indignitate. I had thought in a green old

---

[1] The enchanter in " The Faërie Queene "

age (oh, green thought !) to have retired to Ponder's
End, — emblematic name, how beautiful ! — in
the Ware Road, there to have made up my accounts
with Heaven and the Company, toddling about between it and Cheshunt, anon stretching, on some
fine Izaak Walton morning, to Hoddesdon or Am-
well, careless as a beggar ; but walking, walking ever,
till I fairly walked myself off my legs, — dying walking ! The hope is gone. I sit like Philomel all
day (but not singing), with my breast against this
thorn of a desk, with the only hope that some pul-
monary affliction may relieve me. *Vide* Lord Pal-
merston's report of the clerks in the War-office
(Debates in this morning's "Times "), by which it
appears, in twenty years as many clerks have been
coughed and catarrhed out of it into their freer
graves. Thank you for asking about the pictures.
Milton hangs over my fire-side in Covent Garden
(when I am there) ; the rest have been sold for an
old song, wanting the eloquent tongue that should
have set them off ! You have gratified me with
liking my meeting with Dodd. For the Malvolio
story, — the thing is become in verity a sad task, and
I eke it out with anything. If I could slip out of it
I should be happy ; but our chief-reputed assistants
have forsaken us. The Opium-Eater crossed us
once with a dazzling path, and hath as suddenly
left us darkling ; and, in short, I shall go on from
dull to worse, because I cannot resist the booksellers' importunity, — the old plea, you know, of
authors ; but I believe on my part sincere. Hartley
I do not so often see, but I never see him in unwel-

come hour. I thoroughly love and honor him. I send you a frozen epistle ; but it is winter and dead time of the year with me. May Heaven keep something like spring and summer up with you, strengthen your eyes, and make mine a little lighter to encounter with them, as I hope they shall yet and again, before all are closed !

Yours, with every kind remembrance,

C. L.

LXIX.

TO JOHN CLARE.[1]

August 31, 1822.

DEAR CLARE, — I thank you heartily for your present. I am an inveterate old Londoner, but while I am among your choice collections I seem to be native to them and free of the country. The quality of your observation has astonished me. What have most pleased me have been " Recollections after a Ramble," and those " Grongar Hill " kind of pieces in eight-syllable lines, my favourite measure, such as " Cooper Hill " and " Solitude." In some of your story-telling Ballads the provincial phrases sometimes startle me. I think you are too profuse with them. In poetry *slang* of every kind is to be avoided. There is a rustic Cockneyism, as little pleasing as ours of London. Transplant Arcadia to Helpstone. The true rustic style I think is

---

[1] The Northamptonshire peasant poet. He had sent Lamb his " The Village Minstrel, and other Poems "

to be found in Shenstone. Would his "School-mistress," the prettiest of poems, have been better if he had used quite the Goody's own language? Now and then a home rusticism is fresh and startling ; but when nothing is gained in expression, it is out of tenor. It may make folks smile and stare ; but the ungenial coalition of barbarous with refined phrases will prevent you in the end from being so generally tasted as you desire to be. Excuse my freedom, and take the same liberty with my *puns*.

I send you two little volumes of my spare hours. They are of all sorts ; there is a Methodist hymn for Sundays, and a farce for Saturday night. Pray give them a place on your shelf. Pray accept a little volume, of which I have a duplicate, that I may return in equal number to your welcome presents. I think I am indebted to you for a sonnet in the "London" for August.

Since I saw you I have been in France, and have eaten frogs. The nicest little rabbity things you ever tasted. Do look about for them. Make Mrs. Clare pick off the hind-quarters, boil them plain, with parsley and butter. The fore-quarters are not so good. She may let them hop off by themselves.

Yours sincerely,

CHAS. LAMB.

LXX

September 22, 1822.

MY DEAR F.,—I scribble hastily at office. Frank
wants my letter presently. I and sister are just returned from Paris![1] We have eaten frogs. It
has been such a treat! You know our monotonous
general tenor. Frogs are the nicest little delicate
things,—rabbity flavored. Imagine a Lilliputian
rabbit! They fricassee them; but in my mind,
dressed seethed, plain, with parsley and butter, would
have been the decision of Apicius. . . . Paris is a
glorious, picturesque old city. London looks mean
and new to it, as the town of Washington would,
seen after *it*. But they have no St. Paul's or Westminster Abbey. The Seine, so much despised by
Cockneys, is exactly the size to run through a magnificent street; palaces a mile long on one side, lofty
Edinburgh stone (oh, the glorious antiques!) houses
on the other. The Thames disunites London and
Southwark. I had Talma to supper with me. He
has picked up, as I believe, an authentic portrait of
Shakspeare. He paid a broker about £40 English for it. It is painted on the one half of a pair of
bellows,—a lovely picture, corresponding with the
Folio head. The bellows has old carved *wings*

---

[1] The Lambs had visited Paris on the invitation of James
Kenney, the dramatist, who had married a Frenchwoman,
and was living at Versailles.

round it, and round the visnomy is inscribed, as near as I remember, not divided into rhyme, — I found out the rhyme, —

> " Whom have we here
> Stuck on this bellows,
> But the Prince of good fellows,
> Willy Shakspere ? "

At top, —

> " O base and coward luck,
> To be here stuck ! "
> POINS.

At bottom, —

> " Nay ! rather a glorious lot is to him assign'd,
> Who, like the Almighty, rides upon the *wind.* "
> PISTOL.

This is all in old carved wooden letters. The countenance smiling, sweet, and intellectual beyond measure, even as he was immeasurable. It may be a forgery. They laugh at me, and tell me Ireland is in Paris, and has been putting off a portrait of the Black Prince. How far old wood may be imitated I cannot say. Ireland was not found out by his parchments, but by his poetry. I am confident no painter on either side the Channel could have painted anything near like the face I saw. Again, would such a painter and forger have taken £40 for a thing, if authentic, worth £4000? Talma is not in the secret, for he had not even found out the rhymes in the first inscription. He is coming over with it, and my life to Southey's "Thalaba," it will gain universal faith.

The letter is wanted, and I am wanted.   Imagine the blank filled up with all kind things.

Our joint, hearty remembrances to both of you. Yours as ever,

C. LAMB.

LXXI.

TO WALTER WILSON.

December 16, 1822.

DEAR WILSON, — *Lightning* I was going to call you. You must have thought me negligent in not answering your letter sooner.   But I have a habit of never writing letters but at the office ; 't is so much time cribbed out of the Company ; and I am but just got out of the thick of a tea-sale, in which most of the entry of notes, deposits, etc., usually falls to my share.

I have nothing of De Foe's but two or three novels and the "Plague History."[1]   I can give you no information about him.   As a slight general character of what I remember of them (for I have not looked into them latterly), I would say that in the appearance of *truth*, in all the incidents and conversations that occur in them, they exceed any works of fiction I am acquainted with.   It is perfect illusion.   The *author* never appears in these self-narratives (for so they ought to be called, or rather auto-biographies), but the *narrator* chains us down to an implicit belief in everything he says.   There

---

[1] Wilson was preparing a Life of De Foe, and had written to Lamb for guidance.

is all the minute detail of a log-book in it. Dates
are painfully pressed upon the memory. Facts are
repeated over and over in varying phrases, till you
cannot choose but believe them. It is like reading
evidence given in a court of justice. So anxious
the story-teller seems that the truth should be clearly comprehended that when he has told us a matter
of fact or a motive, in a line or two farther down
he *repeals* it with his favorite figure of speech, " I
say " so and so, though he had made it abundantly
plain before. This is in imitation of the common
people's way of speaking, or rather of the way in
which they are addressed by a master or mistress
who wishes to impress something upon their memories, and has a wonderful effect upon matter-of-fact
readers. Indeed, it is to such principally that he
writes. His style is everywhere beautiful, but plain
and *homely.* "Robinson Crusoe " is delightful to all
ranks and classes ; but it is easy to see that it is written in phraseology peculiarly adapted to the lower
conditions of readers, — hence it is an especial favorite with seafaring men, poor boys, servant-maids, etc.
His novels are capital kitchen-reading, while they
are worthy, from their deep interest, to find a shelf
in the libraries of the wealthiest and the most
learned. His passion for *matter-of-fact narrative*
sometimes betrayed him into a long relation of common incidents, which might happen to any man,
and have no interest but the intense appearance of
truth in them, to recommend them. The whole
latter half or two-thirds of " Colonel Jack " is of
this description. The beginning of " Colonel Jack "

is the most affecting natural picture of a young thief
that was ever drawn. His losing the stolen money
in the hollow of a tree, and finding it again when
he was in despair, and then being in equal distress
at not knowing how to dispose of it, and several
similar touches in the early history of the Colonel,
evince a deep knowledge of human nature, and
putting out of question the superior *romantic* interest of the latter, in my mind very much exceed
"Crusoe." "Roxana" (first edition) is the next in
interest, though he left out the best part of it in
subsequent editions from a foolish hypercriticism of
his friend Southerne. But "Moll Flanders," the
"Account of the Plague," etc., are all of one family,
and have the same stamp of character. Believe
me, with friendly recollections — *Brother* (as I used
to call you), Yours,

C. LAMB.

LXXII.

TO BERNARD BARTON.

December 23, 1822.

DEAR SIR, — I have been so distracted with business and one thing or other, I have not had a quiet
quarter of an hour for epistolary purposes. Christmas, too, is come, which always puts a rattle into
my morning skull. It is a visiting, unquiet, un-
quakerish season. I get more and more in love
with solitude, and proportionately hampered with
company. I hope you have some holidays at this
period. I have one day, — Christmas Day; alas!

too few to commemorate the season. All work and no play dulls me. Company is not play, but many times hard work. To play, is for a man to do what he pleases, or to do nothing, — to go about soothing his particular fancies. I have lived to a time of life to have outlived the good hours, the nine-o'clock suppers, with a bright hour or two to clear up in afterwards. Now you cannot get tea before that hour, and then sit gaping, music-bothered perhaps, till half-past twelve brings up the tray; and what you steal of convivial enjoyment after, is heavily paid for in the disquiet of to-morrow's head.

I am pleased with your liking " John Woodvil," and amused with your knowledge of our drama being confined to Shakspeare and Miss Baillie. What a world of fine territory between Land's End and Johnny Groat's have you missed traversing! I could almost envy you to have so much to read. I feel as if I had read all the books I want to read. Oh, to forget Fielding, Steele, etc., and read 'em new!

Can you tell me a likely place where I could pick up cheap Fox's Journal? There are no Quaker circulating libraries? Elwood, too, I must have. I rather grudge that Southey has taken up the history of your people; I am afraid he will put in some levity. I am afraid I am not quite exempt from that fault in certain magazine articles, where I have introduced mention of them. Were they to do again, I would reform them. Why should not you write a poetical account of your old worthies, deducing them from Fox to Woolman? But I remember you did talk of something of that kind, as a counterpart to the " Ecclesiastical Sketches." But would not a poem be more consecutive than a string of sonnets? You have no martyrs *quite to the fire*, I think, among you, but plenty of heroic confessors, spirit-martyrs, lamb-lions. Think of it ; it would be better than a series of sonnets on " Eminent Bankers." I like a hit at our way of life, though it does well for me, — better than anything short of *all one's time to one's self;* for which alone I rankle with envy at the rich. Books are good, and pictures are good, and money to buy them therefore good ; but to buy *time*, — in other words, life !

The " compliments of the time " to you, should end my letter ; to a Friend, I suppose, I must say the " sincerity of the season : " I hope they both mean the same. With excuses for this hastily penned note, believe me, with great respect,

C. LAMB.

LXXIII.

TO MISS WORDSWORTH.

MARY perfectly approves of the appropriation of the *feathers*, and wishes them peacock's for your fair niece's sake.

Christmas, 1822.

DEAR MISS WORDSWORTH, — I had just written the above endearing words when Monkhouse tapped me on the shoulder with an invitation to cold goose pie, which I was not bird of that sort enough to decline.

Mrs. Monkhouse, I am most happy to say, is better. Mary has been tormented with a rheumatism, which is leaving her. I am suffering from the festivities of the season. I wonder how my misused carcase holds it out. I have played the experimental philosopher on it, that's certain. Willy shall be welcome to a mince-pie and a bout at commerce whenever he comes. He was in our eye. I am glad you liked my new year's speculations; everybody likes them, except the author of the " Pleasures of Hope." Disappointment attend him ! How I like to be liked, and *what I do* to be liked ! They flatter me in magazines, newspapers, and all the minor reviews; the Quarterlies hold aloof. But they must come into it in time, or their leaves be waste paper. Salute Trinity Library in my name. Two special things are worth seeing at Cambridge, — a portrait of Cromwell at Sidney, and a better of Dr. Harvey (who found out that blood was red) at Dr. Davy's; you should see them. Coleridge is pretty well; I have not seen him, but hear often of him from Allsop, who sends me hares and pheasants twice a week ; I can hardly take so fast as he gives. I have almost forgotten butcher's meat as plebeian. Are you not glad the cold is gone? I find winters not so agreeable as they used to be " when winter bleak had charms for me." I cannot conjure up a kind similitude for those snowy flakes. Let them keep to twelfth-cakes !

Mrs. Paris, our Cambridge friend, has been in town. You do not know the Watfords in Trumpington Street. They are capital people. Ask anybody you meet, who is the biggest woman in Cambridge, and I'll hold you a wager they'll say Mrs. Smith; she broke down two benches in Trinity Gardens, — one on the confines of St. John's, which occasioned a litigation between the Societies as to repairing it. In warm weather, she retires into an ice-cellar (literally !), and dates the returns of the years from a hot Thursday some twenty years back. She sits in a room with opposite doors and windows, to let in a thorough draught, which gives her slenderer friends tooth-aches. She is to be seen in the market every morning at ten cheapening fowls, which I observe the Cambridge poulterers are not sufficiently careful to stump.

Having now answered most of the points contained in your letter, let me end with assuring you of our very best kindness, and excuse Mary for not handling the pen on this occasion, especially as it has fallen into so much better hands ! Will Dr. W. accept of my respects at the end of a foolish letter?

C. L.

LXXIV.

TO MR. AND MRS. BRUTON.[1]

January 6, 1823.

THE pig was above my feeble praise. It was a dear pigmy. There was some contention as to who should have the ears ; but in spite of his obstinacy

---

[1] Hertfordshire connections of the Lambs.

(deaf as these little creatures are to advice), I contrived to get at one of them.

It came in boots, too, which I took as a favor. Generally these petty-toes, pretty toes ! are missing; but I suppose he wore them to look taller.

He must have been the least of his race. His little foots would have gone into the silver slipper. I take him to have been a Chinese and a female.

If Evelyn could have seen him, he would never have farrowed two such prodigious volumes, seeing how much good can be contained in — how small a compass !

He crackled delicately.

I left a blank at the top of my letter, not being determined which to address it to ; so farmer and farmer's wife will please to divide our thanks. May your granaries be full, and your rats empty, and your chickens plump, and your envious neighbors lean, and your laborers busy, and you as idle and as happy as the day is long !

VIVE L'AGRICULTURE !

> How do you make your pigs so little ?
> They are vastly engaging at the age :
>   I was so myself.
> Now I am a disagreeable old hog,
> A middle-aged gentleman-and-a-half ;
> My faculties (thank God !) are not much impaired.

I have my sight, hearing, taste, pretty perfect, and can read the Lord's Prayer in common type, by the help of a candle, without making many mistakes.

Many happy returns, not of the pig, but of the

New Year, to both. Mary, for her share of the pig
and the memoirs, desires to send the same.

Yours truly,

C. LAMB.

LXXV.

TO BERNARD BARTON.[1]

January 9, 1823.

THROW yourself on the world without any rational
plan of support beyond what the chance employ of
booksellers would afford you !

Throw yourself, rather, my dear sir, from the
steep Tarpeian rock slap-dash headlong upon iron
spikes. If you had but five consolatory minutes
between the desk and the bed, make much of them,
and live a century in them, rather than turn slave to
the booksellers. They are Turks and Tartars when
they have poor authors at their beck. Hitherto
you have been at arm's length from them. Come
not within their grasp. I have known many authors
want for bread, some repining, others envying the
blessed security of a counting-house, all agreeing
they had rather have been tailors, weavers, — what
not, — rather than the things they were. I have
known some starved, some to go mad, one dear
friend literally dying in a workhouse. You know
not what a rapacious, dishonest set these book-

---

[1] The Quaker poet. Mr. Barton was a clerk in the bank
of the Messrs. Alexander, of Woodbridge, in Suffolk. Encouraged by his literary success, he thought of throwing up
his clerkship and trusting to his pen for a livelihood, — a
design from which he was happily diverted by his friends.

sellers are. Ask even Southey, who (a single case
almost) has made a fortune by book-drudgery, what
he has found them. Oh, you know not — may you
never know ! — the miseries of subsisting by authorship. 'T is a pretty appendage to a situation like
yours or mine, but a slavery, worse than all slavery,
to be a bookseller's dependant, to drudge your
brains for pots of ale and breasts of mutton, to
change your free thoughts and voluntary numbers
for ungracious task-work. Those fellows hate *us.*
The reason I take to be that, contrary to other
trades, in which the master gets all the credit (a
jeweller or silversmith for instance), and the jour-
neyman, who really does the fine work, is in the
background, in *our* work the world gives all the
credit to us, whom *they* consider as *their* journeymen,
and therefore do they hate us, and cheat us, and
oppress us, and would wring the blood of us out,
to put another sixpence in their mechanic pouches !
I contend that a bookseller has a *relative honesty*
towards authors, not like his honesty to the rest of
the world. Baldwin, who first engaged me as Elia,
has not paid me up yet (nor any of us without repeated mortifying appeals). Yet how the knave
fawned when I was of service to him ! Yet I daresay
the fellow is punctual in settling his milk-score, etc.

Keep to your bank, and the bank will keep you.
Trust not to the public ; you may hang, starve,
drown yourself, for anything that worthy *personage*
cares. I bless every star that Providence, not seeing good to make me independent, has seen it next
good to settle me upon the stable foundation of

Leadenhall. Sit down, good B. B., in the banking-office ; what ! is there not from six to eleven P. M. six days in the week, and is there not all Sunday? Fie ! what a superfluity of man's time, if you could think so, — enough for relaxation, mirth, converse, poetry, good thoughts, quiet thoughts. Oh, the corroding, torturing, tormenting thoughts that disturb the brain of the unlucky wight who must draw upon it for daily sustenance ! Henceforth I retract all my foul complaints of mercantile employment ; look upon them as lovers' quarrels. I was but half in earnest. Welcome, dead timber of a desk. that makes me live ! A little grumbling is a wholesome medicine for the spleen, but in my inner heart do I approve and embrace this our close, but unharassing, way of life. I am quite serious. If you can send me Fox, I will not keep it *six weeks*, and will return it, with warm thanks to yourself and friend, without blot or dog's-ear. You will much oblige me by this kindness.

Yours truly,

C. LAMB.

LXXVI.

● TO MISS HUTCHINSON.

April 25, 1823.

DEAR MISS H., — Mary has such an invincible reluctance to any epistolary exertion that I am sparing her a mortification by taking the pen from her. The plain truth is, she writes such a mean, detestable hand that she is ashamed of the formation of her letters. There is an essential poverty and abjectness in the frame of them. They look like begging letters. And then she is sure to omit a most substantial word in the second draught (for she never ventures an epistle without a foul copy first), which is obliged to be interlined, — which spoils the neatest epistle, you know. Her figures, 1, 2, 3, 4, etc., where she has occasion to express numerals, as in the date (25th April, 1823), are not figures, but figurantes; and the combined posse go staggering up and down shameless, as drunkards in the daytime. It is no better when she rules her paper. Her lines " are not less erring " than her words ; a sort of unnatural parallel lines, that are perpetually threatening to meet, — which, you know, is quite contrary to Euclid. Her very blots are not bold, like this [*here a large blot is inserted*], but poor smears, half left in and half scratched out, with another smear left in their place. I like a clear letter ; a bold, free hand and a fearless flourish. Then she has always to go through them (a second operation) to dot her *i*'s and cross her *t*'s. I don't think she could make a corkscrew if she tried, — which has such a fine effect at the end or middle of an epistle, and fills up.

There is a corkscrew ! One of the best I ever drew.[1] By the way, what incomparable whiskey that was of Monkhouse's ! But if I am to write a letter, let me begin, and not stand flourishing like a fencer at a fair.

[1] Lamb was fond of this flourish, and it is frequently found in his letters.

April 25, 1823.

Dear Miss H., — It gives me great pleasure [the letter now begins] to hear that you got down so smoothly, and that Mrs. Monkhouse's spirits are so good and enterprising.[1] It shows, whatever her posture may be, that her mind at least is not supine. I hope the excursion will enable the former to keep pace with its outstripping neighbor. Pray present our kindest wishes to her and all (that sentence should properly have come into the postscript; but we airy, mercurial spirits, there is no keeping us in). "Time" (as was said of one of us) "toils after us in vain." I am afraid our co-visit with Coleridge was a dream. I shall not get away before the end or middle of June, and then you will be frog-hopping at Boulogne. And besides, I think the Gilmans would scarce trust him with us; I have a malicious knack at cutting of apron-strings. The saints' days you speak of have long since fled to heaven with Astræa, and the cold piety of the age lacks fervor to recall them; only Peter left his key, — the iron one of the two that "shuts amain," — and that is the reason I am locked up. Meanwhile, of afternoons we pick up primroses at Dalston, and Mary corrects me when I call 'em cowslips. God bless you all, and pray remember me euphoniously to Mr. Gruvellegan. That Lee Priory must be a dainty bower. Is it built of flints? and does it stand at Kingsgate?

[1] Miss Hutchinson's invalid relative.

LXXVII.

TO BERNARD BARTON.

September 2, 1823.

DEAR B. B., — What will you not say to my not writing? You cannot say I do not write now. Hessey has not used your kind sonnet, nor have I seen it. Pray send me a copy. Neither have I heard any more of your friend's MS., which I will reclaim whenever you please. When you come Londonward, you will find me no longer in Covent Garden; I have a cottage in Colebrook Row, Islington, — a cottage, for it is detached; a white house, with six good rooms. The New River (rather elderly by this time) runs (if a moderate walking pace can be so termed) close to the foot of the house; and behind is a spacious garden with vines (I assure you), pears, strawberries, parsnips, leeks, carrots, cabbages, to delight the heart of old Alcinous. You enter without passage into a cheerful dining-room, all studded over and rough with old books; and above is a lightsome drawing-room, three windows, full of choice prints. I feel like a great lord, never having had a house before.

The "London," I fear, falls off. I linger among its creaking rafters, like the last rat; it will topple down if they don't get some buttresses. They have pulled down three, — Hazlitt, Procter, and their best stay, kind, light-hearted Wainewright, their

Janus.[1] The best is, neither of our fortunes is concerned in it.

I heard of you from Mr. Pulham this morning, and that gave a fillip to my laziness, which has been intolerable; but I am so taken up with pruning and gardening, — quite a new sort of occupation to me. I have gathered my jargonels; but my Windsor pears are backward. The former were of exquisite raciness. I do now sit under my own vine, and contemplate the growth of vegetable nature. I can now understand in what sense they speak of father Adam. I recognize the paternity while I watch my tulips. I almost fell with him, for the first day I turned a drunken gardener (as he let in the serpent) into my Eden; and he laid about him, lopping off some choice boughs, etc., which hung over from a neighbor's garden, and in his blind zeal laid waste a shade which had sheltered their window from the gaze of passers-by. The old gentlewoman (fury made her not handsome) could scarcely be reconciled by all my fine words. There was no buttering her parsnips. She talked of the law. What a lapse to commit on the first day of my happy " garden state " !

I hope you transmitted the Fox-Journal to its owner, with suitable thanks. Mr. Cary, the Dante man, dines with me to-day. He is a mode of a country parson, lean (as a curate ought to be), modest, sensible, no obtruder of church dogmas,

[1] Wainewright, the notorious poisoner, who, under the name of " Janus Weathercock," contributed various frothy papers on art and literature to the " London Magazine."

quite a different man from Southey. You would like him. Pray accept this for a letter, and believe me, with sincere regards, yours,

C. L.

LXXVIII.

TO MRS. HAZLITT.

November, 1823.

DEAR MRS. H., — Sitting down to write a letter is such a painful operation to Mary that you must accept me as her proxy. You have seen our house. What I now tell you is literally true. Yesterday week, George Dyer called upon us, at one o'clock (*bright noonday*), on his way to dine with Mrs. Barbauld at Newington. He sat with Mary about half an hour, and took leave. The maid saw him go out from her kitchen window, but suddenly losing sight of him, ran up in a fright to Mary. G. D., instead of keeping the slip that leads to the gate, had deliberately, staff in hand, in broad, open day, marched into the New River.[1] He had not his spectacles on, and you know his absence. Who helped him out, they can hardly tell; but between 'em they got him out, drenched thro' and thro'. A mob collected by that time, and accompanied him in. " Send for the doctor ! " they said; and a one-eyed fellow, dirty and drunk, was fetched from the public-house at the end, where it seem he lurks for the sake of picking up water-practice,

---

[1] See Elia-essay, " Amicus Redivivus."

having formerly had a medal from the Humane Society for some rescue. By his advice the patient was put between blankets; and when I came home at four to dinner, I found G. D. a-bed, and raving, light-headed with the brandy-and-water which the doctor had administered. He sang, laughed, whimpered, screamed, babbled of guardian angels, would get up and go home; but we kept him there by force; and by next morning he departed sobered, and seems to have received no injury.[1] All my friends are open-mouthed about having paling before the river; but I cannot see that because a . . . lunatic chooses to walk into a river, with his eyes open, at mid-day, I am any the more likely to be drowned in it, coming home at midnight.

[1] In the "Athenæum" for 1835 Procter says: "I happened to call at Lamb's house about ten minutes after this accident; I saw before me a train of water running from the door to the river. Lamb had gone for a surgeon; the maid was running about distraught, with dry clothes on one arm, and the dripping habiliments of the involuntary bather in the other. Miss Lamb, agitated, and whimpering forth 'Poor Mr. Dyer!' in the most forlorn voice, stood plunging her hands into the wet pockets of his trousers, to fish up the wet coin. Dyer himself, an amiable little old man, who took water *in*ternally and eschewed strong liquors, lay on his host's bed, hidden by blankets; his head, on which was his short gray hair, alone peered out; and this, having been rubbed dry by a resolute hand,— by the maid's, I believe, who assisted at the rescue,— looked as if bristling with a thousand needles. Lamb, moreover, in his anxiety, had administered a formidable dose of cognac and water to the sufferer, and *he* (used only to the simple element) babbled without cessation."

LXXIX.

January 9, 1824.

DEAR B. B., — Do you know what it is to suc-
cumb under an insurmountable day-mare, — "a
whoreson lethargy," Falstaff calls it, — an indisposition to do anything or to be anything; a total
deadness and distaste; a suspension of vitality;
an indifference to locality; a numb, soporifical
good-for-nothingness; an ossification all over; an
oyster-like insensibility to the passing events; a
mind-stupor; a brawny defiance to the needles
of a thrusting-in conscience? Did you ever have
a very bad cold, with a total irresolution to submit to water-gruel processes? This has been for
many weeks my lot and my excuse. My fingers
drag heavily over this paper, and to my thinking
it is three-and-twenty furlongs from here to the end
of this demi-sheet. I have not a thing to say;
nothing is of more importance than another. I am
flatter than a denial or a pancake; emptier than
Judge Parke's wig when the head is in it; duller
than a country stage when the actors are off it, —
a cipher, an o! I acknowledge life at all only by
an occasional convulsional cough and a permanent
phlegmatic pain in the chest. I am weary of the
world; life is weary of me. My day is gone into
twilight, and I don't think it worth the expense
of candles. My wick hath a thief in it, but I can't

muster courage to snuff it. I inhale suffocation; I can't distinguish veal from mutton; nothing interests me. 'T is twelve o'clock, and Thurtell[1] is just now coming out upon the new drop, Jack Ketch alertly tucking up his greasy sleeves to do the last office of mortality; yet cannot I elicit a groan or a moral reflection. If you told me the world will be at an end to-morrow, I should just say, " Will it? " I have not volition enough left to dot my *i*'s, much less to comb my eyebrows; my eyes are set in my head; my brains are gone out to see a poor relation in Moorfields, and they did not say when they 'd come back again; my skull is a Grub Street attic to let, — not so much as a joint-stool left in it; my hand writes, not I, from habit, as chickens run about a little when their heads are off. Oh for a vigorous fit of gout, colic, toothache, — an earwig in my auditory, a fly in my visual organs; pain is life, — the sharper the more evidence of life; but this apathy, this death! Did you ever have an obstinate cold, — a six or seven weeks' unintermitting chill and suspension of hope, fear, conscience, and everything? Yet do I try all I can to cure it. I try wine, and spirits, and smoking, and snuff in unsparing quantities; but they all only seem to make me worse, instead of better. I sleep in a damp room, but it does me no good; I come home late o' nights, but do not find any visible amendment! Who shall deliver me from the body of this death?

It is just fifteen minutes after twelve. Thurtell is

---

[1] Hanged that day for the murder of Weare.

by this time a good way on his journey, baiting at Scorpion, perhaps. Ketch is bargaining for his cast coat and waistcoat; and the Jew demurs at first at three half-crowns, but on consideration that he may get somewhat by showing 'em in the town, finally closes.

C. L.

LXXX.

TO BERNARD BARTON.

January 23, 1824.

My dear Sir, — That peevish letter of mine,[1] which was meant to convey an apology for my incapacity to write, seems to have been taken by you in too serious a light, — it was only my way of telling you I had a severe cold. The fact is, I have been insuperably dull and lethargic for many weeks, and cannot rise to the vigor of a letter, much less an essay. The " London " must do without me for a time, for I have lost all interest about it; and whether I shall recover it again I know not. I will bridle my pen another time, and not tease and puzzle you with my aridities. I shall begin to feel a little more alive with the spring.

Winter is to me (mild or harsh) always a great trial of the spirits. I am ashamed not to have noticed your tribute to Woolman, whom we love so much; it is done in your good manner. Your friend Tayler called upon me some time since, and seems a very amiable man. His last story is pain-

---

[1] Letter LXXIX.

fully fine. His book I "like;" it is only too stuffed
with Scripture, too parsonish. The best thing in it
is the boy's own story. When I say it is too full of
Scripture, I mean it is too full of direct quotations;
no book can have too much of silent Scripture in it.
But the natural power of a story is diminished when
the uppermost purpose in the writer seems to be to recommend something else, — namely, Religion. You
know what Horace says of the *Deus intersit?* I am
not able to explain myself, — you must do it for me.
My sister's part in the "Leicester School" (about
two thirds) was purely her own; as it was (to the
same quantity) in the "Shakspeare Tales" which
bear my name. I wrote only the "Witch Aunt,"
the "First Going to Church," and the final story
about "A little Indian girl" in a ship. Your account
of my black-balling amused me. *I think, as Quakers,
they did right.* There are some things hard to be
understood. The more I think, the more I am
vexed at having puzzled you with that letter; but I
have been so out of letter-writing of late years that
it is a sore effort to sit down to it; and I felt in
your debt, and sat down waywardly to pay you in
bad money. Never mind my dulness; I am used
to long intervals of it. The heavens seem brass to
me; then again comes the refreshing shower, —

"I have been merry twice and once ere now."

You said something about Mr. Mitford in a late
letter, which I believe I did not advert to. I shall
be happy to show him my Milton (it is all the show
things I have) at any time he will take the trouble

of a jaunt to Islington. I do also hope to see Mr.
Tayler there some day. Pray say so to both. Coleridge's book is in good part printed, but sticks a
little for *more copy*. It bears an unsalable title, —
"Extracts from Bishop Leighton;" but I am confident there will be plenty of good notes in it, —
more of Bishop Coleridge than Leighton in it, I
hope; for what is Leighton? Do you trouble yourself about libel cases? The decision against Hunt
for the "Vision of Judgment" made me sick. What
is to become of the good old talk about our good
old king, — his personal virtues saving us from a
revolution, etc.? Why, none that think can utter it now. It must stink. And the "Vision" is as
to himward such a tolerant, good-humored thing!
What a wretched thing a Lord Chief Justice is,
always was, and will be!

Keep your good spirits up, dear B. B., mine will
return; they are at present in abeyance, but I am
rather lethargic than miserable. I don't know but
a good horsewhip would be more beneficial to me
than physic. My head, without aching, will teach
yours to ache. It is well I am getting to the conclusion. I will send a better letter when I am a
better man. Let me thank you for your kind concern for me (which I trust will have reason soon
to be dissipated), and assure you that it gives me
pleasure to hear from you.

Yours truly,

C. L.

LXXXI.

April, 1824.

Dear B. B., — I am sure I cannot fill a letter, though I should disfurnish my skull to fill it; but you expect something, and shall have a notelet. Is Sunday, not divinely speaking, but humanly and holiday-sically, a blessing? Without its institution, would our rugged taskmasters have given us a leisure day so often, think you, as once in a month? or, if it had not been instituted, might they not have given us every sixth day? Solve me this problem. If we are to go three times a-day to church, why has Sunday slipped into the notion of a *holi*day? A Holy-day, I grant it. The Puritans, I have read in Southey's book, knew the distinction. They made people observe Sunday rigorously, would not let a nursery-maid walk out in the fields with children for recreation on that day. But *then* they gave the people a holiday from all sorts of work every second Tuesday. This was giving to the two Cæsars that which was *his* respective. Wise, beautiful, thoughtful, generous legislators! Would Wilberforce give us our Tuesdays? No; he would turn the six days into sevenths, —

> " And those three smiling seasons of the year
>   Into a Russian winter."
>   Old Play.

I am sitting opposite a person who is making strange distortions with the gout, which is not un-

pleasant, — to me, at least. What is the reason we
do not sympathize with pain, short of some terrible
surgical operation? Hazlitt, who boldly says all he
feels, avows that not only he does not pity sick
people, but he hates them. I obscurely recognize
his meaning. Pain is probably too selfish a consideration, too simply a consideration of self-atten-
tion. We pity poverty, loss of friends, etc., — more
complex things, in which the sufferer's feelings are
associated with others. This is a rough thought
suggested by the presence of gout; I want head to
extricate it and plane it. What is all this to your
letter? I felt it to be a good one, but my turn,
when I write at all, is perversely to travel out of
the record, so that my letters are anything but
answers. So you still want a motto? You must
not take my ironical one, because your book, I take
it, is too serious for it. Bickerstaff might have used
it for *his* lucubrations. What do you think of (for
a title) Religio Tremuli? or Tremebundi? There
is Religio Medici and Laici. But perhaps the
volume is not quite Quakerish enough, or exclusively
so, for it. Your own " Vigils " is perhaps the best.
While I have space, let me congratulate with you
the return of spring, — what a summery spring too!
All those qualms about the dog and cray-fish[1] melt
before it. I am going to be happy and *vain* again.

A hasty farewell,

C. LAMB.

---

[1] Lamb had confessed, in a previous letter to Barton, of
having once wantonly set a dog upon a cray-fish.

LXXXII

May 15, 1824.

DEAR B. B., — I am oppressed with business all day, and company all night. But I will snatch a quarter of an hour. Your recent acquisitions of the picture and the letter are greatly to be congratulated. I too have a picture of my father and the copy of his first love-verses; but they have been mine long. Blake is a real name, I assure you, and a most extraordinary man, if he is still living. He is the Robert [William] Blake whose wild designs accompany a splendid folio edition of the "Night Thoughts," which you may have seen, in one of which he pictures the parting of soul and body by a solid mass of human form floating off, God knows how, from a lumpish mass (fac-simile to itself) left behind on the dying bed. He paints in water-colors marvellous strange pictures, visions of his brain, which he asserts that he has seen; they have great merit. He has *seen* the old Welsh bards on Snowdon, — he has seen the beautifullest, the strongest, and the ugliest man, left alone from the massacre of the Britons by the Romans, and has painted them from memory (I have seen his paintings), and asserts them to be as good as the figures of Raphael and Angelo, but not better, as they had precisely the same retro-visions and prophetic visions with themself [himself]. The painters in oil (which he will have it that neither of them practised) he affirms to have been the ruin of art, and affirms that all the while he was engaged in his Welsh paintings, Titian was disturbing him, — Titian the Ill Genius of Oil Painting. His pictures — one in particular, the Canterbury Pilgrims, far above Stothard — have great merit, but hard, dry, yet with grace. He has written a Catalogue of them, with a most spirited criticism on Chaucer, but mystical and full of vision. His poems have been sold hitherto only in manuscript. I never read them; but a friend at my desire procured the "Sweep Song." There is one to a tiger, which I have heard recited, beginning, —

> " Tiger, Tiger, burning bright,
>   Thro' the deserts of the night,"

which is glorious, but, alas! I have not the book; for the man is flown, whither I know not, — to Hades or a madhouse. But I must look on him as one of the most extraordinary persons of the age. Montgomery's book[1] I have not much hope from, and the society with the affected name[2] has been laboring at it for these twenty years, and made few converts. I think it was injudicious to mix stories, avowedly colored by fiction, with the sad, true statements from the parliamentary records, etc. But I wish the little negroes all the good that can come from it. I battered my brains (not buttered them, — but it is a bad *a*) for a few verses for them, but

---

[1] "The Chimney-Sweeper's Friend, and Climbing-Boy's Album," — a book, by James Montgomery, setting forth the wrongs of the little chimney-sweepers, for whose relief a society had been started.

[2] The Society for Ameliorating the Condition of Infant Chimney-Sweepers.

I could make nothing of it. You have been luckier. But Blake's are the flower of the set, you will, I am sure, agree; though some of Montgomery's at the end are pretty, but the Dream awkwardly paraphrased from B.

With the exception of an Epilogue for a Private Theatrical, I have written nothing new for near six months. It is in vain to spur me on. I must wait. I cannot write without a genial impulse, and I have none. 'T is barren all and dearth. No matter; life is something without scribbling. I have got rid of my bad spirits, and hold up pretty well this rain-damned May.

So we have lost another poet.[1] I never much relished his Lordship's mind, and shall be sorry if the Greeks have cause to miss him. He was to me offensive, and I never can make out his real *power*, which his admirers talk of. Why, a line of Wordsworth's is a lever to lift the immortal spirit; Byron can only move the spleen. He was at best a satirist. In any other way, he was mean enough. I daresay I do him injustice; but I cannot love him, nor squeeze a tear to his memory. He did not like the world, and he has left it, as Alderman Curtis advised the Radicals, "if they don't like their country, damn 'em, let 'em leave it," they possessing no rood of ground in England, and he ten thousand acres. Byron was better than many Curtises.

Farewell, and accept this apology for a letter from one who owes you so much in that kind.

Yours ever truly,

C. L.

[1] Byron had died on April 19.

LXXXIII

TO BERNARD BARTON.

August, 1824.

. . . . . .

I CAN no more understand Shelley than you can ; his poetry is "thin sown with profit or delight." Yet I must point to your notice a sonnet conceived and expressed with a witty delicacy. It is that addressed to one who hated him, but who could not persuade him to hate *him* again. His coyness to the other's passion — for hate demands a return as much as love, and starves without it — is most arch and pleasant. Pray, like it very much. For his theories and nostrums, they are oracular enough, but I either comprehend 'em not, or there is "miching malice" and mischief in 'em, but, for the most part, ringing with their own emptiness. Hazlitt said well of 'em : "Many are the wiser and better for reading Shakspeare, but nobody was ever wiser or better for reading Shelley." I wonder you will sow your correspondence on so barren a ground as I am, that make such poor returns. But my head aches at the bare thought of letter-writing. I wish all the ink in the ocean dried up, and would listen to the quills shivering up in the candle flame, like parching martyrs. The same indisposition to write it is has stopped my "Elias ;" but you will see a futile effort in the next number,[1] "wrung from me with slow pain." The

[1] The essay "Blakesmoor in Hertfordshire," in the "London Magazine" for September, 1824.

fact is, my head is seldom cool enough. I am dreadfully indolent. To have to do anything — to order me a new coat, for instance, though my old buttons are shelled like beans — is an effort. My pen stammers like my tongue. What cool craniums those old inditers of folios must have had, what a mortified pulse ! Well, once more I throw myself on your mercy. Wishing peace in thy new dwelling,

C. LAMB.

LXXXIV.

TO BERNARD BARTON.

December 1, 1824.

.   .   .   .   .

TAYLOR and Hessey, finding their magazine [1] goes off very heavily at 2*s.* 6*d.*, are prudently going to raise their price another shilling; and having already more authors than they want, intend to increase the number of them. If they set up against the "New Monthly," they must change their present hands. It is not tying the dead carcase of a review to a half-dead magazine will do their business. It is like George Dyer multiplying his volumes to make 'em sell better. When he finds one will not go off, he publishes two; two stick, he tries three; three hang fire, he is confident that four will have a better chance.

---

[1] Taylor and Hessey succeeded John Scott as editors of the "London Magazine" (of which they were also publishers), and it was to this periodical that most of Lamb's Elia Essays were contributed.

And now, my dear sir, trifling apart, the gloomy catastrophe of yesterday morning prompts a sadder vein.   The fate of the unfortunate Fauntleroy [1] makes me, whether I will or no, to cast reflecting eyes around on such of my friends as, by a parity of situation, are exposed to a similarity of temptation.   My very style seems to myself to become more impressive than usual, with the change of theme.   Who, that standeth, knoweth but he may yet fall?   Your hands as yet, I am most willing to believe, have never deviated into others' property; you think it impossible that you could ever commit so heinous an offence.   But so thought Fauntleroy once; so have thought many besides him, who at last have expiated as he hath done.   You are as yet upright; but you are a banker, — at least, the next thing to it.   I feel the delicacy of the subject; but cash must pass through your hands, sometimes to a great amount.   If in an unguarded hour — But I will hope better.   Consider the scandal it will bring upon those of your persuasion.   Thousands would go to see a Quaker hanged, that would be indifferent to the fate of a Presbyterian or an Anabaptist.   Think of the effect it would have on the sale of your poems alone, not to mention higher considerations !   I tremble, I am sure, at myself, when I think that so many poor victims of the law, at one time of their life, made as sure of never being hanged as I, in my presumption, am too ready to do myself.   What are we better than they?   Do we come into the world with

---

[1] The forger, hanged Nov. 30, 1824.   This was the last execution for this offence.

different necks? Is there any distinctive mark under our left ears? Are we unstrangulable, I ask
you? Think of these things. I am shocked sometimes at the shape of my own fingers, not for their
resemblance to the ape tribe (which is something),
but for the exquisite adaptation of them to the purposes of picking fingering, etc. No one that is so
framed, I maintain it, but should tremble.

C. L.

LXXXV.

TO BERNARD BARTON.

March 23, 1825.

DEAR B. B., — I have had no impulse to write, or
attend to any single object but myself for weeks
past, — my single self, I by myself, I. I am sick
of hope deferred. The grand wheel is in agitation
that is to turn up my fortune ; but round it rolls,
and will turn up nothing. I have a glimpse of freedom, of becoming a gentleman at large ; but I am
put off from day to day. I have offered my resignation, and it is neither accepted nor rejected. Eight
weeks am I kept in this fearful suspense. Guess
what an absorbing stake I feel it. I am not conscious of the existence of friends present or absent.
The East India Directors alone can be that thing to
me or not. I have just learned that nothing will
be decided this week. Why the next? Why any
week? It has fretted me into an itch of the fingers ; I rub 'em against paper, and write to you,
rather than not allay this scorbuta.

While I can write, let me adjure you to have no doubts of Irving. Let Mr. Mitford drop his disrespect. Irving has prefixed a dedication (of a missionary subject, first part) to Coleridge, the most beautiful, cordial, and sincere. He there acknowledges his obligation to S. T. C. for his knowledge of Gospel truths, the nature of a Christian Church, etc., — to the talk of Samuel Taylor Coleridge (at whose Gamaliel feet he sits weekly), rather than to that of all the men living. This from him, the great dandled and petted sectarian, to a religious character so equivocal in the world's eye as that of S. T. C., so foreign to the Kirk's estimate, — can this man be a quack? The language is as affecting as the spirit of the dedication. Some friend told him, "This dedication will do you no good," — *i. e.,* not in the world's repute, or with your own people. "That is a reason for doing it," quoth Irving.

I am thoroughly pleased with him. He is firm, out-speaking, intrepid, and docile as a pupil of Pythagoras. You must like him.

Yours, in tremors of painful hope,

C. LAMB.

LXXXVI.

TO WORDSWORTH

April 6, 1825

DEAR WORDSWORTH, — I have been several times meditating a letter to you concerning the good thing which has befallen me; but the thought of

poor Monkhouse[1] came across me. He was one
that I had exulted in the prospect of congratulating
me. He and you were to have been the first par-
ticipators; for indeed it has been ten weeks since
the first motion of it. Here am I then, after thirty-
three years' slavery, sitting in my own room at
eleven o'clock this finest of all April mornings, a
freed man, with £441 a year for the remainder of
my life, live I as long as John Dennis, who outlived
his annuity and starved at ninety: £441; *i. e.*,
£450, with a deduction of £9 for a provision secured to my sister, she being survivor, the pension
guaranteed by Act Georgii Tertii, etc.

I came home FOREVER on Tuesday in last week.
The incomprehensibleness of my condition over-
whelmed me; it was like passing from life into
eternity. Every year to be as long as three, *i. e.*,
to have three times as much real time — time that
is my own — in it! I wandered about thinking I
was happy, but feeling I was not. But that tumul-
tuousness is passing off, and I begin to understand
the nature of the gift. Holidays, even the annual
month, were always uneasy joys, — their conscious
fugitiveness; the craving after making the most
of them. Now, when all is holiday, there are no
holidays. I can sit at home, in rain or shine, without a restless impulse for walkings. I am daily
steadying, and shall soon find it as natural to me
to be my own master as it has been irksome to
have had a master. Mary wakes every morning

---

[1] Wordsworth's cousin, who was ill of consumption in
Devonshire. He died the following year.

with an obscure feeling that some good has happened
to us.

Leigh Hunt and Montgomery, after their release-
ments, describe the shock of their emancipation
much as I feel mine. But it hurt their frames. I
eat, drink, and sleep sound as ever. I lay no anxious schemes for going hither and thither, but take
things as they occur. Yesterday I excursioned
twenty miles; to-day I write a few letters. Pleas-
uring was for fugitive play-days; mine are fugitive
only in the sense that life is fugitive. Freedom
and life co-existent!

At the foot of such a call upon you for gratula-
tion, I am ashamed to advert to that melancholy
event. Monkhouse was a character I learned to
love slowly; but it grew upon me yearly, monthly,
daily. What a chasm has it made in our pleasant
parties! His noble, friendly face was always coming
before me, till this hurrying event in my life came,
and for the time has absorbed all interest; in fact,
it has shaken me a little. My old desk companions,
with whom I have had such merry hours, seem to
reproach me for removing my lot from among them.
They were pleasant creatures; but to the anxieties
of business, and a weight of possible worse ever
impending, I was not equal. Tuthill and Gilman
gave me my certificates; I laughed at the friendly
lie implied in them. But my sister shook her head,
and said it was all true. Indeed, this last winter I
was jaded out; winters were always worse than
other parts of the year, because the spirits are
worse, and I had no daylight. In summer I had

daylight evenings. The relief was hinted to me from a superior power when I, poor slave, had not a hope but that I must wait another seven years with Jacob; and lo! the Rachel which I coveted is brought to me.

· · · · · · · ·

LXXXVII.

TO BERNARD BARTON.

April 6, 1825.

DEAR B. B., — My spirits are so tumultuary with the novelty of my recent emancipation that I have scarce steadiness of hand, much more mind, to compose a letter. I am free, B. B., — free as air!

> " The little bird that wings the sky
> Knows no such liberty." [1]

I was set free on Tuesday in last week at four o'clock. I came home forever!

I have been describing my feelings as well as I can to Wordsworth in a long letter, and don't care to repeat. Take it, briefly, that for a few days I was painfully oppressed by so mighty a change; but it is becoming daily more natural to me. I went and sat among 'em all at my old thirty-three-years' desk yester-morning; and, deuce take me, if I had not yearnings at leaving all my old pen-and-ink fellows, merry, sociable lads, — at leaving them in

---

[1] " The birds that wanton in the air
Know no such liberty."
LOVELACE.

the lurch, fag, fag, fag! The comparison of my own superior felicity gave me anything but pleasure.

B. B., I would not serve another seven years for seven hundred thousand pounds! I have got £441 net for life, sanctioned by Act of Parliament, with a provision for Mary if she survives me. I will live another fifty years; or if I live but ten, they will be thirty, reckoning the quantity of real time in them, — *i. e.*, the time that is a man's own. Tell me how you like " Barbara S. ; "[1] will it be received in atonement for the foolish "Vision," — I mean by the lady? *A propos*, I never saw Mrs. Crawford in my life; nevertheless, it's all true of somebody.

Address me, in future, Colebrooke Cottage, Islington. I am really nervous (but that will wear off); so take this brief announcement.

Yours truly,

C. L.

LXXXVIII.

TO BERNARD BARTON.

July 2, 1825.

.   .   .   .

I AM hardly able to appreciate your volume now;[2] but I liked the dedication much, and the apology for your bald burying grounds. To Shelley — but *that* is not new. To the young Vesper-singer, Great Bealings, Playford, and what not.

If there be a cavil, it is that the topics of religious consolation, however beautiful, are repeated till a

---

[1] The Elia essay. Fanny Kelly was the original of " Barbara S."

[2] Barton's volume of Poems.

sort of triteness attends them. It seems as if you were forever losing Friends' children by death, and reminding their parents of the Resurrection. Do children die so often and so good in your parts? The topic taken from the consideration that they are snatched away from *possible vanities* seems hardly sound; for to an Omniscient eye their conditional failings must be one with their actual. But I am too unwell for theology.

Such as I am,

I am yours and A. K.'s truly,

C. LAMB.

LXXXIX.

TO BERNARD BARTON.

August 10, 1825.

WE shall be soon again at Colebrooke.

DEAR B. B., — You must excuse my not writing before, when I tell you we are on a visit at Enfield, where I do not feel it natural to sit down to a letter. It is at all times an exertion. I had rather talk with you and Anne Knight quietly at Colebrooke Lodge over the matter of your last. You mistake me when you express misgivings about my relishing a series of Scriptural poems. I wrote confusedly; what I meant to say was, that one or two consolatory poems on deaths would have had a more condensed effect than many. Scriptural, devotional topics, admit of infinite variety. So far from poetry tiring me because religious, I can read,

and I say it seriously, the homely old version of the
Psalms in our Prayer-books for an hour or two
together sometimes, without sense of weariness.

I did not express myself clearly about what I
think a false topic, insisted on so frequently in consolatory addresses on the death of infants. I know
something like it is in Scripture, but I think humanly spoken. It is a natural thought, a sweet
fallacy, to the survivors, but still a fallacy. If it
stands on the doctrine of this being a probationary
state, it is liable to this dilemma. Omniscience, to
whom possibility must be clear as act, must know of
the child what it would hereafter turn out: if good,
then the topic is false to say it is secured from falling into future wilfulness, vice, etc. If bad, I do
not see how its exemption from certain future overt
acts by being snatched away at all tells in its favor.
You stop the arm of a murderer, or arrest the finger
of a pickpurse; but is not the guilt incurred as
much by the intent as if never so much acted?
Why children are hurried off, and old reprobates of a
hundred left, whose trial humanly we may think was
complete at fifty, is among the obscurities of providence. The very notion of a state of probation has
darkness in it. The All-knower has no need of
satisfying his eyes by seeing what we will do, when
he knows before what we will do. Methinks we
might be condemned before commission. In these
things we grope and flounder; and if we can pick
up a little human comfort that the child taken is
snatched from vice (no great compliment to it, by
the by), let us take it. And as to where an untried

child goes, whether to join the assembly of its elders who have borne the heat of the day, — fire-purified martyrs and torment-sifted confessors, — what know we? We promise heaven, methinks, too cheaply, and assign large revenues to minors incompetent to manage them. Epitaphs run upon this topic of consolation till the very frequency induces a cheapness. Tickets for admission into paradise are sculptured out a penny a letter, twopence a syllable, etc. It is all a mystery; and the more I try to express my meaning (having none that is clear), the more I flounder. Finally, write what your own conscience, which to you is the unerring judge, deems best, and be careless about the whimsies of such a half-baked notionist as I am. We are here in a most pleasant country, full of walks, and idle to our heart's desire. Taylor has dropped the " London." It was indeed a dead weight. It had got in the Slough of Despond. I shuffle off my part of the pack, and stand, like Christian, with light and merry shoulders. It had got silly, indecorous, pert, and everything that is bad. Both our kind *remembrances* to Mrs. K. and yourself, and strangers'-greeting to Lucy, — is it Lucy, or Ruth? — that gathers wise sayings in a Book.

C. LAMB.

XC.

TO SOUTHEY.

August 19, 1825.

DEAR SOUTHEY, — You'll know whom this letter comes from by opening slap-dash upon the text, as in the good old times. I never could come into the custom of envelopes, — 't is a modern foppery; the Plinian correspondence gives no hint of such. In singleness of sheet and meaning, then, I thank you for your little book. I am ashamed to add a codicil of thanks for your " Book of the Church." I scarce feel competent to give an opinion of the latter; I have not reading enough of that kind to venture at it. I can only say the fact, that I have read it with attention and interest. Being, as you know, not quite a Churchman, I felt a jealousy at the Church taking to herself the whole deserts of Christianity, Catholic and Protestant, from Druid extirpation downwards. I call all good Christians the Church, Capillarians and all. But I am in too light a humor to touch these matters. May all our churches flourish ! Two things staggered me in the poem (and one of them staggered both of us) : I cannot away with a beautiful series of verses, as I protest they are, commencing " Jenner." 'T is like a choice banquet opened with a pill or an electuary, — physic stuff. T' other is, we cannot make out how Edith should be no more than ten years old. By 'r Lady, we had taken her to be some sixteen or upwards. We suppose you have only chosen the round number for the metre. Or poem and dedication may be both older than they pretend to, — but then some hint might have been given; for, as it stands, it may only serve some day to puzzle the parish reckoning. But without inquiring further (for 't is ungracious to look into a lady's years), the dedication is eminently pleasing and tender, and we wish

Edith May Southey joy of it. Something, too, struck us as if we had heard of the death of John May. A John May's death was a few years since in the papers. We think the tale one of the quietest, prettiest things we have seen. You have been temperate in the use of localities, which generally spoil poems laid in exotic regions. You mostly cannot stir out (in such things) for humming-birds and fire-flies. A tree is a Magnolia, etc.—Can I but like the truly Catholic spirit? " Blame as thou mayest the Papist's erring creed," — which and other passages brought me back to the old Anthology days and the admonitory lesson to " Dear George " on " The Vesper Bell," a little poem which retains its first hold upon me strangely.

The compliment to the translatress is daintily conceived. Nothing is choicer in that sort of writing than to bring in some remote, impossible parallel,—as between a great empress and the inobtrusive, quiet soul who digged her noiseless way so perseveringly through that rugged Paraguay mine. How she Dobrizhoffered it all out, it puzzles my slender Latinity to conjecture. Why do you seem to sanction Landor's unfeeling allegorizing away of honest Quixote? He may as well say Strap is meant to symbolize the Scottish nation before the Union, and Random since that Act of dubious issue ; or that Partridge means the Mystical Man, and Lady Bellaston typifies the Woman upon Many Waters. Gebir, indeed, may mean the state of the hop markets last month, for anything I know to the contrary. That all Spain overflowed with romancical books (as

Madge Newcastle calls them) was no reason that Cervantes should not smile at the matter of them; nor even a reason that, in another mood, he might not multiply them, deeply as he was tinctured with the essence of them.   Quixote is the father of gentle ridicule, and at the same time the very depository and treasury of chivalry and highest notions.   Marry, when somebody persuaded Cervantes that he meant only fun, and put him upon writing that unfortunate Second Part, with the confederacies of that unworthy duke and most contemptible duchess, Cervantes sacrificed his instinct to his understanding.

We got your little book but last night, being at Enfield, to which place we came about a month since, and are having quiet holidays.   Mary walks her twelve miles a day some days, and I my twenty on others.   'T is all holiday with me now, you know; the change works admirably.

For literary news, in my poor way, I have a one-act farce[1] going to be acted at Haymarket; but when? is the question.   'T is an extravaganza, and like enough to follow "Mr. H."   "The London Magazine" has shifted its publishers once more, and I shall shift myself out of it.   It is fallen.   My ambition is not at present higher than to write nonsense for the playhouses, to eke out a something contracted income.   *Tempus erat.*   There was a time, my dear Cornwallis, when the muse, etc.   But I am now in Mac Flecknoe's predicament, —

"Promised a play, and dwindled to a farce."

[1] Probably "The Pawnbroker's Daughter," which happily was not destined to be performed. — AINGER.

Coleridge is better (was, at least, a few weeks since) than he has been for years. His accomplishing his book at last has been a source of vigor to him. We are on a half visit to his friend Allsop, at a Mrs. Leishman's, Enfield, but expect to be at Colebrooke Cottage in a week or so, where, or anywhere, I shall be always most happy to receive tidings from you. G. Dyer is in the height of an uxorious paradise. His honeymoon will not wane till he wax cold. Never was a more happy pair, since Acme and Septimius, and longer. Farewell, with many thanks, dear S. Our loves to all round your Wrekin.

Your old friend,

C. LAMB.

XCI.

TO BERNARD BARTON.

March 20, 1826.

DEAR B. B., — You may know my letters by the paper and the folding. For the former, I live on scraps obtained in charity from an old friend, whose stationery is a permanent perquisite; for folding, I shall do it neatly when I learn to tie my neckcloths. I surprise most of my friends by writing to them on ruled paper, as if I had not got past pothooks and hangers. Sealing-wax I have none on my establishment; wafers of the coarsest bran supply its place. When my epistles come to be weighed with Pliny's, however superior to the Roman in delicate irony, judicious reflections, etc., his gilt post will bribe

over the judges to him.   All the time I was at the
E. I. H. I never mended a pen; I now cut 'em to
the stumps, marring rather than mending the primitive goose-quill.   I cannot bear to pay for articles I
used to get for nothing.   When Adam laid out his
first penny upon nonpareils at some stall in Meso-
potamos, I think it went hard with him, reflecting
upon his old goodly orchard, where he had so many
for nothing.   When I write to a great man at the
court end, he opens with surprise upon a naked
note, such as Whitechapel people interchange, with
no sweet degrees of envelope.   I never enclosed
one bit of paper in another, nor understood the
rationale of it.   Once only I sealed with borrowed
wax, to set Walter Scott a-wondering, signed with
the imperial quartered arms of England, which my
friend Field bears in compliment to his descent, in
the female line, from Oliver Cromwell.   It must
have set his antiquarian curiosity upon watering.
To your questions upon the currency, I refer you to
Mr. Robinson's last speech, where, if you can find a
solution, I cannot.   I think this, though, — the best
ministry we ever stumbled upon, — gin reduced four
shillings in the gallon, wine two shillings in the
quart!   This comes home to men's minds and
bosoms.   My tirade against visitors was not meant
particularly at you or Anne Knight.   I scarce know
what I meant, for I do not just now feel the griev-
ance.   I wanted to make an *article.*   So in another
thing I talked of somebody's *insipid wife* without a
correspondent object in my head; and a good lady,
a friend's wife, whom I really *love* (don't startle, I

mean in a licit way), has looked shyly on me ever since. The blunders of personal application are ludicrous. I send out a character every now and then on purpose to exercise the ingenuity of my friends. " Popular Fallacies " will go on ; that word "concluded" is an erratum, I suppose, for " continued." I do not know how it got stuffed in there. A little thing without name will also be printed on the Religion of the Actors ; but it is out of your way, so I recommend you, with true author's hypocrisy, to skip it. We are about to sit down to roast beef, at which we could wish A. K., B. B., and B. B.'s pleasant daughter to be humble partakers. So much for my hint at visitors, which was scarcely calculated for droppers-in from Woodbridge ; the sky does not drop such larks every day. My very kindest wishes to you all three, with my sister's best love.

C. LAMB.

XCII.

TO J. B. DIBDIN.

June, 1826.

DEAR D., — My first impulse upon seeing your letter was pleasure at seeing your old neat hand, nine parts gentlemanly, with a modest dash of the clerical ; my second, a thought natural enough this hot weather : Am I to answer all this ? Why, 't is as long as those to the Ephesians and Galatians put together : I have counted the words, for curiosity. . . . I never knew an enemy to puns who was not an ill-natured man. Your fair critic in the coach reminds me of a Scotchman who assured me he did not see much in Shakspeare. I replied, I daresay *not.* He felt the equivoke, looked awkward and reddish, but soon returned to the attack by saying that he thought Burns was as good as Shakspeare. I said that I had no doubt he was, — to a *Scotchman.* We exchanged no more words that day. . . . Let me hear that you have clambered up to Lover's Seat; it is as fine in that neighborhood as Juan Fernandez, — as lonely, too, when the fishing-boats are not out; I have sat for hours staring upon a shipless sea. The salt sea is never as grand as when it is left to itself. One cock-boat spoils it; a seamew or two improves it. And go to the little church, which is a very Protestant Loretto, and seems dropped by some angel for the use of a hermit who was at once parishioner and a whole parish. It is not too big. Go in the night, bring it away in your portmanteau, and I will plant it in my garden. It must have been erected, in the very infancy of British Christianity, for the two or three first converts, yet with all the appurtenances of a church of the first magnitude, — its pulpit, its pews, its baptismal font; a cathedral in a nutshell. The minister that divides the Word there must give lumping pennyworths. It is built to the text of "two or three assembled in my name." It reminds me of the grain of mustard-seed. If the glebe-land is proportionate, it may yield two potatoes. Tithes out of it could be no more split than a hair. Its First fruits must be its Last, for 't would never produce a couple. It is truly the strait and narrow way, and few there be (of London visitants) that find it.

The still small voice is surely to be found there, if anywhere. A sounding-board is merely there for ceremony. It is secure from earthquakes, not more from sanctity than size, for 't would feel a mountain thrown upon it no more than a taper-worm would. *Go and see, but not without your spectacles.*

* * * * * * * *

XCIII.

TO HENRY CRABB ROBINSON.

January 20, 1827.

DEAR ROBINSON, — I called upon you this morning, and found that you had gone to visit a dying friend. I had been' upon a like errand. Poor Norris[1] has been lying dying for now almost a week, — such is the penalty we pay for having enjoyed a strong constitution! Whether he knew me or not, I know not, or whether he saw me through his poor glazed eyes; but the group I saw about him I shall not forget. Upon the bed, or about it, were assembled his wife and two daughters, and poor deaf Richard, his son, looking doubly stupefied. There they were, and seemed to have been sitting all the week. I could only reach out a hand to Mrs. Norris. Speaking was impossible in that mute chamber. By this time I hope it is all over with him. In him I have a loss the world cannot make up. He was my friend and my father's friend all the life I can remember. I seem to have made foolish friendships ever since. Those are friend-

[1] Randal Norris, sub-treasurer of the Inner Temple, an early friend of the Lambs.

ships which outlive a second generation. Old as I
am waxing, in his eyes I was still the child he first
knew me. To the last he called me Charley. I
have none to call me Charley now. He was the last
link that bound me to the Temple. You are but of
yesterday. In him seem to have died the old plain-
ness of manners and singleness of heart. Letters he
knew nothing of, nor did his reading extend beyond
the pages of the "Gentleman's Magazine." Yet
there was a pride of literature about him from being
amongst books (he was librarian), and from some
scraps of doubtful Latin which he had picked up in
his office of entering students, that gave him very
diverting airs of pedantry. Can I forget the erudite look with which, when he had been in vain
trying to make out a black-letter text of Chaucer in
the Temple Library, he laid it down and told me that
" in those old books, Charley, there is sometimes
a deal of very indifferent spelling ; " and seemed to
console himself in the reflection ! His jokes — for
he had his jokes — are now ended ; but they were old
trusty perennials, staples that pleased after *decies
repetita*, and were always as good as new. One
song he had, which was reserved for the night of
Christmas Day, which we always spent in the Temple.
It was an old thing, and spoke of the flat-bottoms
of our foes and the possibility of their coming over
in darkness, and alluded to threats of an invasion
many years blown over; and when he came to
the part —

" We 'll still make 'em run, and we 'll still make 'em sweat,
　In spite of the devil and ' Brussels Gazette,' " —

his eyes would sparkle as with the freshness of an impending event. And what is the "Brussels Gazette" now? I cry while I enumerate these trifles. "How shall we tell them in a stranger's ear?" His poor good girls will now have to receive their afflicted mother in an inaccessible hovel in an obscure village in Herts, where they have been long struggling to make a school without effect; and poor deaf Richard — and the more helpless for being so — is thrown on the wide world.

My first motive in writing, and, indeed, in calling on you, was to ask if you were enough acquainted with any of the Benchers to lay a plain statement before them of the circumstances of the family. I almost fear not, for you are of another hall. But if you can oblige me and my poor friend, who is now insensible to any favors, pray exert yourself. You cannot say too much good of poor Norris and his poor wife.　　　　Yours ever,

CHARLES LAMB.

XCIV.

TO PETER GEORGE PATMORE.

LONDRES, *Julie* 19th, 1827.

DEAR P., — I am so poorly. I have been to a funeral, where I made a pun, to the consternation of the rest of the mourners. And we had wine. I can't describe to you the howl which the widow set up at proper intervals. Dash [1] could; for it was not unlike what he makes.

---

[1] A dog given to Lamb by Thomas Hood. See letter to Patmore dated September, 1827.

The letter I sent you was one directed to the care of Edward White, India House, for Mrs. Hazlitt. *Which* Mrs. H. I don't yet know; but Allsop has taken it to France on speculation. Really it is embarrassing. There is Mrs. present H., Mrs. late H., and Mrs. John H.; and to which of the three Mrs. Wigginses it appertains, I know not. I wanted to open it, but 't is transportation.

I am sorry you are plagued about your book. I would strongly recommend you to take for one story Massinger's "Old Law." It is exquisite. I can think of no other.

Dash is frightful this morning. He whines and stands up on his hind legs. He misses Becky, who is gone to town. I took him to Barnet the other day, and he could n't eat his vittles after it. Pray God his intellectuals be not slipping.

Mary is gone out for some soles. I suppose 't is no use to ask you to come and partake of 'em; else there is a steam vessel.

I am doing a tragi-comedy in two acts, and have got on tolerably; but it will be refused, or worse. I never had luck with anything my name was put to.

Oh, I am so poorly! I *waked* it at my cousin's the bookbinder, who is now with God; or if he is not, 't is no fault of mine.

We hope the Frank wines do not disagree with Mrs. Patmore. By the way, I like her.

Did you ever taste frogs? Get them if you can. They are like little Lilliput rabbits, only a thought nicer.

How sick I am!—not of the world, but of the Widow Shrub. She 's sworn under £6,000; but I think she perjured herself. She howls in E *la*, and I comfort her in B flat. You understand music?

If you haven't got Massinger, you have nothing to do but go to the first Bibliothèque you can light upon at Boulogne, and ask for it (Gifford's edition); and if they have n't got it, you can have "Athalie," par Monsieur Racine, and make the best of it. But that "Old Law" is delicious.

"No shrimps!" (that's in answer to Mary's question about how the soles are to be done.)

I am uncertain where this wandering letter may reach you. What you mean by Poste Restante, God knows. Do you mean I must pay the postage? So I do, — to Dover.

We had a merry passage with the widow at the Commons. She was howling, — part howling, and part giving directions to the proctor, — when crash! down went my sister through a crazy chair, and made the clerks grin, and I grinned, and the widow tittered, and then I knew that she was not inconsolable. Mary was more frightened than hurt.

She'd make a good match for anybody (by she, I mean the widow).

> "If he bring but a *relict* away,
>   He is happy, nor heard to complain."
>   SHENSTONE.

Procter has got a wen growing out at the nape of his neck, which his wife wants him to have cut off; but I think it rather an agreeable excrescence, — like his poetry, redundant. Hone has hanged himself for debt. Godwin was taken up for picking pockets. Moxon has fallen in love with Emma, our nut-brown maid. Becky takes to bad courses. Her father was blown up in a steam machine. The coroner found it "insanity." I should not like him to sit on my letter.

Do you observe my direction? Is it Gallic, classical? Do try and get some frogs. You must ask for "grenouilles" (green eels). They don't understand "frogs," though 't is a common phrase with us.

If you go through Bulloign (Boulogne), inquire if Old Godfrey is living, and how he got home from the Crusades. He must be a very old man.

. . . .

XCV.

TO BERNARD BARTON.

August 10, 1827.

DEAR B. B., — I have not been able to answer you, for we have had and are having (I just snatch a moment) our poor quiet retreat, to which we fled from society, full of company, — some staying with us; and this moment as I write, almost, a heavy importation of two old ladies has come in. Whither can I take wing from the oppression of human faces? Would I were in a wilderness of apes, tossing cocoa-nuts about, grinning and grinned at!

Mitford was hoaxing you surely about my engraving; 't is a little sixpenny thing,[1] too like by half, in

---

[1] An etching of Lamb, by Brooke Pulham, which is said to be the most characteristic likeness of him extant.

which the draughtsman has done his best to avoid
flattery. There have been two editions of it, which
I think are all gone, as they have vanished from the
window where they hung, — a print-shop, corner
of Great and Little Queen Streets, Lincoln's Inn
Fields, — where any London friend of yours may
inquire for it; for I am (though you *won't understand it*) at Enfield Chase. We have been here
near three months, and shall stay two more, if
people will let us alone; but they persecute us from
village to village. So don't direct to *Islington*
again till further notice. I am trying my hand at a
drama, in two acts, founded on Crabbe's " Con-
fidant," *mutatis mutandis.* You like the Odyssey:
did you ever read my " Adventures of Ulysses,"
founded on Chapman's old translation of it? For
children or men. Chapman is divine, and my
abridgment has not quite emptied him of his divinity. When you come to town I 'll show it you.
You have well described your old-fashioned grand
paternal hall. Is it not odd that every one's earliest recollections are of some such place? I had
my Blakesware [Blakesmoor in the " London "].
Nothing fills a child's mind like a large old mansion;
better if un — or partially — occupied, — peopled
with the spirits of deceased members of the county
and justices of the quorum. Would I were buried
in the peopled solitudes of one, with my feelings at
seven years old! Those marble busts of the em-
perors, they seemed as if they were to stand forever, as they had stood from the living days of
Rome, in that old marble hall, and I too partake of

their permanency. Eternity was, while I thought not of Time. But he thought of me, and they are toppled down, and corn covers the spot of the noble old dwelling and its princely gardens. I feel like a grasshopper that, chirping about the grounds, escaped the scythe only by my littleness. Even now he is whetting one of his smallest razors to clean wipe me out, perhaps. Well !

XCVI.

TO THOMAS HOOD.

September 18, 1827.

DEAR HOOD, — If I have anything in my head, I will send it to Mr. Watts. Strictly speaking, he should have all my album-verses ; but a very intimate friend importuned me for the trifles, and I believe I forgot Mr. Watts, or lost sight at the time of his similar " Souvenir." Jamieson conveyed the farce from me to Mrs. C. Kemble ; *he* will not be in town before the 27th.

Give our kind loves to all at Highgate, and tell them that we have finally torn ourselves outright away from Colebrooke, where I had *no* health, and are about to domiciliate for good at Enfield, where I have experienced *good.*

> " Lord, what good hours do we keep !
> How quietly we sleep ! " [1]

See the rest in the " Compleat Angler."

[1] By Charles Cotton.

We have got our books into our new house. I am a dray-horse if I was not ashamed of the indigested, dirty lumber, as I toppled 'em out of the cart, and blessed Becky that came with 'em for her having an unstuffed brain with such rubbish. We shall get in by Michael's Mass. 'T was with some pain we were evulsed from Colebrooke.

You may find some of our flesh sticking to the doorposts. To change habitations is to die to them; and in my time I have died seven deaths. But I don't know whether every such change does not bring with it a rejuvenescence. 'T is an enterprise, and shoves back the sense of death's approximating, which, though not terrible to me, is at all times particularly distasteful. My house-deaths have generally been periodical, recurring after seven years; but this last is premature by half that time. Cut off in the flower of Colebrooke! The Middletonian stream and all its echoes mourn. Even minnows dwindle. *A parvis fiunt minimi!*

I fear to invite Mrs. Hood to our new mansion, lest she should envy it, and hate us. But when we are fairly in, I hope she will come and try it. I heard she and you were made uncomfortable by some unworthy-to-be-cared-for attacks, and have tried to set up a feeble counteraction through the "Table Book" of last Saturday. Has it not reached you, that you are silent about it? Our new domicile is no manor-house, but new, and externally not inviting, but furnished within with every convenience, — capital new locks to every door, capital grates in every room, with nothing to pay for incoming, and the rent £10 less than the Islington one.

It was built, a few years since, at £1,100 expense, they tell me, and I perfectly believe it. And I get it for £35, exclusive of moderate taxes. We think ourselves most lucky.

It is not our intention to abandon Regent Street and West End perambulations (monastic and terrible thought!), but occasionally to breathe the fresher air of the metropolis. We shall put up a bedroom or two (all we want) for occasional ex-rustication, where we shall visit, — not be visited. Plays, too, we'll see, — perhaps our own; Urbani Sylvani and Sylvan Urbanuses in turns; courtiers for a sport, then philosophers; old, homely tell-truths and learn-truths in the virtuous shades of Enfield, liars again and mocking gibers in the coffee-houses and resorts of London. What can a mortal desire more for his bi-parted nature?

Oh, the curds-and-cream you shall eat with us here!

Oh, the turtle-soup and lobster-salads we shall devour with you there!

Oh, the old books we shall peruse here!

Oh, the new nonsense we shall trifle over there!

Oh, Sir T. Browne, here!

Oh, Mr. Hood and Mr. Jerdan, there!

Thine,

C. (URBANUS) L. (SYLVANUS) — (ELIA ambo).

. . . .

XCVII.

September, 1827.

DEAR P., — Excuse my anxiety, but how is Dash? I should have asked if Mrs. Patmore kept her rules and was improving; but Dash came uppermost. The order of our thoughts should be the order of our writing. Goes he muzzled, or *aperto ore?* Are his intellects sound, or does he wander a little in *his* conversation. You cannot be too careful to watch the first symptoms of incoherence. The first illogical snarl he makes, to St. Luke's with him! All the dogs here are going mad, if you believe the overseers; but I protest they seem to me very rational and collected. But nothing is so deceitful as mad people, to those who are not used to them. Try him with hot water; if he won't lick it up, it 's a sign he does not like it. Does his tail wag horizontally or perpendicularly? That has decided the fate of many dogs in Enfield. Is his general deportment cheerful? I mean when he is pleased, for otherwise there is no judging. You can't be too careful. Has he bit any of the children yet? If he has, have them shot, and keep *him* for curiosity, to see if it was the hydrophobia. They say all our army in India had it at one time; but that was in *Hyder*-Ally's time. Do you get paunch for him? Take care the sheep was sane. You might pull his teeth out (if he would let you), and then you need not mind if he were as mad as a Bedlamite.

It would be rather fun to see his odd ways. It might amuse Mrs. P. and the children. They'd have more sense than he. He'd be like a fool kept in a family, to keep the household in good humor with their own understanding. You might teach him the mad dance, set to the mad howl. *Madge Owlet* would be nothing to him. " My, how he capers ! " (*In the margin is written " One of the children speaks this."*) . . . What I scratch out is a German quotation, from Lessing, on the bite of rabid animals ; but I remember you don't read German. But Mrs. P. may, so I wish I had let it stand. The meaning in English is : "Avoid to approach an animal suspected of madness, as you would avoid fire or a precipice," — which I think is a sensible observation. The Germans are certainly profounder than we. If the slightest suspicion arises in your breast that all is not right with him, muzzle him and lead him in a string (common packthread will do ; he don't care for twist) to Mr. Hood's, his quondam master, and he'll take him in at any time. You may mention your suspicion, or not, as you like, or as you think it may wound, or not, Mr. H.'s feelings. Hood, I know, will wink at a few follies in Dash, in consideration of his former sense. Besides, Hood is deaf, and if you hinted anything, ten to one he would not hear you. Besides, you will have discharged your conscience, and laid the child at the right door, as they say.

We are dawdling our time away very idly and pleasantly at a Mrs. Leishman's, Chase, Enfield,

where, if you come a-hunting, we can give you cold
meat and a tankard. Her husband is a tailor; but
that, you know, does not make her one. I know a
jailor (which rhymes), but his wife was a fine lady.

Let us hear from you respecting Mrs. P.'s regi-
men. I send my love in a —— to Dash.

C. LAMB.

XCVIII.

TO BERNARD BARTON.

October 11, 1828

A SPLENDID edition of Bunyan's Pilgrim![1] Why,
the thought is enough to turn one's moral stomach.
His cockle-hat and staff transformed to a smart
cocked beaver and a jemmy cane; his amice gray
to the last Regent Street cut; and his painful
palmer's pace to the modern swagger! Stop thy
friend's sacrilegious hand. Nothing can be done
for B. but to reprint the old cuts in as homely but
good a style as possible, — the Vanity Fair and the
Pilgrims there; the silly-soothness in his setting-
out countenance; the Christian idiocy (in a good
sense) of his admiration of the shepherds on the
Delectable mountains; the lions so truly allegorical,
and remote from any similitude to Pidcock's; the
great head (the author's), capacious of dreams and
similitudes, dreaming in the dungeon. Perhaps you
don't know my edition, what I had when a child.

---

[1] An *édition de luxe*, illustrated by John Martin, and
with an Introduction by Southey. See Macaulay's review
of it.

If you do, can you bear new designs from Martin,
enamelled into copper or silver plate by Heath,
accompanied with verses from Mrs. Hemans's pen?
Oh, how unlike his own !

> " Wouldst thou divert thyself from melancholy?
> Wouldst thou be pleasant, yet be far from folly ?
> Wouldst thou read riddles and their explanation ?
> Or else be drowned in thy contemplation ?
> Dost thou love picking meat ? or wouldst thou see
> A man i' the clouds, and hear him speak to thee ?
> Wouldst thou be in a dream, and yet not sleep ?
> Or wouldst thou in a moment laugh and weep ?
> Or wouldst thou lose thyself, and catch no harm,
> And find thyself again without a charm ?
> Wouldst read *thyself*, and read thou knowest not what,
> And yet know whether thou art blest or not
> By reading the same lines ? Oh, then come hither,
> And lay my book, thy head, and heart together."

Show me any such poetry in any one of the fifteen
forthcoming combinations of show and emptiness
'yclept "Annuals."   So there's verses for thy
verses ; and now let me tell you that the sight of
your hand gladdened me.   I have been daily trying
to write to you, but [have been] paralyzed. You
have spurred me on this tiny effort, and at intervals
I hope to hear from and talk to you.   But my spirits
have been in an oppressed way for a long time, and
they are things which must be to you of faith, for
who can explain depression? Yes, I am hooked
into the "Gem," but only for some lines written on
a dead infant of the editor's,[1] which being, as it
were, his property, I could not refuse their appearing ; but I hate the paper, the type, the gloss,

----

[1] Hood's.

the dandy plates, the names of contributors poked
up into your eyes in first page, and whisked through
all the covers of magazines, the barefaced sort of
emulation, the immodest candidateship. Brought
into so little space, — in those old " Londons," a
signature was lost in the wood of matter, the paper
coarse (till latterly, which spoiled them), — in short,
I detest to appear in an Annual. What a fertile
genius (and a quiet good soul withal) is Hood!
He has fifty things in hand, — farces to supply the
Adelphi for the season ; a comedy for one of the
great theatres, just ready ; a whole entertainment
by himself for Mathews and Yates to figure in ; a
meditated Comic Annual for next year, to be nearly
done by himself. You 'd like him very much.

Wordsworth, I see, has a good many pieces an-
nounced in one of 'em, not our " Gem." W. Scott
has distributed himself like a bribe haunch among
'em. Of all the poets, Cary [1] has had the good
sense to keep quite clear of 'em, with clergy-gentle-
manly right notions. Don't think I set up for being
proud on this point ; I like a bit of flattery, tickling
my vanity, as well as any one. But these pompous
masquerades without masks (naked names or faces)
I hate. So there 's a bit of my mind. Besides,
they infallibly cheat you, — I mean the booksellers.
If I get but a copy, I only expect it from Hood's
being my friend. Coleridge has lately been here.
He too is deep among the prophets, the year-ser-
vers, — the mob of gentleman annuals. But they 'll
cheat him, I know. And now, dear B. B., the sun

[1] The translator of Dante.

shining out merrily, and the dirty clouds we had yesterday having washed their own faces clean with their own rain, tempts me to wander up Winchmore Hill, or into some of the delightful vicinages of Enfield, which I hope to show you at some time when you can get a few days up to the great town. Believe me, it would give both of us great pleasure to show you our pleasant farms and villages.

We both join in kindest loves to you and yours.

C. Lamb *redivivus*.

XCIX.

TO PROCTER.

January 22, 1829.

Don't trouble yourself about the verses. Take 'em coolly as they come. Any day between this and midsummer will do. Ten lines the extreme. There is no mystery in my incognita. She has often seen you, though you may not have observed a silent brown girl, who for the last twelve years has rambled about our house in her Christmas holidays. She is Italian by name and extraction.[1] Ten lines about the blue sky of her country will do, as it's her foible to be proud of it. Item, I have made her a tolerable Latinist. She is called Emma Isola. I shall, I think, be in town in a few weeks, when I will assuredly see you. I will put in here loves to

---

[1] Emma Isola, Lamb's ward, daughter of one of the Esquire Bedells of Cambridge University, and granddaughter of an Italian refugee. The Lambs had met her during one of their Cambridge visits, and finally adopted her.

Mrs. Procter and the Anti-Capulets [Montagus], because Mary tells me I omitted them in my last. I like to see my friends here. I have put my law-suit into the hands of an Enfield practitioner, — a plain man, who seems perfectly to understand it, and gives me hopes of a favorable result.

Rumor tells us that Miss Holcroft is married. Who is Baddams? Have I seen him at Montacute's? I hear he is a great chemist. I am sometimes chemical myself. A thought strikes me with horror. Pray Heaven he may not have done it for the sake of trying chemical experiments upon her, — young female subjects are so scarce ! An't you glad about Burke's case? We may set off the Scotch mur-ders against the Scotch novels, — Hare the Great Unhanged.[1]

Martin Burney is richly worth your knowing. He is on the top scale of my friendship ladder, on which an angel or two is still climbing, and some, alas ! descending. I am out of the literary world at pres-ent. Pray, is there anything new from the admired pen of the author of "The Pleasures of Hope"? Has Mrs. He-mans (double masculine) done any-thing pretty lately? Why sleeps the lyre of Hervey and of Alaric Watts? Is the muse of L. E. L. silent? Did you see a sonnet of mine in Blackwood's last?[2] Curious construction ! *Elaborata facilitas !* And now I 'll tell. 'T was written for "The Gem;" but the editors declined it, on the plea that it would *shock all mothers;* so they published "The Widow"

---

[1] Burke and Hare, the Edinburgh resurrection-men.
[2] The Gypsy's Malison.

instead. I am born out of time. I have no conjecture about what the present world calls delicacy.
I thought "Rosamund Gray" was a pretty modest
thing. Hessey assures me that the world would not
bear it. I have lived to grow into an indecent character. When my sonnet was rejected, I exclaimed,
"Damn the age ; I will write for Antiquity !"

Erratum in sonnet. Last line but something, for
"tender" read "tend." The Scotch do not know
our law terms, but I find some remains of honest,
plain old writing lurking there still. They were not
so mealy mouthed as to refuse my verses. Maybe,
't is their oatmeal.

Blackwood sent me £20 for the drama. Somebody cheated me out of it next day; and my new
pair of breeches, just sent home, cracking at first
putting on, I exclaimed, in my wrath, "All tailors
are cheats, and all men are tailors." Then I was
better.

C. L.

C.

TO BERNARD BARTON.

ENFIELD CHASE SIDE,
Saturday, 25th of July, A. D. 1829, 11 A. M.

THERE ! a fuller, plumper, juicier date never
dropped from Idumean palm. Am I in the *date-
ive* case now? If not, a fig for dates, — which is
more than a date is worth. I never stood much
affected to these limitary specialities, — least of all,
since the date of my superannuation.

> "What have I with time to do?
> Slaves of desks, 't was meant for you."

DEAR B. B., — Your handwriting has conveyed much pleasure to me in respect of Lucy's restoration. Would I could send you as good news of *my* poor Lucy![1] But some wearisome weeks I must remain lonely yet. I have had the loneliest time, near ten weeks, broken by a short apparition of Emma for her holidays, whose departure only deepened the returning solitude, and by ten days I have passed in town. But town, with all my native hankering after it, is not what it was. The streets, the shops, are left, but all old friends are gone. And in London I was frightfully convinced of this as I passed houses and places, empty caskets now. I have ceased to care almost about anybody. The bodies I cared for are in graves, or dispersed. My old clubs, that lived so long and flourished so steadily, are crumbled away. When I took leave of our adopted young friend at Charing Cross, 't was heavy unfeeling rain, and I had nowhere to go. Home have I none, and not a sympathizing house to turn to in the great city. Never did the waters of heaven pour down on a forlorner head. Yet I tried ten days at a sort of a friend's house; but it was large and straggling, — one of the individuals of my old long knot of friends, card-players, pleasant companions, that have tumbled to pieces, into dust and other things; and I got home on Thursday, convinced that I was better to get home to my hole at Enfield, and hide like a sick cat in my corner. Less than a month, I hope, will bring home Mary. She is at Fulham, looking better in her health than

[1] Mary Lamb.

ever, but sadly rambling, and scarce showing any
pleasure in seeing me, or curiosity when I should
come again.   But the old feelings will come back
again, and we shall drown old sorrows over a game
of piquet again.   But 't is a tedious cut out of a
life of fifty-four, to lose twelve or thirteen weeks
every year or two.   And to make me more alone, our
ill-tempered maid is gone, who, with all her airs, was
yet a home-piece of furniture, a record of better
days; the young thing that has succeeded her is
good and attentive, but she is nothing.   And I have
no one here to talk over old matters with.   Scolding
and quarrelling have something of familiarity and a
community of interest; they imply acquaintance;
they are of resentment, which is of the family
of dearness.

．　　．　　．　　．　　．　　．　　．　　．

I bragged formerly that I could not have too
much time; I have now a surfeit.   With few years
to come, the days are wearisome.   But weariness is
not eternal.   Something will shine out to take the
load off that flags me, which is at present intolerable.   I have killed an hour or two in this poor
scrawl.   I am a sanguinary murderer of time, and
would kill him inch-meal just now.   But the snake
is vital.   Well, I shall write merrier anon.   'T is
the present copy of my countenance I send, and to
complain is a little to alleviate.   May you enjoy
yourself as far as the wicked world will let you, and
think that you are not quite alone, as I am !   Health
to Lucia and to Anna, and kind remembrances.

Your forlorn   C. L.

CI.

November 30, 1829.

DEAR G., — The excursionists reached home and the good town of Enfield a little after four, without slip or dislocation. Little has transpired concerning the events of the back-journey, save that on passing the house of 'Squire Mellish, situate a stone bow's cast from the hamlet, Father Westwood,[1] with a good-natured wonderment, exclaimed, "I cannot think what is gone of Mr. Mellish's rooks. I fancy they have taken flight somewhere; but I have missed them two or three years past." All this while, according to his fellow-traveller's report, the rookery was darkening the air above with undiminished population, and deafening all ears but his with their cawings. But nature has been gently withdrawing such phenomena from the notice of Thomas Westwood's senses, from the time he began to miss the rooks. T. Westwood has passed a retired life in this hamlet of thirty or forty years, living upon the minimum which is consistent with gentility, yet a star among the minor gentry, receiving the bows of the tradespeople and courtesies of the alms-women daily. Children venerate him not less for his external show of gentry than they wonder at him for a

---

[1] Lamb's landlord. He had driven Mary Lamb over to see Coleridge at Highgate. The Lambs had been compelled, by the frequent illnesses of Mary Lamb, to give up their house-keeping at Enfield and to take lodgings with the Westwoods.

gentle rising endorsation of the person, not amount-
ing to a hump, or if a hump, innocuous as the hump
of the buffalo, and coronative of as mild qualities.
'T is a throne on which patience seems to sit, — the
proud perch of a self-respecting humility, stooping
with condescension. Thereupon the cares of life
have sat, and rid him easily.   For he has thrid the
angustiæ domûs with dexterity.   Life opened upon
him with comparative brilliancy.   He set out as a
rider or traveller for a wholesale house, in which capacity he tells of many hair-breadth escapes that befell him, — one especially, how he rode a mad horse
into the town of Devizes; how horse and rider arrived in a foam, to the utter consternation of the
expostulating hostlers, inn-keepers, etc.   It seems
it was sultry weather, piping-hot; the steed tormented into frenzy with gad-flies, long past being
roadworthy : but safety and the interest of the house
he rode for were incompatible things ; a fall in serge
cloth was expected ; and a mad entrance they made
of it.   Whether the exploit was purely voluntary, or
partially ; or whether a certain personal defiguration
in the man part of this extraordinary centaur (non-
assistive to partition of natures) might not enforce
the conjunction, I stand not to inquire.   I look not
with 'skew eyes into the deeds of heroes.   The
hosier that was burned with his shop in Field Lane,
on Tuesday night, shall have passed to heaven for
me like a Marian Martyr, provided always that he
consecrated the fortuitous incremation with a short
ejaculation in the exit, as much as if he had taken
his state degrees of martyrdom *in formâ* in the

market vicinage. There is adoptive as well as acquisitive sacrifice. Be the animus what it might, the fact is indisputable, that this composition was seen flying all abroad, and mine host of Daintry may yet remember its passing through his town, if his scores are not more faithful than his memory.

. . . .

To come from his heroic character, all the amiable qualities of domestic life concentre in this tamed Bellerophon. He is excellent over a glass of grog; just as pleasant without it; laughs when he hears a joke, and when (which is much oftener) he hears it not; sings glorious old sea-songs on festival nights; and but upon a slight acquaintance of two years, Coleridge, is as dear a deaf old man to us as old Norris, rest his soul! was after fifty. To him and his scanty literature (what there is of it, *sound*) have we flown from the metropolis and its cursed annualists, reviewers, authors, and the whole muddy ink press of that stagnant pool.

. . . .

CII.

TO WORDSWORTH.

January 22, 1830.

AND is it a year since we parted from you at the steps of Edmonton stage? There are not now the years that there used to be. The tale of the dwindled age of men, reported of successional mankind, is true of the same man only. We do not live a year in a year now. 'T is a *punctum stans*. The seasons

pass us with indifference. Spring cheers not, nor
winter heightens our gloom ; autumn hath foregone
its moralities, — they are " heypass repass," as in a
show-box. Yet, as far as last year, occurs back —
for they scarce show a reflex now, they make no
memory as heretofore — 't was sufficiently gloomy.
Let the sullen nothing pass. Suffice it that after sad
spirits, prolonged through many of its months, as it
called them, we have cast our skins, have taken a
farewell of the pompous, troublesome trifle called
housekeeping, and are settled down into poor board-
ers and lodgers at next door with an old couple, the
Baucis and Baucida of dull Enfield. Here we have
nothing to do with our victuals but to eat them, with
the garden but to see it grow, with the tax-gatherer
but to hear him knock, with the maid but to hear
her scolded. Scot and lot, butcher, baker, are
things unknown to us, save as spectators of the pa-
geant. We are fed we know not how, — quietists,
confiding ravens. We have the *otium pro digni-
tate*, a respectable insignificance. Yet in the self-
condemned obliviousness, in the stagnation, some
molesting yearnings of life not quite killed rise,
prompting me that there was a London, and that I
was of that old Jerusalem. In dreams I am in Fleet
Market ; but I wake and cry to sleep again. I die
hard, a stubborn Eloisa in this detestable Paraclete.
What have I gained by health? Intolerable dulness.
What by early hours and moderate meals? A total
blank. Oh, never let the lying poets be believed
who 'tice men from the cheerful haunts of streets,
or think they mean it not of a country village. In

the ruins of Palmyra I could gird myself up to solitude, or muse to the snorings of the Seven Sleepers;
but to have a little teasing image of a town about
one, country folks that do not look like country
folks, shops two yards square, half-a-dozen apples
and two penn'orth of over-looked gingerbread for
the lofty fruiterers of Oxford Street, and for the immortal book and print stalls a circulating library that
stands still, where the show-picture is a last year's
Valentine, and whither the fame of the last ten
Scotch novels has not yet travelled (marry, they
just begin to be conscious of the " Redgauntlet "), to
have a new plastered flat church, and to be wishing
that it was but a cathedral! The very blackguards
here are degenerate, the topping gentry stock-
brokers; the passengers too many to insure your
quiet, or let you go about whistling or gaping, — too
few to be the fine indifferent pageants of Fleet
Street. Confining, room-keeping, thickest winter is
yet more bearable here than the gaudy months.
Among one's books at one's fire by candle, one is
soothed into an oblivion that one is not in the
country; but with the light the green fields return,
till I gaze, and in a calenture can plunge myself into
St. Giles's. Oh, let no native Londoner imagine
that health and rest and innocent occupation, interchange of converse sweet and recreative study, can
make the country anything better than altogether
odious and detestable. A garden was the primitive prison, till man with Promethean felicity and
boldness luckily sinned himself out of it. Thence
followed Babylon, Nineveh, Venice, London; haber-

dashers, goldsmiths, taverns, playhouses, satires, epi-
grams, puns, — these all came in on the town part
and the thither side of innocence.   Man found out
inventions.   From my den I return you condolence
for your decaying sight, — not for anything there is
to see in the country, but for the miss of the pleasure
of reading a London newspaper.   The poets are as
well to listen to ; anything high may — nay, must
be read out ; you read it to yourself with an imaginary auditor : but the light paragraphs must be glid
over by the proper eye ; mouthing mumbles their
gossamery substance.   'T is these trifles I should
mourn in fading sight.   A newspaper is the single
gleam of comfort I receive here ; it comes from rich
Cathay with tidings of mankind.   Yet I could not
attend to it, read out by the most beloved voice.
But your eyes do not get worse, I gather.   Oh, for
the collyrium of Tobias enclosed in a whiting's liver,
to send you, with no apocryphal good wishes !   The
last long time I heard from you, you had knocked
your head against something.   Do not do so ; for
your head (I do not flatter) is not a knob, or the
top of a brass nail, or the end of a ninepin, — unless a Vulcanian hammer could fairly batter a " Re-
cluse " out of it ; then would I bid the smirched god
knock, and knock lustily, the two-handed skinker !
Mary must squeeze out a line *propriâ manu ;* but
indeed her fingers have been incorrigibly nervous to
letter-writing for a long interval.   'T will please you
all to hear that, though I fret like a lion in a net,
her present health and spirits are better than they
have been for some time past ; she is absolutely

three years and a half younger, as I tell her, since we have adopted this boarding plan.

Our providers are an honest pair, Dame Westwood and her husband, — he, when the light of prosperity shined on them, a moderately thriving haberdasher within Bow bells, retired since with something under a competence ; writes himself parcel-gentleman ; hath borne parish offices ; sings fine old sea-songs at threescore and ten ; sighs only now and then when he thinks that he has a son on his hands about fifteen, whom he finds a difficulty in getting out into the world, and then checks a sigh with muttering, as I once heard him prettily, not meaning to be heard, " I have married my daughter, however ; " takes the weather as it comes ; outsides it to town in severest season ; and o' winter nights tells old stories not tending to literature (how comfortable to author-rid folks !), and has *one anecdote*, upon which and about forty pounds a year he seems to have retired in green old age. It was how he was a rider in his youth, travelling for shops, and once (not to balk his employer's bargain) on a sweltering day in August, rode foaming into Dunstable [1] upon a mad horse, to the dismay and expostulatory wonderment of inn-keepers, ostlers, etc., who declared they would not have bestrid the beast to win the Derby. Understand the creature galled to death and desperation by gad-flies, cormorant-winged, worse than beset Inachus's daughter. This he tells, this he brindles and burnishes, on a winter's eve ; 't is his star of set glory, his rejuvenescence to descant

[1] See preceding letter.

upon. Far from me be it (*dii avertant!*) to look a gift-story in the mouth, or cruelly to surmise (as those who doubt the plunge of Curtius) that the inseparate conjuncture of man and beast, the centaur-phenomenon that staggered all Dunstable, might have been the effect of unromantic necessity; that the horse-part carried the reasoning willy-nilly; that needs must when such a devil drove; that certain spiral configurations in the frame of Thomas Westwood, unfriendly to alighting, made the alliance more forcible than voluntary. Let him enjoy his fame for me, nor let me hint a whisper that shall dismount Bellerophon. But in case he was an involuntary martyr, yet if in the fiery conflict he buckled the soul of a constant haberdasher to him, and adopted his flames, let accident and him share the glory. You would all like Thomas Westwood. [   ] [1] How weak is painting to describe a man ! Say that he stands four feet and a nail high by his own yard-measure, which, like the sceptre of Agamemnon, shall never sprout again, still, you have no adequate idea; nor when I tell you that his dear hump, which I have favored in the picture, seems to me of the buffalo, — indicative and repository of mild qualities, a budget of kindnesses, — still, you have not the man. Knew you old Norris of the Temple, sixty years ours and our father's friend? He was not more natural to us than this old Westwood, the acquaintance of scarce more weeks. Under his roof now ought I to take my rest, but that back-looking ambition tells me I might yet be a

---

[1] Here was inserted a sketch answering to the description.

Londoner! Well, if we ever do move, we have encumbrances the less to impede us; all our furniture has faded under the auctioneer's hammer, going for nothing, like the tarnished frippery of the prodigal, and we have only a spoon or two left to bless us. Clothed we came into Enfield, and naked we must go out of it. I would live in London shirtless, bookless. Henry Crabb is at Rome; advices to that effect have reached Bury. But by solemn legacy he bequeathed at parting (whether he should live or die) a turkey of Suffolk to be sent every succeeding Christmas to us and divers other friends. What a genuine old bachelor's action! I fear he will find the air of Italy too classic. His station is in the Hartz forest; his soul is be-Goethed. Miss Kelly we never see,—Talfourd not this half year; the latter flourishes, but the exact number of his children, God forgive me, I have utterly forgotten: we single people are often out in our count there. Shall I say two? We see scarce anybody. Can I cram loves enough to you all in this little O? Excuse particularizing.

C. L.

CIII.

TO MRS. HAZLITT.

May 24, 1830.

MARY's love? Yes. Mary Lamb quite well.

DEAR SARAH,—I found my way to Northaw on Thursday and a very good woman behind a counter. who says also that you are a very good lady, but that the woman who was with you was naught.

. . . .

We travelled with one of those troublesome fellow-passengers in a stage-coach that is called a well-informed man. For twenty miles we discoursed about the properties of steam, probabilities of carriages by ditto, till all my science, and more than all, was exhausted, and I was thinking of escaping my torment by getting up on the outside, when, getting into Bishops Stortford, my gentleman, spying some farming land, put an unlucky question to me, — What sort of a crop of turnips I thought we should have this year? Emma's eyes turned to me to know what in the world I could have to say; and she burst into a violent fit of laughter, maugre her pale, serious cheeks, when, with the greatest gravity, I replied that it depended, I believed, upon boiled legs of mutton. This clenched our conversation; and my gentleman, with a face half wise, half in scorn, troubled us with no more conversation, scientific or philosophical, for the remainder of the journey.

Ayrton was here yesterday, and as *learned* to the full as my fellow-traveller. What a pity that he will spoil a wit and a devilish pleasant fellow (as he is) by wisdom! He talked on Music; and by having read Hawkins and Burney recently I was enabled to talk of names, and show more knowledge than he had suspected I possessed; and in the end he begged me to shape my thoughts upon paper, which I did after he was gone, and sent him " Free Thoughts on Some Eminent Composers."

" Some cry up Haydn, some Mozart,
    Just as the whim bites. For my part,

I do not care a farthing candle
For either of them, or for Handel," etc.

Martin Burney [1] is as odd as ever. We had a dispute about the word "heir," which I contended
was pronounced like "air." He said that might
be in common parlance, or that we might so use
it speaking of the " Heir-at-Law," a comedy ; but
that in the law-courts it was necessary to give it
a full aspiration, and to say *Hayer;* he thought
it might even vitiate a cause if a counsel pronounced it otherwise. In conclusion, he "would
consult Serjeant Wilde," who gave it against him.
Sometimes he falleth into the water, sometimes
into the fire. He came down here, and insisted
on reading Virgil's " Æneid " all through with me
(which he did), because a counsel must know
Latin. Another time he read out all the Gospel
of St. John, because Biblical quotations are very
emphatic in a court of justice. A third time he
would carve a fowl, which he did very ill favoredly,
because we did not know how indispensable it
was for a barrister to do all those sort of things
well. Those little things were of more consequence than we supposed. So he goes on, har-
assing about the way to prosperity, and losing it.
With a long head, but somewhat a wrong one, —
harum-scarum. Why does not his guardian angel
look to him? He deserves one, — maybe he has
tired him out.

I am tired with this long scrawl; but I thought

[1] Martin Burney, originally a solicitor, had lately been
called to the Bar.

in your exile you might like a letter. Commend
me to all the wonders in Derbyshire, and tell the
devil I humbly kiss my hand to him.

Yours ever,   C. Lamb.

CIV.

TO GEORGE DYER.

December 20, 1830.

Dear Dyer, — I would have written before to
thank you for your kind letter, written with your
own hand.   It glads us to see your writing.   It will
give you pleasure to hear that, after so much illness,
we are in tolerable health and spirits once more.
Miss Isola intended to call upon you after her
night's lodging at Miss Buffam's, but found she was
too late for the stage.   If she comes to town before
she goes home, she will not miss paying her respects to Mrs. Dyer and you, to whom she desires
best love.   Poor Enfield, that has been so peace-
able hitherto, that has caught an inflammatory fever,
the tokens are upon her; and a great fire was blazing last night in the barns and haystacks of a farmer
about half a mile from us.   Where will these things
end?   There is no doubt of its being the work
of some ill-disposed rustic; but how is he to be
discovered?   They go to work in the dark with
strange chemical preparations unknown to our fore-
fathers.   There is not even a dark lantern to have
a chance of detecting these Guy Fauxes.   We are
past the iron age, and are got into the fiery age,
undream'd of by Ovid.   You are lucky in Clifford's

Inn, where, I think, you have few ricks or stacks worth the burning. Pray keep as little corn by you as you can, for fear of the worst.

It was never good times in England since the poor began to speculate upon their condition. Formerly they jogged on with as little reflection as horses; the whistling ploughman went cheek by jowl with his brother that neighed. Now the biped carries a box of phosphorus in his leather breeches; and in the dead of night the half-illuminated beast steals his magic potion into a cleft in a barn, and half the country is grinning with new fires. Farmer Graystock said something to the touchy rustic that he did not relish, and he writes his distaste in flames. What a power to intoxicate his crude brains, just muddlingly awake, to perceive that something is wrong in the social system; what a hellish faculty above gunpowder!

Now the rich and poor are fairly pitted, we shall see who can hang or burn fastest. It is not always revenge that stimulates these kindlings. There is a love of exerting mischief. Think of a disrespected clod that was trod into earth, that was nothing, on a sudden by damned arts refined into an exterminating angel, devouring the fruits of the earth and their growers in a mass of fire! What a new existence; what a temptation above Lucifer's! Would clod be anything but a clod if he could resist it? Why, here was a spectacle last night for a whole country, — a bonfire visible to London, alarming her guilty towers, and shaking the Monument with an ague fit: all done by a little vial of phosphor in a clown's fob ! How he must grin, and shake his empty noddle in clouds, the Vulcanian epicure ! Can we ring the bells backward ? Can we unlearn the arts that pretend to civilize, and then burn the world ? There is a march of Science : but who shall beat the drums for its retreat ? Who shall persuade the boor that phosphor will not ignite ?

Seven goodly stacks of hay, with corn-barns proportionable, lie smoking ashes and chaff, which man and beast would sputter out and reject like those apples of asphaltes and bitumen. The food for the inhabitants of earth will quickly disappear. Hot rolls may say, " Fuimus panes, fuit quartern-loaf, et ingens gloria Apple-pasty-orum." That the good old munching system may last thy time and mine, good un-incendiary George, is the devout prayer of thine, to the last crust,

CH. LAMB.

CV.

TO DYER.

February 22, 1831.

DEAR DYER, — Mr. Rogers and Mr. Rogers's friends are perfectly assured that you never intended any harm by an innocent couplet, and that in the revivification of it by blundering Barker you had no hand whatever. To imagine that, at this time of day, Rogers broods over a fantastic expression of more than thirty years' standing, would be to suppose him indulging his " Pleasures of Memory " with a vengeance. You never penned a line which for its own sake you need, dying, wish to blot. You mistake your heart if you think you *can* write a lampoon. Your whips are rods of roses.[1] Your spleen has ever had for its objects vices, not the vicious, — abstract offences, not the concrete sinner. But you are sensitive, and wince as much at the consciousness of having committed a compliment as another man would at the perpetration of an affront. But do not lug me into the same soreness of conscience with yourself. I maintain, and will to the last hour, that I never writ of you but *con amore;* that if any allusion was made to your near-sightedness, it was not for the purpose of mocking an infirmity, but of connecting it with scholar-like habits, — for is it not erudite and scholarly to be somewhat near of sight before age naturally brings on the malady? You could not then plead the *obrepens senectus.* Did I not, moreover, make it an apology for a certain *absence,* which some of your friends may have experienced, when you have not on a sudden made recognition of them in a casual street-meeting; and did I not strengthen your excuse for this slowness of recognition by further account-

---

[1] Talfourd relates an amusing instance of the universal charity of the kindly Dyer. Lamb once suddenly asked him what he thought of the murderer Williams, — a wretch who had destroyed two families in Ratcliff Highway, and then cheated the gallows by committing suicide. "The desperate attempt," says Talfourd, "to compel the gentle optimist to speak ill of a mortal creature produced no happier success than the answer, 'Why, I should think, Mr. Lamb, he must have been rather an eccentric character.'"

ing morally for the present engagement of your mind
in worthy objects?   Did I not, in your person, make
the handsomest apology for absent-of-mind people
that was ever made?   If these things be not so, I
never knew what I wrote or meant by my writing,
and have been penning libels all my life without
being aware of it.   Does it follow that I should have
expressed myself exactly in the same way of those
dear old eyes of yours *now*, — now that Father
Time has conspired with a hard taskmaster to put a
last extinguisher upon them?   I should as soon have
insulted the Answerer of Salmasius when he awoke
up from his ended task, and saw no more with
mortal vision.   But you are many films removed
yet from Milton's calamity.   You write perfectly
intelligibly.   Marry, the letters are not all of the
same size or tallness ; but that only shows your pro-
ficiency in the *hands*, — text, german-hand, court-
hand, sometimes law-hand, and affords variety.   You
pen better than you did a twelvemonth ago ; and if
you continue to improve, you bid fair to win the
golden pen which is the prize at your young gentlemen's academy.

.   .   .   .

But don't go and lay this to your eyes.   You
always wrote hieroglyphically, yet not to come up
to the mystical notations and conjuring characters
of Dr. Parr.   You never wrote what I call a school-
master's hand, like Mrs. Clarke ; nor a woman's
hand, like Southey ; nor a missal hand, like Porson ;
nor an all-on-the-wrong-side sloping hand, like Miss
Hayes ; nor a dogmatic, Mede-and-Persian, peremp-

tory hand, like Rickman : but you wrote what I call
a Grecian's hand, — what the Grecians write (or
wrote) at Christ's Hospital ; such as Whalley would
have admired, and Boyer[1] have applauded, but Smith
or Atwood [writing-masters] would have horsed you
for. Your boy-of-genius hand and your mercantile
hand are various. By your flourishes, I should think
you never learned to make eagles or cork-screws, or
flourish the governor's names in the writing-school ;
and by the tenor and cut of your letters, I suspect
you were never in it at all. By the length of this
scrawl you will think I have a design upon your
optics ; but I have writ as large as I could, out of
respect to them, — too large, indeed, for beauty.
Mine is a sort of Deputy-Grecian's hand, — a little
better, and more of a worldly hand, than a Grecian's,
but still remote from the mercantile. I don't know
how it is, but I keep my rank in fancy still since
school-days ; I can never forget I was a Deputy-
Grecian. And writing to you, or to Coleridge,
besides affection, I feel a reverential deference as
to Grecians still.[2] I keep my soaring way above
the Great Erasmians, yet far beneath the other.
Alas ! what am I now? What is a Leadenhall clerk
or India pensioner to a Deputy-Grecian? How art
thou fallen, O Lucifer ! Just room for our loves to
Mrs. D., etc.

C. LAMB.

---

[1] Whalley and Boyer were masters at Christ's Hospital.

[2] "Deputy-Grecian," "Grecian," etc., were of course forms,
or grades, at Christ's Hospital.

TO MR. MOXON.[1]

February, 1832.

DEAR MOXON, — The snows are ankle-deep, slush, and mire, that 't is hard to get to the post-office, and cruel to send the maid out. 'T is a slough of despair, or I should sooner have thanked you for your offer of the " Life," which we shall very much like to have, and will return duly. I do not know when I shall be in town, but in a week or two at farthest, when I will come as far as you, if I can. We are moped to death with confinement within doors. I send you a curiosity of G. Dyer's tender conscience. Between thirty and forty years since, George published the " Poet's Fate," in which were two very harmless lines about Mr. Rogers; but Mr. R. not quite approving of them, they were left out in a subsequent edition, 1801. But George has been worrying about them ever since; if I have heard him once, I have heard him a hundred times express a remorse proportioned to a consciousness of having been guilty of an atrocious libel. As the devil would have it, a fool they call Barker, in his " Parriana " has quoted the identical two lines as they stood in some obscure edition anterior to 1801, and the withers of poor George are again wrung, His letter is a gem; with his poor blind eyes it has

---

[1] Lamb's future publisher. He afterwards became the husband of Lamb's *protégée*, Emma Isola.

been labored out at six sittings.   The history of the
couplet is in page 3 of this irregular production, in
which every variety of shape and size that letters
can be twisted into is to be found.   Do show *his*
part of it to Mr. Rogers some day.   If he has
bowels, they must melt at the contrition so queerly
charactered of a contrite sinner.   G. was born, I
verily think, without original sin, but chooses to
have a conscience, as every Christian gentleman
should have ; his dear old face is insusceptible of
the twist they call a sneer, yet he is apprehensive of
being suspected of that ugly appearance.   When he
makes a compliment, he thinks he has given an
affront, — a name is personality.   But show (no hur-
ry) this unique recantation to Mr. Rogers : 't is like a
dirty pocket-handerchief mucked with tears of some
indigent Magdalen.   There is the impress of sincerity in every pot-hook and hanger ; and then the
gilt frame to such a pauper picture !   It should go
into the Museum.

.   .   .   .

.

CVII.

TO MR. MOXON.

July 24, 1833.

For God's sake give Emma no more watches ;
one has turned her head.   She is arrogant and insulting.   She said something very unpleasant to our
old clock in the passage, as if he did not keep time ;
and yet he had made her no appointment.   She

takes it out every instant to look at the moment-hand. She lugs us out into the fields, because there the bird-boys ask you, " Pray, sir, can you tell us what 's o'clock? " and she answers them punctually. She loses all her time looking to see "what the time is." I overheard her whispering, " Just so many hours, minutes, etc., to Tuesday ; I think St. George's goes too slow." This little present of Time, — why, 't is Eternity to her !

What can make her so fond of a gingerbread watch?

She has spoiled some of the movements. Between ourselves, she has kissed away " half-past twelve," which I suppose to be the canonical hour in Hanover Square.

Well, if " love me, love my watch," answers, she will keep time to you.

It goes right by the Horse-Guards.

DEAREST M., — Never mind opposite nonsense. She does not love you for the watch, but the watch for you. I will be at the wedding, and keep the 30th July, as long as my poor months last me, as a festival gloriously.

                    Yours ever,

                                        ELIA.

THE END.